The Holy City

ALSO BY MEG HENDERSON

Finding Peggy: A Glasgow Childhood

The Holy City

A Tale of Clydebank

Meg Henderson

Flamingo
An Imprint of HarperCollinsPublishers

Flamingo
An Imprint of HarperCollins*Publishers*
77–85 Fulham Palace Road,
Hammersmith, London W6 8JB

Published by Flamingo 1997
3 5 7 9 8 6 4

The Author and Publisher would like to thank Popperfoto for permission
to reproduce the photograph of Clydebank riveters on p.viii, the West
Dunbartonshire Libraries and Museums Department for permission to reproduce the photograph of the *Queen Mary* polishers on p. 174, and the Commando Association for permission to reproduce the photograph of the
Commando Monument on p. 311.

A catalogue record for this book
is available from the British Library

ISBN 0 00 225435 2

Set in Bembo by
Rowland Phototypesetting Ltd, Bury St Edmunds, Suffolk

Printed and bound in Great Britain by
Caledonian International Book Manufacturing Ltd, Glasgow

ACKNOWLEDGEMENTS

This book is the result of my obsession and affection for Clydebank, dating from the years of my childhood spent in Drumchapel on the outskirts of the town. The Glaswegians who were exiled to this far-flung outpost were not universally welcomed, indeed the Chief Constable of Dunbartonshire remarked that Clydebank would feel 'the full impact of having these criminal elements on its borders'. But the ordinary 'Bankies were warm and friendly people and I still have many happy memories of the town and its citizens.

There are of course people who should be thanked for their help with the book, and they fall into the categories of relatives, friends, acquaintances, and total strangers who only stopped me in the street to ask for directions, then found themselves being debriefed of everything they had ever heard about Clydebank. Anyone who has ever told an anecdote about the town will recognise parts of it here, as will those who have related their own stories to me or to anyone else in the media, because of my inability to leave anything out without throwing a tantrum.

Special thanks must go to John McCalman and Sheila Duffy of Radio Clyde, John MacKay and Stephen McCrossan of Scottish Television, Trevor Royle, Alan McKinlay and Hamish Henderson, all of whom generously allowed me to use the fruits of their labour, and Sir Gavin Laird, Michael Shea, Betty Brown, Fred Forrester, for parts of their lives. Also my agent Giles Gordon, AKA the Sophisticated Rottweiler, without whose devilish mischief the lives of his clients would be infinitely duller and less rewarding.

Thanks are due in huge measures to the staff of Clydebank Central Library for various snippets, and the wonderful Pat Malcolm in particular, who knows everything and gives of her time and knowledge with patience and good humour to all who ask. The award for specialist Gaelic knowledge goes to Belinda MacDougall, and the lifetime award for endurance to my husband and family, who somehow put up with my obsessions whilst a book is in progress and then suffer through the cold turkey when it's finished.

SOURCES

The History of Clydebank, compiled by John Hood (Parthenon Publications: Clydebank District Libraries, 1988)

Making Ships, Making Men, Alan McKinlay

The Clydebank Blitz, I. M. M. McPhail (W. Hodge, 1974)

The Clydebank Rent Strikes, Sean Damer

'Scottish Reporters', John MacKay, STV

'Scotland's War', STV

'The 'Bankies Blitz', Radio Clyde

For Rab the Rhymer,
with love as always.

I

It was Tuesday, of that she was sure. Tuesday was library day, and that was the last thing she remembered, being on her way to the library, books to be returned tucked under her right arm. Puffing a bit, but then these days she tended to, and she *had* walked all the way from the Holy City. Not that many called it the Holy City these days, not now that private houses had gone up on the site of the tenements that had been bombed during the War. There were people living there now who had no connection with Clydebank and didn't know its history, but she had been raised in one of those tenements, and as a child she had been trapped under it for hours in the Clydebank Blitz of 1941. She had been thinking about it a lot lately, with this special anniversary coming up there was so much in the press and on the radio, bringing it from the back of your mind to the front. Strange to think that more than fifty years on she was now living in one of the new houses on top of the old Holy City. She had tried to locate the exact spot where her childhood home had stood, using the few clues that still existed, the gap where the church hall had been in Crown Avenue for instance, but she was never sure. It all looked so much smaller than it did then, the years had shrunk everything.

She shouldn't have walked all the way, of course, but it was Tuesday, so she had had plenty of time. The postman came just after 7.30 in the morning, and these days there were often envelopes too big for the letter box, which meant she had to answer his knock at the door and take them from him. Papers, assignments from the Open University mostly, addressed to her, and though she tried to deny it to herself, the thought of it made her smile.

She had done her Highers at the age of fifty, then her A Levels, now it was the Open University. Her, Marion Katie MacLeod, studying for a degree, and not for the first time she wondered what her family would have made of it. But her great-grandfather, old Archie MacLeod, had always said she had an inquiring mind. Sometimes she liked to play devil's advocate by asking herself why she was doing this; getting an education at her age, a waste of money and resources surely? And the answer was always the same. At first it was to prove to herself that she wasn't stupid, then it was because she enjoyed it. Besides, it was hardly her fault that the War had cheated her of her chance first time round. And she was on her own these days; what was she supposed to do, vegetate till the grim reaper came a-knocking?

The bulk of Open University material seemed to arrive, for some reason, on a Tuesday, so she had to be up, dressed and looking respectable just in case. She hated the thought of anyone seeing her straight from bed, half-asleep, unready, caught off guard somehow; that was a hangover from the Blitz, she knew that, she had worked it out long ago and accepted that she couldn't get rid of it. What was that saying about the wisdom to accept what you can't change? Well, she had that wisdom nowadays; she wasn't as lithe as she used to be, but she was wise, after a fashion. Was it a fair exchange, she wondered, smiling to herself as she visualised an essay in the making. She had established a routine of being up and ready, and after the postman had gone she went to the library.

And that was how it had been today. Up, wash, dress, brush her long hair back – she refused to give in to a granny perm, or even a granny bun – go slowly with the brush at the back to avoid the raised bump on that big scar just under the hairline. Sometimes if she was in a hurry she forgot, even after all these years, and grazed the bump, making it bleed. You couldn't forget, you shouldn't forget, but maybe the bumpy scar was there to make sure. She looked in the mirror and examined her reflection, a mixture of the women in her life. Granny Mirren's red hair, though salt and pepper now, considerably more salt if the truth were told; a look of Granny Kate's defiant smile, the green eyes of her big sister Frances and their mother Jean, though not quite the beauty of either, alas, she smiled wryly. And, God forbid, but she had to admit it, on a bad day, even Auntie Maggie was in there somewhere. Then she had toast and coffee – she had never got into the way of breakfast, that was something else she had accepted long ago: you don't have to break the habits of a lifetime if you're comfortable with them.

She could account for every second coming down Kilbowie Road. It was a crisp, frosty morning, so like March 1941 that she could account for every thought; every memory heightened by the approaching events to mark the anniversary. And there was someone she was hoping to see there, someone she was hoping would still be alive, and in her mind she was rehearsing their reunion, as she had done over and over again all these years. Across Dumbarton Road to where Woolworth's stood on the corner, where Woolworth's *had* stood. Puffing slightly from hurrying between the traffic, that was all. She did these days, she was no spring chicken. Then – then what? A blank. Something had happened to her obviously, but what?

She was lying down and there were people around her, and she took stock as best she could. A harsh sound, like the weariest wind you ever heard, and voices in the distance. As she came to, she decided to keep quiet until she had her bearings, no point in making a fool of herself. There was someone above, talking down to her, but she couldn't make out a word. It was like being in a tunnel. She smiled to herself at that. C'mon, Marion Katie, she told herself, you can at least be original, and the fact that the thought occurred reassured her that she was still herself. She kept her eyes closed to gather her thoughts before attempting to answer the earnest-sounding chap above her. Whatever he wanted he could wait till she had her bearings. That was another gain from ageing, you could get away with ignoring people if you wanted to; getting on meant younger people thinking you weren't all there, and you could use that to your advantage sometimes.

She felt for her coat, to make sure she was decent, then she lay still and mentally visited her body, checking for damage. There was a pressure around her chest, not a pain, but something holding her down, and she knew with instant clarity when she had felt that before. It had happened when she was trapped under the debris of her home in Second Avenue in the Holy City during the Clydebank Blitz, and the sensation was so strong, so familiar, that for a moment she wondered if she was still there. She heard her mother's voice in the dark and the silence, trying to stop her panicking, 'Jist take wan breath at a time, Marion Katie, jist keep breathin',' and she was once again that scared eleven-year-old, confused and injured, trapped under tons of rubble. Well, she had survived that, she told herself, so whatever this was, she would survive that too.

'Can ye hear me, love?' She opened her eyes and saw the earnest-sounding chap who had been speaking to her. 'You're OK, don't be frightened. Ye had a wee turn in the street an' ye're in an ambulance. That thing on your face is an oxygen mask, it's helpin' ye to breathe, so don't panic, just take wan breath at a time. We'll soon be at the hospital. You're doin' fine, OK?' Marion shut her eyes again, stemming the panic. She had to be well if she was to see Marek, she couldn't be in hospital, but if there was one thing she had learned long ago, it was to relax when there was no alternative. There was no point in causing a fuss if someone

4

was already in charge, and whatever had happened to her to land her in an ambulance, she knew she would need all her resources to cope with the aftermath. She had learned that too, learned it the hard way. With the anniversary of the Blitz so near, the memories had been creeping into her mind for weeks, just as the bombing had been on the minds of other 'Bankies who had lived through it or heard tales of it. Even now when a plane passed overhead, people of her generation would catch one another's eye and shiver. No need for words, the fear, the pain, the loss, it was all there in the look that passed between them. The strange thing was that she hadn't heard the bomb either, it had come like a bolt out of the blue, just as this 'wee turn' had. One minute she had been in a makeshift bed in the lower flat of the tenement, and the next she was awake and unable to move in the black silence. She did what any eleven-year-old would do, she screamed for her mother. She didn't know how long she had been shouting, but suddenly, from below some-where, came Jean MacLeod's voice. It calmed her as surely as any lullaby, telling her stories of Clydebank, of the family, reassuring her that help would come, and telling her at all costs to take one breath at a time, to keep calm and just breathe.

It was a wartime ritual in every home in the land. Every night at 9 o'clock everyone huddled round the wireless for the News on the BBC Home Service to hear about the latest bomb raids. 'Oh my God,' Jean MacLeod would say, 'they poor people doon there . . .' and everyone would nod their heads in silent agreement, feeling for the cities over the border where the German bombs were falling. They never thought it could happen to them, but then it's the same with every-thing in life. Clydebank was getting on with its life that night, its folk thinking of those worse off than themselves, with no reason to suspect that within minutes of the News starting it would *be* themselves. Marion had just come back from the

La Scala; what was the film? Shirley Temple, that was it, she sang 'On the Good Ship Lollipop'. Marion was singing it to her mother, trying to remember all the words, and Jean was laughing and shushing her away. She was baking scones and trying to listen to the News, absently wondering when her elder daughter Frances would be home. Frances was out dancing with a nice lad called Marek, a sailor off the ORP *Piorun*, a Polish destroyer in Brown's for a refit . . . Marek, who would haunt Marion's dreams for the next fifty years . . . The rest of the family was at home, listening to Joseph MacLeod reading the News. The RAF had had a good night bombing Berlin, Bremen and Hamburg; a German destroyer and a sub sunk; the 'Help your Neighbour' scheme was to end. Funny the things you can recall in detail while others you can't remember at all, another sign of age probably. The siren sounded, but sirens had been sounding for years and nothing had happened . . .

'Listen, love – whit's her name, constable?' It was the earnest-looking ambulanceman again, dragging her back from her memories.

'Marion,' said another voice. 'Just said Marion an' then passed oot again. Any idea whit it is?'

'Could be something or nothing,' replied the ambulanceman diplomatically. 'Marion, Ah'm takin' your blood pressure, you'll feel something tight round your arm.'

She had had that before, many times, but of course the ambulanceman wasn't to know that; he was following procedure, by explaining everything carefully and simply. There was a pumping sound, followed by a low swish. 'Ninety over seventy,' he murmured.

'Will she make it?' asked the other voice.

'First things first,' replied the ambulanceman quietly. 'We don't know whit's wrong wi' her yet, that's why we have doctors. We'll try the Western Infirmary first, see if they have a bed, or if we have to do a grand tour of every hospital in Glasgow till we hit the jackpot. Do you know her address or her age?'

'No; she had some library books, my mate's checking it out for an identity.'

She couldn't tell them, but she was listening, and she knew how old she was too. If only this feeling in her chest would let her take a deep breath and speak. Marion Katie MacLeod, born in February 1930, the fourth child of Jean and Thomas MacLeod, or as her father put it, their 'wee surprise'. Her brother Colin was nine years old at the time, Iain was eight and her sister Frances was seven. So after giving birth to three children in three years, Jean MacLeod had a rest of seven years before her 'wee surprise' arrived on the scene. 'Ah'm the man wi' the seven-year itch,' her father used to joke, which made his wife blush and tell him to 'Wheesht before the bairns hear ye.' That was one of her mother's sayings, but it never prevented Tommy from saying exactly what he liked.

Four generations of MacLeods lived at 70 Second Avenue, in what was called the Holy City. The flat-roofed tenements were built by McAlpine's in the early 1900s, the same McAlpine's that had built the Singer's sewing machine factory just down the hill on Kilbowie Road. The houses were built in tiers on the slope of the hill, and the story was that a returning seaman remarked that they looked like the real Holy City of Jerusalem, and that was how they were known by native 'Bankies, even decades after what was left after the raids was demolished.

Archie MacLeod, the father of the clan, was born on Hougharry in the north of Uist, a tiny speck of an island in the Western Isles, where the way of life was crofting and fishing and where the people of the north were implacably Protestant. South Uist, where Marion MacDonald lived, was equally implacably Roman Catholic, and though never the twain were allowed to meet, Marion, or Mirren as she was known all her life, and Archie, not only met but caused a great scandal by wanting to get married. There was no way that the two religions could intermarry, so Archie and Mirren ran away from Uist when he was nineteen and she was eighteen and got married in Glasgow. Though they lived to see eighty, they never again returned to Uist and mentioned it only in passing. Neither did they see their families again, and as no Uist MacLeod or MacDonald ever tried to make contact with them, the arrangement obviously suited all concerned. All Mirren brought with her was her mother's gold crucifix which she always wore around her neck.

When young Marion Katie was a child listening to these stories she would cry to think of them being without their relatives for ever. Being part of a big family, it seemed terribly sad to think of them being so young and alone in what must have seemed like a foreign land. Their story of heady love and passion coloured her entire outlook, making her a tireless searcher for romance all of her life. Jean MacLeod would shake her head and say to her husband, 'Granda Archie an' Granny Mirren have a lot tae answer for, Tommy, they've fair wasted oor Marion's heid. Talk aboot *Gone wi' the Wind*!' And without lowering his newspaper Tommy would reply, 'Aye, Jeannie, an' the auld fella looks jist like Rhett Butler tae, hauf asleep, wi' his pipe hingin' fae the coarner o' his mooth!' 'Wheesht, Tommy,' Jean would say, 'the bairns will hear!' and they would laugh together. Marion stored this snippet in her head until the day came when she could use it. It was either luck or, as she was only eight years old, a child's deadly instinct for the right wrong moment that ensured the attendance of the entire family.

'Granda,' she said to the old man, 'have we got relatives in Uist called Butler?'

Suddenly there was total silence. Granda Archie sucked on his clay pipe thoughtfully and then slowly shook his head. 'No, no, wee one, no Butlers.'

'Well how is it then that you look jist like Rhett Butler?'

Granda had never heard of Rhett Butler and hadn't a clue what the child was prattling on about, so he gave her a beaming smile of confusion and affection and smoothed her hair gently with his big, rough hand. 'She has an inquiring mind, oor bairn,' he smiled proudly. 'That's a good thing.'

'Aye,' her father replied, in a cool voice, 'an' a great big pair o' lugs for a bairn o' her size, Granda, lugs on hur like a bat. An' mibbe an even bigger mouth.'

Archie and Mirren refused to let their children learn Gaelic. 'If ye want to be a Gael,' the old man would say, in his soft, almost polite island accent, 'then go an' live in Gaeldom. Ye're Lowlanders; the Gaelic will do you no good down here.' But they spoke it between themselves, especially during marital disagreements, thinking that they couldn't be understood by their children. No matter what the argument was about, at some stage Archie would refer to their eldest son's black hair. As they were both blue-eyed with reddish-fair hair, why, Archie would ask, full of righteous wrath, had Mirren produced this *ille dubh* – this black-haired laddie? He knew for a certain fact that there were many black-haired men in South Uist, and he had his suspicions, let there be no doubt about that.

This abominable slur drove Mirren into a paroxysm of rage and grief, during which she pointed out, in the interests of fairness, that at least her laddie wasn't hairy-arsed like all the men of North Uist, so his southern blood was something to be grateful for. And how, Archie would demand, did she know that *all* the men of the north were hairy-arsed, and for that matter, how did she know that *all* of the men in the south weren't hairy-arsed, when she *claimed* to have known – in the biblical sense presumably – only one man: him? And so the battle would rage, with each insult stronger and more profane than the one before.

As a result the MacLeod offspring picked up only the choicest aspects of the language, and all their lives they, and eventually their children, used the Gaelic insults illicitly gleaned from Archie and Mirren's domestic disputes. Tommy MacLeod used to say that all his Highland ancestry had bequeathed to him was the ability to curse in Gaelic. His bilingual skills enabled him to call a daft old bitch '*òinsich na galladh*', and many a hat-man in John Brown's would be addressed as '*amadain an diabhoil*' – a stupid old bastard. It was just luck, he said, that those on the receiving end of his third-generation insults weren't Gaelic speakers too.

Archie became a carpenter with Thomson's, the forerunner of John Brown's shipyard on the Clyde, while Mirren stayed at home and had children, though like many women in those days, she had several stillbirths. Only two of her babies made it to adulthood, John, Marion's grandfather, and his younger brother, Kenny. John became a joiner in the new Singer sewing machine factory in Kilbowie Road, but Kenny inherited the defiantly independent streak that ran through the MacLeods. Kenny, like his father, worked in Thomson's, and he was by all accounts a cheerful lad, but a bit of a loner. One day Mirren asked him to go to the shops for some sausages, and Kenny agreed without a murmur. But he didn't come back, well, not in time for tea anyway. Unknown to anyone Kenny had that morning signed up as a crew member of the ship he had been working on, and instead of fetching Mirren's sausages, he had sailed off into the sunset. He returned three years later, put a package on the table and said, 'There's your sausages, Mirren.'

Kenny was always referred to as 'Big Kenny', a term of esteem unconnected with his size, and he was a hero to the younger MacLeods, though few actually saw him, because he rarely came home. He was a romantic figure who bestrode the globe, forever involved in intrigue and adventure, living the life they would have liked to live. Once he arrived in the uniform of a Canadian Mountie, and whenever the tale was recounted Marion pictured Big Kenny in his Smokey-the-Bear hat, red tunic, riding britches and high boots, standing on the tenement doorstep three floors up, complete with his horse. No one ever mentioned the horse, but it was a known fact that a Mountie would never go anywhere without his trusty steed. Every few years postcards would arrive from exotic places like Valparaiso or Ecuador, to prove that Big Kenny was real.

If Big Kenny was an inspiration to those living humdrum lives, his brother John more than made up for his adventurous spirit. So passive was he that when she was a child Marion often wondered if her grandfather could possibly be a MacLeod, and if he was, then what, she mused, had happened to him? It took her many years to understand that a quiet man is not necessarily a weak man, and that his marriage to Granny Kate was a perfect match. There had, by all accounts, been no fireworks to mark their courting, they had met at the Band of Hope and after a respectable time they had married. But if Kate had once sung hymns, she marched to a different tune thereafter, and Granda John never raised a word of protest.

In the 1920s Kate MacLeod had been one of the leaders of the Clydebank Rent Strikes, when the landlords tried to raise the rents on housing they hadn't maintained or improved for years, at a time when the tenants were suffering from the unemployment of the Depression. There were pro-test meetings in Glasgow at the time, but when the rent-collectors came round, Glasgow meekly caved in. But Clydebank didn't. The women organised themselves with guile to fight the sheriff officers who came to evict families in arrears, hounding them and shouting abuse as they threw the hapless debtor's meagre furniture into the street, not that it often came to that. The women organised a 24-hour vigil, to be on hand at the first scent of an attempted eviction. Kate would be out in the streets with a huge handbell to summon the others, and they would make their way to the home of the intended victim, blocking the close and barricading the house. Kate and her co-rebels thought up many ploys to frustrate the sheriff officers, they changed the names on the doors, so that instead of informing Mrs MacGregor that she was being officially made homeless, they found themselves talking to Mrs Stevenson, and if that wasn't the name on their piece of paper, there could be no eviction. If however the sheriff officers succeeded, the furniture would be moved back in again by the next day. And they bought replacement windows and doors from a local builder, so that no sooner was an eviction enforced than it was reversed. When the landlords began to win, as it was inevitable they would, the homeless families were given bell tents in McLean's Park across the canal, and fed with stews and soups made by the women with bones from the butcher. Granny Kate used to say that she had no real understanding of the class system until the Rent Strikes. 'Ah had nae idea that there was a working class, or that Ah belonged tae it, but wance Ah found oot that it was Us against Them, Ah never forgot it.' From hymns at the Band of Hope, Marion often thought with a smile, to 'The Red Flag'.

Sitting by the window of her fancy flat in the Holy City, thinking back over her life and her family, Marion would recall Granny Kate, a tiny, birdlike soul, her eyes shining with conviction, a woman who had discovered who she was and never lost her pride in the knowledge. And then she thought of Granda John, quiet, gentle Granda John, who sat by his fireside, smiling and saying little, and she recognised the part he had played. He was proud of Kate, and he supported her, never once disagreeing with her or objecting when his dinner wasn't on the table after a long day working at Singer's. In an age when men headed the family and made all the decisions, when they expected their wives to confine themselves to the home and hearth, Granda John had indeed been different, but not in the negative way Marion had once thought. Granda John was a big man in his own way, because he enabled Kate to be who she was, and not for the first time or the last, Marion ached to have known him longer and better.

Tommy MacLeod was John and Kate's only child, something that struck Marion as very, very odd. Everyone around her had big families, and she almost felt sorry for her father. 'How have ye no' got brothers and sisters, Da?' she would demand, as he slouched in his armchair, holding his newspaper to hide his face. He was rarely without a newspaper, it was the stage from which he teased his wife, or shielded himself from the wrath he deliberately induced. Glancing at his wife to make sure she was on edge for his answer, he would reply, 'Ah think ma mother tried it wance, hen, an' didnae like it.'

'Didnae like whit, Da?'

'Thomas John MacLeod!' Jean would warn sternly – you always got your full name when Jean MacLeod meant business – 'If ye know whit's good for ye, ye'll haud your tongue! Ah'm warnin' ye, noo!' Tommy MacLeod would laugh quietly behind the newspaper, and after what he considered a suitable agony of suspense for his wife, he would put the paper down and scoop Marion up onto his knee.

'Ye know that a' mammies stay at hame an' look after the bairns, jist like your mammy does? Ah mean, there couldnae be bairns if there was nae mammy at hame tae look after them, right?'

Marion would nod gravely. 'Well, your Granny Kate was too busy puttin' the fear o' God intae sheriff officers tae stay at hame, wasn't she? She was savin' people fae bein' put oot ontae the street, wasn't she?'

Marion would nod again. 'So if she couldnae be at home, she couldnae have ony merr bairns. Ye see?'

Marion loved the sense of it, the sheer, pure logic, though she had still wondered what it was that Granny Kate had 'tried wance' and hadn't liked, and she hoped that one day, if her mother wasn't around to stop him, her father would tell her.

2

Her father's family were the ones Marion knew best, her
mother's side were no more than sketches. Jean's father had
died in the earliest days of the First World War, leaving his
wife, Norah, and two daughters, Maggie and Jean. Norah,
as they say, liked a dram, but she still managed to bring her
daughters up, in a hand-to-mouth kind of way. She cleaned
other people's stairs, did their washings, anything to keep
her daughters fed, a hard life of poverty and drudgery that
gradually led to more boozing and finally to her death from
TB, a 'dirty' disease that the poor were ashamed of. Over
the years, Maggie had to care for her younger sister when
she was still a child herself, and by the time Norah died
Maggie was to all intents Jean's mother. It wasn't a role she
welcomed and it made Maggie a bitter woman all her life,
hard and unforgiving, and Tommy MacLeod only had to
threaten his children with a visit to Auntie Maggie's to ensure
instant obedience.

Maggie was sixteen when her mother died, five years older
than Jean, and at an age when she had reason to expect a
life of her own. Instead she had to shoulder the burden of
providing for her eleven-year-old sister for the foreseeable
future. She had few assets, least of all in her looks: 'a match
wi' the wid scraped aff' was how Tommy MacLeod described
her. She always wore her mousy hair pulled severely back
from her pinched face, emphasising the resentful look in her
eyes. It was the first thing you noticed, then her tight, thin
lips; Maggie was not an attractive woman to say the least.
And to give her yet more reason to feel hard-done-to, her

unwanted charge was the opposite. Jean grew into an auburn-haired beauty.

Jean married Tommy MacLeod when she was only seventeen; he used to tease her by saying she'd have taken the ragman's horse to get away from life with her sister, and escape from Maggie was certainly a reason to marry sooner rather than later. Ever on the lookout for romance, Marion cast her father as Young Lochinvar, arriving on his white charger to rescue the beautiful but tortured damsel Jean from life with Auntie Maggie. Depending on the circumstances a romantic streak can be either a great handicap or a great life enhancer, and Marion often looked back and admitted to herself that she hadn't always judged those circumstances correctly. She judged with her heart, and even though she clearly heard her head calling her a fool, she did so all her life. Stupid she would admit to, perhaps reckless at times, but deep down she was still not convinced heart over head was necessarily wrong. And anyway, she thought to herself, I am what I am.

Once she got Jean off her hands, poor, dreaded Auntie Maggie married a much older man she cleaned for, believing him to be rich, or at least, richer than her. By all accounts she gave him a life of loveless hell, making him eat alone, sit alone, and presumably sleep alone, until he died, as Tommy always said, 'gratefully'. That's when the old man got his own back on Maggie, because there was just enough money to keep her living very frugally, though for many people of the time that would have been a luxury, and once again she was thrown back on her own meagre talents. 'He didnae leave hur much, bit Ah bet it still wisnae value for money,' Tommy would say. 'The poor auld bugger woulda got merr for his pennies doon the docks than he ever got frae Maggie,' and Jean would blush bright red and say, 'Wheesht, Tommy! The bairns are listenin'!'

The widow Maggie lived alone in Jellicoe Street in nearby Dalmuir, rarely seeing the family and rarely seen by them, until Jean, overcome by guilt, enforced a duty visit. Maggie obviously found these occasions as awful as the family did, as they sat through long spells of uneasy silence, counting the ticks of the big Gingerbread clock on the mantelpiece, hoping that after it struck the next half-hour the agony would be over. There was nothing out of place in her house; the range was polished till it shone, as was the kettle that sat upon it just so, like an ornament. No speck of dust would have dared settle anywhere, but she hovered around anyway, clad in a pristine overall, duster in hand, ready to pounce. Young Marion would be allotted a chair from which, and in which, she dared not move, and was barked at repeatedly to 'Sit up straight, lassie!' – Maggie never once called her by her name – at the slightest twitch of a sagging muscle.

Just for the hell of it Tommy would drip tea onto the polished table, or stand on the polished hearth, for the joy of watching Maggie fuss around, instantly cleaning up the damage, her thin lips contracting even more than usual till they almost disappeared with distaste and annoyance. He would say the most outrageous things to her, which he covered with an easy innocence. 'My, Maggie,' he would say with duplicitous admiration, 'Ah don't know how ye've no' been snapped up long ago by some lucky man, yur hoose has such a homely feel tae it.' It had all the warmth of a morgue. 'Ye're that good wi' bairns tae,' he'd lie, as gasps of amazement fought to escape the gritted teeth of all present, 'ye're a real mother earth gaun' tae waste. Ah aye say that tae Jeannie, daen't Ah, Jeannie? An' ye're still a fine-lookin' wumman, ye hiv a bloom aboot ye, Maggie. Ah hiv this mate at Broon's, Ah'm sure thur's still time fur ye yit . . .'

Each visit started with threats from Jean about what would befall him if he 'gied Maggie ony lip', and after he had done so, Jean would lay into him. 'For God's sake, wumman,' he'd say, 'it's the only excitement the auld biddy gets. An' besides, Ah don't know whit ye bother for, a' she ever gave ye wis guilt.'

'She didnae need tae look after me, Tommy,' Jean would protest. 'Maggie gied up hur ain life fur me!'

'An' by Christ she makes sure we a' know aboot it! She's like wannae they vampires, she lives aff your guilt, Jeannie, she feeds aff it. Ye'd have been better aff sleepin' in the gutter fur a' the auld bugger cared aboot ye. That's the truth, Jean, an' ye know it fine!'

'Thomas John MacLeod,' Jean would hiss angrily, 'Maggie's a harmless widow wumman!'

'Harmless, Jeannie? Harmless?' he'd demand. 'Sure the neighbours take their milk off the step afore she goes oot in the mornin' in case she turns it soor wi' wan look! If a cat passes her door its hair falls oot, in fact if Ah pass her door mine damn near falls oot! Christ, if we drapped her by parachute ower Berlin Hitler wid gie up on the spot!'

Looking back through the years at Auntie Maggie, Marion came to almost understand the old woman, and that in fact her father had come closer than most to what made her tick. Even as a child Marion had felt sorry for her despite fearing her, and she always suspected that though Maggie, one of life's natural victims, played for sympathy, she hated those who pitied her. She almost had the feeling that Maggie sensed her pity and seethed with resentment against it; she was more comfortable with Tommy's dislike, and had more respect for his veiled taunts. Some people make the best of what they have, some the worst, and Maggie had been one of the latter. It was her nature, exacerbated by events, and Maggie could be blamed for neither. Jean on the other hand had reacted to the bleakness of her childhood by finding the close warmth of the MacLeods and going on to create another generation; her children would have what she had missed. In fact, looking back, Auntie Maggie wasn't an ogre, she was a poor, sad, lost soul, and the older Marion got, the more she wept for her.

Tommy MacLeod was a riveter in Brown's, part of 'the Black Squad' who were always filthy, and his arms were so muscled by the work that they looked carved from wood. Riveters were paid per rivet, with no allowances made for bad weather, the difficulty of working in certain areas, like the cramped bulkheads, or any other delay; problems were the riveter's loss, not the yard's. The rivets were heated in a small fire, then the 'hauder-oan' would push them red-hot through a hole in the steel plating covering the ship, where the riveter waited with a hammer to beat the rivet into a flat, polished button holding the ship's shell together. The hammering could be heard all over the yard, adding to the clatter and racket of the other trades. In time the noise affected the men's hearing, but health and safety played no part in the yards. Shipyard workers were hard men, but they had to be, they had a hard life. There was no job security; they were laid off as soon as a ship was completed, and when there was work again the powerful, bowler-hatted foremen chose who got the chance to feed their families. There was nowhere to eat, whatever sandwiches the men brought in were eaten amid the dust and mess where they worked and in all weathers, which in the west of Scotland meant a great deal of rain. Teabreaks didn't exist either, and if they brewed an illicit can of tea on a cold, wet morning in a riveter's brazier, the foremen, those 'bastards in bowlers', deliberately knocked them over. Toilets consisted of a long platform over a trough, with the holes cut out in a row, and as the men sat down the apprentices would launch a piece of burning paper from one end and watch the chain reaction as it sailed to the other, scorching exposed flesh as it passed. It was a joke handed down from one generation of apprentices to another that never lost its appeal because the result was so instantly and painfully obvious.

In later years the men themselves were blamed for the downfall of the yards, because of the frequent strikes caused by their rigid adherence to who did what, and their determination not to give an inch in disputes. But when you thought of the way they were treated, you began to wonder if that attitude was their reaction to that treatment. They were regarded by the bosses as no more than animals, given no dignity and less respect, and when it came to recognising the skills that created the big ships, even that was claimed by the bosses. Little wonder then that the men found ways to hit back, even if the rest of the world didn't understand. Years later, when Tommy MacLeod was no longer alive, Marion saw a film about shipbuilding on the Clyde, and there was her father among a group of men sitting by the river during their thirty-minute lunch break, his small, muscular frame, the dark hair and those blue eyes, crinkled with humour, so real she felt she could reach into the screen and touch him again. With great tenderness and affection he and the other men were sharing their sandwiches with some of the hundreds of feral cats that lived in the yard. Men hardened in body and spirit by the work and the life, yet they cared for stray cats. Maybe that was a reaction too, a means of finding some humanity, a solidarity with other creatures like themselves, living a hand-to-mouth existence with no control over their lives or futures.

And the harshness of their working conditions was reflected in the hard humour of the yards, and the ways the men found to get one over on the bosses. Tommy MacLeod told his family some of the stories, the ones his wife would not disapprove of too strongly. Of Eric in the carpenter's shop, who took orders and made gate-leg tables, which were then smuggled in pieces past the guards at the gates by the other workers. 'Aye,' he would grin, 'many a man had merr than wan leg doon his troosers.' Or Big Malky the engineer, who spent his entire working day collecting bets for his workmates and running to and from the illegal bookies outside the yard gates. And the men called 'the Dummies', deaf and dumb men conscripted to work in the shipyard, who, like everyone else, had their weaknesses leapt upon. The other men would hide their tools till one of the 'Dummies' lost his temper, and as Tommy said, 'if wan went, they a'' went!' In no time the frustration that the deaf often feel in a hearing world turned into full-scale warfare, as the chain reaction spread and their tormentors ran for any cover they could find.

'That's no' funny, Tommy!' Jean would say. 'How would you like tae be deaf an' tae be made a fool o'? Ye should a' be ashamed o' yersels. Ye shouldnae mock the afflicted!'

'Away wi' ye, wumman,' Tommy would grin, 'everybody gets made a mug o'. We don't mean ony herm, we treat the Dummies the same as oorsels, only different.'

But Tommy MacLeod had lived through the Depression of the twenties and thirties when entire families were unemployed in Clydebank. In 1930 Brown's order book was empty and the shipyard had very nearly closed, until they got the contract for No. 534 – the *Queen Mary*. It had looked as though for the next three or four years families could be reasonably sure of survival, but it didn't happen. The money ran out and for two and a half years all work on 534 was suspended and the workers thrown onto the humiliation of the dole once again. It wasn't until April 1934 that work resumed, and the men stood like cattle while the foremen, the 'bastards in bowlers', walked up and down the lines of desperate faces, picking and choosing who would work, and who wouldn't. It was no wonder they were so hated, and why their bowler hats, their badges of authority, doubled as safety helmets too. As they walked through the yards hot rivets, spanners and hammers often landed on or near them from the ships in progress hundreds of feet above, all by accident of course. The men trod a fine line between keeping on the right side of the foremen because their work and their family's survival depended on them, and hating them for the same reason. That they had to bend the knee to men they had little respect and less liking for, ate away at their pride, making the bitterness they felt towards them that much sharper. No. 534 had been built with a high level of apprentice labour, because they were cheaper than journeymen, a practice that continued until the yards had had their day. As soon as an apprentice informed the foreman that his 'time was out' he would be sacked and another apprentice taken on. Apprenticeships contained no formal training, the lads learned from journeymen on the job and years before their apprenticeship was officially over they were skilled workers themselves – for considerably less money. It wasn't uncommon for an apprentice to conceal that his time was out though, because an apprentice's wage was better than no wage at all. They would only own up when they were about to get married, because in their culture apprentices did not marry, only journeymen. The chances were high, therefore, that they would become skilled tradesmen, married men and unemployed men in one swift move.

Tommy MacLeod had worked on 534 though, and he remembered the launch in September 1934, and the mixed feelings of pride and apprehension, because now that the *Queen Mary* had been built, who knew when there would be more work? The MacLeods had survived because they were a big family and they had diversified. Quite simply, while those in the yards were out of work, the others working in Singer's had supported them. But Tommy wanted better for his sons, and that lesson in survival had struck home. So when the time came for Colin to enter the yards, Tommy made sure his son became an apprentice electrician. The year after that, Iain joined them in Brown's as an apprentice carpenter, skills that could be used outside the yards. But Colin had either inherited a streak of adventure from Big Kenny, or else his father's tales of him had infected the boy, which was Jean's preferred version. Colin was a younger edition of his father, with a shock of dark, nearly black, hair falling across his forehead, and the brightest, most vivid blue eyes, alive with his dreams of adventure. He it was who led expeditions on the tramcar to alien and far distant Glasgow, and organised perilous voyages by raft on the canal, his eyes shining with the joy of it no matter what sanctions were forthcoming. 'It's *in* him,' Tommy would say to his wife, not altogether disapprovingly, 'the boy cannae help it.'

'Aye, Thomas John MacLeod,' Jean would retort sharply, 'and we a' know where *that* comes frae, don't we?'

The house at Number 70 was a two-room-and-kitchen with a shared toilet on the landing. Tommy and Jean slept in a set-in bed in the room that doubled as a dining and living room, while Colin and Iain shared one bed in the bedroom, and Frances and Marion another; no one thought of privacy in those days, it hadn't been invented. Every night the four MacLeod offspring fell asleep listening to Colin's tales, of his plans for the future, the great, exciting things he would do. It didn't cross his mind that he would be a shipyard electrician for the rest of his life, he was meant for better things, or at least, more exciting ones.

Colin was part of a gang of three, though there were other privileged members occasionally admitted for certain expeditions. They lived directly above each other, Jimmy Ryan on the first floor of the tenement at 70 Second Avenue, above the ground-floor flat of old Archie and Mirren, Gino Rossi on the second, and Colin and the other MacLeods on the third. Across the narrow landing from them was the home of John and Kate. Little wonder that Marion thought of Number 70 as 'theirs', and all the other tenants as the guests of the MacLeods. Jimmy Ryan's wee brother, Davy, who was five years younger than Marion, was a constant thorn in her flesh, stealing the balls when she bounced them against the gable end as she sang street songs, breaking in when the girls played with skipping ropes, and rubbing out the chalk beds they scrawled on the pavement to play peevers. Convinced that the MacLeods ruled Number 70, she would plead with the various adults in her family to have Davy thrown in the canal, on the sound grounds that Mrs Ryan had Jimmy, and so she didn't need another son, and especially not Davy, not that one.

'Ye're right, wee Marion,' her father would say, the muscles in his face working hard to keep the laughter back, 'these criminals need tae be taught a lesson! Ah guarantee that Davy won't bother ye ony merr wance he's drooned in the canal!'

'Thomas John MacLeod!' Jean would enunciate, 'whit a thing tae teach the bairn! You go away oot noo, Marion, an' don't you tell Mrs Ryan whit your Da says aboot droonin' Davy. Wee Davy's jist a wee boy, he's only playin'.'

Colin, Jimmy and Gino were revered by the other children in the neighbourhood, and their frequent exploits regarded with respect. They were 'the big boys' who were forever involved in something, and no matter what punishment was meted out each time, everyone knew there was another 'something' round the corner. Together they walked to Radnor Park, the Proddie school just up the hill, they sat together, played together and when school finished they walked back home together. Even in the crowd of brothers, sisters and other Holy City children walking along with them, the three lads were side by side and inseparable. Jimmy Ryan's widowed mother worked in Singer's and Gino's parents, Alfredo and Anna, were Italians and ran a tiny café beside the factory.

'They talk funny, they Eyetalians,' Tommy MacLeod would say to annoy his wife. There was silence. Jean always made it a point of honour to hold out as long as she could before rising to the bait and answering back. 'Ah mean,' he persisted, 'ye canny say the Rossis are the same as us, noo can ye?'

'How no'?' Jean would finally demand, as he grinned slyly behind his newspaper.

'C'mon noo, Jeannie, they're a different colour for a start!'

'So whit? They're handsome folk the Italians, an' the Rossis are awfy nice people, they'd help onybody, *that's* how they're no' the same as the likes o' you!'

24

'Aye, bit Jeannie, they're different, an' they *dae* talk funny, ye hivtae admit that, they talk funny!'

'So dae the Irish,' Jean would reply, mindful of her Irish background and the prejudice that came with it. 'Ye'll be sayin' next that the Irish arenae as good as you because *they* talk funny!'

'Well, noo ye come tae mention it, that's a point, Jean. But don't you worry, hen, Ah've made ye respectable by takin' pity oan ye an' changin' your name tae MacLeod. Ah should get a medal for takin' in an orphan!'

Jean, who knew from years of experience where these racial slurs were leading, always had a rolled-up newspaper at hand and would then attempt to whack her husband over the head with it. 'Dae ye think ye're the only wan that can use a paper, Tommy MacLeod,' she'd shout, 'swine that ye are?'

Tommy would then jump to his feet, roll his own newspaper up and they would fence each other until Jean collapsed in a breathless, laughing heap. It was a scene that was enacted so many times in the MacLeod household throughout Marion's childhood that she could recall the sight and the sound of their voices at will for the rest of her life. Years later, reflecting on her own marriage, she realised that her parents had argued constantly, yet she couldn't recall ever hearing a truly angry word between them. Their verbal sparring and their newspaper duels always dissolved into laughter, laughter that lived on in her heart and her dreams, long, long after Tommy and Jean were gone.

If Colin was Big Kenny two generations on, then Iain was Granda John, a quiet, thoughtful lad, content with his lot, slow to anger and quick to smile. He had reddish hair, pale blue eyes, and a slow, gentle smile. Looking back, Marion couldn't recall Iain having an enemy, and the only childhood fight he had ever been involved in was when one of Colin's famous bogey designs was criticised. Any child building a bogey enlisted the assistance and advice of the master, but Colin was as adventurous in this as he was in everything else, innovative even, placing the old pram wheels in locations about the wooden body not thought of before, just 'tae see whit happens'. Naturally, not every design worked out, and one disgruntled customer made his disappointment too obvious, by calling the bogey master 'an eejit'. He was promptly felled by the normally quiet, smiling Iain, who was always there in the background to minimise any problems his older brother encountered.

With Colin there was a hint of danger, a feeling that he was slightly out of control, that you never really knew what he would be up to next, whereas with Iain there was dependability. He was happy to work in the shipyard beside his father and brother in a trade that suited his calm, careful personality. As Tommy often remarked, he was 'wanna nature's carpenters'. Marion always felt that this was said not altogether in admiration, and looking back she would smile at what was clearly Tommy's secret indulgence in hell-raising by proxy, in his love of Big Kenny's adventures and Colin's more amateur exploits. He would have defended Iain to the death, as he would all of his children, but it was fair to say that he identified more closely with Colin, not that he would ever have admitted it. Certainly Iain gave his mother no cause for concern; perhaps having grown up with Jean's constant anxiety over Colin, he had compensated by being the good boy, or maybe he was just a chip off that other MacLeod old block. But he never showed any resentment of Colin, in fact he tried to cover up for his brother whenever another row loomed. He would smile his shy smile, shake his head and then plan the defence, while Colin was already into his next adventure. There was something missing in Colin, he never foresaw difficulties and was always shocked when he landed in hot water, a trait that was missing in turn from Iain's make-up. That at least was Tommy MacLeod's tacit opinion. He knew that Colin was in trouble too often, though he never admitted it outright, and he perhaps suspected that Iain lacked spirit, though he never admitted that either. 'Put the two o' them taegither,' he'd say, getting as near as he ever would to acknowledging his inner thoughts, 'split them doon the middle, an' ye'd have two perfect laddies.'

Jean would give a derisive 'Humph. They're MacLeods aren't they?' she'd say. 'They're perfect already, surely?'

'Aye, right enough, Jeannie,' Tommy would reply, ignoring her sarcasm, 'it's just that Ah never thought ye could understaun' that . . . ye bein' Irish an' that. Well done, lass!'

3

While Iain made furniture for the ships built by Brown's, Granda John made cabinets for Singer's sewing machines, and Frances worked in Department 47 making the electrical motors. There were two marks on the skyline that proved you were in Clydebank: the huge ships under construction towering over the tenements, and the 200-feet-high square Singer's clock, each of its four faces 26 feet in diameter. In the shadow of the clock was 47, known as 'the Beauty Parlour', because the superintendent chose only the best-looking girls to work in his department.

Every year Singer's had a beauty pageant where the wives of the directors perused the girls who had been nominated by each department and voted one Queen. The outfits for the Queen and her attendants were made in the factory and the crowning ceremony took place on the sports field. Thereafter there was a dance that the workforce looked forward to every year, at which the newly crowned Queen took pride of place. That year Frances was the nominee of Department 47, all of them acknowledged to be the cream of the available beauties, so it was a fair bet that she would be Queen. This came as no surprise to her adoring younger sister, because Frances, with her thick auburn hair and green eyes, was the most beautiful creature Marion had ever seen, and her dearest wish was to grow up to look just like her. The seven years between the sisters meant that they were far enough apart for there to be no rivalry, and apart from the times when Marion tried on her sister's clothes, or worse, her scarce supply of make-up, there was no friction between them. Frances was perfect in Marion's eyes, she was the pattern she hoped to follow into adulthood and there was no doubt in her mind that Frances would be Queen. Jean thought so too and wept a few tears of pride.

'Ye're no' greetin' are ye, Jeannie?' Tommy demanded.

'Naw, Ah'm no'!' Jean lied vehemently, which made Tommy wonder aloud what kind of state she would get into when her elder daughter sailed down the aisle on his arm one day. Jean cried even more at that thought.

'Don't worry aboot yer Ma,' Tommy advised no one in particular, 'she's been choppin' onions. Is that no' right, Jeannie?' and he laughed quietly to himself when no reply was forthcoming from his overcome wife. 'Ah don't know,' he said softly, 'youse wimmen jist havtae think o' a posh frock an' ye a' go tae pieces!'

Tommy was less affected by the news, it was to him simply another public statement of the position as it had always been. His Frances, he knew, wasn't blessed with brains, and he secretly acknowledged to himself that though she had Jeannie's looks, she hadn't her character. His Frances was a nice lassie though, a kind lassie, and aye, his Frances was a stunner, and he sometimes had to bite his lip when he saw how men looked at her. Frances was the kind of lassie who aspired to marriage and motherhood; unlike the wean, Marion, who asked questions about everything and read anything that her eyes fell on, Frances's only real ambition was to find a good man and raise a family, and given her exceptional looks she had a better choice than most. But she was afraid to tell her grandmother about the forthcoming beauty pageant. Granny Kate was regarded as a Communist, because in those days anyone with strength of character and a mind of their own was regarded as a Communist, indeed all the people of Clydebank had long had the reputation of being Communists. The truth was that Clydebank was a town of workers, constructed for and made by workers, and there were no middle or upper classes to dilute their power. And the way the houses had been built meant that workers from Brown's, or Beardmore's or Singer's tended to live together, which added to the feeling of solidarity, but the Red Clydeside label had stuck. Granny Kate fitted the label as the label fitted her, and Granny Kate disapproved of Department 47 being called the Beauty Parlour, so she would not, Frances knew, approve of her granddaughter entering a beauty contest. Her father's advice was not to tell her until she had to.

'Listen, hen,' he said, 'Granny Kate worked in Department 19 straightening sewing needles wi' a wee hammer, Granny Kate would never have got intae 47.'

'That's a helluva thing tae say aboot your ain mother,' Jean said, finished wiping her eyes. 'Auld Kate is a fine-lookin' wumman!'

'Aye, but, Jeannie, wi' the best will in the world, she wisnae a great beauty,' Tommy replied. 'A' the good looks in the family come frae the MacLeod side, an' she only married a MacLeod.'

'Dear God in heaven, wid ye listen tae the man! He's beginnin' tae believe that nonsense! Oor Frances hasnae got the MacLeod looks, she looks like *me*, she's got ma colourin', she's the double o' me when Ah wis her age! Ah only married a MacLeod tae, God help me!'

'But when you were seventeen, ye had time tae become a MacLeod, didn't ye? Ye kinda grew intae perfection,' Tommy replied, retiring behind his newspaper to wait for the onslaught his illogical explanation was designed to provoke. Her mother's mistake, Marion knew, was in using logic against Tommy's deliberately silly pronouncements, therefore she could never hope to win. It ended as these things always did, with her mother unable to counter Tommy's endless stream of lunacy and launching herself at him instead. They would wrestle in Tommy's armchair as he let out mock appeals for help, and then he would say 'Noo, Jeannie, ye know whit'll happen!'

'Naw Tommy, naw!'

'Ye leave me nae choice!' he would announce, then he

30

would tickle her till she gave in. It was amazing how she was transformed by the breathless laughter this produced into, well, into a girl was the only way Marion could describe it. These battles with Tommy brought out the carefree teenager she must have been before she became a mother of four. Sitting in her rocking chair calling up her memories decades later, Marion recognised that as a mark of a good relationship, when one could still find the person they had married, even after years of struggle and worry. She had wanted the kind of closeness and love her parents had, that had cushioned and protected her childhood. Had that been too much to ask, she wondered?

But that particular spat between Tommy and Jean mattered little in the end, because Frances was conscripted and sent to work in munitions – in Singer's sewing machine factory. The War had changed the rules and she was no longer the leading beauty of 47, so she wouldn't have to tell her militant Granny that she was about to be made Queen. Maybe next year . . .

In the meantime there were other pressing problems. Eric, he of the thriving gate-leg table export business in Brown's, had taken an order that was proving difficult to deliver. Getting gate-leg tables out past the guards on the gates was always successful, thanks to the ingenuity and co-operation of his workmates, but in a rash moment he had agreed to make a big, fixed-leg table. And he had made a fine job of it, everyone agreed, rarely had workmanship like it been seen outwith the big liners like the *Queens*. The problem was how to get something of this scale past the guards at the gates who were employed by the management to cut the level of pilfering from the yard. The matter had been exercising the finest minds in the yard for weeks, and Tommy MacLeod's especially, as Iain had assisted the master craftsman in the making of the table.

'Why is it ony o' your business?' Jean demanded.

'Jeannie, Jeannie,' he sighed, 'wan o' these days somebody's gonny hear ye askin' things like that, an' it'll look bad for me! As ma mither aye says, "It's Us an' Them. Noo that would be reason enough, but oor Iain here helped tae make this table, so that's another reason. But the main wan is that Eric has an order tae fill an' we canny let the customer doon, noo can we?'

'Well, Iain shouldnae have got involved!'

'Eric's his boss, wumman!' Tommy replied, shaking his head.

'An' Ah still don't see why you, the great Tommy MacLeod, should have anythin' tae dae with this. Ye're a bloody riveter for God's sake!'

Tommy threw his hands out to the rest of the family, appealing for the support of his audience. 'Have Ah no' jist explained a' that?' he demanded. 'Whit merr can Ah say tae make the wumman understand?'

As the weeks passed the logistical difficulties of how to get the table out of the yard were discussed back and forth, plans were assessed, discarded and thrown back, until the night Tommy arrived home with the light of genius burning in his eyes.

'Right, Jeannie lass, all hands tae the deck! Ah need your auld pinnies an' things.'

'Aye, Tommy, Ah'm sure ye dae, but Ah'm wearin' ma auld pinnies an' things.'

'Noo, Jeannie, we've nae time for your impression o' Auld Maggie the Martyr, jist get yersel' busy an' help the War effort! Ah've had an idea!'

'Holy Jesus, Mother o' God!' Jean moaned. 'We're a' done for noo, he's had an idea!'

Tommy's solution to the great table problem was, like all brilliant ideas, astonishingly simple. The now famous table was so big that each leg was supported by a small castor, in other words, it was mobile and could be pushed out of the yard. The next thing had been to think of items that could be legitimately wheeled out, and that was where Tommy's spark of genius came into play: a bridal party.

When women were leaving work on the last day before getting married, they were traditionally dressed up as babies by their workmates, dummies in their mouths, frilly bonnets on their heads and a chamber pot, a chanty, on their laps. They would then be pushed out of their workplace and through the town in a pram, their friends singing songs as raucous and risqué as possible. Every male they encountered, even if they had to be dragged out of all the pubs en route, was forced to kiss the 'baby' and drop a donation into the chanty for the pleasure. Then the blushing bride would be returned home, usually several hours later, red about the face but with a little bit extra with which to start her married life. If such a bride could be found and the rest of the work-force invited to join in, then the plan could proceed, Tommy decided, and if there was no one about to marry, a volunteer would be press-ganged. An idea so simple that it had to work, but for Tommy it was too simple. 'If somethin' is tae be done,' he said, 'it's tae be done well,' and when no genuine bride-to-be was found, he decided that the volunteer bride should be male. He had been determined to give the starring role to the biggest, ugliest, dirtiest man in the yard, but even Tommy had to toe the line somewhere, so he reluctantly settled for one of the less muscled apprentices. What he needed now was female clothes, and as he was gathering Jean's, others were finding camouflage material for the table itself.

When Friday came around the plan was put into action. They would exit through the smaller gate near the Town Hall rather than the bigger, better-policed one along Dumbarton Road. The 'bride' was dressed and made up by the women in the cleaning shop and the bridal carriage assembled, covered by purloined sheets and tablecloths and decorated with streamers of crepe paper in different colours. When the hooter sounded to mark the end of the working day a heavy entourage surrounded the table with the blushing bride on top and pushed it through the yard, all of them shouting, cheering and singing, and the unsuspecting guards laughingly waved them through.

It was too easy for Tommy though, the lack of challenge was almost an insult. He decided that the guards had to be tested, so to everyone's horror he halted the procession in its tracks, and insisted that the two guards had to kiss the bride and give a donation. One by one they were encouraged to climb on top of Eric's table, kiss the unfortunate apprentice and throw some money into the chanty on his lap. And no quick peck was accepted, Tommy insisted that only the most passionate of kisses would be allowed, as it was, he commented, 'probably the last chance the poor lassie will get'. Only when he was satisfied did the bridal party proceed past the gate and on into the safety of the town. As a parting gesture he greeted both the guards warmly in Gaelic and slapped each of them on the back for being such good sports. Eric's mammoth table was delivered, the apprentice was allowed to keep the cash in return for losing his dignity, and honour was satisfied all round.

It was a victory, one-up for 'Us' in the constant war between 'Us an' Them', and there were precious few of those.

4

As Tommy MacLeod made his way home at the end of his shift he was accompanied more often than not by Danny Boyle, who lived in Crown Avenue. Danny was the other riveter on the squad, the left-hander to Tommy's right hand, and he also 'kicked wi' the left foot', an expression that indicated that he was a good Catholic boy. 'Left of foot, left of hand and left of nature!' as Tommy used to say. Because of this his nickname was, without offence being intended or taken, 'Danny the Pape', which over time had been shortened to 'Pape'. Tommy and Danny Boyle would separate where Second Avenue met Kilbowie Road, where Marion waited every night for her father, while Danny walked on up the hill to Crown Avenue.

''Night, Tam, see ye in the mornin',' Danny would say.

'Aye, bright an' early, Pape,' Tommy would respond, clasping his daughter's clean hand in his huge, rough, filthy paw.

'It'll be the golden rivet the morra then, Tam, Ah feel it in ma bones.'

'Me tae, Pape, the morra without a doubt. It's the golden rivet for us an' it's you an' me for the good life. Night, Pape!'

'Da,' Marion would ask, 'whit's the golden rivet?'

'It's a secret, hen!' Tommy would whisper, his eyes darting here and there for eavesdroppers. 'When me an' Pape find it we'll let you see it first, a'right?'

But she of the inquiring mind couldn't let the question of

the golden rivet go and took it to her mother as Jean was going through the ritual of cleaning out the fire.

'Whit's the golden rivet?'

'Where did ye hear o' that?' Jean asked, poking the ashes through into the ash can below.

'Da and Pape talk aboot it every night, bit Da won't tell me whit it is.'

Jean turned round to face her daughter with the expression Tommy called her 'shocked missionary face'. 'Well, first of a', Marion Katie MacLeod,' she said sternly, 'you will *not* call Danny Boyle "Pape". Is that understood?'

'Da calls him "Pape".'

'Ah don't care if the Pope hissel' calls him "Pape", you *don't*! Understood? The last thing we want is you goin' aroond copying anythin' that daft Da o' yours says or does, or ye'll end up as daft as him. Danny Boyle is Mr Boyle tae you!'

'Well why does Da call him "Pape", then?'

'Holy Jesus, Mother of God!' said Jean in her own mother's Irish accent.

'Mammy, Jesus wasnae the Mother of God.'

'Ah know that fine!' Jean retorted, struggling up from her knees with the ashes from the fire. 'An' don't think Ah don't know where ye heard *that*! Whit Ah'm sayin' is there isnae always a reason why your Da does or says anythin', an' jist because he does, disnae mean you havtae dae the same, does it?'

Marion's brow furrowed, trying to work out where this conversation was going and why. 'But –'

'Marion, will ye let it drop? Listen; it's wan thing for your Da tae call Danny Boyle "Pape" but quite another for you to call him "Pape". That's a' ye need tae know!'

Marion gave the matter some more thought and decided to abandon the 'Pape' issue till a more auspicious moment. 'An' whit aboot the golden rivet, well?'

'Whit golden rivet?'

'The golden rivet Da and Pa– Mr Boyle talk aboot.'

'Och, Marion, Ah *tellt* ye! Ah don't have an explanation for every daft thing your Da comes up wi'? Noo run away oot an' play, Ah've tae get the dinner oan in a minute!'

Marion made her way to the door, deep in thought, then she turned back. 'Mammy?'

'Holy Jesus, Mother of God! – an' nae smart answers! Whit is it *noo*, Marion?'

'When Ah'm aulder will Ah get tae call Mr Boyle "Pape"?'

'Aye,' said Jean heavily, 'when ye grow up an' you're a riveter in Broon's, ye can call Danny Boyle "Pape". But for noo it's Mr Boyle, OK?'

But Marion's questions about Pape Boyle didn't stop there. She thought he looked like a badger. He was small and stocky with brown eyes, black hair beginning to turn silver at the temples and a complexion like Cary Grant, the film star, that looked like a permanent suntan. Like her father, Pape's upper body was heavily muscled from the work he did, with strong arms that seemed to run into his neck without any clear division. His nickname should, she thought, have been Brock, but she sensed that her mother would have been just as reluctant to discuss this, however important the matter was to herself, and so she decided to let the matter rest there for the moment. But she still wished she knew what the golden rivet was . . .

Auntie Maggie, like Frances, worked in Singer's. In a job custom-made for her, she polished the finished sewing machines before they were shipped to the far corners of the earth. Maggie spent her entire life vainly trying to cleanse her existence of the shabbiness of her early life, her mother's drinking and TB, the constant poverty. Everything in her home shone and sparkled. It was almost an obsession, and Singer's paid her to do it, until the War intervened, and she too was diverted into the production of bullets and guns. Whoever was shot by one of Maggie's bullets would at least have the satisfaction of knowing that it was a clean bullet.

'They should just shove Maggie intae a shell case and send that ower,' Tommy MacLeod muttered. 'If she exploded ontae the Germans they'd surrender soon enough.'

Jean looked up from where she was ironing, a look of warning that Tommy knew well and constantly ignored. He turned the page of his newspaper. 'Ah mean,' he continued with studied casualness, 'wan look frae they eyes wid turn the Gerries tae liquid, never mind a pillar o' salt.'

Jean was keeping her counsel, the only sign that she was annoyed a louder thud than normal of the flat iron, first on the range then onto the clothes.

'Either that,' her husband continued, flicking from one page of his newspaper to another, 'or they could let her loose wi' her dusters an' she could polish the hell oota them till they gie in.'

Jean lifted the flat iron from the range where it had been heating up and stood over him. 'That tongue o' yours could dae wi' a good ironin',' she said. 'It might get rid o' a lot o' the rubbish ye speak, Tommy MacLeod!'

'Ye see whit Ah mean?' Tommy appealed to no one in particular. 'Violence jist gallops in that family! See whit damage Maggie could dae?'

Frances had met Marek Nowak the way most young people of the age met, at the dancing. He was one of the *Piorun*'s crew, and while the little destroyer was being refitted he was more or less free to enjoy himself after a year at sea. He was part of the Polish fleet that had escaped as Germany invaded, and thereafter they served alongside the British navy. In 1941 Marek was a tall lad of nineteen, a year older than Frances, the exact ages, Marion's romantic heart couldn't help but notice, that Granda Archie and Granny Mirren had been when they fled from Uist all those years ago. Apart from that he spoke good English with an accent that intrigued Marion; often she would ask him questions just to hear him talk. He was fair-haired and blue-eyed and he was always bright and cheerful, unlike poor Jimmy Ryan who was so tongue-tied when Frances was around. Unusually Tommy, always protective of his beautiful daughter, took to Marek straight away, partly because the Polish seamen were well regarded in Clydebank, and there was sympathy for them too over what had happened to their country after the German invasion. Even so, when the two went out Marion was often sent along too, though it was many years before she realised that she was chaperoning the young lovers. Whatever Marek and Frances might want to get up to, Marion's constant questions could easily distract them. They went to the High Park, or the Bluebell Woods in Dalmuir, with the little burn running through what was known as Lover's Walk, where it always seemed to Marion that she had entered an enchanted land, with the tinkle of the water and the perfume of the bluebells. She often wondered if crushed bluebells could be made into perfume, but she could never bring herself to try it, the little flowers were so delicate and helpless somehow; roses at least had thorns to protect them. She took little notice of Frances and Marek on their walks, nobody had told her to keep an eye on them after all, but her presence must have been something they could have done without.

On really special days they went on the train to Helensburgh, six long miles away. Before the War and the rationing there was a delicacy her mother often talked of; it came in a little tartan cardboard handbag, and was called Edinburgh Rock. Marion had no memory of ever seeing one let alone sampling the contents, sweets were, after all, strictly rationed, but she knew from listening to the rest of the family that Edinburgh Rock was wonderful and in normal times could be found in Helensburgh. She simply assumed that

Edinburgh was a suburb of Helensburgh, because Scotland's capital city was a long way from Clydebank and therefore well outside the boundaries of her life. Whenever Edinburgh was mentioned in school she placed it on her mental map alongside Helensburgh station, the place famous for its rock.

She was used to hearing and seeing the steam engines in their black LNER livery, their chuff-chuff noises and plumes of smoke were part of normal life that she would only notice once they had disappeared for ever, but somehow if you were going on a trip the ordinary became special. Jean made up sandwiches that were wrapped in the waxy paper loaves of bread came in, and sometimes she managed to come by a few eggs to boil for the feast. Jean felt sorry for her elder daughter; courting was a hard enough business without this damned War laying down impossible rules. Any lad she met might be called up and gone for years, perhaps even killed in action, and Marek would leave as soon as the *Piorun* was ready for service. Who knew if he would ever be seen again? Everything had changed with the War; people behaved in different ways when there was a possibility they might be killed or not meet again. Look at the way some married women found themselves other men as soon as their own went off to fight. Like 'that Sal Devlin' down the road who had gone to school with Frances. Such a bright-eyed, innocent wee thing she had been in those days, yet look what she had become. Marion listened hard whenever Sal Devlin's name was mentioned, while trying to appear absorbed in other matters, because Sal was discussed in special, hushed, adult voices. She was aware that her parents talked about Sal in a kind of code whenever she was around, but she could never figure out why.

Sal was a big-boned girl who seemed years older than she actually was, with the kind of make-up that seemed a touch heavier than the norm, and hair blonder than was considered natural. Innocent she may have looked once, but from her early teens on she had a knowing look in her eye and a wry smile on her lips, as though she was well aware of what the other women thought of her but didn't care over much. Marion liked her though, she liked the fact that Sal never passed you in the street without asking how you were doing, and how Frances was, and she always had a stick of gum when no one else had, a stick of gum, moreover, that she generously handed over. Marion somehow knew without being told that she had to hide the gum from her mother and she didn't mention her meetings with Sal as she wandered up the hill from her shift at Singer's. There was a definite atmosphere when Sal's name was mentioned in those peculiar hushed adult tones, and it was mentioned frequently by the local women when they met in queues, in the street or halfway up a close. She was known as 'that Sal Devlin', even after she had married a local lad, Tony Gallagher, a foundryman in Singer's, just before he went away to the army. Many girls did the same, and having had no time to experience marriage nor tangible proof of being married, some, like Sal, continued to behave as though they were still single 'only merr so', as Tommy would say with a sly grin. There was a constant stream of visitors to Sal's home in Second Avenue, all of them servicemen and all of them foreign. It was also noticed that Sal was rarely short of rationed goods, even those so scarce that they couldn't even be rationed.

'Ah see that Sal Devlin had another Yank in her hoose last night,' Jean would say quietly to Tommy.

'Noo, Jeannie, the lassie's only daein' her bit for the War effort. He wis likely a poor laddie away frae hame for the first time, feelin' homesick an' Sal took pity oan him. Ah'm sure she gied him a nice tea an' sent him oan his way.'

'A nice tea? He wis there a' night! He wis seen leavin' at six o'clock, her hingin' oot the windae wavin' tae him an' him wavin' back, happy as Larry!'

'Well, there ye are then, he must've enjoyed his tea as much as Larry did!' Tommy turned the page of his newspaper. 'Whitever it is she serves up, Ah jist wish Ah could hiv a bite, Ah'll tell ye that. Ye never see them leavin' withoot a big grin oan their faces onywey!'

'Ye whit?' Jean rounded on him. 'A bite? Ah'll gie ye a crack oan the ear if Ah hear any merr o' your cheek, Thomas John MacLeod! An' Ah hope ye've had a word wi' oor Colin an' Iain tae keep away frae her, we don't want them getting caught up wi' the likes o' her.'

'Ach, Jeannie, sounds tae me as if ye're jealous o' the lassie's currant bun. Why dae ye no' jist ask her for the recipe an' then ye can have a' the Yanks beatin' a path tae your door tae?'

There then followed a swift, furious struggle as Jean launched herself at Tommy and Tommy caught her around the waist and wrestled with her. Marion ignored them and tried to work out what exactly it was that 'that Sal Devlin' did and why she was so obviously disapproved of by the local women. As she went over the conversation again in her mind for clues missed the first time round, the familiar scene she had witnessed many times was taking place. Jean would eventually call a halt and stand up, smoothing her apron down with one hand, her hair with the other, as she caught her breath. As always she would hiss 'Swine!' at Tommy, as he gathered up his newspaper again and resumed his seat by the fire, and as always he would reply with a grin, 'That's me, hen, Swine MacLeod!'

Jean was constantly torn between urging Frances not to befriend 'that Sal Devlin' to protect her daughter's virtue and reputation, and trying to indulge her need for romance and excitement. Tommy, being her Da, was like all Das through-out the ages, only interested in protecting her virtue and reputation.

'Ah used tae be a laddie masel',' he'd say mysteriously. 'Ah know whit they're like. It would take a clever wan tae get by me!'

'Listen tae him!' Jean would say. 'The last of the red-hot lovers! Clydebank's ain Rudolph Valentino!'

'Well, if you say so, Jeannie, though Ah wouldnae make such claims masel',' he grinned. 'The trick is tae fool the lassie intae thinkin' ye know nothin'. If ye know nothin' then ye canny dae her any herm.'

'Well, in that case you had a head start,' Jean replied. 'Ye *did* know nothin'!'

The excitement of a trip to Helensburgh was all Marion could think of, and the days before dragged so much it seemed life was in slow motion. The feeling built gradually so that on the night before she could hardly sleep, then it was up and get ready in her best clothes, and collect the ancient battered metal bucket and spade that she had from prewar days. Once trips like this were almost so frequent they were mundane, hard as that was to imagine now. Standing waiting for the train to stop at the platform was almost too much to bear, and there was a feeling that if you didn't jump on that very second it might take off without you. With her stomach full to bursting with butterflies, she would climb aboard the brown carriage and sink into the blue moquette seats, hopefully one beside a window. Then waiting for the first glimpse of the sea, watching impatiently as each station slid past always too slowly, asking every few minutes, 'Are we near yet?' Then there it was, the vast sea, almost alive, moving in a way the canal didn't, and not even the River Clyde did. This was an altogether more exotic entity, with crabs and waves and seaweed, and that delicious rush of terror that you might go out too far, or that some unknown creature might come up through the deep and get you. This was The Seaside. She was almost exhausted with excitement by the time she dug her spade into the sand, and no matter what time of year it was, she had to don her knitted costume and take to the water. The times she had spent standing in the freezing water, determined to enjoy it, even if her teeth chattered uncontrollably, her nose ran, and goosebumps the size of grapes stood out all over her body, just to say she had been in the sea. And running around, doing everything, because not a moment could be wasted at the seaside, and then huddling under coats to protect them from the wind while they ate their picnic. And trying to get the sand out of places it was never intended to be; she often wondered why it was so difficult to get the grains out of certain crevices when they had found their way in so easily in the first place. When the time came to board the train for the return journey she would be so exhausted that she slept all the way back, so in reality Frances and Marek could easily have abandoned themselves in any number of lustful urges for all the good she was as a chaperone.

5

One of Marion's favourite pastimes was watching her elder sister get ready for a night out. Frances, being the undisputed beauty of the area, had been the focus of male attention all through her life, but her main concern was that she smelt of oil. All Singer's employees did, the fine scent of machine oil identified them wherever they went, as surely as a chimney sweep was unmasked by his sooty appearance, or a nurse by the fine scent of disinfectant. For Frances, feminine to the ultimate extent, the smell of the oil was an unwanted accessory, and much time was spent concocting mixtures to mask it. Marion would be sent into the park to collect the blossoms of every flower in bloom, or maybe lavender seeds, which she and Frances would infuse in various ways to produce a perfume. Rosewater was the aim, or some variation thereof, but despite their best efforts, their father pronounced every attempt 'Essence of Cabbage', and so the quest went on. There was face powder and rouge to apply, but not so thick that her Da in particular could object – that was always a fine judgement – and a little block of black stuff that had to be spat on and rubbed with a little brush to produce mascara. A touch of eyebrow pencil, and finally lipstick as red as Frances thought her parents would let her away with, which was applied after leaving home and removed before returning, just in case. It struck Marion that 'that Sal Devlin' never removed her make-up, though too much make-up made you a hussy, and being a hussy brought disgrace upon the entire family. As ever, each generation's idea of 'too much' of anything differed sharply, just as Sal's did.

The main problem that occupied the minds of all females during the War was getting enough nylons, and much discussion went into whether to ignore a run in your last pair, which implied that it had only just happened and you were therefore absolved of blame, or to attempt a repair, which might equally imply that they *were* your last pair, and that pointed to poverty, which was shameful. Frances had a bottle of stuff for when she had no nylons left, a kind of make-up that looked better on the legs than it did on the face to tell the truth. You put some on both hands, then smoothed it over your legs, and only experience plus great care helped you avoid telltale streaks from the operation. Next was the creation of the seams every stocking had, by applying a line of eyebrow pencil from heel to thigh, to make it look like a perfect nylon. This too was fraught with difficulties. First of all there was a question mark over anyone's ability to apply the line straight enough, thick or thin or dark enough, and if all that was accomplished, sitting down brought new problems, as the line tended to become smudged when touched. The only way to avoid this was to spend the entire night on your feet avoiding any surface that might compromise the 'seam', and after a long shift at whatever factory you worked in, standing when you weren't actually dancing was not an attractive proposition. The alternative was to go bare-legged, which brought you back to hussy territory, as it was a well-known fact that only a hussy would venture forth bare-legged.

The nylon problem was to haunt every female throughout the War years, unless of course, you knew an American GI particularly well, because GIs all had an endless supply of nylons, as did 'that Sal Devlin'. But if you went with a Yank you were considered as much a hussy as if you had gone out bare-legged, probably more so, thereby cancelling out any benefit. Frances, though, knew Marek and the Poles were safer, because though they were over here, they weren't regarded as overpaid or oversexed. Apart from his interesting

46

accent and the prospects of good days out that he presented, Marek meant no more to Marion than any other friend of her big sister's, and being so much younger than Frances, Marion had better things to occupy her time with. And though he wore an unusual uniform, Clydebank was a busy port, and unusual uniforms had always been around. Funny to think that someone she had hardly noticed at the time would take up so much of her thoughts as she grew older.

Clothing was a problem too, but like most other women of that time, Jean MacLeod was a dab hand at dressmaking, so for the big dance at the Masonic Hall Frances was to have a new dress – clothing coupons permitting. The three of them went out to look for material, Marion, Frances and Jean, and after much searching and discussion, a satiny green material was chosen. Granny Mirren was horrified, it was common knowledge that green was bad luck, the lassie couldn't wear green!

'But, Granny Mirren,' Frances had protested, 'it goes wi' my eyes!'

'It's ill luck, lassie,' the old woman insisted in mystical Celtic tones. 'No good will come of it!'

'Whit aboot the luck o' the Irish?' Tommy asked from his usual position by the fire.

Jean, her attention on the discussion in hand, was off guard for once. 'Whit on earth are ye talking aboot? Whit has luck o' the Irish tae dae wi' anythin'?'

'Well, they a' wear green,' he said, 'the leprechauns an' little people, they a' wear wee daft green jerseys an' hats, daen't they? An' they're aye findin' gold at the end o' rainbows, so it canny be a' that unlucky, can it?'

'Away tae Hell!' Jean replied, annoyed at herself for being distracted by Tommy's nonsense. 'If ye've nothin' tae say, say *nothin'*, Tommy MacLeod!'

'An' there's that other bit o' Irish luck tae take intae account,' he said, slipping the punchline into place without raising his eyes from his paper. 'You're Irish, an' look at your luck – ye got tae marry above your station, ye married a MacLeod. Noo if that's no' a crock o' gold, Ah don't know whit is!'

'Merr a crock o' –'

'Wheesht noo, Jeannie,' he said slyly, 'the bairns will hear ye!'

Once commonsense had been restored after Tommy's interruption, the discussion on the luck or otherwise of wearing green continued and, as ever, the entire clan had to have their say. This led to Granny Mirren being outvoted, on account of Gaelic superstitions being as defunct in the Lowlands as she and Granda Archie had declared the Gaelic language. Even so, she got the last word by repeating once again in those mystical tones that 'No good will come of it!' and insisted that Frances should also wear the crucifix she had brought from Uist all those years ago. To Granny Mirren's sure and certain knowledge, only the crucifix had protected the family since she and Archie had fled from the island, and when anyone ventured forth into unknown territory, the crucifix was bestowed upon them to guide them safely through what lay ahead. Reminders, usually by her grandson Tommy, that Big Kenny had always managed to turn up like a bad penny down the years without the talisman effect of the crucifix, were treated by Granny Mirren with a sweet smile, denoting that she hadn't heard and furthermore wouldn't hear, so there was no point in him repeating the slur. With the matter settled, the creation of the gown could go ahead, though as they left to return to their own home Granda Archie was heard to mutter a few choice words the rest of the family weren't supposed to understand, but did. 'Òinsich na galladh!' muttered the old man to his wife, to which Granny Mirren replied, 'Pòg mo thòn! Amadain an diabhoil!'

'Tell ye whit,' Tommy MacLeod called after his grandparents, 'Ah agree wi' baith o' ye!'

*   *   *

The phoney war had gradually given way to reality, and soon families all over the country began to feel its effects. In September 1940 Mussolini declared war on the Allies, and soon afterwards events took place that would affect the residents of 70 Second Avenue thereafter. Firstly 70's gang of three, Colin, Jimmy Ryan and Gino Rossi, temporarily expanded to four for a special mission. With Iain they went to volunteer for the Forces. Jean sobbed and protested, and Tommy, for once in logical mode, told her to relax. All of the lads were apprentices involved in work crucial to the war effort and so would be sent back home, but it was important for them to have the pride of volunteering. He was half-right. The workings of the military mind were never as logical as even Tommy MacLeod.

Jimmy and Gino were both accepted and set off immediately for their basic training with the Argyll and Sutherland Highlanders at Stirling Castle. Colin, as a nineteen-year-old apprentice electrician, and Iain, as an eighteen-year-old apprentice carpenter, were both doing the work of time-served tradesmen in the yards, so both were considered, as their father had predicted, to be in reserved occupations and rejected for the forces.

Iain accepted the decision with his usual stoicism, but Colin was bereft. Enlisting was a huge adventure to him, it was his way out of the yards, his escape from the mundane and ordinary existence he had struggled against all his life. His disappointment affected everything about him; the way he looked, the way he talked and the way he walked showed his desolation. It was as though someone had thrown a switch and dimmed down his entire personality. Had they all been rejected he might have reluctantly come to terms with it, but his lifetime pals had gone, leaving him almost alone, and however relieved his mother was, the change in her once bright, troublesome and exasperating son still worried and saddened her. At first she thought he was just missing his pals, as in fact the entire family did, because Gino and Jimmy

49

were part of the MacLeods too, especially Jimmy, as quiet and reserved as Colin was outgoing. Jimmy's father had been an Irish American who had been sent from the American headquarters of Singer's to help the 'Bankies set up and run a modern production line. In Clydebank he had married a woman from Orkney and had a son, Jimmy. Then after eleven years and several stillbirths, Wee Davy arrived, the bane of Marion's life. Their father died of TB, that dreaded scourge of the working classes, just months before his youngest son arrived, so Mrs Ryan hadn't had the happiest or luckiest of lives, which was perhaps why, like Queen Victoria, she dressed in black for the rest of her life. Maybe it was her perpetual mourning that sent Jimmy to the lively MacLeods, or as Tommy maintained, the torch he held for the beautiful Frances.

Whatever the reason, Jimmy was always there, a good-looking boy with dark hair and brown eyes. Though he was always part of Colin's harebrained schemes, there was a feeling of dependability about him too. Iain was the one who smoothed over Colin's troubles after they had happened, but however insane Colin's activities were, Jimmy would put some sort of brake on them at the time, if he could. Many's the time Jean would look at Jimmy after some escapade and say with quiet disappointment, 'Jimmy, how did ye no' stop him?' What Colin might get up to now that Jimmy was gone worried Jean, once he had recovered from the shock of it at any rate.

For the present though there were no more stories in the bedroom, and Marion found it hard to sleep without her brother's voice conjuring up the exotic adventures he knew waited for him, someday.

Then the second thing happened. It began as any other day, people were going to work, children getting ready for school, mothers going about their housework, when the police arrived at Number 70 and knocked on the door of Alfredo and Maria Rossi. The Rossis were Italian nationals which apparently made them enemy aliens after Mussolini's declaration of war. Their café beside the Singer's factory had already been boarded up, and the Rossis were to accompany the police to Barlinnie Prison. If ever there was a situation crying out for Granny Kate, this was it, and the hapless policemen didn't have long to wait. Kate was on them in a second, closely followed by the other tenement dwellers. The police were local men, most on first-name terms with the people they lived and worked among because they had grown up together and gone to school together.

'Is that you, Gus Whyte?' she demanded, rounding on one constable. 'Whit are you daein' here botherin' decent folk?'

'Noo, Mrs MacLeod, don't get involved in this,' he said, looking embarrassed, 'there's nothin' can be done aboot this.'

'Dae ye hear yersel'?' she demanded. 'Ye go intae the Rossis' café every day o' your life, Ah've seen ye there maself, talkin' tae them, jokin' wi' them, buyin' your fags. And yet here ye staun', tellin' them that they're the enemy an' ye're takin' them tae prison? Does your mother know whit ye're tryin' tae dae here the day?'

'Mrs MacLeod,' said another, 'Gus is right, there's nothin' we can dae aboot it, the Law is the Law an' we a' have tae obey it, especially at times like these.'

'The Law is an arse, Sandy Duncan,' she stated, 'an' you know it as well as Ah dae. Ye should be bloody ashamed o' yersel' tae. Your laddie's in the Argylls, isn't he? Well, so is the Rossis' son! Their Gino's fighting alangside your Alec! The Law is it? Well, when the Law is an arse ye don't obey it, ye gie it a damn good kick!'

But the policemen were not to be dissuaded, so the residents of Number 70 did what they did during the Rent Strikes of the twenties, it was all they knew to do. They forced the policemen out of the close and blocked it so that they couldn't get back in, as the Rossis sat shocked inside their home.

'Tell me, why are ye takin' oor neighbours tae the jile?' Tommy MacLeod asked, his piece-bag over his shoulder as usual, ready for another day's work until this crisis had thrown itself at him.

'They're enemy aliens,' the police repeated, 'they could be passing secrets back tae Italy.'

'Away ye go, ya big clown!' Granny Kate shouted. 'They run a wee café! Whit secrets dae ye think they have? That every packet o' needles that leaves Singer's has three inside? Is that the kind o' secret ye don't want Mussolini tae have? Well Ah've jist gied that secret away, are ye gonny take me tae the jile as well?'

Tommy was struggling to put his case with a civility he didn't feel. 'Ma mother might be puttin' it a wee bit colourfully,' he smiled tightly, 'but she has a point, dae ye no' think so? These people are our friends, they've been here a' the years that Ah can remember, a' the years you can remember tae, eh, Sandy? An' you tae, Gus, seeing as we went tae school thegither.'

The policemen looked at him then turned their gaze away. 'We are only doin' oor job,' Gus Whyte said, relying on pomposity, because he had nothing else to defend himself with. The outraged stares of Number 70's inhabitants did nothing to make him feel any better, in fact he was stung into threats he didn't mean but couldn't recall once they had been uttered. 'And if the rest o' youse don't step back and let us dae it, we'll lift every wan o' ye!'

Tommy's struggle to keep the dialogue amicable collapsed then despite his best efforts, 'Whit would ye dae this for?' he demanded, raising his voice. 'Take them tae Barlinnie, among murderers and thieves? Are ye no' right in the heid or whit?'

'Look, Tommy,' Gus Whyte pleaded, 'Ah keep tellin' ye, this isnae up tae you or me, this is somethin' we havtae dae an' nothin' can stop it. Ah'm tellin' ye, if ye don't stand back ye'll a' land in the jile.'

All of Tommy's tactical diplomacy had been deserted. 'An' this is whit we're fightin' for, is it?' he shouted, inches from the policeman's face. 'This is whit ma family an' me are workin' a' the hours that God sends for, so the likes o' ye can persecute decent people? Ye're like the bloody Gestapo yersels, dis that no' strike ye? Well, pish tae your Law, and pish tae ye tae, Gus Whyte, an' the same tae the rest o' ye heroes. Ye're no' takin' the Rossis away unless ye've got a Black Mariah that'll take the rest o' us tae! Bugger aff, ye're no' gettin' in!'

Then a cheer went up that made the hair on Marion's neck stand on end, just as fifty years later the memory of it brought tears to her eyes, as the people she had known all her life stood together, refusing to allow the hapless Rossis to be led away like criminals.

But just as the cheer of defiance rang out, Alfredo and Maria Rossi pushed their way through the crowd blocking the close, their bags packed, their eyes downcast. 'You will get in trouble, my friend,' Alfredo told Tommy, with a sad smile. 'We won't cause you trouble that can be avoided.' And with that they left voluntarily with the police, leaving the residents of Number 70 seething with silent, impotent rage. Except for Tommy MacLeod that is.

'We won't let them away wi' this, Freddie,' he said. 'We'll get in touch wi' Gino, he'll get it sorted oot. An' jist you remember!' he called after the police escort, 'there won't always be a war oan, an' we'll a' be meetin' again, an' Ah for wan won't forget each wan o' ye!'

'Ah tellt ye, didn't Ah, son?' Granny Kate said bitterly. 'It's them an' us. Nothin' changes.'

It was the only time Marion ever saw her father in tears. Tommy MacLeod, who met the world with jokes, wisecracks and laughter, cried that day for the fate of the innocent Rossis, and for his guilt at being able to do so little to change it.

The neighbours in Second Avenue spent the next few days subdued by the tragic little scene they had witnessed, and then suddenly there was great commotion down the road at the close where 'that Sal Devlin' lived. In the early hours of the morning a stranger was seen to run out of her door, down the stairs, through the close and along the street. Two things caught the attention. First of all he was screaming and holding his backside, and secondly, he was stark naked. Then Tony Gallagher appeared in close pursuit, throwing bits of a foreign serviceman's uniform after the screaming, naked figure who was departing at speed down Kilbowie Road. Tony, it seemed, had come home on leave to surprise his pining bride as she lay in bed alone. Only Sal was neither pining nor alone, though she was certainly surprised, if not as surprised as her companion. Much to the amusement of all the neighbours who had gathered to witness the spectacle, the foreigner had been ejected from the marital bed and chased off, with bits of his uniform following behind. As the neighbours returned reluctantly to their own homes, Sal was seen hanging over the windowsill, laughing as mirthfully as any of them.

The next evening Marion overheard her mother and father discussing the previous night's entertainment, and she took a step back outside the living room so that she could hear the uncensored version.

'It seems,' said Tommy, chuckling quietly, 'that Big Tony crept intae the bedroom in the dark an' pulled back the blankets, an' whit does he see but a big arse up in the air. At first he thinks it's Sal's, but then he notices that it's a big hairy arse, an' as far as he can remember, Sal hasnae got a big hairy arse.'

'Whit happened then?' Jean whispered.

'Whit happened then? He booted the bloke oot, whit dae ye think?'

'Good for him!' Jean announced righteously.

'Mind you,' said Tommy, 'whitever the bloke does tae fight the Gerries, Ah hope he disnae need tae sit doon tae dae it. No' for a while anyway.'

'How? Whit did Big Tony dae?'

'Well,' said Tommy, relishing every moment of the performance, 'he twigged whit wis goin' oan, an' the poor
bugger an' Sal were kinda too involved in other thoughts
tae notice Big Tony, so he went back tae the fireplace, picked
up the poker an' the next time the arse hove intae view, so
tae speak, he rammed the poker –'

'Oh, for God's sake, Tommy!' Jean protested, 'there's nae
need tae hammer it hame!'

'Well, funny enough, Jeannie, that's exactly whit Big Tony
did. Did ye no' hear the other poor bugger screamin' a' the
wey doon Kilbowie Road?'

'That's enough, Tommy, ye're enjoyin' this!'

'Again, so wis the other bloke until – Christ, Jeannie, ye
wurnae hidin' under the bed yersel', wur ye? Cos that's *exactly*
whit Big Tony said tae the guy, so they tell me, "Ye're
enjoyin' this, pal, well enjoy this poker right up your –"'

'Thomas John MacLeod! Wheesht, the bairns will hear
ye!'

Despite Big Tony's intervention, peace prevailed thereafter, or at least until he had gone back to rejoin his unit,
but once he was safely out of Clydebank, the familiar stream
of foreign callers again found its way back to sample his wife's
special teas and legendary currant bun. And 'that Sal Devlin'
still had a grin and a stick of gum for the local kids that they
never told their mothers about.

6

So life went on in Clydebank, not normally, but normally for the times, though there was concern that nothing seemed to be happening apart from the ever longer hours being worked. Part of the problem was the town's reputation as the Red Clydeside; the myth had to be lived up to by the local politicians, and that may well have helped the town to be ill-prepared for what was coming. The Labour councillors, puffed up with their own rhetoric, decided that protecting the people from aerial bombardment was tantamount to condoning the government's foreign policy. They wanted appeasement, not war, and like politicians of any age, they deluded themselves that what they wanted would happen, simply because they had made a speech.

While other parts of the country made preparations from 1935, when Germany began to rumble and war looked likely, Clydebank waited until compulsory measures were introduced in 1938. It saved the faces of the Clydebank politicians if the truth were told; they had talked themselves into a corner that their rhetoric couldn't get them out of, and the compulsory orders saved them from the humiliating climb-down they deserved.

And oh, the terror of that wireless broadcast on 3 September 1939, when Chamberlain finally admitted that his bit of paper was worthless and that the country was now at war. It had been as though the Germans were knocking on your door and their planes just minutes behind. Clydebank, having been pushed into preparations, seemed to take to it with a will, and many children had been evacuated a few days before

Chamberlain's declaration, their Mickey Mouse gas masks in boxes hanging by their sides. Marion was the only one in the family below working age and Jean MacLeod decided not to send her away. 'If we go,' she said, 'we'll a' go the-gither.' Marion assumed that she meant they should all be evacuated together or not at all, but the unspoken fear in her mother's mind was that Marion would be all alone in the world if she were to survive outside Clydebank, while the rest of the family were bombed. Tommy quickly dispelled the confusion though, by putting his wife's fears into words. 'Jist think, Marion, if we wur a' deid, they might send ye to live wi' yur Auntie Maggie. A fate worse than death, eh?' At the mention of Auntie Maggie's name Marion instantly sat up straight. 'Aye,' said her father, chuckling quietly, 'Ah know whit ye're thinking, hen. Ah'd rather face the Luftwaffe tae, than risk havin' tae stey wi' Auntie Maggie!'

It was easy to joke about what would never happen.

Clydebank was suddenly fired with enthusiasm. Anderson shelters were dug into gardens where possible or wanted, and they weren't always. For tenement dwellers, shelters were built in the back courts to take everybody. Constructed of brick and ferro-concrete, they had no lights; dark, damp, windowless blocks with chemical toilets, that everyone hated. Marion looked at the shelter behind her home and mused that she would be less scared bumping into Hitler coming up Kilbowie Road, or even Auntie Maggie come to that, than of spending an hour in one of those scary, dank, brick boxes.

The other kind of protection involved reinforcing the tenement closes with steel scaffolding, and building baffle walls feet from the front and back closes, to stop a bomb blast being funnelled up through the building. The idea was that if a raid should happen, everyone in the tenement would come down and sit inside the fortified close at ground level. The baffle walls brought cursing to Marion's attention for the first time, because adults didn't swear in front of children back then, and being in English as opposed to Gaelic, it sounded harsher somehow. People were forever walking into the baffle walls during the blackout; first came a yell of pain, then an oath screamed loudly in rage, closely followed by the laughter of anyone in earshot.

The folk did what they could in the time available, but what they didn't have were the necessities; they didn't even have enough stirrup pumps, though the official line was that every home should have one. But there again, the official advice from the Civil Defence hierarchy was that no raids of any severity were expected in Clydebank, so perhaps the belief that nothing would happen contributed to the chaos when it did. Organisation was poor and, as usual, the authorities blamed the people, but as the entire population was working such long hours they could hardly be available for every lecture on extinguishing incendiaries – especially as they stood little chance of having the equipment to do it with. As well as the lack of stirrup pumps and sandbags, they didn't have enough fire hoses either; the Ministry refused to pay for them.

Tommy MacLeod expressed the thoughts of many in his own individual style. 'Whit dae they expect us tae dae – get thegither in a big line an' pish oan the fires?' On receiving one of his wife's disapproving stares he later added an alternative version of this to his repertoire, one suitable for more delicate ears: 'spit oan the fires'. Naturally, his children chose only to repeat his first attempt to each other and their friends.

But despite the work going on nothing happened; Hitler didn't knock on any door in the town and no bombers came to call either. It was the time of the 'phoney war', and because nothing had happened, the children started to filter back home. By Christmas most of them were back once more with their families, and Jean MacLeod felt vindicated in not sending her bairn away in the first place.

*　　　*　　　*

The Civil Defence HQ was situated in the basement of the Public Library, right in the middle of the expected target area. The Government bureaucrats had fixed ideas on the size of room required, and quite simply the basement was just that size, though the local people knew it defied logic. Those going about their business that Thursday night didn't know it at the time, but the HQ had been told by the War Room in Glasgow at 7.30 pm that 'the beam was on', that Clydeside would be hit on 13 March. But it was classified information, and not only were the citizens of Clydebank not to be told, but neither were the emergency services.

Since the declaration of war German planes were a common sight high over the town, people glanced at them then ignored them. They were on reconnaissance missions, taking pictures to form precise mapping for the raids no one seriously thought would come. Forty or more times the sirens had wailed their warnings as the Germans snapped away over Clydebank, and on that crisp, frosty March night they had their reward, they even had a 'bomber's moon'. Sometimes you wonder if there is anyone up there, and if there is, what kind of sense of humour the Almighty possesses.

With precise co-ordinates the Germans were able to send out a radio-navigational beam to the target area for their bombers to follow. The boffins on our side could not only pick it up, but they could 'bend' the beam, to send the bombers to the wrong destination. But not in Scotland, only in the South. Hindsight is a wonderful thing, but no matter how many times Marion considered it over the years since, it seemed incredible, unforgivable, that no one thought Clydebank would one day get hit. There was all that important industry, the shipyards and the munitions factories on the Clyde, and by 'bending the beam' away from English cities, like London, Liverpool, Manchester and Birmingham, the Luftwaffe had a clear run to Clydeside. Why did no one spot it?

The year before, when 'the beam was on' for Liverpool,

the population was told, and predictably fled the city, causing the bureaucrats' worst nightmare combination, panic and uncontrolled movement of large numbers of people, at a time when freedom of movement was very restricted. So the military and the police were ordered to set up roadblocks, and the terrified Liverpudlians were caught and forced back into the city. By their desperate flight they had missed one night of bombing, but the German pattern was to come back for a second night, and when they did, the hapless people were like sitting ducks, or perhaps lambs to the slaughter would be a more accurate description. Thus the myth of 'We can take it' was born. The reality was that there was no choice; the people took it because they were forced to take it.

And there was another strand to the tale. Though it wasn't official policy, it was accepted by both sides that civilians would die in great numbers during aerial bombardment, and that terror bombing was a legitimate tactic, to lower morale and make the civilian populations less enthusiastic about continuing the War. Having accepted this, it was an easy step for the RAF to believe that as German planes would fly over Britain anyway, this presented an opportunity to attack them, and even if British nightfighters were not particularly accurate and 'kills' were few, the possibility put the fear of death into the German pilots. But if the bait had been forewarned and had fled as a result, the Germans would have less reason to terror bomb. 'We escaped ha ha' would have been more likely to rally the country, when the preferred result was a population demoralised upon hearing that hundreds of people had been wiped out by the enemy. If the bait wasn't in place then the Germans might think twice about risking their planes, and that fear had led to Hermann Goering, the Luftwaffe chief, abandoning daylight raids in favour of night raids. And the simple fact was that if the German planes didn't come, the RAF would lose the chance to destroy them, or at least scare the German pilots into thinking it was a possibility.

The bombing of Clydebank was a terror mission. Let the

scholars and the intellectuals say what they would. The people who were there, the ones who ran screaming in terror or spent hours trapped under debris, and those who spent weeks looking for families blown into so many pieces that they were never found; they knew better. Hitler had given up any idea of invading the British mainland and had by that time turned his attention towards Russia. The German intention was to cause as much damage and social disruption as possible, to terrorise and demoralise the population, the same motivation as for the British attack on Dresden some years later. Therefore it was in the RAF's interests that the bait was in place, but the bait consisted of people, families like the MacLeods and their neighbours, grandparents, mothers, fathers, brothers and sisters, all pawns in a great big war game. As the uniformed men were cannon fodder, the civilians were bomber fodder.

But of course the ordinary people knew nothing of this at the time, their minds were on other things, particularly at 70 Second Avenue. The removal of Alfredo and Maria Rossi had shocked them all, and there was a mixture of anger, sadness and guilt. From Colin MacLeod, Granny Kate got Gino's address, but letters took a long time to arrive, and before Gino knew about what had happened to his parents, they had been interrogated at Barlinnie Prison and then moved to an internment camp somewhere in Argyll. There was a sense of anxiety at Number 70, the injustice of what had happened to their neighbours occupied their minds much more than any possible threat from the skies. There was an expectation that news, any news, would arrive at any moment, and neighbours, meeting in the street or in the narrow close, looked each other in the eyes hoping for some word, then passed on with a helpless shake of the head. It seemed odd to them that the rest of the world was going on as usual, while such a terrible thing had happened. Normally you would go to the police and get them to sort such things out, but what did you do when the police had taken part?

And while they were thinking of how to get the Rossis

back home, Colin staged his own drama. His disappointment at being made to stay at home making ships instead of going off to war had been heightened by news from Jimmy Ryan. Jimmy had volunteered to be a Commando, the new, specialist fighting force formed in 1940, and had survived the exacting training course at Achnacarry near Spean Bridge, emerging as one of the truly elite. He came home on leave before being posted abroad, wearing the coveted green beret with the Argylls' badge pinned to it. And there was a subtle change in Jimmy, something in his bearing as well as the green beret had transformed him into a real live hero. Marion couldn't take her eyes off him, and even Tommy MacLeod seemed slightly awed by the boy who was now so obviously a man. He stayed until Frances came home from her shift at Singer's, and that was when Marion knew her father had been right. There are some things that children, with their black-and-white approach to life, see far more clearly than adults. That day Marion saw an expression in Jimmy Ryan's eyes when he looked at her big sister that she would never forget, a look of such concentrated admiration and devotion that she was surprised that no one else commented on it. Even Frances seemed unaware of it, but then Frances was probably used to adoring looks from the male population. For Marion though it became a defining moment. She would, she vowed, one day marry the man who looked at her like that, or remain a spinster. Young Lochinvar on his white charger or no one. If her mother had known she would have blamed Granny Mirren and Granda Archie, who between them had 'wasted oor Marion's heid' with romance. Marion carried two pictures of Jimmy Ryan in her mind for the rest of her life; one of a lithe, fit, uniformed hero with that look in his eyes when he saw Frances, and the other the Jimmy she was to know after the War. It was, she often thought, like looking at pictures of two different people.

Then Jimmy left, henceforth to be involved in the kind of excitement and adventure that Colin, a Dan Dare figure all his life, could only dream of as he fiddled with electrical wire and switches. And these days there was precious little of that to keep him occupied, because the apprentices had gone on strike. It was the usual story, and one that would continue to surface for many years. The lads served apprenticeships that were deliberately kept longer than necessary, thereby also keeping their wages at an apprentice's level, years after they were actually doing a tradesman's work.

The hours hung heavy on Colin's mind and on his hands after Jimmy's news came, and with Gino, the other part of the gang, also away, there was precious little to occupy him. He would go walking in the Old Kilpatrick Hills from early in the morning till late at night, as other 'Bankies had done during the Depression, thinking of the adventures the shipyard was cheating him of, and the irony was that he wasn't even doing anything in the yard. It made the taste in his mouth even worse; while his pals were off fighting, he was roaming the hills to pass the time. Then one morning Colin wakened Marion before he set off for his day in the hills, and thrust a note under her pillow.

'Marion,' he whispered, 'gie this tae Da when he gets back fae the yard the night.'

Marion nodded sleepily and turned over.

'Mind, noo, the night. Don't gie it tae Ma, gie it tae Da the night. Right?'

Marion hadn't suspected anything at the time, she was used to Colin's derring-do exploits, and besides, there had been no precedent in her young life for what her brother had in mind. She had only the vaguest memory of watching him go out the door that morning as usual, his piece-bag containing his lunch sandwiches over his shoulder. Then she forgot all about the whispered conversation and the note under her pillow.

That night she waited at the end of the road for the familiar sight of her father coming home with Pape Boyle after a double shift at Brown's, then she skipped beside Tommy along Second Avenue and up the close at Number 70. She remembered noticing with a shock for the first time that he looked tired; he had always just been her Da before and he never looked any different. As he sat down in his armchair by the fire, the ever-present newspaper in his hand, he engaged in the usual banter with his wife as she got his meal ready. She mentioned that Colin was late, which prompted Tommy to suggest with a wink at Marion, that 'Mibbe the boy's visiting his Auntie Maggie.'

Jean attacked him immediately. 'Don't you start!'

'Whit?' he demanded, opening his arms to the room for defence, his eyes wide with innocence. 'Are ye sayin' the lad widnae visit his favourite Auntie Maggie then?'

Still Marion didn't remember the note. In fact it wasn't till she was getting ready for bed and reached under the pillow for her pyjamas that she felt the piece of paper in her hand and instantly recalled the early-morning conversation. Even all these years later she couldn't explain why she had frozen with fear, how she had known this was bad news. She had walked into the sitting room and wordlessly held out the note to her father.

'Whit's this? Somethin' ye did at school?' he asked, laying his paper down. 'Ye're that smart, oor Marion, Ah don't know if Ah'll understaun it, mind!' Her eyes never left his face as he read Colin's note. 'Jeannie,' he said quietly.

'Whitever ye're uptae, Tommy, Ah don't have time!' she replied, the familiar teasing slotting into place; first a remark from him, then one from her, then –

'Jeannie, ye'd better come here, lass, it's aboot Colin.'

The silence lasted for ever, and Marion stood watching as the drama unfolded. 'Sit doon, Jeannie,' Tommy told her.

'Tommy . . . Tommy, whit is it? Is he hurt?' Her left arm wrapped itself around the front of her waist, grasping at the apron string, while her right flew to her throat to contain a cry, stopping it from escaping and confirming her fears. Tommy handed her the note, but panic made her blind and she couldn't see the words. 'Jist *tell* me, for God's sake! Is he hurt?'

'He's run away tae join the army.'

The silence and the stillness stretched, with Tommy and Jean staring wordlessly into each other's eyes, then Tommy turned to his daughter, the note in his hand. 'Where did ye find this, hen?' he asked. Marion, lost in terror and guilt and fear, could barely get the words out. 'Don't be scared, hen, jist tell me.'

She told them of being wakened by Colin that morning, of his insistence that she give the note to their Da when he came home.

'How did ye no' tell me earlier?' Jean shouted at her savagely. 'Ah've been askin' aboot him a' night an' ye never said a word!' She lashed out at Marion, just missing her bare arm. The scared child turned and ran out of the house, instinctively fleeing downstairs to Granny Mirren and Granda Archie. Behind her she could hear her father's voice raised in real anger for the first time she could ever recall, and her mother plaintively calling her name as she ran to the safety of the old MacLeods. And then there was more anger, more panic than she thought could exist, as the various members of the clan ran between each other's homes, demanding explanations, arguing, shouting, crying and remonstrating with one another.

Iain was summoned, but Iain knew nothing, though he tried to make his brother's return path easier. 'He'll jist be away for a walk,' he said, feigning unconcern, 'ye know whit he's been like since Jimmy an' Gino went away.'

'He's gone away tae fight,' Tommy said, his eyes scanning the note again, as though it would suddenly burst into speech and tell him where Colin was. Jean sank into a chair with a stifled moan. 'He says we've no' tae try an' find him, he'll be back efter the War.'

A brief smile flashed across Iain's face; it was so like Colin, just the kind of heroic words you would expect from him.

'How did ye no' give us this earlier?' Jean rounded again on Marion, who stared back wordlessly, clinging to Granny Mirren's skirts, confused and shocked.

'Stop it, Jean!' Tommy said. 'It's no' the bairn's fault, she wisnae tae know whit Colin was aboot. That's why he gave her the note, she's too wee tae be suspicious.'

Jean MacLeod pulled her daughter to her, hugged her and cried.

Days later she tried to make her peace with her daughter. 'Colin's no' like the rest o' ye,' she said. 'Colin gets intae trouble because he disnae understand things, he disnae know how tae deal wi' things.' Marion looked at her blankly. 'Ach, ye'll understand whit Ah mean when ye have bairns o' yer ain,' Jean smiled sadly. 'There's aye wan ye havtae look oot for, nae matter how auld they are.'

So now Number 70 was missing several residents: those legitimately at war, one not, and two lawfully but unjustly removed; and the latter three had to be brought home, whatever the effort needed. Colin had gone to a recruitment centre in Glasgow, and given his real name with a fictitious address and occupation, and in his mind he would be many miles away before anyone found out that he should be working at John Brown's instead, or at least on strike.

At his home in Second Avenue life stood still. Every knock at the door was instantly answered by an anxious face, looking for news, as the minutes dragged painfully into hours then days, with no one eating or sleeping. Lots of families had waved their sons off to war, but it was inexplicably worse if the son wasn't supposed to have gone. Colin had run away, he hadn't gone in the usual, accepted manner, so somehow the anxiety every family lived with in wartime was heightened. All they could think of was that he was out there somewhere, and they had him at risk from every danger, as though the sons of others were not. There's no logic when it's your own.

The police meantime had acted more calmly, by alerting the military to be on the lookout for a Colin MacLeod. He had nearly pulled it off though, he had been accepted by the Argyll and Sutherland Highlanders, assigned a unit and a number and taken to Stirling Castle to be kitted out for his basic training before he was discovered. The redcaps who escorted him home had given him respect and admiration for his determination; he was, in their eyes, a man. Jean greeted the news of his imminent return with a mixture of rage and relief, in her eyes he was the same daft laddie he had always been and he deserved a good skelp. But Tommy stopped her. 'There will be nae rows, Jean,' he stated in that unusually quiet and serious voice. 'The laddie is creased, he's hurtin' ower this. An' for that matter he isnae a laddie any merr, he's a man noo, an' mammies don't skelp men.'

When he was brought home under military escort though, Colin still looked like a laddie, his eyes shining once again as they used to; he had had an adventure.

As the rest of the family tried to appear as if they were busy about the house, Tommy spoke to his son alone in the bedroom, and they emerged looking subdued but almost happy. His father had told Colin that he was old enough to consider his mother's feelings, and if he ever did anything of that sort again, he would take him into the back court and they would sort it out, man-to-man. In other words, a man's skelp. If he didn't want to be an electrician that was fine, but he had to stick it out till the end of the War. He was doing his bit as surely as Jimmy or Gino, and after the War he would have earned the right to decide for himself; he could take wings and fly, with his father's, though probably not his mother's, blessing. Tommy MacLeod had grown up with Big Kenny ever present in his life, he had actually seen him the time he came home dressed in the Mountie's uniform, with or without his horse, and he understood the wanderlust, the need to move on.

Jean, shocked and angry, rushed to the Grandas and

Grannies for support. 'Tommy's tellt him he disnae havtae stey at Broon's efter the War,' she told them incredulously. 'He says Colin can go away!'

Granda Archie puffed on his pipe, a man who had taken flight from kith and kin when he was a lad too. 'Aye, well, Jean,' he said slowly, 'Tommy has a point, I never realized he had that much sense, him always makin' a laugh at everythin'. Jist goes tae show ye, ye don't always give folk credit, especially not your own!' and he chuckled to himself.

'Granda Archie, he's sendin' the lad away!'

'No, no, lass,' the old man replied kindly, 'he's lettin' him go, because go he will anyway. Sometimes ye havtae let them go to be sure they'll come back.'

Jean looked to Granny Kate. 'The auld fella's right, Jean,' Granny Kate said. 'Colin's no' a laddie noo, ye cannae tell him whit tae dae any longer, ye jist keep yer fingers crossed behind yer back that he'll be safe, an' ye listen while he tells you whit he'll dae. And ye'll listen, or ye'll lose him for good. Ye cannae protect him a' his life, Jean, lass, or even a' yours.'

But Jean's worries were those of any mother who knows that there's 'something missing' in their child. With Colin it was a sense of caution, of awareness of danger and his own mortality. All his life he had got into one scrape after another, and that was with her there. He might look like a man, but he was still her bairn, her first born, and she could recall, as though it were yesterday, every milestone in his life since he drew enough breath for that first yell. All through his childhood every time he grazed a knee she was cut to the bone, every bumped head or hurt feeling made her wince too. What would befall him if he were out in the big wide world without her? She knew that Granny Kate was right, she couldn't protect him for ever, but she wanted to, even if it was just for a wee while longer . . .

So there was much to think about in the days after Colin returned from his biggest adventure yet, as life returned to normal, if a new normal. And a week later the Rossis came home too; they just walked up the street and let themselves into their home below the MacLeods' without any fuss. But the news travelled fast and everyone in Number 70 descended on them offering them food, drink, whatever they needed, and demanding to be told how their release had come about. Granny Kate's letters had, it seemed, reached Gino, though his to her had never arrived, and he had pleaded with his commanding officer to do something to help his parents. It had taken a couple of months, but the CO had really moved things, and at first it was agreed that the old couple should be released from the internment camp, but not allowed to return to Clydebank, because of its military importance. The CO had fought that one too, pointing out that their son was risking his life for his country, and it was an obscenity for that country to first jail, then detain, and finally to think of exiling his parents from their home. On the morning of Monday 10 March the Rossis were simply told that they were free to go, the camp gates were unlocked, and they went home to Second Avenue.

7

So there they all were on the following Thursday evening, the residents of 70 Second Avenue now recovered from their various upsets, doing the ordinary things that ordinary people were doing all over Clydebank, all over the country; baking scones, knitting, getting children ready for bed, trying to remember the words of 'On the Good Ship Lollipop', and listening to the Nine o'Clock News as usual. When the siren sounded they took no notice, again as usual, while a mile or so down the road, the warning that this time it was for real had arrived ninety minutes earlier. Yet some had premonitions. 'Get intae the shelter,' one mother told her children, 'an' you can a' have a good laugh at your Mammy in the mornin' when it's another false alarm.'

The German pathfinder unit arrived first, just as it had in Coventry four months before, dropping incendiaries to start the fires that would guide the bombers to their targets. They lit the town as though it was daylight, sheets of flame sending burning rain to illuminate every street, marking out where the Heinkel 111s and the Junkers 88s should drop their bombs. The planes arrived at 9.30 to find that bomber's moon, on a clear, crisp, frosty March night. They came from exotic-sounding places that Big Kenny would doubtless have known well and Colin only dreamed of, names that would send a shiver through every 'Bankie who lived through that night. From Beauvais in northern France, Stavanger in Norway, Aalborg in Denmark, from Holland and North Germany they came, and as they passed over the rest of Scotland to converge on the Clyde, the noise of their engines could be heard in Edinburgh and in Aberdeen.

By the time Clydebank realised it wasn't just another siren the bombers were upon them. They sheltered as best they could, under tables, in shelters if they had them, or like the residents of 70 Second Avenue, in the lower flats of the tenement. As they waited to die mothers prayed and children were sick with fear. Just before midnight Jean MacLeod tucked Marion into a makeshift bed in old Archie and Mirren's home and went to the closemouth to watch out for Frances, the only one not at home. They were three hours into a raid that would last all night and everyone was scared, listening for every bomb whistling down, then holding their breath as the thud reverberated, making desperate deals with fate – 'If this wan misses us, we're a' right' – as buildings collapsed all around. Marion wondered if it was like thunder and lightning; did you count the seconds between the whistle and the thud to judge how near you were to oblivion? She remembered looking round the gloom and picking out the faces of her family, her brothers Colin and Iain, Granda Archie, Granny Marion, Granda John and Granny Kate. Click! a snapshot for the family album of her mind as they all tried their best to give reassuring smiles despite the carnage and the noise all around. Tommy, as ever, was making light of it. 'Ah told that lassie,' he said, ' "If that Marek brings ye hame late frae the dancin', a' Hell will break loose." Was Ah right or whit?' It was all so clear, she recalled them as though the scene had happened an hour ago. She had looked at Colin. 'Colin, tell me a story.' He and Iain exchanged a look and laughed, then they moved over to her makeshift bed and Colin began. She remembered drifting off to sleep hearing his voice as she always had, but she didn't hear the bomb.

In the years afterwards, the family album would fall open as she slept and she saw them all together just as they were that night. The snapshot would come to life and they would be with her so clearly, their voices so distinct, but before she could move towards them they were gone in less than the blink of an eye. Click! As if someone had switched a light out, or the film had moved on, and the image was gone in an instant. Each time she tried desperately to wake up, but she was never quick enough and the scene just vanished. But it's so real, so real.

The pathfinder unit did a good job, first setting fire to forty acres of timber stored at the Singer's factory. The wood was intended for the sewing machine cabinets Granda John made, though the factory had largely turned to making armaments, tank tracks and Sten guns. Once ablaze it was the perfect beacon, a torch so massive that it burned for ten days. One poor man desperately tried to put the flames out with all he had, a stirrup pump and a bucket of sand. Then Yoker Distillery was hit, the flames and smoke from the burning spirit marking out the east of the town, sending a pall of whisky fumes across the town for days, while in the west three Admiralty oil tanks at Dalnottar were set ablaze on that first night. Little wonder then that with such helpful illumination the Luftwaffe concentrated on Clydebank rather than on Glasgow, and with the fires still raging, why they found their way again so easily on the second night. Eight more Dalnottar oil tanks went up on the Friday night, plus two at nearby Old Kilpatrick; so massive was the blaze that the glow could be seen from Aberdeen. That someone was getting it was clear, but there was no way of knowing precisely who, because all newspapers and radio broadcasts were censored.

And with so many water mains blown apart there was little the firefighters could do as everything burned, aided by the burst gas mains. Those who made it through the craters found that their hose-couplings didn't fit, because there was no uniformity anywhere in the country, and anyway, the hydrants that still had a water supply couldn't be located, because they weren't painted to make them stand out. In desperation the men pumped water from the nearby Forth and Clyde Canal, but the hoses were badly punctured by being dragged over the debris of glass shards and sharp stones. The hoses on the trailer pumps that could be dragged over the terrain were too short and anyway couldn't distribute water over a large enough area. It seemed that no matter how hard they tried, something, or several somethings, were against them. There were firemen on duty so long that they slumped on the ground from exhaustion, local volunteers who had no knowledge of what had become of their own families. But still they, and the units that came from outside to help, battled in relays and shrugged off their own injuries; heroism comes in small actions by little people. They knew the bombers would undoubtedly be back on Friday night too, as they were . . .

In the Dalmuir Masonic Temple, where Frances was dancing with Marek, once it was understood that the town was under attack the dance music stopped and the dancers started to sing 'Abide With Me'. Marek and Frances tried to make their way back to Second Avenue, dodging incendiaries and bombs dropped by planes diving so low that they looked certain to crash.

Marek's boat, the *Piorun*, Polish for Thunderbolt, had just finished a refit and was sitting at a berth in Rothesay Dock. At the next berth was the newly constructed battleship, HMS *Duke of York* which, being a prime target, was under attack. The *Piorun*'s crew quickly formed themselves into impromptu gun crews, regardless of what their on-board jobs were, and fired on the German planes attacking the *Duke of York*. The Polish seamen, most in their teens, blazed away at the bombers with ack-ack guns that could be heard all over the town. When the *Duke* was hit and set on fire some of the *Piorun*'s crew fought the blaze. They used sand and whatever they could find, and when that ran out they used their bare hands to put the fires out to save the new battleship, while the others continued to fight off the German bombers, the bombs and parachute mines falling all around them. And Marek was one of them, Marek who had stood before Marion in her dreams so many times over the last fifty years. A quick snap of him standing there crying. Click! She reaches out to him, trying to comfort him and to hear what he's saying, but the film moves on and he's gone too.

Clydebank was ablaze, and in what was left of their homes people were dead, dying and injured. Because no one, apart from the officials, had been seriously expecting the raid, in many cases people didn't even bother going to whatever shelters they had. And families were not always together, so it took some days or weeks to discover if their relatives were dead or alive.

First-aid workers trained to deal with minor injuries found themselves amputating limbs and delivering premature babies. One 94-year-old woman, given a tot of whisky to help her cope with shock, immediately decided that she must be having a baby; an unlikely event doubtless more believable to her than what was really happening.

And amid the death and destruction ordinary people with no experience of rescue work did whatever was necessary to get others out of the debris. Two passing bus conductresses rolled up their sleeves and started digging, and when another blast blew them off their feet, they got up again and carried on working. A local policeman climbed into a ruined building and pulled out an old man who was trapped beside an unexploded bomb. People leaving their houses grabbed whatever they could, the canary in its cage or a prized fur coat, and a policeman's daughter grabbed her father's hat. Later, finding her home a burning ruin, she wondered what good a police hat was to her and threw it on the flames too.

Those searching for their families were confronted by the full horror. Bodies lay everywhere, some unmarked, killed by the blast, others blown apart, sights that some were never able to talk about. Marion didn't hear the bomb that hit her home in Second Avenue. One minute she was looking at her family as she listened to one of Colin's stories, and the next she was awake in the darkness. It was incredibly hot so, half-asleep, she tried to pull the blankets off and found that she couldn't move. She tried pulling her legs out from under the blankets and couldn't, because the blankets were huge slabs of masonry. She pushed with her arms to lever herself out, and that's when the pain hit, around her chest. Well, not pain exactly, more a pressure, something catching her, holding her down. Must get out! Have to get out! She was scared, so she did what any eleven-year-old does when they're scared, she yelled for her mother. In the far distance she could hear thuds and the thought went through her mind that the thunderstorm had passed over them. It was silent and dark, and there was a smell of gas. 'Mammy! Mammy!' There was no reply. She shouted again, as loud as the tightness around her would allow, 'MAMMY! MAMMY!'

Then she heard a voice slow and quiet, from somewhere nearby. 'Ah'm here, Marion,' Jean MacLeod said. Relief running through her, she tried to find her mother with her eyes, but it was too dark, and the panic welled up again. 'Marion, listen tae me,' her mother said, 'everythin's a'right. They'll come an' get ye in a wee while, ye've jist got tae stay calm and breathe nice an' easy. D'ye hear me, Marion? Jist stay still an' keep breathin', jist take wan breath at a time, nice an' easy, noo.' She began to lose consciousness, lulled as much by the sound of her mother's voice as the gas escaping from severed pipes, fading and drifting off into oblivion.

She had no idea what time was passing, she was only aware of sleeping and waking for what seemed an eternity. Every time she opened her eyes she saw only blackness, and as pain gave way to numbness she wanted to sleep more, but her mother wouldn't let her.

'Marion! Marion! Are you still there?' Marion heard her in the hazy distance but didn't reply. 'Marion Katie MacLeod! If you don't wake up Ah'll give ye what for!' It was too hard, Marion Katie MacLeod didn't want to be awake, but being addressed by her full name had the desired effect, it made her break through the dense cloud that was in her mind. 'They'll be here tae get ye soon,' Jean told her, 'and ye'll need tae help them. Ye canny go to sleep. Tell me about the day ye were born. Marion Katie! Tell me what happened on the day ye were born!'

'Ah don't remember.'

'Aye ye do! Ye remember fine! Where was your Da?'

'Da . . . Da was at work . . .'

'Should he have been at work?'

'Naw, he was on the back shift, but Granny Kate put him oot an' said he wasnae needed.'

'That's right, an' what happened then?'

'He worked right through two shifts, an' Granda John had tae go an' get him tae tell him he had a wee lassie.'

'An' what did he say when he saw ye?'

'He said . . . he said . . . "Another wee carrot top like Granny Mirren, but she's got Granny Kate's cheeky wee face," so Ah was called efter the two grannies.'

Whenever it seemed as if Marion would drift once again into unconsciousness, Jean would waken her by telling her stories or demanding that Marion tell her, and so it went on, till at last there were voices up above. 'Shout, Marion! Shout an' let them know where ye are!' her mother urged, and Marion yelled as loud as she could. Then a man's voice somewhere above answered.

'We hear ye, lass, we're comin'!' Somewhere in the blackness, high, high up above, was a chink of light, and she kept her eyes on it and forced herself awake. Three times the man told her he was throwing a rope down, but Marion couldn't see it let alone reach it. Then there was a sound from underneath, like a great big mole burrowing, and suddenly up beside her popped two men with miner's helmets on their heads, their faces and bodies black with mud and soot. One of them shone his light on her. 'Hello, lass,' he said brightly, as though he had met her in Dumbarton Road, 'who are you?' Marion was so astonished that she stared back silently for a moment.

'Tell them who ye are!' her mother said beside her.

She took as deep a breath as the clamp around her chest would allow and announced, 'Ah'm Marion Katie MacLeod of 70 Second Avenue.' Then it all faded again.

Teams of miners from West Lothian had volunteered to help search for survivors the day after the first raid, and when they reached Marion she had been trapped for more than twelve hours. Their methods were different from the amateurs. Instead of standing on top of the debris and lifting pieces off till they reached someone, the miners dug a tunnel straight through which they supported with wooden struts, they went straight to the centre. The two who had popped up beside Marion then had the problem of what to do with her. The debris pinning her by the chest was easily enough removed, but her legs were caught by large pieces of masonry, heavy beams and metal pipes, and they couldn't use anything with a naked flame to cut through, because of the risk from escaping gas. Marion was vaguely aware of frantic discussions taking place between the two miners and the men up above, but she was too far gone to connect it with herself or her situation.

'Christ, Ah dinny ken how we can get the bairn oot. Whit aboot her legs?' said one voice.

'Well, it's either her life or her legs, that's the choice. It's no' an easy choice, but it's a' we have,' replied the other. 'If she was your bairn, whit would ye dae?'

'Ah'd say "Bugger her legs, get her oot."'

'So would Ah, let's get oan wi' it before the whole place caves in on top o' us.'

Eventually she was aware of clean air hitting her nostrils and flooding her lungs, but as she tried to breathe it down the pain in her chest hit again, and she went out like a light. They took her to Radnor Park Church Hall, which had been set up as a first-aid post. During the night an off-duty nurse had arrived and found no one medically qualified there, and an endless stream of devastatingly injured casualties coming in. She had gone to the Western Infirmary, described the scenes she had seen and pleaded for help, and a bunch of final year medical students had volunteered to go to Clydebank. Their superintendent had refused to take any responsibility for them, and he refused to give them any medical supplies, but a nursing sister had wrapped whatever they might need in sheets. Everything that was except morphia, because student doctors weren't allowed to administer morphia. The people of Clydebank would get treatment, but no pain relief, because of the rules.

The brave little band of medics dodged bombs, mines and craters that night, walking with their supplies on their backs, and when they reached Radnor Park Church Hall they worked hour after hour. The more serious cases they sent to hospital in whatever vehicles they could find, driven by volunteers, and by the time Marion was dug out, the worst of the casualties had been cleared. One of the student doctors took one look at the now deeply unconscious child and was so horrified by her injuries that he went with her to the Western Infirmary. She had too many injuries to log, there were fractures to the skull, breastbone and ribs, and multiple fractures to the pelvis and the legs the miners had fought not to leave behind if they could avoid it. The young student gazing sadly at her singed red hair matted with blood and dirt had little hope for her, but he had witnessed scenes of carnage and death all night, he wanted the little girl to live, if that were possible. 'And we'll take the wee boy to the Western too,' he had said, 'the boy Ryan, David Ryan.'

Marion knew nothing of this, that day or for many, many more afterwards. She thought of those months as lost from her life and would smile wryly to herself every birthday and reflect that she was actually months, if not years, younger.

There had been moments of wakefulness, but they were like dreams, and moments that *were* dreams; the problem was telling one from the other. People appeared and disappeared with confusing regularity, as she tried to struggle back to a world she could understand, the real world. Did Marek stand beside her crying, and was that wee pest Davy Ryan really there every time she opened her eyes? Or had she dreamt it all up?

One day the dreaming phase would be over, and she and wee Davy would have to come to terms with being Number 70's only survivors. And then they would wish they could escape back into their dreams for ever.

The bomb had hit the left side of Number 70, the side where Granda Archie, Granny Mirren, the Ryans, the Rossis and Tommy and Jean and their family had their homes. Granda John and Granny Kate had taken refuge there too, the MacLeods all huddled together as they always did in times of crisis, waiting for the noise and the danger to end. Some people were found in bits, some never found at all, becoming part of the 'disappeared' that became a feature of the Clydebank bombing.

The amateur rescuers and the east coast miners who had earlier found the wee lassie and the wee boy went on with their work. Apart from the two as yet unidentified children only bodies had been found at Number 70. The diggers were ordinary people who had reacted instinctively to the problem. Those working shifts in the factories, in the yards or at Singer's, were more likely to be safe, because the industrial sites were relatively unscathed. As they emerged they saw the carnage, looking on a familiar landscape now rendered unrecognisable and horrific. Their neighbours and work-mates were trapped inside the heaps of rubble and they had to be got out, so they dug with their bare hands. When one band reached Tommy MacLeod he was so badly mutilated that they gave him up for dead. Each time they located someone their hopes soared, but each time there was no sign of life the weariness fell heavier on them. Bowing their heads with resignation they left this latest find where he was and went on with the next task. Then they heard a hoarse voice demanding, 'Where's ma family?' and were shocked to find the dead man talking to them. The rescuers formed a circle around him, and stood looking helplessly and silently at the mortally injured man. Then one spoke up in a deliberately casual voice.

'Who are ye, pal? Whit's yer name? Ah'm Geordie, by the way.'

'Thomas John MacLeod,' he said, and they could have sworn that he laughed quietly. 'Ma family. Are they a' right, Geordie?'

The rescuers looked at each other again. He was so badly injured he should be dead, certainly he had only minutes left. What could they say?

'Aye,' Geordie lied cheerfully, 'they're a' fine. Cuts an' bruises, that kinda thing, Tam. They're worried aboot ye, mind, Ah'll jist send somebody tae tell them ye're a' right. They're hivin' a cuppa tea while they wait for ye.' A kindness to a dying man.

'Tell them Ah love them, Geordie,' Tommy said. 'Tell them Ah love them a'.' And then he died.

The only one not found within the ruins of the building was Jean. Standing at the closemouth keeping watch for Frances coming up the road, the blast had thrown her outwards and a long distance forward as the building collapsed on those who were inside. She had been the first to be found, and it was obvious she had died instantly, long before her youngest daughter had been found, and a longer way from her. Tommy was the last, apart from Frances, that is, who was never found. The only survivor of the MacLeod family was Marion, though it was to be many, many months before she knew it.

In the years that had passed since, many things had puzzled Marion. She had clearly heard her mother's voice talking her into surviving while she was trapped, yet Jean was nowhere near, in fact she was already dead. She thought about it often, but then she just accepted it because she didn't need an explanation. She *knew* what she had heard, and in moments of crisis during the rest of her life she would hear it again. 'Just keep breathin', Marion, just take wan breath at a time . . .'

But what about Frances? Where was she and what had happened to her? Obviously she had died that night too, but no trace of her older sister was ever found; Frances would remain one of Clydebank's 'disappeared'. Marion could lay flowers on the mass grave where the rest of the family were buried, but she could bring no posies for Frances, because Frances had simply ceased to be, and that was hard to come to terms with. She remembered watching her go off that night on the arm of Marek, wearing her new green dress, Granny Mirren's gold crucifix from Uist around her neck to ward off the evil eye, her auburn hair swinging free, her green eyes shining. In her memory she followed them along their route many times, as though somehow an elusive clue would suddenly appear if she looked hard enough, but she always lost them at the same spot. Arm in arm they went, Frances into oblivion, and Marek into the snapshot album Marion carried in her mind, all of them trapped together somewhere between reality and nightmare.

8

'Hello, Marion?'

She opened her eyes and found a young lad bending over her.

'Marion, you're in the Western Infirmary. Do you remember what happened?'

She was aware that she was staring at him stupidly and felt embarrassed. She wanted to say, 'I was trapped after the bombing,' but the words wouldn't come out, stopped by whatever was grasping her chest, squeezing out everything but the effort to take the next breath.

'Don't worry,' said the lad, putting a stethoscope into his ears, 'I think you're having some breathing problems, we'll do what we can to sort you out.' He turned to the man in the green overall she remembered from before. 'I can hear her chest from here,' he said, 'it's almost waterlogged.' Then to Marion he said, 'Have you had a chest infection lately, y'know, bronchitis or pneumonia?'

She nodded.

'Many? Say in the last year, more than one?'

She nodded again, struggled to speak, then held up three fingers. Three chest infections in the last year to be exact. Her GP had said she should maybe have an x-ray sometime, just in case, but there was no urgency.

'Does chest trouble run in your family?' the lad asked, and her eyes filled up. How many times had she been asked questions like that over the years, and had to reply that she didn't know, she had had no family after the age of eleven? Well, there was Auntie Maggie, but she could hardly be called family . . . The lad took her tears as the fear of a scared old lady. 'It's OK, Marion,' he smiled. 'Have you been breathless recently?'

She nodded, closing her eyes. 'No wonder he thinks you're a daft auld biddy,' she thought. 'So wrapped up in your memories of fifty years ago that you missed that one.' Aye, she'd been breathless recently, now that she thought about it, it had been worse over the last three or four days. Her mind had been on the 50th anniversary though, and she hadn't given it a thought, hadn't realised it was another chest infection. 'No' fit to be let oot alone!' she thought.

'I think you've got another one, Marion,' the lad said. 'I'll give you an injection to make you more comfortable, then we'll see about finding you a bed.'

In the distance she heard a discussion that she felt must be about her, but she was too weary to stay awake.

'We don't have any beds here,' the lad said, 'I've got CVAs and infarctions backed up on trolleys along the corridor. I'm pretty sure it's a chest infection, but she seems to think she's had a few recently. She should be investigated in case there's anything nasty there. I'll call the Royal, see if they can take her.'

The green-suited paramedic sighed heavily and shook his head. 'Another "See the sights of Glasgow" effort,' he said. 'Ah used tae be a paramedic in the auld days, y'know, noo Ah'm a tour guide. Ah'm thinking of charging the patients for my services.'

'Why not?' the young doctor shrugged. 'The way things are going they'll soon have to pay for the petrol as well.'

Then she was aware of movement, and realised she was back in the ambulance.

The day after the first night of bombing, those who weren't engaged in rescue work moved out of the town and headed to whatever safety they hoped existed. Some went to Glasgow, just five miles along the Clyde, to seek out relatives, hoping that the city wouldn't be as devastated as their own streets but fearful that it would be. What they found was another world untouched by the previous night's carnage, where people stared in shock at their rags and their distress and wondered what had happened to them. Others saw only odd characters wearing nightclothes in the middle of the day in city streets and laughed at them. Glasgow had been largely untouched by the Luftwaffe, and the Glaswegians hadn't been told of what had befallen Clydebank because press reports had been censored to ensure that there was no mention of the raid or its results. Even so, the laughter had remained in the mind of the refugees long after they had an explanation for it. The physical wounds would heal in time, but the assault on the spirit would not, and being laughed at was part of it. 'Bankies had always guarded their independence, the biggest insult you could use was to say Clydebank was in Glasgow, and it seemed to the bedraggled refugees that the difference between them and the city that had begotten their town was even more marked that morning. They had stepped out of a nightmare into an unknown land of strangers who were even more strange than usual.

While they were being stared at or laughed at, those at home gathered about them what family they still had and what possessions they could carry and jumped aboard any transport that happened along. Cars, lorries and buses evacuated the townspeople, so that by Saturday a population of nearly 50,000 had been reduced to around 10,000. For many of those fleeing what they knew would be a second night of bombing, the transport they took out of Clydebank that day, headed for destinations all over Scotland, determined where they would live and what they would do with the rest of their lives. More than one family left with the fate of relatives still unknown, and some wouldn't find out for weeks, others would never know, just as Marion didn't know about Frances, and would live with the unease of unfinished business all their lives.

During the Depression of the twenties many 'Bankies had got into the habit of heading for the hills, unwittingly spearheading the Scottish hillwalking and climbing movement. After the horrors of Thursday they instinctively moved out of the town into the hills, to what they thought would be safety. Instead they walked straight into the decoy towns of lights and fires, codenamed 'Starfish', intended to lure the second wave of bombers away from the town. And there were already fires burning in the hills, caused by bombers dumping what was left of their payload on the previous night, so when the planes returned on Friday night some bombed the decoy towns because they looked like Clydebank. So many of those who had lived through the first raid were killed in the second raid, in the hills where they had fled looking for sanctuary.

For those who remained in the town the priorities were finding survivors, repairing water, electricity and gas mains, and bomb disposal. And as much of the industrial base had escaped intact, most factories were able to resume production, with the workers bussed in each day from wherever they had been evacuated.

Gino Rossi had been given leave from the Argylls to search for his parents, Alfredo and Anna. He spent weeks scouring what was left of his home town, joining the groups hauling boulders away with their bare hands and in desperation, viewing every mangled body that was dug out from ruins far from Second Avenue, as the clearing up continued. He never did find them, and he would live for the rest of his life with the agony of knowing that if he hadn't fought so hard to get them released from internment they would have survived the War. To his mind he had got them home just in time to get them killed, or at least to join the growing list of disappeared, and even though he came through his army service unscathed, that scar of grief and guilt would inevitably mark him for ever. Jimmy Ryan, serving with the Commandos, was engaged in extraordinary war work, if any could be called ordinary, and wouldn't find out for many months that apart from his young brother, Davy, lying alongside Marion in hospital as they both clung to life, he too was alone in the world. The extra little twist of the knife that Fate held in store for Marion was that she had one relative, her dreaded Auntie Maggie, who had been working her shift in Singer's when the bombing started, and so had survived. Her house had been cleaved in half, and after the 'all clear' she stood staring up at her black-leaded range balanced precariously near to the edge, its brightly polished kettle still sitting on top, both of them covered in dust and debris. Tears poured down her face; that the world should witness the mess her home was in, and her so houseproud that never a speck of dust was allowed to settle in peace. Oh the shame of it!

In Clydebank the living got on with burying the dead. There was an atmosphere of rawness, of every movement and thought being achieved through physical pain. Nothing came naturally, all was awkwardness and it hurt so badly. The familiar landscape had gone, not just in terms of what buildings should stand where, but in terms also of the normal running of day-to-day life – the people you saw on your way to work, the banter, the discussions men had about football, and women had about their families or news of the latest queue that heralded something could be got if you stood long enough, ration book in hand. There was no routine any longer, all was shock, grief and pain, on a scale they could never have imagined. It rendered them almost paralysed yet they had to carry out impossible tasks, like burying their entire families. Everyone had experience of death, it was always, as the local clergymen were to intone many times in the weeks to come, in the midst of life, and the community dealt with it as their beliefs dictated. But how did you cope with it on this scale, when the community was no longer there to support you, and the normal rites that helped you bear it had been destroyed? There was no time to come to terms with the death or deaths within your family; burial had to take place as soon as possible to lessen the very real risk of contagious disease, and for a great many that meant a mass grave. Everyone felt the pain of it, but none more than Pat Rocks, who had come off his shift to find his home in Jellicoe Street gone, and with it thirteen members of his family; yet somehow he had to function, to do what had to be done. They all had to, whatever the scale of their loss. Do what had to be done now, and suffer later when there was once again time to think and you couldn't put it off any longer. The goodbyes not said, the harsh words not retrieved, forgiven or forgotten, the 'if onlys' and 'maybes' that would haunt them long after their loved ones had ceased to be affected by hurts, real or imagined.

Everyone has something to reproach themselves with when a loved one dies, but the people of Clydebank faced so many deaths at once, so many hurts and guilts, and some never recovered. Those able to claim the bodies of their relatives made arrangements for family funerals, while mass graves were dug at Dalnottar Cemetery for those unclaimed or unrecognisable. They went to their graves ignominiously covered in sheets tied with string round the waist and neck, because the Department of Health had refused requests made long before the raids to provide cardboard or papier-mâché coffins. Most of the families and neighbours of 70 Second Avenue were among them, including all the MacLeods except Marion, who was expected shortly to join them. Where Frances was no one knew, except possibly Marek.

Then the counting began of those who had died, and a legacy of bitterness was added to injury for the survivors. The official figures didn't add up and it was a strongly-held conviction that the carnage had been deliberately under-estimated to avoid denting morale in the rest of the country. To the people of Clydebank, who could see for themselves the extent of the death and destruction, each updated figure was an insult. At one stage 500 casualties was the official estimate, to which one Home Guard asked with bitter sarcasm, 'Which street?' The Imperial War Graves Commission gave the final total as 448. Clydebank was not only obliterated, but its suffering was belittled and its dead demeaned. Sometimes you wondered who the true enemy was . . .

Not of course that death was confined to the dates of the March raids or the second two-night assault in early May; the dying went on for weeks, months and years afterwards. In September of that year the tug *Atlantic Cock* was working in Beardmore's old basin in the Clyde when it hit a parachute mine dropped in March. The tug landed on the other side of the river and nine of her crew were killed, including one man who was thrown seventy feet into the air. And the mental and emotional deaths were uncounted in the official figures, however wrong they were.

By the weekend after the bombing, much to the dismay and disgust of those still searching the ruins, crowds from Glasgow turned up to stare at the little piles of recovered belongings denoting where once homes had stood, full of bustling, lively families. It was assumed by the exhausted and distraught rescuers still looking for survivors that the sightseeing was ghoulish, and it certainly hampered the work going on. But people show sympathy in different ways, and perhaps for at least some of the unwelcome Glaswegians this intrusion was as near as they could get to expressing theirs. Perhaps they were just being there, bearing witness, and by all accounts what they saw, the long lines of 'Bankies streaming out of their town in a continuous procession lasting a full day, carrying whatever they had salvaged of their former lives, the sad little bundles of clothes and shoes sitting among the ruins, left an indelible impression on their memories. For others though, the jackals in every society, the tragedy offered an opportunity for gain, and looters arrived from Glasgow under the guise of humanitarian aid, sometimes with vans, to steal whatever they could. It was of course a myth of the War that looting did not take place anywhere; wherever the vulnerable are to be found there will also be those who feed off their misery. It was ever so, and still is.

As the dead were buried, exotically-coloured pet canaries and budgies sang in the trees overhead. Liberated from their cages by the bombs that had killed their owners, they were now free to fly over the remains of the town. And pet dogs and cats roamed the streets, driven mad by fear, hunger and thirst. Dogs formed packs, and after one was spotted searching for food near a makeshift mortuary an animal clinic was set up to destroy them. Five hundred were painlessly put to sleep immediately and, by the end of 1941, 1,800 family pets had been destroyed.

Meanwhile the evacuated searched for homes, and the Laird family, a mother with two little boys, a baby girl in a pram and their red setter, Crumpet, had been evacuated to Kirkintilloch, a douce settlement of wealth and respectability outside Glasgow. Kirkintilloch, where until 1970 the citizens would not permit a pub within their community, for fear that the riffraff on the outside would enter their boundaries and bring drunkenness and debauchery to mar their genteel sensibilities. Instead the riffraff of Kirkintilloch took their own drunkenness and debauchery outside to the surrounding areas, where it so obviously belonged. That Mrs Laird had no idea that day what had become of her husband was bad enough, but she and her children were taken around Kirkintilloch's grand villas, and bungalows with villa aspirations, in an attempt to find someone who would offer them a roof over their heads. But the God-fearing residents who obviously had room to spare didn't even offer a stable, at least not to the mother and her children. The red setter dog was something else though; they were prepared to offer Crumpet a home. Eventually a miner and his wife, living in a council house with three children of their own, welcomed the Lairds into their home without a second thought and cared for them, Crumpet too. The younger of the Laird boys, Gavin, then eight years old, was years later to become a trade union leader.

In Jellicoe Street, the lad who lived above Auntie Maggie emerged from his shelter to find the building split in two and in immediate danger of falling down. He stared up at his kitchen, left open to the elements by the bombs, and on the table was his newly-bought wireless. It broke his heart to be able to see it but not to rescue it; the wireless was a much-prized and costly item. It was too much to bear. Suddenly he dashed up what was left of the communal stairs, grabbed the wireless, and in the same movement, turned and headed down again, with the stairs collapsing behind him as his feet cleared each one. The wireless, though, was undamaged, and worked perfectly for many years afterwards. And many toothless 'Bankies emerged that morning to look for the glasses their false teeth had been soaking in when the bombs had started to fall, including one old chap who had been stopped by his son from re-entering his home during the raid to find his gnashers. 'It's bombs they're throwin', no' pies!' the son said wryly, firmly steering him back to the safety of the shelter.

In another street a lad visited the charred remains of his home, where an incendiary had arrived down the chimney the previous night. He was looking for his golf clubs, and found them still in their bag, the shafts melted and the heads drooping forlornly, looking for all the world like wilted flowers in a vase. He headed for the damaged but still habitable home of a pal, where he found the Irish Catholic mother of the family blessing the darkened house with Holy Water. 'Wait tae she goes intae the kitchen,' said the pal with a wink, 'Ah've got a half bottle o' whisky planked, we can hiv a dram.' When the bottle was retrieved and a hearty swig taken, they realised with horror that they were drinking Holy Water, while the mother blessed her home with the finest Johnnie Walker.

These were the 'lucky' ones, the ones who could summon up a smile in their darkest moments to stop tragedy claiming total victory. A few months later though there was one strike back on behalf of Clydebank, thanks once again to ORP *Piorun*, which had returned to sea after her refit. In May the *Piorun* was on convoy duty to Gibraltar not long after the horrific sinking of HMS *Hood* by the super-battleship *Bismarck*, making the German ship top of the most wanted list, as well as the pearl of the German fleet. The convoy was in the English Channel late one dark, drizzly night when one of the *Piorun*'s crew spotted the *Bismarck*. The find was reported, and the *Piorun*, low on fuel, engaged the battleship, drawing its fire to give the other ships time to prepare and the hastily scrambled British planes time to mount an attack. The Polish Thunderbolt was also under attack throughout by the German planes protecting the *Bismarck*, but it kept up the attack until the *Bismarck* was duly torpedoed and sunk by another ship. An RAF squadron leader whose wing had taken part in the operation later recorded in his report: 'It is the biggest mystery of the seas how this small ship could attack the *Bismarck* and survive.' To the people of Clydebank who knew the crew and the ship, however, it wasn't such a big mystery.

There was a crackling sound, with a distant voice mixed in with it. 'Her name's Marion MacLeod,' said the policeman. 'She lives at 35 Second Avenue.'

'No I don't!' Marion thought. 'I live at 70 Second Avenue!' Her breathing was easier, the wind she heard didn't sound as weary, but instinct made her lie still and quiet. She'd sort this out later, meantime she would concentrate on taking one breath at a time. There was a creaking sound as the ambulance brakes bit, then she was aware of being lifted and the cool air touched her cheeks. She looked up and she could see the sky, light and bright above her after the darkness, and knew she was safe.

There was no way of keeping track of the months that followed after the miners dug her out, she floated in time, touching base then moving again, whether back in time or forward she never knew. Faces appeared then disappeared, voices spoke then stopped, pain came and went. She was aware of being moved, of being wheeled along corridors and then going into a blessed, pain-free oblivion, then waking again and being sick, but she had no idea of whether it happened once, twice, or many times, or indeed if it was all part of some pointless dream and hadn't happened at all. The local minister appeared before her looking serious and sad, he mouthed something she couldn't quite make out and then left. Another time she opened her eyes to find Marek standing beside her crying; she blinked and he was gone. Other faces, faces she didn't know, appeared, smiling, saying words she couldn't understand because they were so jumbled up and sounded like they were coming through a tunnel, but the tone of the voices was soothing, kind, so she relaxed into floating sleep again. Sometimes she wondered where her mother, her father and the rest of the family were, but they had never been far from her throughout her life, so it simply didn't enter her mind that they weren't there. Besides, she could hear their voices talking and laughing, so they were nearby, even if she couldn't see them. She was vaguely aware of the small body in the next bed to her and noticed one day that it was that nuisance Davy Ryan, but before she could tell him to jump in the canal she drifted off on another journey. Sometimes she heard him crying and wondered if she'd hit him and if she would get in trouble for it, even if she couldn't remember doing it. And mixed in with it all was the clean, sharp smell of disinfectant. She remembered a conversation between Frances and their mother. Frances had hated smelling of oil from the factory and Jean had sympathised, but said she should count herself lucky. Nurses, she said, smelt of disinfectant, even when they were off duty you could still smell it; but Marion wasn't sure if the conversation had happened in the past or the present, and while she was still wrestling with that question, it floated out of her mind. Once she opened her eyes and found another strange man beside her, but there was something familiar about him. He looked like Granda Archie, only younger. He said he was 'Uncle Kenny', and she stared at him for what seemed a very long time. *Uncle* Kenny? Did he mean *Big* Kenny? She wasn't sure if she said the words or just thought them: 'Where's your horse?'

Gradually, over many months, the conversations around her became clearer, the faces came into focus for longer and longer spells. She couldn't hold conversations at first; when she tried to speak, the words in her mind somehow refused to come out of her mouth, but she could nod her head. Then one word, then two, then, as the floating feeling disappeared, sentences. She understood that she was in hospital, that she had been very sick and still was, but that she would be all right. There was no sign of her family, though she asked about them every time someone spoke to her. The nurses and doctors didn't reply, so she often wondered if she had actually asked, or had only thought the words, then one day the hospital chaplain appeared and sat between the two beds in the little room she and Davy Ryan shared. And he told them. They were all gone, Granny Mirren, Granda Archie, Granda John, Granny Kate, Tommy and Jean. Colin, Iain, and Frances too, as well as the Rossis and Mrs Ryan. All Davy had in the world was his brother Jimmy, and all things considered there was no way of knowing how long he would have him. Marion, like her mother before her, had only Auntie Maggie.

It was a strange sensation watching the chaplain as he spoke. She felt almost detached, a watcher rather than a key player in the little tragedy being enacted in the room. She could hear the words, knew what each one meant and understood the sentences. It was just the reality she couldn't quite grasp; nothing his words conveyed connected to anything real. She watched his mouth move, saw his eyes try to maintain contact with her own and shy away despite his best intentions when he couldn't help it; she almost felt sorry for him. His quiet voice droned on, rising and falling inside a kind of vacuum, the words interrupting for a moment and then vanishing as if they had never been spoken. When he finished giving the news he seemed reluctant to stop talking, afraid of what might take the place of his voice, until finally, exhausted of things to say, he sat looking bleakly from Marion to Davy and back again. If he expected a reaction he didn't get it, both children lay back in their beds and stared at him intently, without giving any indication that they had heard a word. Nonplussed he got up and left, intending to find a nurse somewhere to take his place.

In the room there was silence, then Davy Ryan began to weep softly. With some difficulty Marion turned over onto her side and went instantly to sleep, the last sound she heard Davy's weeping, giving way to rising sobs then screams. She didn't want to deal with this now, she'd deal with it some other time.

9

Over the next few days none of the staff at the hospital made any reference to what the chaplain had told them, they simply left the two bereaved and shocked children to cope with it in any way they could. They weren't being cold-hearted, they were simply giving them time to adjust to their new situations in life; there would be time later for crying and comforting. But Marion had other ideas; if they were alone then they would cope with it themselves, they didn't need anyone telling them what to feel, how to react or what to do. She was still immobile, but wee Davy's legs hadn't been as badly broken as Marion's so they had healed faster, and when he cried in the night she got him over to her bed and cuddled him till he calmed down and went to sleep. For some reason that she couldn't explain even to herself, she didn't want outsiders involved with their grief. Wee Davy was too young to look after himself, and until he could, she decided, she would look after them both.

Something happened to Marion Katie MacLeod then. It was as if all her life till now the Granny Mirren side of her nature had been in control, pleasant, sweet though sometimes a little risqué, especially in the Gaelic, and now it was time for the Granny Kate genes to take over, battling, fiercely independent and determined. Confined to a hospital bed she may be, but she would make the decisions, she would take control, and it would be as well for anyone planning to do it for her not to look at her and see a pathetic, badly injured thirteen-year-old. She wasn't a child any longer, no one would protect her or patronise her, she was very firmly in charge. Wee Davy, who was only eight years old, reacted to the loss of his mother and the life he had known by regressing to babyhood, while Marion leapt forward in time. When the little boy refused to take his medicine Marion dealt with him, firmly pushing the nurses away. 'I know you're angry, Marion,' said one kindly, 'but don't be angry at us, we're here to help.' 'We don't need your help,' Marion replied calmly. And when Davy fell when he was trying to walk again, it was Marion who forced herself out of bed to lift him. 'That's our job,' said the nurse. 'No, it's not,' she replied, 'it's mine. Davy is mine.' Where before she had been a biddable child who would do as she was asked, now she queried everything, wanted to have it all explained and then made her own decision, not theirs.

Oh she was a bitch during that time all right, she gave no quarter and caused the kindly nurses a lot of trouble. 'Why do you hate us so much?' they would ask, and she would shrug her shoulders. 'Ah don't hate you, Ah jist don't need you,' she replied quietly but firmly. 'Away an' help people that need it.' It took her a long time to work it out. Somehow she had known that she had to develop her strength, that her survival and Davy's would depend on her, and if she let herself rely on their kindness and care she couldn't get the strength she would need for what lay ahead. There was hatred of course, and anger that came in waves and stages. Hatred of the Germans, naturally, and illogically, anger at her family for leaving her alone, especially her mother. 'If we go,' Jean had said, 'we'll a' go thegither.' Well they hadn't, had they? They had all gone together, but they had left her behind. And her father had joked about her being left alone with Auntie Maggie, 'a fate worse than death', he had called it, yet he'd gone off and left her to it as well. Traitors, that's what they were, every one of them a traitor!

There was anger too when she discovered that Big Kenny had indeed been by her bed. His latest performance was as the skipper of a Canadian merchant ship escorting Atlantic convoys. He had arrived in Scotland just after the Clydebank Blitz and decided to find out what had happened to his family. He had sat by Marion's bed for two nights during the months she had been semiconscious and then had to return to his ship, but he had left her a letter. 'My Dear Marion,' it said, 'I'm sorry I have to leave now before you are well, but I know you will get better. We MacLeods find our own way and you will find yours. When the War is over I will come back, but I have left money for you with the hospital chaplain. It's £500, don't let him tell you it is any less. From your Uncle Kenny.' Five hundred pounds was a great, unimaginable fortune, Big Kenny had obviously prospered; she was rich, but the money meant nothing then. To have missed meeting Big Kenny! She was angry at herself, angry at the nurses, angry at Big Kenny and at anyone and everyone who approached her. What good was his money, what good were his promises to come back one day, beside the ultimate experience of meeting the man himself, the man she always thought her mother didn't really believe existed. Jean always suspected that Big Kenny was a carefully crafted figment of Tommy's rich imagination that the rest of the family had simply gone along with – sometimes it was easier to go along with her Da. But Big Kenny was real, and if she had seen him she could have told her mother so . . . if her mother had been alive to tell of course. And had she *really* asked where his horse was?

The staff were so concerned about the change in her attitude to the world that they brought the chaplain back again, presumably to offer sympathy and understanding, and to see if he could make her more sociable. Poor man! What could he do but tell her she would be reunited with her family once again at the great rollcall in the sky, and push the line about the Almighty having a master plan unknown to lesser mortals? 'Fine,' thought Marion. 'If He had a part in this Ah'll deal wi' Him tae!' 'Bugger your God!' she said, staring him right in the eye, and grabbing the Bible he had doubtless brought to give her comfort, she threw it against the wall. 'Anythin' else?' she asked. The minister tried again. 'One day, when you're older . . .' and Marion responded with a loud, continuous, piercing scream delivered from within two inches of his right ear, making him leap feet in the air before hastily departing. Davy looked over at her from his bed, his eyes wide with surprise, and then they both started laughing so hard that they had to hold all their aching bits. When the nurses arrived in response to the scream and the minister's hasty departure, Marion and Davy were rolling about their beds laughing, and saying 'Ouch!'

Oh, it was unfair! Often these days she sat by her window in the new Second Avenue, in the rocking chair she bought to ease the arthritis in her back, and recalled those raw, angry days when she insulted and upset perfectly nice people who didn't deserve it, who were only trying to help, and she blushed scarlet. But on the other hand, it did teach her that help should only be offered when it was wanted, and she had never forgotten that. It's something there to be taken, not to be forced, no matter how good the intentions of the giver or how pure their motives. And the arrogance of them always assuming that religion was everyone's answer! It had caused a great deal of grief to the MacLeods, and as a result the family Archie and Mirren went on to found on the mainland did not necessarily regard religion as a good thing. She remembered one of her Da's favourite pronouncements from behind his newspaper, 'Show me a tambourine basher an' Ah'll show you a heidbanger!' To which her mother had always replied, 'Aye, an' Ah'll show ye somebody that managed it *withoot* the tambourine!' But all the same, the minister had only tried to comfort her all those years ago, he didn't deserve to be attacked. 'Poor man!' she'd think, then she'd laugh despite herself.

*   *   *

The convalescence of Davy and Marion continued, but slowly. There was little in the way of physiotherapy, and there were no hospital swimming pools to help the muscles relax and recover their former strength. She wrote to Jimmy Ryan when an address became available telling him what had happened to Number 70 and its occupants, though he had already been notified. She told him she was taking care of Davy and he wrote back months later, a sad little note of a few lines, saying he would see them as soon as he could. Davy, a scared little lad, had focused his mind on his brother's return; everything, he knew, would be wonderful again as soon as Jimmy came home, and he looked at her to read out what Jimmy had said about him, which was nothing. She looked back at the little eager face. How she had hated that face a few years ago when he was rubbing out her beds, stealing her balls and jumping into her skipping ropes! But her mother had been right, Davy was 'jist a wee boy' after all. 'He says,' Marion lied, scanning the note, 'tell Davy to be good and that I'll be home very soon. Tell him that he has to get his legs really better so that we can play football in the High Park, and tell him that everything is OK, that we'll get another house and live in it together.' Davy smiled with delight; she remembered that smile too, every time he spoiled one of her games, and now here she was, protecting him!

The correspondence continued spasmodically, because there was still a war going on and Jimmy was still fighting in it, but at least she kept him informed of what was happening, while for her, Jimmy Ryan was a link to her former life, however tenuous. Two years after the bombing they were sent to a convalescent home in Saltcoats on the Ayrshire coast, where Marion had to fight to make them put her and Davy in the same room. When she was nearly fourteen and Davy nine it was decided that they could be discharged. The physical wounds had knitted together as well as they could, and now it was a question of building up the strength in wasted muscles and reconstructed limbs. Out of the blue

Auntie Maggie came to see her, and it struck Marion that she hadn't been expecting her and was surprised, shocked even, when she turned up. Something else surprised her: she was no longer afraid of Auntie Maggie.

'Ah'm sorry aboot . . .' She looked so old, yet by Marion's calculations she could only be in her early fifties, but there again, she had looked old all the years that she'd known and feared her. Marion stared at her coolly.

'Aboot whit?' she asked her.

'Well . . . aboot your Mammy an' . . .'

'Ye mean aboot *your* sister, Auntie Maggie?'

'Aye, aye . . .'

'Well, don't let it worry ye, it was a long time ago.'

'Aye, well, Ah shoulda been sooner, bit Ah've been busy, ye see . . .'

'Aye, Auntie Maggie, Ah can imagine.' She couldn't understand why she was turning the screw on Maggie. It wasn't as if she had missed her; she hadn't given her a first thought never mind a second in all that time. Maybe it was revenge for all those duty visits to Maggie's now demolished house when she had yelled 'Sit up straight, lassie!' to make her jump. These days Marion took potshots at everybody, just to warn them not to come too close.

'The thing is, Marion' – Jesus! Maggie knew her name! – 'they've asked me tae take ye in when ye leave here.'

Marion was horrified. 'Well, naebody's asked me, Auntie Maggie, so ye can jist forget aboot it an' go oan wi' your polishin' wherever ye live noo.'

'Campbell Street,' she said. 'They gied me a hoose in Campbell Street.'

'Makes nae odds tae me,' Marion replied casually, 'Ah'll no' be livin' there.'

'Bit, lassie, ye'll havtae, it's that or the poorhoose at Barnhall. Besides, Ah owe it tae your Mammy tae take ye in.'

The old duty thing, Marion thought bitterly, Da was right,

it's her only enjoyment in life tae feel a put-upon victim! 'It's a wee bit late tae think o' ma Mammy, Auntie Maggie, ye never gied her as much as a smile while she was alive! An' whit aboot Davy? Who looks efter him tae Jimmy comes hame?'

Maggie looked stunned. 'The boy's nothin' tae dae wi' me, Ah'm no takin' him in an' a'!'

'Davy goes wi' me, an' Ah'm no' goin' wi' you,' Marion said firmly, trying hard to keep her voice from rising. 'Thanks for comin', Auntie Maggie. Mibbe see ye again wan o' these years.'

'Tae Jimmy comes hame,' that was what she had said to Auntie Maggie. What had she really been thinking? That Jimmy would look after her too? That somehow they would all set up home together and – then what? She would think about that later too, in the meantime nobody was separating her and Davy, and that was final. But it wasn't that simple; you could take potshots at ministers, nurses and Auntie Maggie, but the blank face of officialdom was too vague a target to aim at with any accuracy. The Almoner came to see her and spelled out the position. If Marion wouldn't live with Maggie then it was the poorhouse, because she was nearly fourteen, the school leaving age, and by then children in homes were expected to be working and to vacate the premises. Because her injuries had been so bad it would take her some time to be strong enough to work, so the poorhouse it would be. And Davy wasn't a relative, Davy would go into a children's home until his brother came to collect him. Marion had heard frightening tales about children's homes, they were terrible places with rules and regulations. There were beatings and the children all wore parish clothes and shoes that cut into your ankles. You could always pick out the children 'on the Parish' at school by those shoes, they came in black or brown and the children's socks were always encrusted with blood at the ankle. The children didn't get enough to eat and they were never allowed out, and even wee ones were made to scrub the floors. That wasn't going to happen to Davy.

'Ah'm lookin' efter Davy for his brother!' Marion protested.

'You can't, Marion, he's not part of your family.'

'Ma family were taken away frae me!' she countered. 'So was Davy's! We're each other's family noo! Ye're no' takin' him tae any home!'

She thought about it for a few days then asked to see the Almoner again. 'If Auntie Maggie takes me *and* Davy, will she get any money for it?' she asked.

'She could get a little for Davy,' said the Almoner, 'but nothing for you, because you're fourteen. But I don't think she will take Davy, Marion, do you?'

'She might.'

Then she asked to see Auntie Maggie, probably the first time in her life anyone had actively sought her company.

'Ah'll come tae live wi' ye if ye'll take Davy tae,' she said bluntly. The older woman opened her mouth, but Marion butted in. 'Ye'll get money for him. An' ma Uncle Kenny left me some money when he was here, ye can have half o' that tae. Ah'll keep the other half to look efter Davy and me till Ah get a job. An' Ah'll look efter him, he's a good wee boy, he won't be any trouble tae you. Ye don't have tae do anythin', an' when Ah can work Ah'll find a place for us tae go. A' Ah'm askin' is that we sleep under your roof in Campbell Street. We don't have tae like each other or even talk tae each other, Davy an' me will keep outa your way.'

Maggie was silent for a moment. 'Aye, a' right,' she said quietly.

Marion stuck her hand out; this was a business arrangement, nothing more. Maggie hesitated for a moment then awkwardly shook her niece's hand. As she turned to leave Marion said sweetly, 'An' jist think how people will talk aboot ye, Auntie Maggie, they'll say you're a good wumman, takin' in two orphans, an' wan no' even related tae ye. It'll make ye a saint.'

She had delivered the parting barb in a tone Tommy MacLeod himself could have used when talking to Maggie, and somewhere in the distance Marion could have sworn she heard him laughing, and her mother launching into him, 'Now you listen tae me, Thomas John MacLeod . . . !' She reached for her writing pad and began a letter to Jimmy Ryan, telling him the good news that she and Davy would be cared for by her kind Auntie Maggie. She just hoped Jimmy didn't remember some of the family stories about that same, kind Auntie Maggie.

Before she and Davy went to Campbell Street, Marion had to see the hospital chaplain.

'Ah'm here for the money my Uncle Kenny left me,' she said. 'An' Ah know it was £500, so nae keepin' a coupla quid back!'

He handed over an envelope, and she opened it, counted the notes carefully, and walked to the door.

'If you ever need any help . . .' he said kindly.

'Ah won't,' she replied firmly and shut the door behind her. Then she hesitated for a second, opened the door again and said, 'Thanks.' It was as near to an apology as she could get, though at the time she didn't realise that was what she was saying; looking back she hoped he had understood. He wasn't really her enemy after all, he was just the unfortunate man who had taken on the task of telling her that her family was dead, not an easy nor an enviable task and one that many would have avoided. And for his trouble he had been abused and insulted. She had shot the messenger, and she knew he hadn't deserved it.

Reality began to hit home as soon as she saw Clydebank again, or what was left of it. Up till then she had been in an artificial world of doctors and nurses, in places and with people she didn't connect with home. Now she was back, seeing once again the town she had known all her life, bits of it still painfully recognisable, but after three years there were huge, ugly gaps where the familiar should have stood. The Holy City was gone. It should have been up there on the hill to the side of Singer's, but all that was left of the demolished buildings were the outlines of the ground floor rooms. There could scarcely be a stone here she hadn't walked on, or passed close by every day and taken for granted, never suspecting for a moment that they wouldn't always be just where they were and as they were. Now they were scattered about the ground and she had a great temptation to try to piece them back together like a giant jigsaw, to somehow reconstruct what had been reduced to pebbles. People she'd known had lived here; people she had grown up with had lived within these outlines, and they were all gone. She was aware of a deafening silence in her mind, an empty expanse of nothing where the noise of those people should be, and instinctively she went to her old home, or where it had been, using the Singer's clock as a compass. In times of trouble you went to your family, everyone knew that, only her family wasn't there. She couldn't quite trace where Number 70 had been, but she knew she was near. In her mind she had created a kind of fantasy that it wasn't true, that there had been some awful mistake and they would all be there, waiting for her to return. A big shout would go up when she appeared and they would all come running, hugging her, crying and demanding to know where she had been. She could see the entire scene played out before her, could hear their voices, but she couldn't make it happen. Instead there was a silence that hurt every muscle in her body; she ached for them all, her Mother and her Da, the Grannies and Grandas, Colin and Iain, and Frances. She felt that they were somehow just out of her reach and sight, separated from her by an invisible wall. They were standing behind that wall, looking at her, willing her to find the loose brick. All she had to do was push it, the wall would fall down and they would be reunited again, the MacLeods all together as they should be. But try as she might she couldn't find the invisible loose brick, she couldn't touch them, couldn't see them and couldn't hear them.

She lay down in the remains of the Holy City and sobbed, the tears streaking the dust across her face and the sobs racking her body. Gus Whyte, one of the policemen who had taken the Rossis to Barlinnie Prison, passed by, and he took a step towards the red-haired figure lying across the stones. Then he stopped and moved on to watch from a distance in case she needed help. It was a scene he had witnessed so many times in different parts of Clydebank over the past three years. People needed to cry; what they didn't need, he knew, was a big polis stopping them and telling them everything was all right when it wasn't.

And the silence continued as she reached the next hurdle, facing life without a big family. Being part of a big family gives you a constant back-up, a reassurance that there's always someone at home, always something going on that you have a part in. The bouts of banter between Tommy and Jean, between Tommy and the world for that matter. You were constantly involved in the concern about Colin and wondering what would happen next in his search for adventure. You listened to Granda Archie and Granny Mirren squabbling in the Gaelic they didn't think you understood, and Granny Kate was always there defending 'Us' against 'Them', with Granda John quietly smoking his pipe in the background. They had been part of each other's lives as of right; never a word was uttered without another voice adding to it, nor an opinion aired that wasn't immediately contradicted, it was the way family life functioned, how things should be. In a big family there were constant dramas, and now she was on her own, her and Davy; she didn't count Auntie Maggie, that was a temporary arrangement. At times she thought the silence would make her scream out loud just to hear some noise, and at other times she felt such terror at the thought of never seeing them again that it made her feel sick with panic. It made no sense; how could all that life and energy just disappear, just vanish without trace?

The thoughts of anger and disbelief plagued her mind for a long time, sometimes they still did, especially in her sleep. Scenes from her childhood would play through her mind, mixed up with other scenes, snapshots from when she was barely alive in the ruins or in the room beside Davy, though she was never sure whether they had actually happened or not. But it was all so real! She would wake up with a jolt, and realising it had been another dream and that they really were all gone, she would shout 'Naw! Naw!' into the darkness of the Campbell Street bedroom. It *couldn't* be true – *how* could it be true? Davy would wake in the bed beside hers, but having grown used to Marion's nightmares he would turn over and go back to sleep; it was part of his new reality after all and he had adjusted to it quicker than she had. He had Marion to look after him, so perhaps that made it easier for him to look to the future, and one day Jimmy would come home, but Marion had no one to care for her in the future, so the past was harder to let go of.

Even as she denied what she had to accept, she knew that she had to get on with whatever life was left, because there was Davy to look after. She was fourteen and hadn't had a school lesson in three years; all hope of an education had to be abandoned. That rankled because, as Granda Archie had said, she had 'an inquiring mind'. Colin, Iain and Frances had worked as soon as they left school, but Jean MacLeod had a secret dream that Marion, their 'wee surprise', might one day become a schoolteacher, the height of respectability and ambition. With the whole family working they could at least afford to keep her at school and out of the factories. And Marion had liked school, she had been good at her lessons and she enjoyed learning. Now all that was finished and she had to swallow her feeling of injustice along with all the other injustices and get on with it. She wouldn't let it happen to Davy though. There was no way of being sure that Jimmy Ryan would come home, so she had to plan to bring Davy up, and there would be no yards, no factories for him. If Davy was clever, then she would make sure there was enough money to give him the chance of an education. So Davy would go back to school, and as soon as she was able, Marion would go into Singer's to make sure he could stay there. Till Jimmy came home . . . Take wan breath at a time . . .

10

The house in Campbell Street had two bedrooms, so Marion and Davy slept in one and Auntie Maggie in the other. They rarely met and never ate together, firstly because that was how Marion had arranged it, and secondly because of their different shifts at the factory. On her first day at Singer's the smell of machine oil had reminded her so strongly of Frances that she was almost reduced to tears. She had whipped round quickly at the first whiff before she had time to gather herself, expecting, hoping, to find her sister there. But it was just Singer's familiar in-house perfume that no amount of 'Essence of Cabbage' ever overcame, and it still clung to the factory and the workers even though most of the sewing machine manufacture had given way to munitions. She almost laughed when she discovered that for the duration of the War she would be polishing bullets like Auntie Maggie.

There was comfort there too though; many of the workers were pre-War 'Bankies she knew from before the Blitz. They had known her family, and most had lost someone, so there was a feeling of support among them. They accepted 'Frances's wee sister', and it helped somehow to be among other women who had known Frances. They would tell her stories of her sister at work, of the grown-up person she was when she wasn't 'Marion's big sister'. They told her of the day a group of them had gone to have their ears pierced, a procedure perilously close to the dreaded hussydom, and they had persuaded Frances to have hers done too. But afterwards her nerve had failed at the thought of what her family might say, especially her Da, and Frances had removed the sleepers before she went home. No one had noticed apparently, and in time the minute holes in her lobes had healed over, so Frances had got away with it. The women would talk about their experiences and wonder together what had become of the disappeared, of whom she discovered, her sister was only one. In her absence they had all gone over the nights of the Blitz many times, stories that Marion was listening to for the first time had been told and retold. She spoke to women who had been at the dance in the Masonic Hall and they told her of seeing Frances leaving that night with Marek, going over every second, knowing that each piece of the jigsaw was precious. As the realisation had dawned that this time the siren's eerie call was no false alarm, Frances had desperately wanted to get home to Second Avenue. She and Marek had left the Masonic Hall heading for the Holy City and that was the last sighting there was. So Marion advanced the film in her mind that had stopped as they set off down Kilbowie Road that Thursday night, Frances in her new green dress with Granny Mirren's Uist crucifix around her neck, her long auburn hair getting caught up in the chain so that she kept having to free it with a frown. Arm in arm with Marek, talking and looking into each other's eyes, the two of them laughing, then the picture froze, darkened and disappeared. Now it had been taken on a few frames, she saw them dancing, enjoying themselves until the siren sounded, followed by the first incendiaries. The dancers started singing 'Abide With Me'; she saw Frances and Marek outside the Masonic Hall heading for the Holy City and then the picture ground to a halt again, but it was still progress of a sort.

At Maggie's home – it wasn't Marion's home – Davy was kept out of the way as much as possible; the last thing she needed was any aggravation from the older woman. She was careful with Big Kenny's money, putting it into the Post Office and living off her wages, which were good because of all the overtime she worked. When she was off shift she took Davy walking along the canal or up to the High Park, and she helped him with his homework, determined that he would get every chance. Together they wrote to Jimmy over the months, waiting anxiously for each reply to confirm that he was still there, even if each letter had been written to them weeks or months before and there was no guarantee that he still *was* there by the time they arrived. It was a period of waiting, of marking time until the War was over and normal life, whatever that might be, could once again be lived. War had become a way of life, it was almost impossible to visualise an end to it, and when VE day finally arrived there was a feeling of disbelief, followed by an almost overwhelming grief in the town. There was dancing in the streets, parties and great joy, but there was also a feeling of despair at the loss of life, at the thought of those who were not there to celebrate. The people of Clydebank who had survived would catch each other's eye and know what thoughts were behind them. The end of the War was wonderful of course, but ... But soon Jimmy would be home, that was the thought she had to hold on to for Davy's sake, she told herself. But what about her? She decided not to think about that till she had to.

Jimmy didn't come marching home triumphantly in his smart uniform with all his medals on his chest. He arrived without any warning very early one morning in 1946, so early that he had slept on the doorstep of the house in Campbell Street rather than wake them. Davy found him and told Marion there was 'a man' lying across the door; it was so long since he had seen his brother that he hadn't recognised him. And besides, the boy had been expecting a uniformed hero, and this was a man in a crumpled suit. Jimmy Ryan was so changed that Marion barely recognised him either. The last time she had seen him was when he was on leave after his Commando training, a lad who had about him a new aura of fitness and assurance, but his new maturity had been tinged with an almost tangible innocence. What she saw that morning was a man, a weary man, who had come home to find everything changed, and not for the better. Whatever dreams of home had kept him going, reality had now intruded upon them, and whereas those at home had lived with that reality since March 1941, Jimmy Ryan was now facing it for the first time, five years on.

Sitting in her rocking chair she would call him to mind as he was that morning, and she would see him again so clearly. What had she felt? Disappointment. Yes, she had felt that keenly, she was ashamed to admit. She had clung on as grimly as Davy to the notion of a heroic Jimmy returning to put their world back together again. She had been too young, too desperate, to consider how the years and his experiences might have changed him, and how this home-coming might not be joyful for him either. And there was another feeling too, one that moved swiftly into the vacuum created by her disappointment: pity. She looked at him, saw how tired he was and the sad, lost expression in his eyes, and a surge of pity had engulfed her. All she could think of was gathering him to her as she had wee Davy, and holding him forever to make it all better. Against that Jimmy Ryan didn't stand a chance. Maternal instinct was such a devious old bitch when you thought about it.

It wasn't much of a proposal when it came, in fact it wasn't a proposal at all. Jimmy Ryan, being a returned serviceman with a dependent younger brother, was offered a house in North Elgin Street. Davy couldn't be separated from Marion and Marion couldn't be separated from Davy, and further-more, she did not want to live with Auntie Maggie for the rest of her life. The solution was obvious: she had to move in to the North Elgin Street house with Davy and Jimmy, and the only way that could be accomplished in 1947 was to get married. There was no bended knee, no impassioned speech, just a logical statement of practicalities. Not that that stopped Marion from donning the rose-tinted spectacles of course. Her mother had married her Da at the age of seventeen, he was Young Lochinvar who had rescued the damsel Jean from life with Maggie, and now Jimmy Ryan was doing the same for her. Granda Archie and Granny Mirren had a lot to answer for, they had indeed 'wasted oor Marion's heid' with their tales of romance. True, when Jimmy looked at her she didn't see that expression in his eyes that he had had for Frances, but she decided that it would come in time as they settled down together. Maybe in her heart of hearts she knew that this marriage was an arrangement between two people who were for each other the remnants of a life and family now gone. Maybe she suspected that had the Blitz never happened, she and Jimmy Ryan would never have ended up together, but if there was one lesson she'd learned, it was that life had to be lived as it was, not as you wished it was. There were flourishing unions founded on less than they had; they were working with the cards fate had dealt them. And that being decided it was but a short step to believing that their being together was fated, written in the stars almost, and after the horrors of the past years, a better life was on the way in a land fit for returning heroes. And home-grown heroines.

Auntie Maggie took the news of the impending nuptials stoically, asking only 'Are ye sure, lassie?' and being silenced with a look that would have done credit to Granny Kate smiting one of 'Them'. There was no mention of a Catholic wedding, though the Ryans were Catholic, or indeed a Protestant one; the deed would be done very quietly at the local registry office. The seventeen-year-old bride and the twenty-four-year-old groom would start their married life in North Elgin Street with twelve-year-old Davy. It wasn't exactly a conventional start to married life, but it was the only one on offer.

On the night before the marriage Maggie had busied herself around the kitchen in Campbell Street, polishing everything in sight as usual. The balance between her and her niece had shifted markedly since the days when she had terrorised the young Marion by shouting 'Sit up straight, lassie!' Marion might have been Jean's daughter, but by then she was Tommy MacLeod's daughter too, and if anything Maggie was slightly wary of her feisty niece.

'Ah was thinkin',' she said, furiously buffing up the ornaments on the mantelpiece, 'aboot ye leavin'.'

Marion was pressing a blue two-piece she had borrowed from a pal in the factory; the days when Jean MacLeod was ever at hand to run up some special creation for her daughters were long gone.

'Don't worry, Auntie Maggie,' she said, 'ye'll soon have the place tae yersel'. An' ye can search Davy an' me if ye like, we're takin' nothin' o' yours wi' us!'

'Naw, naw, Ah wisnae meanin' . . .' She thrust her hand into the pocket of her apron and brought something out, pushing it into Marion's hand as though it might explode.

'Whit's this?' Marion asked.

'It's your Uncle Kenny's money,' old Maggie said, turning away and redoubling her efforts with the duster towards an unfortunate 'wally dug' that was in danger of having the glaze rubbed off.

Marion stared at the bundle of bank notes. 'Naw, Ah gied that tae ye for lettin' Davy an' me stay here. It's your money.' She tried to force it back at Maggie, but the older woman grabbed her outstretched hand, the first time Marion could ever remember them ever actually touching.

'Ah never wanted it, Marion,' she said, 'an' you an' the laddie have been nae trouble tae me, in fact . . . in fact, Ah'll miss ye.' Marion didn't know what came over her, indeed if anyone had accused her in the future of what she did next she might very well have been moved to physical violence. She put her arms round old Maggie's thin, hard body and hugged her. Maggie quickly pushed her away.

'Don't be daft, noo!' she said. 'Ye'll need a' the money ye can get tae start your new life. Ah wish ye everythin' Ah never had masel'.'

'But, Auntie Maggie,' Marion said quietly, 'ye never wanted married life.'

'Who told ye that?'

'Well . . .'

'Listen, Marion, Ah was that jealous o' your Mammy sometimes Ah'm surprised Ah didnae turn green!'

Marion stared at her.

'Your Da was the best man Ah ever knew, cheeky wee bugger though he wis. Your Mammy had it a', Tam MacLeod, a family. An' whit did Ah have? A nice shine tae ma hoose!'

'But, Auntie Maggie, ye coulda found somebody!'

'Naw Ah couldnae, lassie! Oor Jean was likeable, she was a bonny, bonny lassie, a' the things Ah never was, and she had the good luck tae find the right man. No' everybody finds the right man. Ah don't know if you have, but if your Jimmy is hauf as good as your Da, ye'll dae a' right.' And with that she disappeared to her bedroom.

Marion was stunned. If Tommy MacLeod had only known! That he was as irresistible to old Maggie as he claimed to be to the female world at large – the Rudolph Valentino of Clydebank as Jean used to call him sarcastically. What might the knowledge of Maggie's high opinion of him have done for him, she wondered, or *to* him? Would he ever have lived it down? It had been a mystery to the entire family why Maggie didn't ever round on him when he lambasted her with his outrageous remarks, but he was more right than he ever knew. 'It's the only enjoyment the auld biddy ever gets,' he used to say, and she *had* enjoyed it. More than he suspected. He would have needed more than his newspaper to protect him if the family had found out years ago, in fact there was every possibility that old Maggie had Tommy MacLeod beaten hands down with that one, and him not around to think up a reply.

Looking back at her wedding day all she felt years later was numbness. The only way to get through the gaps, the silence where their families should have been, was to steel yourself not to think about it. They went through the brief ceremony like robots, making the correct responses, smiling where and when it was called for; stiff, determined smiles they were, the kind that made your face ache. That was her main memory, that smile and the hope that she would get through it without breaking down and making a fool of herself. She remembered a moment of panic when she suddenly thought that it was all so unreal that it couldn't be happening, when she wanted to shout 'STOP!' because letting it continue was tantamount to accepting the situation. In her mind it was as though any future appeal might be blocked by an authoritative voice saying, 'But you raised no objection at the time. Appeal denied.' It really was, as the cliché said, like a bad dream that she expected to wake up from at any moment. And yet logically she knew it was futile; this was reality. There was no appeal; they *were* all gone. Yet somehow she had lived the rest of her life hoping to wake up from the dream that wasn't.

She had had no idea what to expect of sex, it wasn't a subject ever raised, except for the banter at the factory, and she had gone along with that to disguise the fact that she knew nothing. The way the other women discussed it, sex was a battleground between men and women; the men always making demands, the women finding ways to refuse them. If you married then you had to put up with it to a certain extent, but there was something not quite respectable about it, not that Marion was ever clear what 'it' was, though she pretended to understand everything she heard. When she and Jimmy decided to get married it had prompted a discussion in the canteen between the women in her department at Singer's and a great deal of advice on how to deal with 'it', which came down to how to refuse 'it'.

'Start as ye mean tae go oan,' Isa advised. 'Get in there first wi' the rules, that's ma advice, Marion, hen,' which caused great roars of laughter from the other women. 'Ma Bobby noo,' Isa continued, 'he's just like a' the rest, thinks o' nothin' bit his oats, his booze, his fags an' his fitba'. Whit ye dae, hen, is keep his mind oan the booze, the fags an' the fitba' an' he'll leave ye in peace.'

'She's right,' Jessie agreed, 'ye tell him straight that he kin hiv it wance a week oan a Setterday, because that's the day fur the booze an' the fitba', an' it's no' your fault if he's in nae fit state oan Setterday night an' canny manage it, is it? Ah'm tellin' ye, hen, anither hauf an' a pint is cheap at the price tae be left alane!' The women around the table were laughing so hard that they were choking on their tea.

'Och, it canny be *that* bad,' Marion said, casually affecting a knowledge of the subject she didn't have. 'Ye a' seem tae have survived it.'

'That's because we've had tae be clever,' Betty explained. 'Took us a while tae learn a' the tricks, but we're learnin' ye noo tae save ye time!' All the women nodded vigorous agreement. 'Take ma Arthur. When Ah think o' a' they years Ah used "the curse" as an excuse tae dodge that look in his eye before Ah screwed the nut! It only worked because he had nae idea how long "the curse" lasted, Ah strung that wan oot for years! Ah hid three bairns before Ah cottoned oan that the ba' wis in ma court. "Right, that's it," Ah said. "Nae merr o' that nonsense for me. We've goat a' the bairns we want, so that's an end tae THAT." "Wait a minute," he says. "There's weys." "Weys?" Ah says. "Weys? This is the wey. It's either that or cut the damn thing aff, the choice is yours, Arthur, son!" Hisnae bothered me since, must be, noo let me think, oor wee yin is fifteen in July, so when Ah fell wi' her wis Arthur's last stand so tae speak.'

'An' does he no' go wi' other wimmen, then?' Marion asked.

'Other wimmen?' Betty's voice screeched with shock. 'Sure, whit other wimmen wants it ony merr than Ah dae?

Unless he peys them of coorse, an' he hisnae the money tae dae that!'

'Ye see whit we mean, hen?' Isa explained. 'Ony money they hiv goes oan the booze, the fags an' the fitba'. They get used tae the fact that they've had a' the oats they're gonny get then they settle doon an' become as hoose-trained as they ever will.'

For the married women in the factory the issue was clear cut. Sex was for getting children, and as soon as you had all you wanted your duty was at an end. But at the same time they laughed and joked, so it was difficult to know if they meant it to be taken seriously. And there was no one to ask, because Marion *had* no one apart from Auntie Maggie, which meant she had no one. Jimmy hadn't even kissed her before they were married, and they had never discussed their hopes, dreams or even their expectations, so she regarded the wedding night with apprehension. It was wasted anxiety as it happened; Jimmy didn't touch her for two months, and she began to wonder if *he* had already learned the lessons her workmates had been trying to teach *her*. Then one night there was some confused fumbling in the dark followed by a sharp pain, and within seconds Jimmy had rolled over and gone to sleep without a word. Next morning Jimmy couldn't or wouldn't meet her eyes and there was no mention of what had happened between them. Was that what Granny Kate had 'tried wance an' didnae like'? She began to wonder if she had dreamt it, but decided that she hadn't, because her dreams were more inventive than that. If that was all there was to 'it', she decided, then the other women were wasting their time trying to avoid 'it'; it would surely take less time and energy to simply go along with 'it' than to think up ways of keeping their men otherwise engaged.

It seemed that all of her life she had been in the dark, she was the one on the outside who didn't know what everyone else did. As a child the world was full of grown-up secrets that one day she would be given access to, only here she was, an adult, and life was still every bit as much a mystery to her. Everywhere she looked there were questions that only she needed to ask and answers only she didn't have.

Six months after she and Jimmy were married a letter arrived, forwarded first from the hospital and then shoved through the letter box by old Maggie. It was from Big Kenny, now safely back in Canada, and he wrote to ask his niece if she would like to live with him there. Marion kept the letter to herself. Even if it had arrived before the ring had been slipped onto her finger she couldn't have gone, she couldn't have let Jimmy or Davy down, but she liked the secret knowledge that she had a choice, even if she hadn't known it at the time. What Colin would have given for that opportunity! It was kind of Big Kenny, but it couldn't have worked, even if she had accepted his offer. How could he swashbuckle and buccaneer about the world with a teenage niece he didn't even know, to nail his boots to the kitchen floor? It was Big Kenny's role in life to bring excitement to others, to expand their dreams by living his own; he was infinitely more valuable out there traversing the globe than looking after an orphaned relative. So she wrote back to Big Kenny, telling him of her recent marriage and thanking him for his kindness. 'But please,' she wrote, 'don't forget that we are family and that I want to hear from you.' Then she thought better of it; it was too pleading, it sounded too vulnerable. She ripped the paper up and wrote on a fresh piece, 'We're all that's left of the MacLeods, we should keep in touch.'

In years to come, when the going got tough, the thought of Big Kenny's letter was like an escape clause in her marriage contract, a cushion when she needed support. It provided a way out that she knew she would never take, but maybe that was the very best kind to have. And besides, it was too late. That single coupling two months after she and Jimmy married had resulted in her being four months pregnant when

Big Kenny's letter arrived. At least now she knew for sure that it hadn't been a dream . . .

When she was moving into North Elgin Street, she was surprised to find 'that Sal Devlin', despite the odds still Mrs Tony Gallagher and now the mother of several children, already in residence. Jean MacLeod would have been horrified to find her daughter living three doors away from the scarlet woman of Second Avenue, but Marion had always liked Sal and was glad to see her waving from her window as the Ryan family moved in. It had been a speciality of Sal's, she remembered with a smile, waving to people from her window after a good currant bun tea, though in those days they had all been male and in assorted military uniforms. Except for the chap Big Tony caught of course, that one had been out of uniform, as he left at least. The North Elgin Street houses were officially regarded as temporary, though they would still be occupied more than fifty years later. They were constructed of steel sheets riveted together, with plasterboard applied to the inside, and they had two bedrooms, a kitchen with a Baby Belling electric cooker, a double sink and a galvanised boiler for doing the washing. They also had an inside toilet with a bath, a sitting room and back and front doors. The only heating was an open coal fire in the sitting room, surrounded by a stylish tile fireplace, and it quickly became apparent that in winter the houses were as cold as the grave, and in summer as hot as a furnace. Marion busied herself making a home for the family, and trying to cope with Davy's jealousy. He had yearned for his big brother to come home, but what he hadn't bargained for was that Jimmy would come between him and Marion after all their years of closeness. And he had expected a hero, a big brother who would tell him tales of adventure, plus a roll call of all the Germans he had killed for him. But Jimmy never talked about what he had done during the War, and he reacted angrily to Davy's perfectly understandable hatred of the enemy that had destroyed Clydebank. Davy was a teenager as argumentative and provocative as any of his own time or since, and there were times when he goaded his brother, said he couldn't have been a Commando, because Commandos had guts, and Jimmy would get up and walk out the front door. Sometimes he didn't come back for an hour, or even a day; shades of things to come, though Marion wasn't to know that at the time. She should have asked him about it then, but she was too young and inexperienced to ask. That was the thing about having a big family, it wasn't just that there's always someone around, it was their experience that was around too, the collective knowledge of the generations to help you think things through, find the proper perspective and make decisions. She had lost all of that; she was adrift without a rudder, trying to fathom the great mysteries of life for herself, and she was never sure what was happening, what her reaction should be, what she was doing or if she should be doing it differently. Still, maybe it *was* a big mistake, not asking him where he went or why, but even though he was her husband and they were about to have a child, she felt she didn't know him well enough to question him. No marriage in her family had been like this she knew, but was that a bad thing? After all, no marriage she knew had been like any other. But she *should* have tried to talk to him about it; maybe it would have helped. But then again, maybe it wouldn't have . . .

11

Jimmy went back to Brown's as a lagger, installing insulation in the ships being built in the yard. Work was easy to get, with big contracts being awarded to replace ships sunk during the War. So though rationing was still in force, money wasn't tight in Clydebank, which was just as well with Marion being pregnant. Not that she had known of course, she hadn't even guessed at first. How could she when there was no one to tell her? She had felt sick and faint occasionally, but she hadn't fully recovered from her injuries though there were some days better than others. The women at work recognised the pattern and told her she was expecting. 'Ye didnae listen tae a word we said!' they chided her, all of them laughing and shaking their heads as they admitted her as a full member of their society. Marion had laughed too and gone along with their assumption that she had given in to her uncontrollably lusty young husband. What else could she do? She was four months gone when she found out, and she spent the next three crying for her mother. The loneliness at that time was so strong she could taste it, yet there she was with a husband, Davy and now a new life begun. But her Da wasn't there to fuss around her; she wouldn't see the Grannies and Grandas smiling proudly, or her brothers grinning at the thought of becoming uncles. And Frances, who might easily have been the one having Jimmy Ryan's baby, and Jean, who should have been there to spoil her and give her advice. She fell into a depression that felt as dark and frightening as the remains of Number 70 had been that March night. She had even lost the surrogate family support she had found with the women in the factory, because being a pregnant woman meant she had to give up work. And that's when she heard the voice again. 'Jist relax, Marion, everythin's a' right. Wan breath at a time noo, don't panic.' Jean was still with her after all, talking her through the crisis.

She had known nothing about married life or what to expect, apart from what she remembered of the marriages around her as a child. The constant banter between Jean and Tommy, the strong, supportive companionship between Granda John and Granny Kate, and the perpetual state of genteel Gaelic warfare that somehow held together the relationship between Granda Archie and Granny Mirren. But what she had with Jimmy bore no resemblance to any of that. She had no idea what indeed they did have, but whatever it was, there was nothing she could relate back to the marriages she had grown up amongst. Jimmy was quiet to the extent of being withdrawn; you would have sworn that though he was there with you, mentally he was somewhere else. And what were you to make of a man who had hardly touched his wife, and when he did, was so overcome with shame and self-disgust that he disappeared for a whole day? There was never a cross word between them, but then that was part of the problem, there were few words of any kind.

Sometimes she would take herself off to the nearby Our Holy Redeemer's Church, not because she had any time for religion, but because it was quiet and cool and she could think, or at least escape from North Elgin Street, where her troubles were centred. A young priest was usually there and at first they would exchange a nod and a smile in passing, till one day he plucked up the courage to talk to her.

'I'm Father Sheridan. Is there anything I can help you with, my child?' he asked.

Marion looked at him in his long black cassock buttoned from neck to toe, with his funny little pom-pommed biretta on his head. It all looked three sizes too big for him; he should be outside playing football with the rest of the lads, not in here, trying to give advice on problems he couldn't hope to understand, now or in the future. Though he had called her 'my child', he could barely be a year or two older than herself, yet because of the gulf between them she almost felt old enough to be his mother. She smiled at his earnest, innocent face. She couldn't call him 'Father', it was too ridiculous, and she could hardly call him 'Sheridan', so she decided to solve the problem by avoiding his name altogether. 'Ah doubt ye can help me,' she said with quiet humour, 'I'm eighteen years old, my entire family was wiped oot in the Blitz, Ah'm married tae a man Ah don't know an' Ah'm expectin' in a few months – an' don't ask me how *that* happened, because Ah barely noticed it – an' Ah don't know where ma life has gone or where it's gonny go. Can ye help me wi' that, then?'

The young priest sat down beside her, desperately trying to hide the fact that he was blushing. 'Have you no one?' he asked.

'Only Auntie Maggie,' she grinned wryly, 'an' she canny help hersel'!'

'Well, sometimes we just have to get on with life,' he said uncertainly. 'When we're going through a rough spell, sometimes we don't see the whole picture at the time.'

She looked at him, and wondered if this was on a par with his usual line in comfort and advice, and if his flock got anything from it. Or did they just smile and thank him, then go out wondering what on earth he meant, but too devout to say so? Did none of them ever say, 'Whit in hell are ye goin' on aboot?' She remembered the minister in the hospital, a different religion, but pretty much the same approach. 'Tell me somethin',' she said. 'Ah've aye been curious aboot people in your line o' work. Is a' this stuff in a book somewhere? Ah mean, dae ye look up the question an' it gies ye the answer? Ma man's brother, oor Davy, he has these logarithms that ye look up. Is that how your lot work?'

Young Father Sheridan looked flustered. 'What I mean is,

we don't always know what the grand plan is, what the Lord has worked out for us, but one day you will look back on this time and see that there was a reason for it all.'

'Listen, son,' Marion said kindly, patting his hand, 'Ah'm no' wanna your lot, Ah jist come here because it's quiet an' it's away frae ma problems. Noo Ah don't mean any offence, Ah hope ye believe that, but does anythin' ye've said make any sense tae ye? Because it's *mince* tae me!'

He looked so shocked and hurt that she was immediately sorry. 'It's jist me, son!' she said, 'Ah come frae a family that argued aboot everythin', an' noo they're a' away Ah have naebody tae argue wi'. Ah don't mean any harm an' Ah don't mean tae insult ye, Ah was jist curious, that was a'. Ye don't have tae talk tae me, Ah'll just sit here if it's a' right wi' you. Ye canny help everybody, ye know, just put me doon as wan o' your failures!' And from then on he left her to sit alone in his church, advice- and mince-free.

But it wasn't the end of her brushes with young Father Sheridan and the 'one true faith', because it came to light that Davy, now thirteen, was having trouble at his new secondary school. A note was put through the door asking why he hadn't been attending school. Marion worked with him every night, and though he was finding maths hard going, he didn't seem to be having so much bother that he should be dogging off school. He left at the same time every morning and came home as usual in the afternoons. That afternoon she showed him the note, and he burst into tears. It was the maths teacher, he said, sometimes he got tired and couldn't do the work, and she screamed and shouted at him if he didn't understand. Marion understood immediately; it was something she thought only she had to put up with at first, but when she mentioned it to one or two other people, she discovered that she was far from alone. One of the side effects of what they had gone through in the Blitz was an intolerance of noise; it was as if their sense of hearing had been heightened, so that ordinary noises sounded louder, and several different noises at once confused her so that she almost felt off-balance. Even the everyday sound of a bus passing her on the road could make her grimace till it had gone, and people shouting could be unbearable, which was why she sought out quiet places, like the church. Davy had the same problem; she had no idea whether it was physical or maybe part of what they called 'shock', but it was something they had to live with. She thought of the teacher shouting at Davy and her blood boiled. She had been one of the bright ones at school, but she could remember the dimmer ones being on the receiving end of some incredible screaming performances by the teachers, and she had wondered even then how yelling at them was supposed to teach them what they hadn't learned, or couldn't learn. The children inevitably went to pieces in front of the entire class, adding public humiliation to the terror of being exposed as stupid and being screamed at by someone with so much power, and from what Marion could see, they learned less thereafter.

But Davy was a clever lad, she wasn't having them turning him against learning. After all he'd been through she wasn't having him going to the yards like so many, as though being working class it was accepted that it was all they were fit for. So gathering as much decorum about her expanding girth as she could, she went down to the school to talk to the teacher concerned. Miss Anderson was a tall, fair-haired woman in her late thirties, with a long neck, big teeth, no wedding ring and a facial expression that explained why. Marion was enraged to find herself being looked down upon by this vision; she read the woman's look, and saw what she had decided to see. From the teacher's point of view Marion was another working-class lassie married and pregnant, or possibly the other way round, with little breeding and even less education. She kept her temper – what was it Granny Kate used to say? 'Keep your powder dry till ye need it.' She asked if Davy was having problems.

'He doesn't understand things first time,' the creature said,

'I have to go over everything for him and I don't have time, there are other children more capable of learning than David who need my time.'

So Davy was a waste of her time, was he? 'And how do you know,' asked Marion, affecting proper English as she was talking to a teacher, 'that Davy isn't capable of learning?'

'Mrs Ryan,' sighed the teacher, 'I have a lot of teaching experience, I know when a child is bright or not, and David isn't, I'm afraid.'

'And tell me, Miss Anderson,' Marion began. She stressed the 'Miss' so that it was understood in the universal language of women that it was meant as an insult, 'when a child isn't bright and can't learn, the accepted way of dealing with him is to scream at him, is it?' Before the teacher could reply, Marion went on. 'Have you any idea what Davy went through in the Blitz, Miss Anderson? His mother was killed and his brother was away for six years all told fighting the Germans. Davy never knew if his brother would come back. He had three years in hospital with nearly every bone in his body broken, three years of operations and more operations just to be able to walk again, three years of no schooling. Where were you *then*, Miss Anderson? We could have done with your shouting then to get us some lessons, both Davy and me! Now he comes back to school with all that to make up, and instead of helping him you decide that he's daft and all he needs is a good yelling at. Well, don't you worry, Miss Anderson,' she said, 'I'll tell you what I'm going to do. Davy won't be coming back here, he'll be going to the Protestant school from now on.' And with that, she swept out.

Marion didn't have long to wait for a reaction. First it was the headmaster at the door. It was usual, he said, in an attempt to establish himself in a position of advantage to look down and reprimand from, for a parent – or guardian, he gave a little laugh here – to present their concerns to the headmaster rather than going straight to the class teacher. He was civilly received in North Elgin Street, but was a little surprised to be told by the young Mrs Ryan, 'I believe in dealing with the one making a mess of the tune – the organ-grinder, not the monkey,' then even more surprised by the speed with which he was assured that the Ryan family had made up its mind on the matter and politely shown the door. Next it was the local parish priest, accompanied by the younger priest who had presented Marion with mince in Our Holy Redeemer's, Father Sheridan. The Roman Catholic establishment was aghast, it seemed, that a Catholic child could be removed from one of their schools and put into a Protestant school. In fact there was no such thing in Scotland; there were either Catholic schools for Catholics, or State schools for everyone else, though these were attended mostly by Protestants. Again assurances were given to the good fathers that the matter had been thought through, that the family had decided it would be in Davy's best interests to give up the faith and be educated alongside Protestants. She had gone to a Protestant school herself, Marion told them and, from her recollection, children who had been so ill that they had missed years of schooling were not labelled as idiots and shouted at. She knew she was lying in her teeth about that; teachers were teachers the world over, and she knew they knew it too. But since setting foot inside a Proddie school would have been heresy to a Catholic priest of the time they could hardly prove her wrong.

Next came a more senior delegation; the local Monsignor and the Canon arrived, accompanied by the headmaster and the priests, asking to see Mr Ryan, the man of the house, the *Catholic* man of the house. Mrs Ryan invited them in and informed them that Mr Ryan was at work, which was just as well, because he would, she said politely, have thrown them off his doorstep. Another lie; Jimmy could barely connect to his family in a normal manner, let alone get involved in Davy's schooling or indulge in casual violence, but the thought of being confronted by a *nasty* Catholic man of the house was a risk she knew they would be reluctant to take. They came with an offer; if Mrs Ryan would agree to Davy staying on in the school, and more importantly, in the faith – if they lost Davy they also lost any family he might have in the future – they would see to it that he had a different teacher. One who would not shout at the boy, which was of course wholly inappropriate and intolerable after all his suffering, and indeed he would get extra teaching where he encountered difficulty.

Mrs Ryan took her time thinking about it as they sat watching her intently, then to general sighs of relief and smiles of approval she gave her reluctant agreement. One Catholic child had been saved plus who knew how many he might one day sire, and everyone was precious. The crisis had been averted. As the Catholic hierarchy were leaving, young Father Sheridan, supplier of mince to non-believers, turned to Marion with a sly smile and winked. The lad was learning, she thought, there might be hope for him yet.

When they had disappeared in a flurry of cassocks, Marion held her arms around her growing stomach as the child inside kicked with gusto, and she laughed till the tears ran down her face. It had been so easy! She hadn't had to hit anyone or even resort to insults. She hadn't even threatened them – apart from the bit about Jimmy throwing them off the door-step of course and that was a tactical lie rather than a threat she decided; that was allowed. She had just stated her inten-tions and let them work it out, let them have the glory of coming up with a solution. How on earth had she known what to do? It must have been all those years listening to the MacLeods. From the histories of the religious nonsense on Uist she had learned how 'their' minds worked and what their priorities were, and from Granny Kate she had picked up the rudiments of battle, of fighting to win rather than just fighting. Maybe in there too were other lessons that could help her make sense of her marriage. She put her hand on her stomach, and felt the child moving about; there was after all another life dependent on her finding a way through this.

In the yards business was booming. Jimmy Ryan became one of 'the white mice', one of the men who lagged the miles of pipes inside a ship with asbestos, who came out of the yard at the end of every shift covered in fine, white asbestos dust. The factory that produced the asbestos was Turner & Newall in nearby Agamemnon Street, supplying all the industry in Clydebank. The houses around Agamemnon Street were covered with the fine white dust and children played in it, throwing wet clumps of it at each other in fights, and people walking their dogs in the area combed the white powder out of their pets' coats in the closemouth before taking them into the house. It was part of the price Clydebank paid for having high employment within the town.

For Marion though the white dust meant one of her least favourite jobs, brushing as much of the dust as possible off Jimmy's overalls then boiling them up in the boiler and putting them through the wringer. The asbestos was so thick in the air that you could see it and smell it; it got everywhere, no matter how hard you tried to get it out or how much you washed it away. The times she struggled with those white overalls in the confined space while heavily pregnant, huffing and puffing as usual on wash day. No washing machines then, not that a washing machine could've coped with heavy overalls anyway, and it was a matter of pride to get them as clean as possible, till next week.

The spirit of the yards continued, even if not everyone working there came from Clydebank any longer. Many travelled in by bus and tram from all over the place; some came originally from outside Clydebank and others were unwilling exiles who had lost their homes in the Blitz and still hoped to return home one day. There had been some rebuilding after the War, but not enough, despite letters constantly arriving at the council offices from exiled 'Bankies asking when they could come home. Inevitably many never did. They had boarded whatever transport was available on the Friday and Saturday after the bombings and made their lives wherever they were taken to. They all left with the firm intention of 'going home' as soon as new houses were built, but those who wanted to return far outnumbered the rebuilding programme, and as their families grew up elsewhere, their ties loosened. There were gaps all over Clydebank where those who remembered the layout of the old town could still identify what had stood and who had lived where. It wasn't uncommon even in the fifties to come across some returned exile standing before a gap in tears, seeing in their memory the home they once lived in, recalling friends and relatives they had lost. It was hard to pick up the pieces when so many of the fallen pieces were still visible.

She had felt a niggly pain in the small of her back all day. It was like a tiny worm made of molten steel, wriggling for a few seconds and then stopping, but there were so many niggly, wriggling pains on the best of days that she only barely registered this one. Her pregnancy had lasted longer than time and she was tired of the moving mass her body had become. Some of Big Kenny's precious money had been invested in impossibly tiny clothes, but she was less than enthusiastic about the forthcoming birth. She couldn't understand it herself; here she was about to reproduce, about to add to a family that had been all but decimated – it was a victory, a triumph, yet she felt no joy. If anything she felt nearer to breaking down emotionally than she had at any time in the last seven years. She sensed it was something to do with the longing for those who weren't there during what should have been an exciting family time, but she didn't hold the thought long because it threatened her composure, and if she lost that who knew where it might lead?

It was the day of the twice-yearly pay-out of the Co-op dividend, when women from all over Clydebank made their way to the Co-op office along from the undertakers in Alexander Street to pick up their 'divi'. The dividend was a percentage calculated from everything you bought at the Co-op stores. When your turn came in the pay-out queue, you quoted your number – 14/1092 in Marion's case. No woman *ever* forgot her number, it was as indelibly etched on the minds of women as the National Service number was on the minds of men. The amount due would be counted out into your hand like a windfall, a present almost. In every case it was earmarked for household use before it was safely in their hands. Children with new shoes were a sure sign of the 'divi'; their mothers treating themselves to a new apron and maybe, if the money stretched that far, a piece of precious net curtain. The 'divi' didn't run to luxuries, but still there was an air of excitement as the women, holding their children by the hands, queued up along the street and around the block. The excitement infected the children too, so there were frequent, vain, threats of retribution if behaviour didn't rapidly and dramatically improve as they waited in line.

The niggly worm in the small of Marion's back was moving further afield as she stood, it was travelling around under her stomach, before easing again. Nothing too bad, just annoying. Gradually though it became more painful until she was holding her breath till each spasm passed. Then a bigger, stronger pain arrived, almost doubling her over, and she felt something inside give way then a rush of liquid running down her legs. She put her hand on the arm of 'that Sal Devlin' beside her. 'Ah'm sorry tae bother ye, Sal,' she said, 'but could ye help me?' 'Oh my God,' Sal exclaimed, 'the poor lassie's waters have broken!' and all the queue of excited housewives abandoned their places and became instant midwives.

Sal took charge of her message bag and her 'divi' book while two other women put their arms around her and helped her inside the Co-op office. The unfortunate office manager, misunderstanding what was going on, tried to stop them. 'If you know whit's good for ye, Mac, ye'll take your ugly wee face oota the wey!' Sal snarled at him. It didn't matter that he had quickly grasped the situation and had already moved his 'ugly wee face' before she had uttered the threat; birth was a time when women were in charge, and before he knew it he was under attack from the rest of the sisterhood.

'Ye're no' so keen in throwing a lassie oot when ye want tae *get* her intae this state!' another woman hissed at him, as though Marion's pregnancy was his fault, 'so jist you bugger aff or ye'll be nursin' your daft wee nose long efter this poor lassie's finished nursin' her wean!' That he was entirely innocent of all charges was neither here nor there; he was a man, in the eyes of the sisterhood he was guilty by association.

'Away an' phone an ambulance for the lassie,' Sal ordered, pushing him into his office, 'an' jist keep oota the wey an' behave yersel' or *you* might need carryin' on a stretcher by the time it gets here!'

Marion was caught between the awful spasms then the lulls before the next one, either laughing at the comments the women were unfairly using against the manager or holding her breath against the growing pain around her body. 'Look at the wee article!' said Sal sarcastically, looking the little man up and down with distaste. 'Ye wonder whit makes us dae it, daen't ye? Ah mean it's no' for their looks, is it?'

'Ye can say that again,' said another, rolling up her coat to make a support for the small of Marion's back as she sat her in a chair. 'An' the business end's even uglier. Ah mind ma first time. Ah didnae know whether tae laugh or feel sorry for the poor bugger havin' tae cart it aroond wi' him!'

'So whit did ye dae?' asked Sal.

'Ah laughed of coorse! He wisnae best pleased neither. Ah said tae him, "If you don't want me tae laugh at it, keep it where Ah canny see it!"'

All the women giggled, but just then another contraction hit and Marion gasped and gripped Sal's hand tightly. 'Look at that!' Sal spat accusingly at the manager. 'See whit ye've done noo!' Having put up with more than enough uncalled-for abuse, he belatedly realised that he could do nothing right in the situation and he turned and fled. 'Aye,' she sneered at his retreating back, 'that's right! You jist bugger aff when things get bad. This is nane o' your business anywey, this is *real* work, women's work! Bit afore ye go, Superman,' she said, 'away an' get this lassie's divi for her, unless of coorse ye intend tae force her tae staun' in line as she gies birth!'

12

They took her to Rottenrow, the Royal Maternity Hospital in Glasgow, though she was only vaguely aware of this or anything that was happening at the time. Her entire existence was centred on the contractions, like steel vices around her body, of getting through one and then waiting in dread for the next, with the waiting time between terrifyingly less and less all the time. This couldn't be normal, she reasoned, no one could survive such pain, and yet those around her, who-ever those hands and encouraging voices belonged to, seemed not in the least perturbed; did they *know* what was happening to her? The pain became an entity in itself, blocking out all thoughts of the baby; all she wanted was to reach the end, but just as one vice-like spasm ended, another began. Why had no one told her it would be like this? Lying under the rubble of Number 70 had been easy compared with what was going on in her body now, the searing, ripping pains that followed one after another. She tried holding her breath each time in an attempt to control it, but it didn't work, and then she couldn't breathe even if she wanted to because the squeezing intensity had shocked her mind into a state of paralysis. A nurse kept instructing her officiously to breathe normally, telling her that she wasn't doing herself any good holding her breath, as though she had any choice. She felt like hitting the idiot and resolved that if she survived it would be the first thing she would do afterwards. Meantime her every available ounce of strength and attention was taken up just trying to survive till the end of this contraction, then this one, and the next. Her reality became the waves of agony she was trapped in, with only glimpses of the rest of the world inexplicably going on as normal. There were snatches of conversation between the nurses and doctors, 'Obstruction . . . mumble mumble . . . foetal distress . . . mumble mumble,' and from nowhere came a flash of Jimmy's pale face with a look of such profound horror that in the split second before he disappeared she actually found herself feeling sorry for *him*. People came and went, some rushing around, some pausing to talk reassuringly to her, but nothing changed. Always, always, there was another contraction . . .

'Mrs Ryan,' a voice said above her. Looking up she stared into two eyes set between a white hat and a mask; she would have been just as unsurprised to see the White Rabbit from *Alice in Wonderland*. 'Mrs Ryan, we're going to have to do a Caesarian section to get baby out.' She couldn't see what this had to do with her; he could don a pair of tap shoes and take off across the floor with Ginger Rogers for all she cared. 'We'll just pop you off to sleep now. I just want you to breathe into the mask.'

But a gigantic swelling of pain surged across her lower body and she was holding her breath against it, and then Jean was beside her. 'Come on, Marion, dae as you're tellt, noo. Take wan breath at a time.' The sound of her mother's voice reached through the agony and she tried to sit up to find where it was coming from, but a shadow fell over her face, covering her nose and mouth. 'That's right, Marion,' Jean's voice echoed through a long, long tunnel, 'wan breath at a time, it'll soon be ower.' And as her mind swirled and the pain receded she seemed to be floating off into another world. The last thought she had was that wherever this pleasant, pain-free place was, she had found her mother again and she wanted to stay there for ever.

'Mrs Ryan? Mrs Ryan, are you awake yet?'

Marion kept her eyes shut. Before she answered the question she wanted to know what the consequences might be, she wanted to take stock. Somewhere in her mind was the memory of being wakened up once before like this, and she hadn't liked what had happened afterwards.

'Mrs Ryan,' the voice persisted, 'open your eyes.'

She wondered irritably why the voice didn't buzz off and find someone else to annoy. If she was asleep she must have a perfectly good reason for being asleep; what skin was it off her nose?

'There's someone here to see you, Mrs Ryan, you've had a wee boy.' Before she could process this piece of information there was a snuffly, mewing sound, followed by a loud, piercing screech. Marion's eyes snapped open, and the first sight she saw was the crumpled, angry face of her newborn son.

'Better than smelling salts!' laughed the nurse holding him. 'Works every time!'

Marion tried to sit up. 'No, no, lass!' the nurse smiled, pushing her gently back down again with one hand, while she cradled the baby in the other. 'You've just had an operation, you can't go jumping about like that!' She put the baby in a cot by Marion's bed and called for another nurse, then taking her under each arm, they eased her into a semi-sitting position. She closed her eyes briefly. The pain across her stomach wasn't like before, but it was bad enough, and there were drips in both hands, one attached to a bottle of blood and the other to a clear fluid. Carefully the first nurse arranged the baby in her arms, avoiding the trailing tubes. He was wrapped tightly in a blanket so that only his head was visible, and a tiny face with a bad-tempered expression. It was the ugliest, most beautiful face she'd ever seen. She eased the blanket to free his arms. 'Don't do that,' chided the nurse, 'he feels more secure being caught tightly.'

But Marion, who knew what it was to be caught tightly, ignored her. 'He'll feel better bein' free,' she said, gazing at her son. 'Take ma word for it.'

His mouth was working all the time, with little tics playing across his features, as though he desperately wanted to say something but hadn't discovered how to yet. Marion looked helplessly at the nurse. 'Whit's up wi' him?' she asked.

'He's hungry,' the nurse said, with the kind of smile that reminded Marion of why she wanted to hit her earlier.

'Great,' she said with a wry grin. 'Ah'm his mother an' Ah don't even know when he's hungry.' They put him to her breast. 'Cut tae bits,' she thought, 'needles and tubes all over, noo he's gonny suck oot whit's left o' me!'

It was just one of those things, the doctor told her later, her records hadn't been passed on in time, what with her having a different name now. Obviously with all the injuries she had received there was no way she could have given birth naturally, only of course, as he said, they weren't to know that at the time, were they? And as soon as her GP had called in and explained the situation they had performed the section. It was just a pity really that her GP hadn't known till next day. 'But all's well that ends well, eh?' And what if the GP hadn't found out she was in labour and called in? 'No point thinking about that, Mrs Ryan!' the consultant boomed from on high. 'You have a healthy son, you should be happy!' and with a godlike smile he swept out of the ward.

After he had departed Marion thought back on the endless pain – what's twenty-four hours between friends after all? – and realised that all those hours of agony had been for nothing. Her pelvis had been crushed into so many pieces under 70 Second Avenue that the baby would have needed a hacksaw to get out that way, and at one point she could have sworn that was what he had been using. She looked at him again; well it hadn't been for nothing she decided, but it could very well have been. She could have lost him, they could both have died, and all because the information hadn't been passed on. Her life seemed to have been dominated by the consequences of information not being passed on.

She had lost track of the time, which consisted anyway of one form of pain taking the place of another, then she opened her eyes to find Jimmy sitting by her bed. He was still wearing his overalls covered in the white asbestos dust, so he must have come straight from work. It flashed guiltily through her mind that she hadn't given him a single thought, her world had contracted to herself and her son. It was, she was to think many times in the years since, the first time they had met each other's gaze for more than a brief half-second.

His eyes filled with tears and his face contorted with anguish. 'Ah'm sorry,' he whispered.

She wondered what he had done. 'For whit, Jimmy?'

'This! A' that!' he said desperately, throwing his hands outwards to encompass the universe. 'It's ma fault!'

'Jimmy, Ah don't know whit ye mean, whit's your fault?'

'You havin' tae go through a' . . . a' THAT!' he said savagely. 'Ah did that!' He got up, sending the chair spinning backwards to the floor and almost ran from the ward, the dust from his overalls billowing around him. She called after him twice, but he didn't turn round. He hadn't even looked at his son.

Sometimes events happen that you realise later were turning points in your life, like a door shutting, only the sound of it takes a long time to reach you. For Marion the moment when she understood that she and wee Davy were Number 70's only survivors was a turning point, it was the moment when she grabbed her destiny by the scruff of the neck and gave it a good shake. Watching Jimmy run from her bedside that night was another, though she didn't know it at the time. Another door had closed, even if she didn't hear the sound of it at the time.

They let her go home after the stitches came out, a procedure so familiar she felt she could do it herself. 'This won't hurt,' that's what they always said as the scissors and forceps got to work; it was a lie of course, it hurt like hell. Before she left with her son the consultant had something to say. He had wanted Mr Ryan to be there too, but Mr Ryan hadn't been seen since he left the ward without looking at his son two weeks before. Marion stared the consultant straight in the eye and said Mr Ryan had been held up and silently dared him to draw any other conclusion. 'What I have to say, Mrs Ryan,' he said, lowering his eyes, 'is that there should not be any more babies. There *must* not be any more babies, or it could kill you. Do you understand?'

Marion said nothing.

'I know this is distressing news for such a young woman – what age are you? Eighteen, nineteen is it? Yes, yes. Well, I appreciate that you would naturally wish to have more children, but you have this wee fellow and that was, well, shall we say fortunate in the circumstances? Ideally you should not have had him, so he's a bonus, isn't he?'

Marion still made no reply, but it crossed her mind that in an ideal world there would have been no War, no Blitz, and she wouldn't be living the life she was living, a life so far removed from the one she had had that sometimes it seemed to her to belong to someone else.

'Which of course is why I would have preferred to speak to Mr Ryan. There are methods, you understand, it is 1948 after all, we're not in the Dark Ages.' He laughed quietly in an attempt to soften the impact of what he was saying. 'Methods that concern Mr Ryan rather than you . . .' His voice trailed off. She could conceive, go through labour and an operation apparently, but when it came to talk of avoiding another pregnancy it could only be discussed man-to-man; it was almost too delicate to be mentioned in front of her, it seemed. She smiled. What would be this man's reaction, she wondered, if he knew that the child he delivered with his scalpel had been the result of her one and only sexual experience? Somehow, after the nature of Jimmy's departure, she thought it was a safe bet that there would be no more babies.

'It's all right, Doctor,' she said quietly, 'I understand. And Mr Ryan is a good man, he'll understand too. He won't want to put me through anything risky again. Anything else?'

'Just make sure that you keep your appointment for the six-week checkup,' he said briskly, 'and do refrain from intercourse until then.'

Marion smiled wryly; that was something she thought she would have no difficulty in complying with.

Davy came to take her home to North Elgin Street. He was growing into a strapping teenager and the difference in their ages was lessening all the time. Once the five-year gap seemed big enough for her to be his mother, then his older sister, and now because, she suspected, of Jimmy's behaviour, Davy was almost her equal. He made no reference to Jimmy, but she felt the anger in his silence, his shame and animosity that his once adored brother had run off and left Marion with their baby.

The first time he had seen his nephew he had watched Marion unwrap him from the layers of nappy, vest, gown, cardigan and shawl to bathe him. He was struck, as everyone always is, by how tiny the baby was, then he drew a finger silently down the little spine, as the naked child shivered slightly at his touch. 'Look at that!' he said, as Marion watched, wondering what Davy was seeing. He took the child's two ankles in his hands and gently moved his legs from side to side, his eyes wide, then he repeated the exercise with the arms, before gently feeling all over the child's skull. The baby stared up at him, looking almost as puzzled as Marion.

'Whit is it?' she asked.

'He's perfect!' Davy said softly. Marion laughed, and he looked up at her bashfully. 'Ah mean he's no' like you an' me, Marion. He's *new*!' Marion, still laughing, looked at him quizzically. 'He hasnae any scars,' Davy explained. 'It's like he's, he's SEAMLESS!'

They took the seamless child home to North Elgin Street. 'Whit's his name?' Davy asked. 'We canny keep callin' him "him", can we?'

Marion had thought about that. She had wanted to call him after all the males in the family she no longer had. Archibald John Kenneth Thomas Colin Iain Ryan. Too much; but what to leave out that would make her feel less than guilty? Then she remembered her father's remark about her brothers, the overly adventurous Colin and the painstakingly cautious Iain. 'Put them taegither,' Tommy MacLeod had said, 'split them doon the middle . . . an' ye'd have two perfect laddies.' Well that was what she had, one perfect laddie, and she knew for sure that she would never have another. 'Ah'm callin' him Colin Iain,' she said, and Davy nodded. Then she thought: Whit the hell? Wan more name won't hurt him. 'Colin Iain David Ryan,' she said. Davy coloured and turned away, his eyes shining.

The first visitor to knock on the door was Sal Devlin, bringing the message bag Marion had left behind in Alexander Street after going into labour. Inside it was her divi. It had come to £2 18s 3d, about a week's wages in 1948, and there was no doubt now where it would go; lace curtains were definitely out. Sal cooed over the baby and proffered a gift of a blanket for the pram and ten silver thrupenny pieces. 'Ah aye put them by when Ah can,' Sal explained, 'so that Ah can gie them tae new babies.' Making conversation with someone she had known to be disapproved of felt odd, but then again, Marion had accepted all those generous sticks of gum that Sal's visitors had left behind, so who was she to judge?

'How many dae ye have yerself, Sal?'

'Six in six years, hen.'

'SIX? My God, Sal, how did ye manage that?'

'Without too much bother, hen, that's the trouble,' Sal grinned. 'Ah fa' wi' a friendly look! An' Big Tony bein' Catholic, he thinks he's daein' his bit for the Pope, an' apart frae that he thinks it makes him look a helluva man.'

'Well, this wan's the only wan Ah'll have,' Marion said.

'It's early days, Marion hen,' Sal said kindly, 'ye'll change your mind later.'

'Naw,' Marion smiled, 'Ah mean Ah canny have any merr, Sal, the doctor tellt me.'

'Oh God, hen, Ah'm sorry! Me an' ma big mouth!'

'It's OK, Sal, honest,' Marion laughed, 'Ah don't think it will bother me. As my Granny Kate might've said, Ah've tried it wance an' Ah didnae like it much!'

'Oh Ah remember your Granny Kate!' Sal said. 'Whit a wumman she wis! But know who Ah *really* liked? Yer Granny Mirren. They a' talked aboot me – oh it's a' right, Marion hen, Ah knew they a' talked, it never bothered me! Ma view was that Ah was young an' any day we might a' be bumped aff, an' we nearly a' were, weren't we? Live for the moment, that's whit Ah believed, take whit's oan offer and let them a' talk, because ye're a long time deid! But your Granny Mirren was a lady tae me. She'd never avoid me, always smiled at me an' said "Nice day, Mistress Gallagher," in that beautiful voice. Was she Highland, your Granny Mirren?'

'Aye,' Marion smiled, picturing the scene, 'her an' ma Granda came frae the Isle o' Uist.'

'Ah knew it was somewhere foreign like that,' Sal said. 'Lovely soft voice she had. "Nice day, Mistress Gallagher," she'd say. Never called me "that Sal Devlin" like the rest o' them, she was always nice tae me. An' your Da, he was a right wee bugger tae, wasn't he? Usedtae wink at me when he passed. "Hav a good night last night then, Sal?" he'd say. "Nane o' your business, ya cheeky wee bugger!" Ah'd say, and he'd say, "Merr's the pity, Sal, merr's the pity!" No' that he'd have been interested, mind ye, it was jist his wey.'

'He usedtae say ye served your visitors tea an' currant bun,' Marion told her, smiling at the memory.

'Currant bun?' Sal bent over, holding her arms around her

waist and laughing. 'Christ, it musta been bloody good currant bun then, 'cos they kept comin' back for merr!'

'Aye, he usedtae say that tae! Told ma mammy they a' left wi' a big grin on their faces an' he wished he could have a bite! Drove her mad!'

'Oh my God!' Sal laughed, wiping her eyes with the hem of her pinny. 'He was a cheekier wee bugger than even Ah thought! Ye must miss them awfy sore, hen.'

'Aye, Sal,' Marion looked down, her eyes filling with tears, 'awfy sore.'

Sal put her arms around her and hugged her. 'You listen tae me, hen,' she said softly. 'Any time ye need somebody tae talk tae, you jist chap on ma door.'

'Thanks, Sal.'

'Ah mean it, noo, anytime, hen. Mind, noo. Look, Ah'll havtae get back tae the hoose. The Pope's man in North Elgin Street will be hame frae work soon an' Ah'd rather feed him than gie him time tae think o' daein' anythin' else.'

In honour of Colin Iain David Ryan's homecoming, Auld Maggie paid her first visit to North Elgin Street. She brought a gift for her great-nephew, a hand-knitted shawl, with a jacket, leggings and bonnet. The shawl was painstakingly and beautifully worked to look like lace.

'Ah didnae know ye could knit like this, Auntie Maggie,' Marion said, genuinely surprised.

'Ah've had a lotta time oan ma hands ower the years, lass,' the older woman replied. 'Ye can learn anythin' well when ye've no' much tae dae.'

'But it's . . . it's a work o' art,' Marion said, 'it's that fine!' and Auld Maggie, who couldn't take a compliment because she wanted one so much, brushed off her niece's flowery words with 'Ach, away wi' ye!' Then looking at the sleeping Colin Iain David, she said, 'Efter a', look whit *you've* made!'

There was no mention of Jimmy till Maggie stopped as she was leaving and asked where he was. 'Oh, he's workin' extra shifts, Auntie Maggie,' Marion smiled. 'We need the money noo that Colin's here.'

Auld Maggie studied her silently for a moment. 'My, lassie, but ye've taken a lot oan. First his brother, then him, an' noo his bairn. An' where is he tae be seen?'

'Ah told ye, Auntie Maggie,' Marion said steadily, 'Jimmy's at work, earnin' money tae keep his brother, his wean an' me. OK?' This far, her tone said, and no further.

Auld Maggie nodded. 'An' ye're nae merr than a bairn yersel'. Ah remember that feelin' well, hen, but Ah think ye're daein' it wi' merr grace than Ah ever did wi' oor Jean.'

Auld Maggie's tone had touched something in her, threatening to breach the barrier Marion had carefully constructed, but she stayed at the living room window, a smile fixed on her face and her hand ready to be raised in a wave in case Auld Maggie turned round at the bottom of the street, which she didn't. Then she sat down by the fire and cried. Davy put his arm around her shoulder. 'It's a' right, son,' she smiled, 'Ah think they call it the baby blues, it happens tae women efter they have a bairn. It's nothin' tae worry aboot.'

But the tears were for herself, for the layer upon layer of responsibilities that had stolen her life, for the loss of that life and the opportunities and chances she might have had. It seemed that she had no control over the doors that started closing with the bombs the Germans had dropped on Clydebank. She had been an innocent, bright-eyed eleven-year-old with 'an inquiring mind' and everything before her, and in one awful night everything had changed for ever without anyone asking her permission. And every time a door closed, she was left with another responsibility, with someone else to take care of, when she wasn't sure she could take care of herself.

There was no one to show Colin to, no family to coo over him and to see likenesses that were or weren't there, or to offer advice, wanted or not. The nearest thing Marion had

had to family support were the women in Singer's, so it seemed entirely natural that she should present her son for their approval at the earliest opportunity. She pushed the pram along Dumbarton Road onto Kilbowie Road and into the factory one lunchtime, and her former workmates in the canteen didn't disappoint her.

Jessie peered into the pram at the sleeping Colin. 'Oh my God!' she shouted. 'Isa! Isa, quick, come here! Come an' look at the bairn! Who does he remind ye o'?' Before Isa could reply Jessie continued, 'It's Tommy MacLeod! He's Tommy MacLeod tae the life, in't he?'

Several more of the women crowded round, nodding in agreement and uttering sounds of amazement. 'Your Da was such a bad wee bugger!' Isa said with admiration. 'Ye never knew whit he'd come oot wi' next!'

'Aye,' said Betty, her voice soft with nostalgia, 'ye hadtae be oan yer toes aroond Tommy, Ah'm tellin' ye, an' hauf the time ye hadtae take his word for whit he was sayin', him speakin' the Gaelic like! Ah usedtae say tae him, "Say somethin' in the Gaelic, Tommy, it sounds that nice," an' he always did it for me.'

Marion turned her face away to hide her laughter. Her Da's knowledge of the Gaelic consisted entirely of curses and insults, and she had a mental image of her Da calling Betty a daft old bitch, and Betty enjoying the nice sound of it.

'Ah heard ye had a bad time, hen,' Isa said.

'Ah havtae admit it wis a wee bit sorer than Ah expected, Isa,' Marion replied. 'Why does naebody tell ye it'll be like that?' All the women hooted with laughter.

'Ye're bloody right, hen,' Betty chuckled, 'an' there's a reason for that! Would ye go through wi' it if ye knew the truth?' And again they all collapsed, giggling and choking on their cigarettes and their tea.

'Ever wondered how it's wimmen that have the bairns?' Isa demanded. ''Cos if men hadtae take a turn the human race would die oot! Ah mind jist before ma youngest was born, ye know that time when ye think ye might as well jist gie in an' split in two? Well, Ah hears this daft voice shoutin' frae ben the hoose, "Ye a' right, Isa?" "Ah'm champion, Bobby son," Ah shouts back. "Nae bother at a', a piece o' cake. An' when this is ower Ah'll get you for this, ya useless randy wee bastard that ye are!"' She waited until the laughter around her had subsided, wiping her own eyes with the hem of her overall. 'Honest tae Christ though, see if Ah'd got ma haunds oan him, he'd have been takin' his last breath as the bairn was takin' her first!'

'Know ma worst time?' Betty said. 'It was when Ah was expectin' ma second, 'cos Ah'd already had wan so Ah knew *exactly* whit tae expect the second time. Ah went aboot in a panic wi' ma legs crossed for aboot eleven months, by the time the bairn was born she was aboot ready tae go tae school!'

'So there ye have it, Marion hen,' Isa said, drawing on her cigarette, her nicotined fingers shining with oil. 'If ye thought the first time was bad, wait tae the second time! How's that for words o' encouragement?'

'Oh there won't be a second time!' Marion said firmly, and the listening women sank into another paroxysm of mirth.

'Dae ye no' think we a' said that?' Betty mocked her gently.

She left Singer's with Colin's pram full of money, thanks to the tradition that no one could pass a new baby without putting silver coins under his pillow. She had kept up the act and said all the right things, and in doing so had passed another initiation rite into the sisterhood, the universal club of women. But her words had been as duplicitous as her Da's Gaelic, and she was aware that her membership wasn't quite as valid as theirs. They, after all, had husbands, whereas she had no idea where her husband was. Neither, for that matter, had she any idea who he was. She was relieved that none of them had mentioned Jimmy, but she would be a great deal older before she understood that the women had been fully aware of the situation and had been sparing her the need to lie. Women instinctively supported each other in such times, knowing it could be their turn next.

She looked at her son still asleep in his pram and tried to see the resemblance to her father, but he looked to her like all babies, like himself. They were going down Kilbowie Road, and on the spur of the moment she turned the pram around and headed back up the hill past Singer's, towards the empty space where Second Avenue had been. Using the Singer's clock as a reference point she worked out as closely as she could where Number 70 had stood.

'This is where ye come frae,' she said quietly to the sleeping baby. 'This is the Holy City, Colin, where you an' me an' Davy belong.' Then she looked up and said aloud, 'This is my son, Colin Iain David.'

She sensed rather than pictured her family standing in a group behind the invisible wall. They were smiling at her, smiling at Colin. 'See, Da?' she said softly. 'Colin Iain, wan perfect laddie, an' Davy, a bit tae spare.' Then she turned down the hill and started the long walk back to North Elgin Street.

13

Colin Iain David Ryan was nearly a month old when his father returned to North Elgin Street. Jimmy was still wearing the working clothes he had on when he ran out of the hospital ward the night his son had been born. He looked as he always did at the end of these expeditions, tired and dirty, and he had lost more weight than on previous absences, but there was calmness about him. There always was. Each time he disappeared there had been a period of tension building up inside him that made him slightly uneasy, and jumpy, it was something Marion sensed rather than saw. Then he would walk out for however long it took and return, if not refreshed, then at least at peace, until the next time.

While he had been away there had been little money coming in, and if it hadn't been for Big Kenny's precious money there was no knowing how they would have survived. Davy had taken on a milk round with Scottish Dairies, rising at four in the morning and getting home again just in time to set off for school. He had wanted to do a paper round too, but Marion had stopped him; she recognised his guilt over his brother's behaviour and his need to do something for the family, but he also needed his energy for his school work. Marion had decided that he would not leave school at fourteen and go into the yards, he would stay on and get his Highers, his passport to a better future, that was what Big Kenny's money was for, the future. She hadn't discussed it with Jimmy, she had simply told him and he had nodded pleasantly but without interest or feeling. He wasn't antagonistic towards his family, he wasn't a drinker, a gambler or a

wife-beater. Some women had all of those problems to con-
tend with and had to put up with them because they were
economically dependent on their men and had no realistic
choice. But Jimmy wasn't like that, maybe that was why
she had never challenged him about his behaviour. He was
pleasant, but he just wasn't there. You had the feeling that
you were talking to him through a mist, that he was thinking
of something else. She knew her father would have been
incensed at any man treating his family as Jimmy did, but
somehow there was something sad about him. You felt that
it wasn't his fault, that whatever was driving him was beyond
his control, and so anger wasn't what she felt. But Davy did.

When Jimmy came back that night Davy rounded on him
with the pent-up rage, shame and guilt that had been building
since Jimmy returned from the War.

'Whit kind o' man are ye,' he demanded, 'leavin' your
wife an' bairn tae fend for themselves? Whit did ye think
they would dae for money?'

Jimmy looked at him silently, his face entirely blank, then
he looked away.

'Answer me, Mr Hero, Mr Commando! Is that how ye
dealt wi' the Germans, by runnin' away?'

'That's enough, Davy!' Marion said.

'Ye're a bloody disgrace!' Davy shouted, and, frustrated
by Jimmy's lack of response, he lunged at his brother and
punched him full in the face. In an instant Jimmy's hands
were round Davy's throat, squeezing so hard that his knuckles
were white and though Davy's face was twisting grotesquely,
there wasn't the slightest expression on Jimmy's. Marion tried
to prise his fingers off Davy's throat one at a time. When
she couldn't she panicked, pushed herself between them and
hit Jimmy's arms outwards as hard as she could. At first his
arms held, then abruptly he dropped his hands to his sides
again as Davy slid to the floor gasping for air. Still there was
no emotion in Jimmy's face, not even a look of mild anger.
There was blood running down from his nose where Davy's

single punch had connected, but he seemed unaware of that too. He stared at Davy, who lay on the floor, his chest heaving with his attempts to drag air into his lungs.

'Ah'm sorry, son,' he said helplessly, 'but ye shouldnae touch me like that ... If ye hadnae touched me ... Ah canny *help* it, see?' He turned away quickly, but Marion was quicker. She threw her arms around him and held him, with all her strength fighting off his attempts to run again, until they were both streaked with his blood. She stroked his hair, at the same time using the only words of comfort she knew.

'It's OK, Jimmy, jist take wan breath at a time, son, it'll be a' right.'

Slowly his head sank onto her breast, and she held him like a child till she felt him relax, then she helped him to bed and tucked him in. He slept all night, and next morning he left for work at the usual time without a word, as though nothing had happened.

And somewhere in her romantic heart Marion thought she had reached him, thought that because she had stopped him leaving that night, that she and Jimmy had become closer, that there would, after all, be a happy ending. Granny Mirren and Granda Archie had indeed a lot to answer for, just as Jean MacLeod had predicted.

For Davy though, sitting by the fire fingering the bruises left the night before by his brother's hands, the matter was more clear cut. Jimmy Ryan was, he decided, insane, and Marion should throw him out immediately in order to save all their lives.

'How dae Ah throw him oota his ain hoose, Davy?' she asked with a smile. 'It's his name oan the door an' oan the rent book, ye know.'

'He's gonny kill wan o' us,' Davy protested. 'Ah'm tellin' ye, Marion, he's mad!'

'But, Davy son,' she reasoned, 'dae ye no' think that somethin' musta happened tae him tae make him the wey he is?'

'Like whit?'

'Ah don't know, Davy, bit he wasnae always like that, was he? Ah mean, before the War, like?'

Davy thought for a moment. 'Ah don't know, Marion,' he said, 'Ah was that young when he went away, Ah don't know whit he was like. You were aulder than me, dae you remember whit Jimmy was like then?'

Marion shook her head. All she remembered was that he was the quiet one of her brother Colin's wee gang, the one who balanced Colin's extrovert streak. In fact the only clear memory she had was of the softness in his eyes when he looked at her sister Frances that time when he was on leave before going abroad. He had been wearing his uniform and green beret and she had never seen anyone so handsome or heroic; it was almost impossible to relate him to the man who had nearly strangled Davy.

'Sometimes,' Davy said quietly, testing the water, 'Ah think he canny be Jimmy. It's like Jimmy went away an' this other man came back in his place.' He searched Marion's face for understanding. 'Know whit Ah mean?'

'Aye,' Marion replied sadly, 'Ah know jist whit ye mean, Ah think the exact same thing masel'. Ah think back tae the days we were a' growin' up in Second Avenue, an' Ah see him an' Colin an' Gino runnin' aboot, an' it's almost like that Jimmy's died as well.'

Davy nodded. 'It's like wanno they science fiction stories, ye know the wans, where an impostor takes ower somebody's life.' They both laughed uncertainly. 'Ah saw Gino the other day,' he continued. 'He asked if Jimmy was a' right, because every time he sees him, Jimmy looks right through him like he doesnae know him. That's how Ah feel about Jimmy. Ah don't know *him*, at least no' this Jimmy.'

'Well, somethin' must've happened tae him while he was away, Davy, an' as far as Ah can see, a' we can dae is wait tae he gets better.'

'But a lotta men went away tae the War, Gino did, an' they arenae like Jimmy, are they? Some men were prisoners o' the Germans an' the Japanese for years an' were tortured, some were badly wounded, an' they're OK. Why should he be any different?'

'We don't know that, Davy, dae we?' Marion said. 'Ah don't tell people ootside whit Jimmy's like, dae you?'

He shook his head.

'Well mibbe other men are like Jimmy, an' their families don't talk aboot it either.'

'Aye, mibbe, Marion,' he said. He sounded as though his suspicions of alien takeover were more likely, but he didn't want to upset her by saying so, and Marion laughed.

'If a wee aerial comes oota his heid we'll think again, OK?' she said, making Davy laugh too. But their conversation had led to a sharing of concerns between them, an acknowledgement that all was worse than it had been, and now it was out in the open Marion was more confused than ever. So much for a trouble shared, she thought.

Confusion, that was the word that best described how she felt during those years. On the outside she seemed to be coping, to know what she was doing, and as far as Davy was concerned, Marion knew best, she would sort everything because she was in charge, as she always had been. But inside it was a different story. She had no idea what was going on most of the time when Jimmy's odd ways dictated their lives, she got by on a wing and a prayer.

Now here she was, lying in a hospital bed all these years later and supposedly wiser, but confused once again, wondering how to cope with yet another crisis. She had been going to the library on Tuesday as usual and it seemed that she had run across Dumbarton Road and passed out at Woolworth's corner. An ambulance had taken her first of all to the Western Infirmary, but there were no beds, so she had gone to the Royal, where two days later, she was more or less with it. Embarrassed of course, felt like a stupid old woman, hoped no one had seen her knickers at any stage of the proceedings, and if they had she at least wanted them to remember how clean they were. It seemed that she had been suffering from a chest infection, which explained the wheezing, and she felt even more of a stupid old woman for not realising she had been ill in the days before the great collapse.

It wasn't as if chest infections were unusual, she had had two or three in the last year alone, which she had put down to the damage done to her lungs while she was under the rubble during and after the Blitz. Plus, she was getting on. They had wanted to know if chest trouble ran in the family, and again like a stupid old woman she had come over all watery-eyed, because she had had no family after the Blitz, and eleven-year-olds take little notice of inherited ailments. Must have been the way she had been feeling, she decided, it wasn't like her to burst into tears, not when anyone was watching at any rate. After she and Davy had been left alone all those years ago it had been a matter of pride to at least appear in control; one moment of weakness and someone else would take over your life, and she wasn't ever going to have that. Wasn't going to have it now either. They had put her on a course of antibiotics and the chest infection was under control; she was feeling better and she wanted to go home as soon as possible. When the Big Chief and his lesser Indians reached her bed that was what she intended telling them; thanks, lads, but I'm fine now, I won't trespass on your hospitality any longer. There were essays for the Open University to do, and more importantly there was the return of the Piorun's *crew, and Marek Nowak might be there. She had to talk to him, if he was alive to talk to, because only he knew where Frances had gone that night.*

'Now, Mrs MacLeod is it?' Her casesheet was open and pieces of paper were handed round. 'How are you?'

She looked at the tall, middle-aged man and wondered how often he had used those words in his career; they'd probably carved a groove in his vocal cords. 'Fine, Doctor,' she said, 'ready to go home right now.'

Then a brief, intense conference. 'I think we'll keep you for a few more days,' he said, 'just to make sure.' He smiled reassuringly and turned to continue his stately progress with his hangers-on.

'No, I don't think so,' Marion replied firmly, 'I think I'll go home as soon as someone gets my clothes. Thanks anyway.'

The doctor stopped, a slight frown playing across his forehead, then he said a few words to the lad who had examined her when she had come in. 'Dr Hall will speak to you,' he said and, taking the rest of his team with him, the consultant swept on.

She liked Dr Hall. Andrew Hall his name was, Drew for short; she had asked him that first day, between wheezes. He was the houseman, you could tell that by the dark circles around his eyes alone, and the fact that every time anyone in the ward opened their eyes, he was still working. They'd had a few chats in the days since the great collapse, usually when he was taking yet more blood or listening to her chest. He had told her that his father was a GP in Govan and that if he survived this year and a half without going barking mad from lack of sleep, he would join him. Most housemen dreamed of becoming hospital consultants, GP posts were considered to be only for the thickest doctors, and even then the wealthier areas were preferred. She had admired him for choosing downtrodden, deprived Govan, the begetter of Clydebank; he'd get no medals working there. And he had a wicked sense of humour.

'Now look here, Marion MacLeod,' he said, sitting on her bed, 'Jesus, what I'd give for a fag!'

'Your lungs maybe?' she asked.

'Saucy cat! Now look here, Marion MacLeod, God up the ward there is none too pleased with patients who don't accept what he says. If God says you have to stay in, then you have to stay in; have you got that? Otherwise he'll have my balls.'

'I don't mind,' she smiled, 'they'd be no great loss to me!'

'You will be force-fed cold mince and tatties for that, mark my words! One day I plan to use those balls, I'll have you know! There are women out there gasping for the end of Drew's slavery, it's a toss-up whether I'll be a GP or a full-time stud!'

'Don't hold your breath,' Marion sneered, 'or anything else for that matter. Look, son, why does Eat-the-Breid want to keep me in?'

'Well, now, it could be for your charm, if you had any,' he said, 'but it's because we want to do a few tests.'

'What kind of tests?'

'We want to find out about these chest infections. Could be absolutely nothing but a thrawn nature and a bad attitude, at least that's what I'm betting, but then again, it could be something else.'

'Like?'

'Well, hell's teeth! That's what we want to find out!'

'Tell the truth, you wee weasel, or I'll have your balls now!'

'A mouth on her like a sewer! OK, brass tacks. We don't know. That's the bottom line. What we're looking out for is a focus for all these infections, something that keeps flaring up, and that something might be a tumour, or it might be nothing at all. Personally I think it's down to your septic personality, but who listens to me?'

'What kind of tests and how long will they take?'

'The usual stuff, x-rays, blowing into a tube to gauge your lung capacity — I'd give you the technical name but you're a daft wee woman and it would only confuse you. Depending on what we find we might have to go in and snip a bit off, but that's the extreme end.'

'What do you think?'

'Now you're confusing me with someone who knows his arse from his elbow! What do you think this is — cross my palm with silver and I'll give you a clean bill of health?'

'OK, Hippocrates, how long do I have to stay in?'

'Oh, classical wit now, is it? Say three or four days for the tests.'

'Well, that's all,' she said, 'I have an appointment with a man and I aim to keep it.'

'Do you charge much?'

'More than you could afford.' She laughed quietly. 'Now run along, your boss looks like he needs his elbow licked!'

'This is what we get for letting the working classes into our nice clean wards, filth!' He turned away from her bed then looked back. 'Don't worry too much,' he said. 'The worst scenario is also the least likely.'

'What do you know?' she replied. 'You're just a wee Govan nyaff!'

'Cow!' he hissed at her. 'It's the bluntest needle for you in the morning!' And he hurried up the ward to rejoin the round.

The breakthrough with Jimmy didn't come, not that she gave up on it for years. Human beings can adapt to almost anything, and the Ryans settled into a pattern of uneasy, bemused coexistence. They lived in the same house, shared the same table, but Marion, Davy and Colin related to each other, while Jimmy was a solitary presence who was somehow not there even when he was. His absences continued, sometimes at a time of stress but more often for no reason that Marion could work out. The only person who knew what triggered his walkabouts was Jimmy, though she doubted that; he didn't seem like a man in control, he seemed like a man in deep trouble who didn't understand it himself or know how to ask for help. He wasn't part of the family; there was a barrier that no one could get through, and the truth was that Davy had long since stopped trying. He put up with Jimmy out of respect for Marion and gave his brother a wide berth. Jimmy was like a living ghost who came and went, taking little interest in his son. Colin learned to walk and to talk with only occasional glances from his father, friendly glances to be sure, but unemotional and uninvolved. Marion worried constantly about the effect on Colin, who was effectively growing up without a father, though Davy, full of guilt and shame over his brother, tried to fill in. He was only a laddie himself though, and he had his studies; his studies were important to Marion. He had decided, he told her, blushing self-consciously, to become a teacher, only too aware, given his earlier experiences with the awful Miss Anderson, why Marion smiled wryly.

'It jist seems tae me,' he explained, 'that there are lotsa rotten teachers that ruin bairns, they treat them like muck, so the bairns think they *are* muck an' that learnin's no' for them, so they gie up. Know whit Ah mean?'

'Ah know whit ye mean, Davy,' she said quietly. 'Ah was jist thinkin' aboot ma mammy. She aye wanted me tae be a teacher, and noo there will be a teacher in the family. She stopped me throwin' you in the canal when ye were a right wee pest, mibbe she knew whit she was doin'.'

'It'll mean years at university,' Davy said, 'wi' me no' earnin' a penny. Ah don't know if we can afford it.'

'Don't you worry aboot that, son, we'll afford it,' she said. 'But wi' Jimmy . . .'

'We've managed wi' Jimmy, or withoot Jimmy, a' this time, we'll go on managin'. Leave the worryin' tae me, we'll manage, Davy.'

Big Kenny's money was lasting quite well in the Post Office, but to preserve it they would need a regular wage coming in, and Jimmy couldn't be counted on. Sometimes he would work for months, bringing his wages home and at least providing for them, but she never knew when he would simply disappear, and when he did, when he would reappear. Before Davy's ambitions became clear her only real concern had been Jimmy's wellbeing, and the fear that one day he might not return and she would never know what had become of him. She knew that they would survive without him, because they had learned to survive despite him, but the secret fear of spending years wondering what had become of him haunted her. It would be like Frances all over again, only worse. She knew that Frances was dead, she just didn't know how or where it had happened, but if Jimmy should walk out one day and never come back, how could she live with the thought of him lost and alone somewhere? She looked on him as a child, not as her husband; he was a lost and troubled child.

'Well, if it isn't Mrs Ryan!' Father Sheridan was picking up stray rose petals along the aisle in Our Holy Redeemer's.

'Aye it's me, son,' Marion replied. 'This you doin' your ain cleanin' noo?'

'We had a High Mass yesterday,' hé said. 'You won't know this, not being "one of my lot", but at the end

157

wee girls go down the aisle dropping rose petals from baskets.'

'Very nice too. Whit for?'

'To look very nice of course!' He mimicked the paternal tone that always made her smile. 'Is there anything I can help you with, my child?'

'Well, for a start, as Ah'm no' wanna your lot, Ah think ye can stop expectin' me tae call ye Father. OK?'

Father Sheridan nodded. 'I grant you special dispensation,' he grinned.

'So whit's it tae be then, Mr Sheridan or whit your mammy calls ye?'

'Gerard to my mother,' he said, lighting up a cigarette and easing himself onto the pew in front of her, his feet on the seat, 'Gerry to my friends.'

'Gerry it is,' she said. 'Ah'm no' auld enough tae be your mammy. In fact Ah'm no' auld enough tae be this wan's mammy.' She nodded towards Colin, fast asleep beside her, exhausted from his determination to walk.

'I take it he hasn't been baptised in the Holy Roman Church?' Gerry Sheridan asked, smiling.

'Or in the unholy Proddie wan,' Marion replied. 'Ye'd havetae prove tae me that there is a God, make him appear in front of me, an' then I'd blacken his eyes for the things he lets happen.'

Father Sheridan chuckled. 'In that case, Lord,' he said looking heavenwards, 'stay where you are! This woman means business, take it from me!' Then he looked back at Marion. '*Is* there anything I can do for you?'

'Well, instead of pickin' up your ain petals, ye could gie me the job. Ah'll clean the place better than any Catholic, because Ah won't aye be adorin' the statues!'

Father Sheridan thought for a moment. 'Do you mean it? Because we do need someone, old Mrs Flynn has gone off to discover if there is a God.'

*　　　*　　　*

158

Marion walked home carrying the still sleeping Colin, wondering if Gerry Sheridan was just being kind, or if he really did need a cleaner. Then she decided it didn't matter; looking at all that gold, marble and glitter, the church could well afford what it would pay her. And besides, it was all in a good cause, it was to help turn out another Catholic teacher, Davy Ryan. It was Marion who had kitted him out for his delayed First Holy Communion and had his photo taken. She had even managed to hide her smile at his pious expression, standing there, his hair Brylcreemed flat, his knees scrubbed clean beneath his shorts, and his hands clasped in front of him with a rosary carefully arranged to fall from his wrists. And it had been a repeat performance for his Confirmation when he was twelve; she had gone along to Our Holy Redeemer's to watch the Archbishop slap him across the face for no reason that seemed sensible, and give him another name. There had been much discussion about which saint's name he should choose to strengthen his resolve through life, to shore up what St David had presumably failed to do. They had settled on Michael, the name of the father Davy had never known, though it did cross Marion's mind that it had done Mr Ryan Senior little good. There he was, a skilled, well-to-do Irish American, sent over for a short time to help set up Singer's production line in the new Clydebank factory. He had every reason to expect to take his wife and two sons back to America with him when the job was done, where Jimmy and Davy would have lived comfortably in the American Dream. Instead TB had carried him off, leaving his wife and sons to a life of poverty, leading to where they now were. On the face of it Michael might not be a great investment in the future, but it was probably as good as any other saint's name. Looking round the people she knew, none of the saints whose names they answered to had exactly come up to expectations, and yet the rituals of the Catholic Church went on reinforcing the belief that only a saint's name would do. Well, it was none of her business she supposed, it didn't *have* to make sense to her, but it still surprised her that it made sense to anyone.

Changing Colin from one arm to the other she laughed. What would Granny Mirren and Granda Archie have thought? They had fled both the Catholic and Protestant religions, and their granddaughter had bolstered up the religious duties of her young stepbrother, and now she was cleaning a Catholic church. She knew that they would not have considered it fitting work for an 'inquiring mind', but there was no alternative until Colin went to school. One day though, she thought, one day it would be her turn and she would maybe get the chance to satisfy her 'inquiring mind'. But for now she had responsibilities to take care of.

14

That Marion's friendship with Sal didn't exactly become the focus of her life, was due mainly to Jean MacLeod's lingering influence. As far as Jean had been concerned, Sal was a brazen hussy, whereas to Granny Mirren she had been 'Mistress Gallagher', but then Granny Mirren, unlike Jean, had herself been a bit of a brazen hussy in her day. Perhaps her elopement with the Protestant Archie wasn't on the same scale of misdemeanours as Sal's assignations, but there was fellow feeling there just the same. Granny Mirren had, after all, broken the worst taboo that any Uist female could and had suffered her own losses as a consequence. And who knew what the young lass who became Granny Mirren felt about missing a traditional wedding? She had no doubt grown up on Uist expecting to go through the same stages and rituals as all the other girls had for generations. Just as Marion had listened at her knee to the tale of Mirren and Archie's elopement, Mirren herself had probably heard stories of courtship, shy glances and true love at her mother's knee. The lass who became Granny Mirren would have had no reason to suppose that when her time came her life wouldn't take a similar path, until she fell in love with a Protestant from the other part of the island. The alternatives were giving him up or running off with him to a place where it mattered less. So she had run off with Archie, but for all anyone knew she had sorely missed the wedding she had a right to. The only finery she had for her marriage was her mother's gold cross, that Marion had last seen snagging Frances's long hair as she set off for the dancing a few short years ago, but on the day

Mirren wore it she was already an outcast. Little wonder then that she alone didn't snub 'that Sal Devlin', because Granny Mirren knew better than anyone that people are bad judges of each other's morals or motives. Thinking about it made Marion ache all over again for the missing women in her life to discuss such things with, for the adult years she would never have with them.

With wartime rationing still restricting a wide range of things, the friendship of the two Second Avenue refugees in North Elgin Street consisted at first of whichever of them had to go into town getting one or two things for the other before the supply disappeared. Time gradually proved that this duty fell more often to Marion, though at first she put Sal's reluctance to going outside down to the fact that she had six very young children, and Marion knew how much time one could take to get ready for an outing. She finally understood the true situation one Monday morning, when Sal stood at her window and beckoned her in.

As ever, the thing that struck Marion about the Gallagher house was the almost desperate air of respectability, the determined feminine touches. There were lace doilies everywhere, exquisitely worked antimacassars on the arms and backs of the armchairs and the couch, brightly coloured plastic flowers precisely placed on most surfaces, and in the centre of the table, on a cloth delicately embroidered with crinoline ladies in a country garden, stood a crystal decanter filled with coloured water that was changed regularly. Marion had once asked Sal where she came by all the different colours she used in her decanter, and being an avid book-reader she was stumped at the reply. Sal apparently ripped book jackets from the main part of the book and soaked them till the dye coloured the water, and when she got fed up with one colour, another book bit the dust without actually being read.

But if Auntie Maggie cleaned and polished her house in an attempt to rid her life of her miserable beginnings, Marion wondered, then perhaps Sal might be filling her home with beauty to atone for what everyone else thought of as her past sins, apart from her sins against literature that is. 'I might have been "that Sal Devlin" once,' was the message, 'but now I am clean and sweet Mistress Gallagher.' And the children forever entwined around Sal's legs, in her arms or clinging to her neck, were as well dressed as any other child, and probably better cared for – a slut, but a good mother, and let no one say otherwise.

'Could ye get me some milk,' Sal asked that Monday, 'an' mibbe some sugar tae if there is any? Ah'm no' feelin' like masel' the day.'

But there was something in her voice that made Marion take more notice of her than usual. 'Whit is it, Sal?'

'Ach, nothing much.' Sal smiled too brightly, smoothing her hands across the antimacassar on the back of the couch, then looking away too soon.

'Sal, whit is it?'

There was a silence, then Sal turned full-face towards her, and Marion found herself totally speechless.

'Noo don't go jumpin' tae conclusions!' Sal said. 'Ah fell an' hit it oan the end o' the table.'

Until that moment Marion hadn't jumped to any conclusions, she had simply been stunned by the bruise all down one side of Sal's face, but she knew instantly, by Sal's preemptive denial, exactly how it had happened.

'When did he dae this?'

'Noo, ye're jumpin' tae conclusions, Marion hen!' Sal was smoothing with renewed vigour, smoothing away the truth.

'Sal, Ah asked ye when he did this?'

Sal looked at her with the sad, defeated eyes of a beaten animal. 'Setterday,' she whispered, 'Setterday night. It's always oan a Setterday night, when he's had a few, see?'

'Whit for?' Marion asked, halfway between fury and pity.

'Noo don't go blamin' big Tony!' Sal protested, one hand raised to fend off the expected verbal attack. 'It's me, Ah make him dae it somehow. Ah don't how, but it must be me, because he's no' like that except when Ah say somethin'. Ah'll need tae watch ma tongue, then it'll be OK.'

'How long has it been goin' oan?'

'Since he came back efter the War. He wasnae like that afore, well no' wi' me, wi' the odd foreigner mibbe when there was a poker handy, but no' wi' me!' She tried a smile that picked up some tears along the way and turned into an ugly grimace. She broke down in loud sobs, forcing her hand to her mouth in an attempt to stem the noise. 'When he came back he would blow up if anybody said anythin' tae him, at work an' that, ye know, said naebody wis gonny tell him whit tae dae any longer. But Ah was the wan nearest at hand, so Ah got it.'

'Have ye tried talkin' tae him aboot it, Sal?'

'Oh he's awfy sorry, Marion. Naw, Ah mean it, ye've never seen a man greetin' so sair, he canny believe he's done it an' he swears it won't happen again.'

'But it does, Sal, doesn't it? The War's been ower for years noo an' he's still hittin' ye!'

'But he'll stoap noo, you'll see, he won't dae it again, he's promised, Marion.'

Marion sat down on the couch and pulled Sal to sit beside her. 'Listen,' she said, holding Sal's hands between her own, 'why dae ye put up wi' it? Ah mean, why dae ye stay?'

'Noo, don't be daft, Marion hen. Ah've got six bairns an' nae money, where am Ah gonny go? An' Ah tellt ye, it's no' just his fault, it's mine tae, it's somethin' Ah dae, it must be. Ah try no' tae say anythin' when he's had a few, but somehow Ah always make him mad! An' Ah couldnae leave him, he's a' Ah've got, in't he?'

She looked at Marion through red-rimmed, tearful eyes, begging her to understand, and Marion nodded to save Sal any more pain. 'So if ye'll jist get the milk an' the sugar, Marion, Ah'd be gateful. The bruisin' disnae last long, but Ah don't want anybody else tae know. Ye know whit they'd

164

say, don't ye? "He's payin' her back for how she behaved during the War, an' she deserves every punch, every kick." Ah won't gie them that satisfaction.'

Marion winced at the picture Sal's words painted in her head. 'It's OK, Sal,' she said, 'Ah won't say anythin'.'

As she turned to go Sal followed her to the door. 'Ye see, no' everybody's as lucky as you, Marion,' she said sadly. 'Ah've never seen your Jimmy wi' a drink in him, he disnae gamble his pay oan the horses or the dugs, an' he disnae chase winmen. He's a nice quiet fella. You've got a man that's good tae ye.'

As Marion pushed the pram along the road towards the shops her eyes filled with tears, eventually forcing her to stop at a shop window and pretend to be looking at the display while she wiped her eyes and got control of herself again. 'Aye,' she thought bitterly, 'ma man's definitely a quiet fella, ma man's good tae me, so he is.' What right had she to ask why Sal put up with being beaten, why she hadn't walked out on Big Tony, when *she* was covering up a married life every bit as abusive and bizarre? Jimmy was so distant that he lived in another world, and even when he wasn't on one of his wanders the only way you knew he was in the house was if you heard that wee cough of his or if you had his overalls to scrub the asbestos dust off at the weekend. They slept in the same bed, but there might as well have been a brick wall running down the centre, because they never touched, not by accident and not by design. But it was a woman's duty to make sure her marriage and her family life ran smoothly, if it didn't then it must be *her* fault, so for all she knew the world might be full of guilty women keeping secrets. She thought again of Sal, pictured the ugly bruise down her face. Granny Mirren had been right: let she who is without secrets cast the first stone.

The early years of the seamless child, Colin Iain David Ryan, consisted of accompanying his mother on a variety of odd jobs, from cleaning Our Holy Redeemer's to cleaning in Janetta Street School, plus other places in between. He had a store of picture books and would occupy himself quietly and without complaint wherever the work took them, but in the back of Marion's mind she knew it wasn't right. Her son had a right to her entire attention and care, as she had had when she was growing up. Jean MacLeod was always at home looking after her house and family, and Marion had the security of taking for granted that, no matter what happened, her mother's comforting presence would always be there. Up till 1941 at any rate. Jean's stay-at-home housewife's role had been dictated partly by the times; she was a wife and mother before the War brought about great changes in women's attitudes and expectations. Women who'd had to work during those years had discovered a new freedom they were reluctant to give up afterwards, but that hadn't been a factor in the MacLeod household. Jean had been a product of the prewar society, and she was also able to remain at home because other members of the family played their parts. The MacLeods had been a traditional family, with Tommy bringing home his wages when there was work at Brown's, and when there wasn't, the grandparents helped out; that was the way of things. As the older children left school and started earning, Jean's role had become more entrenched and life in Second Avenue more comfortable. Marion, being the youngest, benefited from having her mother always at home without the strain of constant financial problems, because there were four wages coming in, even if two were apprentices' pennies. It was the only model Marion had for family life and one she naturally wanted to recreate, but the Ryan family didn't operate in that way, because it couldn't.

There was full employment in Clydebank after the War, in fact there was a shortage of labour, thanks to the glut of work in the yards. Order books were booming with replacements for merchant and Admiralty ships lost, and the reconversion of civilian ships that had seen wartime service. And in those days before long-haul air travel, passenger liners were still needed in large numbers. Clydebank had suffered greatly in the Blitz and the town had been changed for ever in ways only suspected at the time, but after the War the people had some compensation in being able to earn good money to help them rebuild their lives. But the Ryan family had taken a less conventional route, partly because of Marion's determination that Davy should get an education instead of entering the yards. Her ambitions would have put a heavier strain on the finances of any working-class family of the time, but the Ryans were not the traditional family either, because of Jimmy's disappearances. If Davy was to continue with his education, and Marion insisted that he would, then she had to work. This meant that her own son would not have the security of spending his early years at home with his mother, as she had. She remembered 'helping' with household chores, polishing the furniture with Jean every Friday, cleaning out the range, setting a fire, going shopping and the endless times hanging onto the handles of Jean's message bag on the way home as her mother conducted in-depth gossip sessions with neighbours they met in the shops, the streets or in the close at Number 70.

Everything was geared to Tommy coming home; his meal would be ready on time, the fire lit so that he could slump in his armchair beside it and survey and attack the world from behind his newspaper. But there had been something else she hadn't realised then. It hadn't been just a build-up of work before Tommy came in the door, but an increase in her mother's anticipation, a kind of happiness that she only now understood as love. Her mother looked forward to her father coming home because she wanted to see him again, because she loved him. The verbal sparring, and the physical kind as well that always ended up in laughter, that had all been part of a good loving relationship, and Marion and the rest of the family had grown up surrounded and protected by that. She didn't know where she had gone wrong, but somehow she had, because there was nothing like that in the Ryan household. Her own son had to follow her around her various jobs outside the home, so he couldn't, as she could at his age, have a nap or look at his picture books in the warmth of his own home if he felt like it. He would have no memory of the routines that led up to his father coming home from work, because there was never any certainty that his father would. For the same reason Colin would remember nothing of his mother's happiness as Jimmy walked in the door, covered in asbestos dust at the end of a hard day at the yard. And even if Jimmy had returned home every night as other fathers did, there was no *frisson* of excitement from either Marion or Jimmy, because there was no love. Marion felt protective towards Jimmy, felt whatever was wrong with him and so with their life together, that somehow she must be at least partly to blame. Davy felt resentment towards Jimmy, shame and guilt that his brother was not the man he wanted him to be, and Jimmy, well, no one knew what Jimmy felt about anything. That was the atmosphere her son was growing up in, and the guilt and regret seared her to the bone. She wondered what Colin would say to his own family when he grew up, what stories he would have to tell of his odd childhood, and she couldn't imagine anything less than censure from him as an adult. There were times when she felt sheer panic at the mess her life was in, and the mess she was sure she was making of her son's life, and yet she could see no alternative. She had a secret resolve inside her to somehow make things better for him in the future, but at the same time she couldn't see how she could achieve it, and all the time his childhood was slipping by.

By the time Colin was five years old and ready to start at Elgin Street School, Davy had passed his Highers in English, History, Geography and Maths – not bad for a laddie who 'couldn't take things in'. He applied for and got a place at

Glasgow University to study for a four-year Master of Arts degree, and he also qualified for a full grant. After that there would be a further year as a postgraduate student at Notre Dame College in Dowanhill, where Catholic teachers finished their training. There was much excitement and satisfaction, it felt to Marion as though life was going in the right direction, that however odd it was, and however tortuous the path, it was at least moving forward. But at the same time life immediately became more difficult on two fronts. Davy would still be living in North Elgin Street, but he would need all his time now for studying, so the money his odd jobs brought in would stop. And while he had been at school himself he had been around more than he would be now, to look after his nephew while Marion took on extra jobs. Now that temporary arrangement would end, and at the same time Colin's starting school meant that Marion could work longer, more settled and therefore better-paid hours. But without Davy's help, the two hours at the end of the day when Colin would be out of school and Marion would still be working, seemed like an insurmountable problem.

If she had learned anything from the Blitz it was that nothing in life could be taken for granted, including life itself. So she had taken a leaf from her father's book and looked outside Clydebank's traditional industries. The day had already come when no one wanted to buy bullets hand-polished by herself or Auntie Maggie from Singer's, and the day must surely come, she reasoned, when the world had all the sewing machines it could ever use. But until her time came to have the life she wanted, she would need to be sure of being in work for everyone's sake. So instead of going back to Singer's she had taken herself in hand and gone after a coveted job in Brown's, as one of the army of women polishers.

When a ship was finished and the black squad and the rest were done, everything had to be cleaned and polished. In the big liners there were dressing tables, wardrobes and chests of drawers in the cabins, and tables and chairs everywhere that had to be perfect before the ship was handed over and paying passengers stepped aboard. The furniture was made and installed by the yard carpenters, but as the various parts of the ship came together, and numerous feet tramped through it, inevitably some damage was done, and rather than replace a piece of furniture, repairs were carried out. So while some of the women cleaned and polished, a small number became skilled French polishers, and that was Marion's aim. It might not be how she intended spending the rest of her life, but it was a skill she could use outside the yards and Singer's, it was an insurance policy, a means of bringing in money to minimise the drip-drip erosion of what was left of Big Kenny's money in the Post Office.

The women were taken on as a ship neared completion and laid off until the next time, but in the days when the big liners were still being ordered they were assured of work in various yards. These jobs were highly sought after and went usually to women who had husbands working in the yards, which qualified Marion, as Jimmy was a 'white mouse' and, in name at least, he was her husband. But her connections were stronger than that, because she was old Archie's great-granddaughter, Tommy MacLeod's daughter, and the sister of Iain as well as Colin, and Iain had been an apprentice carpenter in Brown's. Even years after they were all dead, they still had influence, because in Clydebank such things still mattered.

The only problem was what to do with her own Colin during those two hours after school. He was too young to be given a key and told to amuse himself till Marion came home. Anything could have happened to him, and apart from that the thought of him coming home to an empty, cold house every day was too much for her to bear; the boy was deprived enough of normal family comforts. And because of the situation in the Gallagher household there was no way she could ask Sal to keep an eye on him, though she knew

Sal would in a minute. The only solution, she decided, was Auntie Maggie.

Auld Maggie was now retired and living on her pension, plus whatever she had secreted away during her working life; certainly she had never been one to splash out on comforts or treats, for herself or anyone else. Marion examined every possibility and then re-examined each one over again before she settled on asking Maggie for help. The very thought went so much against the grain that she started out on the road to Campbell Street three times then turned back again before going through with it at the fourth attempt out of absolute necessity.

If Maggie was pleased to see her only niece on her doorstep she didn't show it, making Marion think again about the horrors she might be consigning her son to. A cold unwelcoming house almost seemed a more cheering prospect for a wee lad than entering Maggie's lair, even braving big Tony Gallagher in fighting mood might not be so bad after all. Auld Maggie had changed little from the thin-lipped, unsmiling woman Marion remembered from those duty visits of her childhood. In the years between there had been odd moments of thawed feelings, but any visible emotions were quickly refrozen in case a vestige of affection took hold. And if age was supposed to mellow, then it had given up on Maggie. The wraparound pinny, the same one, Marion could have sworn, still swathed the thin body, and Maggie's skin didn't seemed so much wrinkled as worn thin; maybe she scrubbed and cleaned her face with Brasso too. And her hair remained in its scraped-back non-style, only there seemed less of it and it was white these days. Inside the Campbell Street house was just as she had left it to marry Jimmy – God, but that seemed a hundred years ago, not six – if a speck of dust had landed in the interim it had, as always, been given short shrift. Maggie invited her in and instinctively she sat up straight in a dining chair. They tried small talk but it quickly dried up, so Marion took a deep breath and explained her predicament. Maggie sat clasping her hands in front of her apron.

'Folk that canny look after bairns right shouldnae have them,' she stated.

'Folk don't always have problems *when* they first have the bairns,' Marion returned, 'but you wouldnae know anythin' aboot that, Auntie Maggie, never havin' had a bairn.'

Maggie ignored the taunt. 'Oor Jean had four o' ye,' she said, 'an' she managed tae look after ye a' fine withoot goin' oot tae work.'

'Christ, whit have we got noo,' Marion said, 'the Jean MacLeod Admiration Society? It's a pity ye never appreciated her while she was alive, no' think so?'

'That's as may be,' Auld Maggie replied quietly, much to Marion's surprise, 'but Ah don't believe in mothers workin' when they have young wans.'

'Mibbe it's ma young wan Ah'm workin' for, Auntie Maggie,' Marion said. 'Mibbe it's tae gie him a better life than Ah had.'

The old woman sat stony-faced, offering no assistance, making Marion ask again, making her beg. 'You auld bitch!' Marion thought, struggling to keep the conversation as civil as she could.

'Whit Ah wanted tae ask, Auntie Maggie, is if Colin can come here tae Ah finish work.'

There was no reply. Marion watched as the thin lips grew thinner, and wondered if her mouth might one day seal up under the pressure. 'It would only be for a coupla hours, Ah'd pick him up as soon as Ah finished work.'

'Ah'm too auld tae put up wi' bairns runnin' aboot ma hoose,' Maggie finally said.

Ye were born too auld, Marion thought sourly. 'Ah'm no' askin' ye tae have bairns runnin' aboot, Ah'm askin' ye tae have wan wee boy sittin' here for a coupla hours, readin' his books or listenin' tae the wireless. He's no Attila the Hun, ye know!'

Auld Maggie sat in silence for what seemed ages, then she

said, 'Aye, a' right, well. We'll see how it goes. But Ah want nae trouble frae him, nae nonsense!'

'Ye won't get any.'

'An' the only reason Ah'm daein' this is because Ah know the trouble you're havin' wi' that good-for-nothin'!'

'Auntie Maggie, Ah don't know whit ye mean,' Marion said, 'an' Ah don't want ye sayin' things like that in front o' the bairn. Look, Ah think we'll jist forget it. Don't bother!' She got up to go, but Maggie pointed to the empty chair and Marion found herself sitting down again.

'Naw, naw,' she said calmly, 'the bairn can come here. He's family after a', he's oor Jean's grandson an' she'd have done the same for him. Ah know ye've always thought Ah had a useless kinda life, Marion MacLeod, but you think on. Your life is nae bed o' roses either, you've nothin' tae be superior aboot, an' jist you remember that!'

Stamping back down the road blinded by tears of rage and humiliation, Marion composed several replies she should have given, the kind of put-downs that never come quickly enough to the mind or the tongue till it's too late. Then a thought struck her. 'The auld bitch!' she thought bitterly. 'She was gonny dae it a' along, but she hadtae put me through it! She couldnae dae somethin' oota common decency an' keep her mouth shut, she hadtae stick the knife in. Well she might *think* she knows, but she never will for sure, Ah'll see tae that!' She stopped pounding the pavement in rage and she thought of the old woman, as alone in the world on her terms as Marion had become in hers, and she couldn't help feeling a grudging admiration for Auntie Maggie. 'The auld bitch!' she said again, shaking her head and laughing as she said it. Then silently she added, 'Good for her!'

Anyhow, it was settled. Someone else would have to clean Our Holy Redeemer's; Marion was going into Brown's to learn the art of French polishing. She would have a full-time job instead of all the part-time bits and pieces the family had survived on up till now. It was time to move on.

15

Going into Brown's she shivered with the feeling of having been there before because of all the stories she had heard all her life. Just as Singer's had revealed fascinating glimpses of Frances's character she had never suspected, being in Brown's was like seeing another side of Granda Archie, her father and her brothers, it was like *déjà vu* by proxy. The first thing that hit her was the noise, a cacophony of unbearable sounds mixed together that hurt her still sensitive ears. The noise reverberated around her head and she had to lean against the wall of the Polishing Shop to steady herself. Then she gritted her teeth and straightened up. What was the alternative – abandon all her plans and dreams for her family because she didn't like the noise? Sometimes there was nothing to do but get on with it, a lesson she had already had to learn.

In the 1950s the number of riveters had dropped dramatically as welders took over, but you could still hear the rhythmic sound of hammer hitting metal coming to you from all over the yard. The men they called 'the Dummies' were still there, most of them time-served joiners, and she understood for the first time that their lack of hearing was no handicap in the yards, because the background noise deafened everyone else just as effectively. The jokes her father described the men playing on 'the Dummies' simply played on an area of weakness or difference, just as they did with everyone else. Everyone carried a scar or a difficulty of some kind, whether visible or not, and it was the way of the men to make fun of them, perhaps because laughter made their lot easier to bear. But she worked alongside one of the men, John Oliver, a skilled French polisher who passed on what he knew with real generosity, and through him she got to know the other 'Dummies'. At first she had been nervous of them, a little embarrassed at not being able to communicate with them, until she noticed that even the hearing often used sign language and mimes because of the noise around them. So she tried to learn sign language and found them to be gentle, friendly, inoffensive men, so she couldn't help feeling her mother's outrage too. Though most had been born deaf, a few of the men had lost their hearing, but whatever the individual reasons, their deafness was not their fault. She thought of her own son who had nearly died as he was being born, and of how she would have felt if he had been deaf and been taunted for it. And she never called them 'the Dummies' again. They all had names, they were all human beings, and each one was some mother's son.

The first ship she worked on was the Royal Yacht *Britannia*, due to be finished and launched to commemorate the coronation in June 1953. Going aboard was like entering another world of wealth and opulence that Marion had never dreamed of. She remembered her father recounting tales of the ships he had worked on, of the luxury he spent his days creating while working in conditions not fit for a dog, then returning to his home, where the accent all his life had been on getting by, on surviving until next payday. Before the War there had been no certainty that payday would come around again either, because the men had been employed on a casual basis up till then. Little wonder that they found ways to supplement their earnings, and why even in the fifties you could tell which ship a man worked on by his DIY efforts around the house. Many a home, it was said, boasted a kitchen similar to the great *Queens*, with the same surfaces and fittings, and the yard electricians even had the bulbs welded into their test lights, or many a house would have been lit courtesy of the yards as well. Anything that could be moved past the guards at the gates *was* moved, with an air less of stealing it than of getting one over on those who had used and abused families for generations.

In the Engineering Shop there was a retail outlet that had nothing to do with management, a kind of corner shop on the premises where the workers could buy whatever they needed on tick, paying for it on Friday, payday. And as they streamed out of the gates on Friday the illegal bookies' runners would be waiting to relieve them of the money they had lost on tick during the week too. Everyone in Clydebank knew to avoid the area around Brown's at ten-past-five every night, the time when the yard hooter went and the men burst forth. Any innocent passerby caught up in that huge mass of humanity desperate to get away from work would be carried along with them in whatever direction they took; it was like being swept away by a huge tidal wave. The first port of call was Connolly's Bar across the road from the yard, where the halfs of whisky were poured out and stood four deep on the bar, along with pint chasers. The men rushed in, threw their drinks down their throats and as they dashed out again to catch a tram home, they handed the money to the man who stood at the door taking up the collection. The refreshed workers would then board the trams waiting to take them home, the service No. 9s and the peak-hour specials put on for the yards. The trams would take off, shimmying from side to side on the rails as they rattled along, bursting at the seams with humanity at its grimiest. Ordinary mortals waiting along the tram route would let the vehicles pass rather than get on, because standing nose-to-nose with a filthy, sweating member of the black squad brought no joy, it was better to be late.

Connolly's was more than a pub to the men of Brown's, Connolly's was a talking as well as a drinking shop. It was where the men settled differences, where information about work in other yards was passed on, where pay lines were split between squads, explanations given and plots hatched. Many of the 'bastards in bowlers', the foremen who allocated work within the yards, expected drinks to be left for them at the bar by the men. Those who did not comply would find themselves assigned to the dirtiest, hardest and lowest-paid work, and if it came to payoffs, they would be first out the door and last to be taken on again. And even though they were employed by the yards rather than taken on as casual labour, once a ship was finished, they would be on the dole again if they couldn't find work at one of the other yards.

The riveters like Tommy MacLeod were still considered the hard men of the yards, but as Marion saw, they had to be. Even in the fifties they still worked in all weathers and often outside, on the deck or on the shell of a ship under construction. In winter they would be holding pneumatic hammers so cold that their hands stuck to the metal and frostbitten fingers were common. They worked with sweat dripping off them from the heat of the rivets and the furnace heating them, while inwardly they froze because of the weather. Often they could be seen balancing on two wooden planks a hundred feet above the ground, the planks bouncing beneath their feet as they worked, and nothing to steady them or break their fall if they lost their footing. Accidents happened all the time, and it was said that there was a death for every ship built. Whenever someone was killed the work-force would take the rest of the day off and within the yard they would take up a collection for the family of the man concerned. But there would be no compensation from the management, and nothing was allowed to stand in the way of shipbuilding, least of all respect from the bosses. She thought back to her father, saw him in her secret store of mental snapshots coming home from work every night, watched as she threw herself into his arms as he turned into Second Avenue. There was always a smile, always a joke, and she wondered how a proud man like Tommy MacLeod had forced himself to put up with worse treatment all his working days than she was seeing in the fifties, because, as everyone told her, there *had* been improvements. He had borne it because he had a family and because there was no alternative, and somehow he had managed to keep his spirit intact, and there was no way she could let him know now how much she admired him. How do you throw yourself into the arms of a memory and hug him till it hurts?

At 7.25 every morning the first hooter sounded at Brown's followed at 7.30, the official starting time, by the second, and the closing of the main gates. At the timekeeper's wooden hut each man was given a small, round, brass disc with his works number stamped on it. But the hut was a good ten minutes' walk from the main gates, and the only way the entire work-force could get through on time was if those who arrived early also passed through early – for no extra pay. A man's working time, and so his pay, began as he picked up his metal check, not as he entered the gates, so if you missed the 7:30 A.M. starting time because of the inevitable queues at the hut, you were deemed to be late and were therefore 'quartered'. This meant that men who had been on company soil for ten minutes had fifteen minutes deducted from every-thing they earned, basic pay, piecework and overtime. So in the perpetual battle between the management and the workforce, a new strategy was worked out. The men who arrived early refused to collect their metal checks until 7.30 on the dot, and the queues that built up were so huge that a great deal of time, and therefore money, was lost processing the workers. This brought the practice of 'quartering' to an end, not because of its basic unfairness, but because the way the men hit back cost the company money. It was a victory though, one of the few the workforce managed to force out of the management.

When work finished for the day the men were held wher-ever they were, even on board half-built ships, until the hooter sounded. Then they would scramble in their thousands down the gangplanks to get home, with accidents avoided only by luck. As they pushed and edged forward the gates would remain firmly closed until the last possible second. You could see them as you passed, crowded behind the gates like cattle, then bursting forth to freedom when the hooter sounded. Yet to hear the grand speeches on launch day, you would think the bosses held the men in the highest esteem; they were the skilled tradesmen who had built the most famous ships sailing the seven seas, as well as the reputations of the yards. It was the law of the yards; words were cheap, but men's sweat, men's lives, were cheaper.

The arrangement with Auntie Maggie seemed to be working well, though Colin had been well warned to behave. He looked at his mother with wide, clear blue eyes and nodded solemnly, the lock of dark hair that always fell across his brow bouncing in time with the movements of his head. He had Tommy MacLeod's eyes, no doubt about that; her old workmates in Singer's hadn't been imagining the resemblance to please her after all, or if they had, she was happy that it had come true. And it made her smile to think what Granda Archie would have made of his granddaughter with the inquiring mind producing another *ille dubh*, another black-haired laddie, and not a South Uist man near her.

'Noo, Auntie Maggie's auld, Colin,' she told her son nervously, wrapping his scarf across his chest and under his arms and then buttoning up his coat on top, 'an' auld folk don't like a lotta noise. So ye'll be quiet, won't ye?'

Colin nodded.

'Ye've got your books an' pencils for colourin'-in, an' before ye know it, Ah'll be there tae take ye hame. OK?'

Again Colin nodded.

But all through that first day her thoughts were on him, watching the minutes crawl past, wondering how he was behaving, wondering how Auld Maggie was behaving, and she had to stop herself running along the road at 5 o'clock to collect him. Standing outside the Campbell Street door she composed herself before knocking, and when Maggie opened the door Marion was determinedly calm and casual. Colin looked up from where he was drawing at the table as she came in, smiled, closed his book and got down from the chair. He put his arms out for a hug then ran to put his coat on. Marion prayed silently that he would remember the little speech they had rehearsed. 'Thank you for letting me stay, Auntie Maggie,' he said formally, 'Ah hope Ah wasn't any bother,' then he looked up for reassurance and smiled when he got a quick nod from his mother. Auld Maggie looked at her too and shook her head with a wry grimace. 'Ye're your Da's daughter right enough, Marion MacLeod,' she said. 'He never missed a trick either!'

At the end of the first week there had been no adverse reports from either Maggie or Colin about the arrangement, and Marion could stand it no longer. 'Has he been OK, Auntie Maggie?' she asked as easily as she could.

'Ah would've been the first tae tell ye if he hadnae,' said Maggie, closing the door behind Marion and Colin. 'Good night tae ye.'

'A vote of confidence if Ah'm no' mistaken,' Marion thought, 'or as near as that auld besom will ever get tae wan!'

Walking along the road hand-in-hand with Colin at the end of the next equally eventless week she asked brightly, 'Whit do you an' Auntie Maggie dae, Colin?'

'We draw pictures,' he replied. 'She gives me biscuits an' milk an' sometimes we sing songs.'

Marion nearly tripped over her own feet. Maggie giving him treats was a big enough shock, but Maggie *drawing*? Maggie *singing*?

'An' she tells me stories aboot Granny Jean an' Granda Tommy. She says Ah would've liked them, an' they'd have liked me.'

She felt the tears prickling behind her eyes.

'Would they have liked me, Mammy?'

'Aye, Colin,' was all she could reply, 'they would've loved ye, son.'

It was so peculiar. Just as you thought you were getting on with life not too badly, something happened or someone said something that brought you face-to-face with the rawness of it all over again. And you realised that the sense of loss never really became easier to deal with. The wound didn't heal, it stayed there under the thin skin that you managed to cover it with, so fragile that the slightest touch, the gentlest word, could effortlessly break through it and leave you hurting again. Even an innocent question from your own child could have you feeling like a sad, lonely and helpless eleven-year-old again.

But the arrangement seemed to be working out with no problems on either side – thus far at any rate. It must be better for Colin, Marion reasoned, to have one safe place to go after school, rather than be trailed around the variety of jobs she'd had to take on before. And it must be good for him to have a wider family, even if that was only Auld Maggie. The War had permanently deprived him of grandparents, aunts, uncles and cousins, though he was certainly not the only child in Clydebank in that position. Not content with that, fate had even conspired to make him an only child, and getting to know Auld Maggie might help him feel less isolated, if indeed he felt isolated. Even so, in her quietest moments she wondered if she were rationalising it, making excuses for herself to latch onto, and she wondered too how her son would remember all of this.

One of the things she loved about being out at work again was being in the company of other women. There was Sal of course, but for once in her life she had found herself reacting to Sal in a way that puzzled her. She was well aware that Tony Gallagher's promises not to lift his hand to his wife again had been broken, either because Sal no longer felt the necessity to hide the bruises from Marion, or because the beatings were increasing; on that Marion had been unable to make up her mind. She knew that Sal needed her help, she knew that she should give it, but somehow she had pulled back. She wasn't proud of it and she didn't entirely understand it, but at the same time she couldn't help it either. It was as if some instinct was telling her that she had enough difficulties of her own and that she had too little time and energy to spare in fighting for Sal, who showed no signs of fighting for herself. Every beating was accompanied by her stout defence of her husband and her total acceptance that his solemn promises had been given and would not be broken this time. It was less a solution than an upholding of the status quo, as though Sal was thinking, 'This is what I've got. It may not be worth a lot, but it's better than nothing.' Certainly however irate the situation made Marion, it seemed to bother Sal considerably less. And besides, she was aware too that her knowledge of normal married life was woefully inadequate and she was terrified of exposing her lack of knowledge lest people might discover the odd life she too had settled for. Maybe some marriages survived beatings, for all Marion knew some marriages positively thrived on violence. Whatever the reason, she had gone with her instincts and put some distance between herself and Sal, and if that was the wrong thing to do, well, she would have to live with that decision.

One of the women in the Polishing Shop was Agnes Boyle, wife of Danny the Pape, 'Left of foot, left of hand and left of nature,' as Tommy MacLeod liked to describe him. Agnes was small and plump, with a hairstyle exactly like Auld Maggie's, but her pleasant face made it look homely on her. She was quietly spoken and always had a smile in her dark eyes, but Agnes Boyle had had her tragedies too. She lost her only brother, Robert Sweeney, in the sinking of HMS *Hood* by the *Bismarck*, and three of her four children had been killed during or after the Blitz in 1941.

They were repairing a scratch on a dressing table on the *Britannia*, Agnes instructing Marion. It had been a deep scratch, so Agnes had sandpapered the area down to the wood, then built up the gouge with beeswax. Now she was applying different waxes, polishing between each layer, to slowly bring the entire surface back to its original level and colour. It was a fascinating process to watch and reminded Marion of the 'before and after' adverts she had seen for invisible mending. You would see a piece of torn material in one picture and beside it another showing the material now supposedly perfectly mended after the 'miracle' potion had been applied. She never believed the adverts, of course, but when Agnes had finished polishing there would be no sign of damage either; it really was like invisible mending.

'Ye'll no' mind o' it, hen,' Agnes said as they worked, 'but Ah went tae see ye when ye were in the Western.'

'Did ye, Agnes?' Marion said. 'God, Ah canny remember that at a'! That was good o' ye though, Agnes.'

'Ah was there every day seein' ma ain bairns,' she said, looking away. Marion knew what that meant; if you were to keep from breaking down even all these years later, the last thing you needed was that look of pity in someone's eyes, or that note of sympathy in their voice, however genuine, in fact *especially* if it was genuine. 'When Ah heard you an' the wee Ryan boy were still alive Ah jist looked in oan ye. Ah didnae expect tae see either o' ye again after that though, the two o' ye were in a bad, bad way!'

'Aye, well, he's no' the wee Ryan boy any longer, Agnes,' Marion smiled, 'he's at the university noo.'

'Away! Is he?'

'Aye, he's gonny be a teacher.' No one would ever know the effort it took to keep her pride in Davy just the right side of smug.

'My but that's good tae hear, hen! Ye've done well by him, your Mammy would be that proud o' ye.'

Now it was Marion's turn to look away.

184

'Ye know we only have the wan noo,' Agnes continued, 'oor Robert. He's ages wi' yersel', Marion, but mibbe ye won't mind him. You went tae Radnor Park School, didn't ye? Oor bairns a' went tae the Catholic school, St Stephen's. He's workin' as an electrician.'

'Here?'

'Aye, here. He did his National Service then came back. Know how they can get it deferred if they're daein' an apprenticeship? Your Davy will likely be the same.'

'Naw, Davy would've had his deferred, but he never passed the medical, no' after the injuries he got in the bombing.'

'Oor Robert passed the medical. He was lucky, mind. He just missed that Korean War. Christ, ye'd think we'd had enough o' war, wouldn't ye? Ye'd think mibbe Clydebank had already done its bit. Robert's injuries were a' deep cuts in the Blitz. Lots o' stitches an' scars, that kinda thing. Got him a helluva time in the army, though. He was in the Royal Signals, an' because he was Scottish wi' scars oan his face the English decided he must be a Glesca hard man, wanna they Teddy Boys wi' chibs. He got challenged by every wee nyaff in the outfit! The scars show up awfy bad in the cauld weather, turn bright red, so they dae. He lets oan he isnae bothered, but he is, of coorse.'

'An' is he quite settled noo?'

'Settled? Oor Robert? My God, hen, he's no' any such thing! The arguments between him an' his faither jist aboot drive ye up the wa', so they dae! The big fella got him his apprenticeship an' as far as he's concerned Robert should be grateful that he's set up in a good trade ootside the black squad him an' your Da were in. Your Da did the same wi' your Colin and Iain tae. Robert, though, he's full o' rebellion, keeps sayin' his faither's yard fodder, that he's let the bosses make a mug o' him a' his life an' they're no' gonny make a mug o' Robert. Ye should hear it in oor hoose some nights, bloody pandemonium, so it is!'

'An' how is, um, Mr Boyle?' Marion asked. She had been about to say 'Pape', but her courage failed her.

'Pape? Och, he's fine,' said Agnes. 'Take merr than a wee war tae finish him aff! Still misses your Da, though. He's had three other right-handers since but naebody ever measures uptae Tam the Teuchtar as far as he's concerned.'

'Tell me somethin', Agnes,' Marion asked, 'have ye ever heard o' the golden rivet?'

'The golden rivet, hen? Aye, of coorse Ah have! Dae ye mean tae tell me that the daughter o' Tam the Teuchtar disnae know aboot the golden rivet?'

'He would never tell me,' Marion laughed. 'He said if him and Mr Boyle ever found it they'd show it tae me first, but it was a secret.'

Agnes chuckled. 'Whit a right wee bugger that man was!' she said. 'Listen, hen, he was havin' ye on, *everybody* knows aboot the golden rivet! A' riveters believe that wan day they'll find a rivet made oota pure, solid gold in amongst the usual wans. An' when they find it, it'll set them up for life. It's an auld, auld story. An' that wee bugger tellt ye it was a secret, did he?'

In the years since the Blitz Marion had met many people who had known her father, and she had become convinced that if he'd had a grave of his own, if he hadn't been buried in a mass plot, the inscription on his headstone should read: 'Here lies Tommy MacLeod. He was a right wee bugger. Sadly missed.' But 'Tam the Teuchtar'?

'Is that whit they called ma Da?' she asked. 'Tam the Teuchtar?'

'They still dae call him that, hen! Ah swear tae God the wee bugger haunts this place, there's no' a day goes by that somebody disnae tell a story aboot him!'

'But why Tam the Teuchtar, Agnes?'

'Because he was that good wi' the Gaelic, wisn't he, hen? Spoke it a' the time.'

Marion started laughing and had to hold on to Agnes's

arm to steady herself. Maybe a PS could be put on that imaginary headstone, 'He also spoke Gaelic, by the way.'

'Agnes,' she gasped, mopping at her eyes, 'Ah'll tell ye a secret aboot ma Da, but promise ye'll no' say tae anybody else?'

Agnes nodded seriously.

'Ma Da, Agnes,' she said, then burst out laughing again, 'ma Da only knew Gaelic cursewords, Agnes, it was the only Gaelic he had! He could say anythin' as long as it was an insult!'

'Away tae hell!' Agnes laughed. 'Is that true, hen?'

'Aye it's true! It was his Granda Archie and Granny Mirren that were teuchtars, ma Da never went further than Glesca Cross a' his days!'

'Folk were always askin' him tae say somethin' in the Gaelic. Dae ye mean he was calling them a' sorts o' –?'

Marion nodded, then the two of them stood laughing and holding each other. 'Whit a wee bugger he was right enough, Marion hen! Wan o' these days ye can tell me whit his Gaelic words meant, there's a few bastards in bowlers Ah'd like to tell!'

16

She didn't have to wait long to meet Robert Boyle, known to one and all, except his parents, as Rab the Rhymer, because he always had a story. She was in the Polishing Shop trying to keep warm, with the air outside so cold that a white plume of steam came from her mouth with every breath, and her hands were too numb to feel what she was doing.

'You Marion MacLeod?' a voice asked behind her, and she looked up to see a blue-eyed, brown-haired young man standing just inside the door. He had Agnes's colouring. He wasn't tall, about 5' 9", but it was still three inches or so taller than herself. He was thin with lanky arms and legs, so that he gave the impression of being a taller man. The first thing she noticed was his eyes, which were a pale but vivid blue, but more than the colour it was the expression, mocking but gentle somehow, that drew her attention. Then she saw the scars on his face. One ran from under his right eye, through his top lip and under his chin; another fell diagonally across his nose, and yet another came from under his chin and up the right side of his face to just beyond his ear. She guessed who he must be, because, as his mother had said, the scars stood out bright red in the cold air.

'Aye,' Marion smiled. 'You must be Robert Boyle?'

'How did ye know?' he asked, grinning. 'Was it the nice designs oan ma physog tipped ye aff?' As Agnes had remarked, he only pretended that the scars didn't bother him, but they did. That was where the mocking look in his eyes came from, a gentle man forced to deflect hurtful comments by being funny.

Marion didn't hesitate. 'Aye, ye canny miss them, can ye?' she said casually. 'But it could be worse, son, ye might no' be here at a'.'

She was banking on him accepting her honesty. Before her hair had regrown to cover her own scars she had had to put up with a variety of reactions to her appearance, and she was sure that he too must have had enough of well-meaning denials. He chuckled softly.

'Thought ye might like tae have this,' he said. 'Ah found it in the Carpentry Shop a while back, been meanin' tae gie it tae ye.' He held out a dark blue hard-backed school exercise book, and watched as she took it, lighting a cigarette and making a great show of not watching. Marion sat down, wiping her hands on her overall. Making a loose fist of her hands she blew between the thumb and first finger of each then tried to rub some feeling into her numb fingers. Then carefully she opened the book. The image hit her like a sudden blow to the stomach, knocking the air out of her. It was a drawing of her Da, caught as he worked on a rivet, and it was as if someone had shouted 'Hey, Tam!', because his face was turned and smiling towards whoever had drawn the picture. It captured her Da so perfectly that a camera couldn't have done better, and she sat staring at it for a long time, tears welling up in her eyes. She wiped the tears away with the back of her hand and turned the page. Now it was her Da with Pape Boyle, both of them resting on their hammers, posing like grinning circus strongmen. On the next page was her brother Colin with that faraway look in his eyes, that promise of the adventures he knew he would have one day.

Robert Boyle had said nothing and neither had Marion, and he must have become sensitive to her silence. 'Look,' he said shyly, 'the book's yours, Ah jist thought ye might like it. Take it hame wi' ye and look at it in peace.'

'Wait a minute, Robert,' she said as he turned to leave. 'Who drew these?'

'Who drew them? Dae ye no' know? Honest?'

She shook her head and turned more pages, to reveal her mother and Frances, their arms around each other's waists, and herself about seven years old sitting on Granny Mirren's knee, with Granda Archie in his armchair across the fire from them, puffing on his pipe.

'It wis Iain, of coorse!' Robert smiled.

'Iain?'

'Aye, Iain. Your brother, Iain MacLeod. Who else would it be?'

'Iain could *draw*?' she asked in a kind of wonder. 'Oor Iain, Robert? Are ye sure?'

'Of coorse Ah'm sure! Dae ye mean ye didnae know Iain could draw?'

Marion shook her head again. Not only didn't she know, but she was sure no one in her family had ever suspected it, no one that was, apart from her Da, and he had never mentioned it. The drawings in the yard had presumably been done at the time, but the ones of the rest of the family must have been from memory, because Iain had never sketched at home. That was something she would have remembered, something the family would have talked about, because these drawings weren't only good, they were brilliant.

'Ah canny believe it. Ah never knew him tae dae anythin' but get Colin oota trouble.' She tried a smile but tears were coursing down her cheeks.

'Take it hame wi' ye, Marion,' Robert said, stamping out a Woodbine on the floor. 'Some bowler hat will creep in any minute, an' if he sees us talkin' as if we've a right tae it would make his day!' He was obviously embarrassed, because as he turned on his heel and disappeared she noticed that the stamped-out Woodbine had only a couple of puffs out of it.

She left the book in her bag under her coat and tried to get on with her work, and at the end of the day she carried it out of Brown's like a priceless jewel. She collected Colin from Auntie Maggie's house and caught the bus home, thankful that he chattered on enough for both of them, because her mouth was too dry and her eyes too wet to keep up a logical conversation. Once home she took the book to her bedroom, guiltily thanking fate that Jimmy was off on one of his mystery jaunts and she could have peace. She closed the door and sat on the bed, and began studying each page in awed silence. They were all there, the entire family, in beautiful, striking detail. It was like breaking through that invisible wall, like finding them again, proving that they really existed and she hadn't imagined them. All the family photos had gone in the destruction of Second Avenue and she had nothing but a child's memory to compare likenesses. Sometimes she would look in the mirror at the slight woman with the golden-red hair she saw there and try to work out who she looked like. She *needed* to look like someone, needed to belong; it was a hunger in her to see her family in her own face, and now there it was, better than photos because Iain's love of them shone through his pencil in a way it couldn't through a photo taken by a box Brownie.

She wanted to show Colin, who hadn't had even her memories of the family he would never know, but the tears wouldn't stop and she would have to control herself enough not to upset him. This was a joyous thing after all, she didn't want her son to look at Iain's drawings and think there was something sad about them. And then a fresh wave hit her; she was looking at Iain's secret skill that he would never have been given the chance to use had he lived. Their world was one where people made things, did things with their hands, produced something functional; being an artist wouldn't have qualified as a bona fide skill. And that brought more tears, for quiet, easy-going Iain, who knew better than to advertise his talent outwith the yard. The chances he would have missed had he lived! A logical voice inside her kept repeating that this was hardly anything to grieve over, because Iain hadn't lived, but that made her grief for him all the more keen. All she could think about was how he had always taken a back seat in the family. Colin was a dare devil, Frances was beautiful and wee Marion had an inquiring mind. And Iain? Well Iain was just Iain; he never upset anyone and tried to pour oil on the troubled waters of everyone else, usually Colin. Yet he had this outstanding skill, this ability to capture people with a pencil in an old school exercise book that was to lie forgotten and undisturbed for years after his death. The book was a slice of the lives he saw around him, packed full of beautifully evocative images of those he had loved as well as she had.

For the first time ever she was able to see in Granny Kate's face an expression she often saw in the mirror, and realised with a rush of exhilaration that she *looked* like Granny Kate! And that tilt of Granny Mirren's head Iain had captured so well, she recognised that too, and the way her mother smiled, and the bright expression in her Da's eyes that she saw in her own son's. And at the very end, just as she was feeling sad that there was no drawing of Iain himself, she came upon a page of self-portraits. Iain from different angles, Iain with smiles, grins and grimaces, all so heartbreakingly lifelike. What she held in her hands was like a series of still movie frames, and it took very little imagination to flick a switch somewhere in her mind – *click!* – and watch them come to life and move across the pages, gloriously real and alive.

When the tears had run their course she took the book of drawings into the living room where Colin was doing his homework, and sat on one of the armchairs on either side of the fire.

'Ye know how you're always askin' what your Granny and Granda looked like?' she said.

Colin nodded.

'Well, look what Ah've got!'

He came over and squashed in beside her and she opened the book and began a narrative of the images on each page.

'That's me when Ah was wee,' she said, 'and that's your Uncle Colin.'

'But he looks like me!' Colin shouted delightedly. He pulled on the lock of hair that always fell over his brow and pointed at an identical one on the page. 'See?'

'Wait till ye see this!' Marion turned to a head-and-shoulders portrait of Tommy MacLeod.

'Now your Uncle Colin looks like this man, doesn't he? Well this man is my Da, your Granda Tommy, and your Uncle Colin is his son, my brother.' Colin's brow furrowed as he tried to keep track of the relationships. 'So if you look like Uncle Colin, an' Uncle Colin looks like Granda Tommy, then you must look like Granda Tommy tae!' Colin laughed out loud, and excitedly turned the pages.

'Who's this man?' he asked, 'pullin' all the different faces?'

'That's your Uncle Iain, he drew these pictures,' Marion said.

'He was a good drawer!'

'Aye, he was.' She swallowed hard.

'Can I have the ones of him an' Uncle Colin an' Granda Tommy?'

'Tell ye whit,' she smiled, smoothing his hair, 'we'll get somebody tae put them in frames an' we'll put them on the wa', so that everybody can see them.'

'But can they *really* be *mine*? My special pictures?'

'Aye, they can be yours.'

The discovery of the drawings had heightened her emotions, and next day she walked about the yard as though she had just been given sight for the first time. She looked at the chalk drawings on the sides of ships under construction, huge caricatures depicting various local worthies. For the first time she saw that they weren't childish daubs, but had been skilfully drawn by someone who knew how to draw, and she remembered other workers who had their own reputations, as fine singers or even as poets. There was the big lad in the Engineering Shop who had taught himself four foreign languages; the boy who played a 'moothie' so well he was said to bring tears to a glass eye, and the chippie who carried a book of Shakespeare's plays in his hip pocket. And she realised that Iain had been at home here with *his* talent, he was accepted as another character and doubtless drew portraits his workmates took home, and cartoons of the bastards in bowlers to amuse the others. The yard was full of men who had skills and talents they would never fully develop, because there were mouths at home to feed. Life was hard and they had to work in harsh conditions to keep it from overwhelming them, and more importantly, their families. There was only time for work, not for what might have been if all things had been equal, because they never were and never would be. It made her feel bitter and desperately sad for them, but at the same time there was a fierce admiration and pride in them too. They were survivors against the odds, she realised, just like Iain's drawings. She knew she was being sentimental, but then she laughed to herself. Why shouldn't she? She had a right, hadn't she.

The next time she saw Robert Boyle at work she called out to him and beckoned him over.

'Robert, Ah jist wanted tae thank ye for the book.'

'Noo, you're no' gonny greet again are ye, Marion?' he grinned, pretending to be prepared for a quick getaway. 'Ah canny stand it when wimmen greet!'

'Dae ye make many wimmen greet then, Robert?' she asked tartly.

'Merr than you think,' he winked, 'an' a damned sight merr than ma Ma knows!'

'Dear God!' Marion said, rolling her eyes heavenwards. 'Another wan that thinks he's Rudolph Valentino!'

'Where dae ye think Ah got these scars?' he demanded. 'In an air raid or somethin'? Well, don't you believe it, hen. Ah jist say that tae kid ma Ma. Every wan was done wi' a sword, ma physog is a map o' a' the duels Ah've fought!'

'Aye,' Marion replied drily, 'an' lost by the looks o' it!'

'Well, you widnae say that if ye had seen the other guys –'

'Shut up, Bamstick! Ah only wanted tae say thanks for the drawin's.'

'Why? Ah didnae draw them!'

'Well, ye couldnae, could ye? No' easy doin' drawin' an' holdin' a sword.'

'Nae bother tae me, hen!'

'Christ, here he goes again! Look, a' Ah'm sayin' is it was kind o' ye, that's a'.'

'Ach away!' he replied, his face flushing.

'Well, noo Ah've seen it a'! Was that why Zorro wore a mask, dae ye think?' Marion laughed. 'Or are you the only famous swordsman who blushes!'

'Don't you believe it!' he replied. 'It's part o' ma charm, it's a' carefully cultivated.'

'Big words frae a big mooth, eh?'

He started to reply but she cut him short. 'An' don't bother tellin' me that isnae the only thing ye have that's big; a' the eejits say that!'

'Aye, but can they *prove* it, Marion?' He winked and took off again into the mêlée of the yard. 'Rab the Rhymer?' she thought. 'They've got that wan dead right, then!'

But underneath the patter and the show she knew – knew without a shadow of doubt – that he was one of the shyest men she had ever encountered. The first time she set eyes on him she saw straight through it all to the kind, sensitive man Robert Boyle was, and it came as a surprise when she realised in time that others saw only Rab the Rhymer. Listening to them discussing him she often wondered if they were talking about the same man, but luckily instinct made her keep her thoughts to herself. Here she was, a wife and mother in her twenties who had never experienced the heady delights of falling in and out of love the way every teenager should. It was hardly her fault she didn't recognise the signs.

*　　　*　　　*

The launch of the Royal Yacht *Britannia* in April 1953 was heralded, as was every launch, by intense activity all over the yard. Men who weren't given a second's breathing space in the great goal of making a profit for John Brown's, were switched to cleaning up wherever a royal eye might fall and be offended. The tracks carrying the yard steam engine were covered in tarmac, lest the VIPs might feel a moment's discomfort as their Daimlers and Rolls-Royces passed over them. Money, it seemed, was no object, except where the safety of the workforce was concerned.

The ship was duly named, the traditional bottle of champagne smashed, and the *Britannia* slipped into the Clyde, cheered on by those who had built her, each one wondering if the event would be marked as usual by lay-offs or transfers to other yards. As soon as the launch party had moved off, the newly-laid tarmac was dug up again and everyone was harried back to work as soon as possible. But only the shell of the *Britannia* had been finished; after the pomp and ceremony ended she was taken to the fitting-out basin to be finished, and it would be November before the snub-nosed tugs pushed and prodded her out of the basin, down the Clyde and out into the open sea. On that April day, though, in the heart of 'Red Clydeside', a place that still made the establishment nervous, the young Queen had gone out of her way to stress that the *Britannia* was not a pleasure craft, that she was in fact 'a Royal Palace-at-sea.' To those who had worked on her, especially those like Marion who had helped fit her out and witnessed the luxury, it was a remark as silly as it was untrue.

The ship had been a replacement for the previous Royal Yacht, the 50-year-old *Victoria and Albert*, and had been ordered for George VI. On his death in 1952, his project, as well as his crown, had been inherited by his daughter. Designed by Sir Victor Shepheard and commissioned in 1951 at a cost of £2.1 million, the 5,769-ton ship had a length of 412' 3". The Royal apartments were astern, while the crew quarters were forward, and for many of those who had been bombed out ten years before and were desperate for decent housing in which to raise their families, even the crew cabins made a nonsense of the remarks made at the launch that this was not a pleasure craft.

But the House of Windsor was then still in recovery from the damage done by the abdication of Edward VIII, and was sensitive to criticism; to a degree at any rate. In another bid to stave off unfavourable comment about the building of the 'Royal Palace-at-sea', it was said that the *Britannia* could also be used as a hospital ship in time of war, and who more than the 'Bankies would appreciate that? In fact, as time would prove, the *Britannia* never served as a hospital ship.

17

The latest postcard from Big Kenny bore on the front a picture of an Argentinian gaucho. 'Why is he wearin' those clothes this time, Mammy?' Colin asked. Marion thought back to the last one, which had a picture of an Alaskan Eskimo, and realised that her son thought they were both photos of Big Kenny. 'Well, why not?' she mused. To her father Uncle Kenny had been a hero, to her mother he was a figment of her father's imagination, while to Marion herself he would for ever be a Canadian Mountie. Big Kenny's function had always been to brighten the lives of others, to fire their dreams and fuel their ambitions. If he was both an Eskimo and a gaucho to Colin that was OK, it was somehow fitting.

She had tried to keep up a correspondence with Big Kenny after the War, but Kenny was a travelling man, he had no time or aptitude for writing long epistles, or any kind of epistles at all come to that. Occasionally a postcard or a Christmas card would arrive, with 'Uncle Kenny' scrawled across it, but beyond confirming that he was still alive, there was never any detail. She still wrote the odd letter, of course, just to keep in touch; he was family after all. And obviously he read her letters, because the postcard had been addressed to the new house.

They had moved to 2E Langfaulds Crescent in Faifley, one of the new council estates or schemes outside the town. At least the new house had a chance of being heated; the old steel houses had been too hot in summer and freezing in winter and she had often wondered how Davy managed to study in his room in North Elgin Street. Not that he had ever complained, he was a good lad; no one would ever have believed how close he came to being thrown in the canal as a troublesome five-year-old. Faifley, immediately and for ever dubbed 'the Fifely', was outside Clydebank's industrial heart, and the red Central SMT double-decker buses ran a shuttle service between the scheme and the town, taking workers to and from work. Many people didn't like being so far from Clydebank itself, there was a certain comfort after all in being near the familiar when so much of life had changed for so many. But Marion approved of the move. The new house was part of a modern tenement housing eight families on the right-hand side of the crescent and there were green fields nearby, room to stretch your eyes and for kids to play, and that had to be better for the generation after hers to grow up in, she thought. And maybe it was better too for those who had survived the horrors of 1941 to be away from the daily reminders, the gaps where buildings had stood that had never been replaced.

There were things she didn't like, of course. The Fifely was built on a hilly site, and the houses on the right had two sets of stairs before you reached the closemouth, and that was before you reached the internal stairs from the first to the top landing. Woe betide anyone with a baby in a pram, or an elderly woman dragging home her groceries, and as there were few shops in the Fifely, women had to drag their shopping all the way from the centre of Clydebank. To get to the washing green at the back there was another flight of steps down, and up of course, so living on the top floor might have been a benefit in that you had no one above you to make noise, but washing day could be exhausting enough without all those stairs. Even so, it *was* better; if only they hadn't squeezed so many people into the available space. But houses were in short supply and there was pressure from exiled 'Bankies to get back home, so perhaps it was under-standable at the time.

And Big Kenny had followed them, in spirit anyway, his

postcards were still reaching them. She had no clear idea what he did for a living, though he must surely be thinking of slowing down soon. He was separated from his brother, her Granda John, by eleven years of Granny Mirren's failed pregnancies, so he would be sixty-six or thereabouts. He did something connected with boats, she thought, but then that was also part of Big Kenny's mystique, and it wouldn't have been half as exciting to know exactly what it was he did do.

'Why, Mammy?' Colin persisted, holding the picture of the gaucho.

'Well, your Uncle Kenny is a special man,' she smiled, 'he can be anything he wants. He's magic! When Ah was wee, Colin, he was a Mountie!'

'On a horse?'

Marion laughed. 'Aye, of course on a horse, he wouldnae be a Mountie if he didnae have a horse, would he?'

It wasn't the first time Colin had been confused, hardly surprising given his background; there was that time at his school. It was Parents' Night and the conversation with his teacher had gone smoothly enough. He was a bright boy who loved books, a bit of a loner, but happy enough in himself. When the other lads were fighting with one another Colin Iain David Ryan was more often than not to be found reading. Not that he was averse to mixing it, he could cause as much mayhem as the rest of them, but not as often, not as badly. He loved travel books and told stories of his Uncle Kenny, who was apparently out there somewhere in the universe, everywhere in the universe, doing amazing things, if Colin were to be believed. Marion was quietly pleased; to have given her son such a high regard for Big Kenny was something to be proud of. Wouldn't Tommy MacLeod have been pleased?

'One thing has been puzzling me though, Mrs Ryan,' said Miss Cairns. 'I don't know quite how to put it, but there seems to be some confusion in his mind about his father.'

'His father?' Marion repeated, feeling distinctly puzzled herself.

'Yes. Someone mentioned it in the staff room,' she gave a nervous little laugh, 'one day he calls his father Davy, and the next, Jimmy. He says he has two daddies, that they both live in the family home.'

'Well?' Marion asked innocently, just for the hell of it.

'Well, I don't mean to pry –'

'I bet you don't!' Marion thought icily.

'But is this Colin's imagination? I mean, I know he has a vivid one, what with Uncle Kenny and all.'

'Well, let me set your curiosity straight, Miss Cairns,' Marion replied, all cool politeness. 'First of all Uncle Kenny *does* exist, and he leads exactly the kind of life my son describes. Secondly, there *are* two men in our house, one called Davy and one called Jimmy. Jimmy is my husband, Colin's father, and Jimmy hasn't had the best of health since he returned from the War. He was a Commando, Miss Cairns. If all the men in uniform did their bit, Jimmy Ryan did his bit and more, and that has taken its toll on his health. The other man is Davy, my husband's younger brother. I brought Davy up, Miss Cairns, he is five years younger than me, and he has always taken on some of the duties of a father when Jimmy wasn't able to. Davy isn't my fancy man, Miss Cairns, he isn't Roger the Lodger.'

'I'm sure I didn't mean to imply that he was, Mrs Ryan,' said the teacher apologetically, her cheeks flushed as she hurriedly straightened the books on the desk in front of her.

'And furthermore, Miss Cairns, Davy Ryan is nearing the end of a four-year MA honours degree at Glasgow University. As a matter of interest, Miss Cairns, did you do an Honours degree?'

'Well, no, I did a straight MA, Mrs Ryan, not that that's of any real importance.' She laughed a little too brightly.

'No,' Marion replied. 'Quite. But I'm sure you'll remember to mention it to the rest of them in the staff room in the morning.'

All the way home she seethed with rage. How dare they

make assumptions about her morals? Give these people a bit of education and they thought they had the right to look down on you. Working class equals the habits of the gutter, that's what they thought. What was it Granny Kate used to say? 'It's Us against Them, an' don't you forget it.' They always assumed that they had higher standards that the working classes could neither understand nor aspire to. God help Davy Ryan if *he* picked up that kind of attitude with his degree! Still, that was *her* in her place, and not a Gaelic phrase used in anger either. Then she saw the funny side of it; the very idea that she and Davy were carrying on together, when the closest contact they had these days was sharing what he was learning at Gilmorehill. He learned, then taught her, and the more she learned the more she hankered to learn. Must be that inquiring mind at work. Still, she hadn't quite lied about Jimmy; he had been ill in ways she couldn't explain since the morning she found him asleep on the doorstep of the Campbell Street house all those years ago, but he had been ill in a way Miss Cairns would understand too.

His periods of absence had continued, and she had given up even wondering where he went, or why. Then there had been an accident at the yard, a boy of fourteen waiting to start his apprenticeship had been working wherever someone needed a hand. He had been helping to carry a sheet of galvanised steel without any protection when he had slipped, and the sheet had cut across his throat. He wasn't badly hurt, a matter of luck rather than anything the management did to safeguard the workforce even in the fifties, but there was a lot of blood. It seemed that Jimmy had witnessed the accident and when Marion had collected Colin from Auntie Maggie's that night and gone home, Jimmy was nowhere to be seen. It had happened so often that she was hardly surprised; what passed through her mind was that at least she wouldn't be scrubbing his damned overalls this weekend.

It lasted three weeks this time, in the middle of a wet and cold winter, then he returned. Usually there was a feeling of calm about him once he had rid himself of whatever he needed to rid himself of, but this time his eyes looked odd and his face flushed and sweaty. She looked up as he came in the door then immediately went over to him and took his arm. He was so fevered that she could almost feel the heat coming from him, and for only the second time in their so-called married life, he leaned against her.

'Dear God, Jimmy! What's happened to ye?'

'Nothing, Marion,' he said. 'Ah jist feel bad.'

She could hear a wheezing from his chest and helped him onto a chair. His clothes, the ones he was wearing when he left, were soaked, and he had no strength to help her remove them.

'Davy! Davy!' He ran from his room, alarmed by the urgency in her voice. 'Davy, take the money oota ma purse, son, an' go an' phone the doctor for Jimmy.'

'Naw, naw,' Jimmy protested feebly, 'Ah don't need a doctor, nae doctor!'

'Go, Davy,' she told him, 'go *now*!'

Marion didn't need the doctor to tell her that Jimmy had double pneumonia, the sound of his moist, laboured breathing was enough. The doctor wanted him to go into hospital, but Jimmy had refused and Marion had said she could take care of him better at home herself.

'How did he get in this state, Mrs Ryan?' The question sounded like an accusation; what he really meant was 'How could *you* let him get into this state, Mrs Ryan?'

'Mr Ryan likes to go away into the hills at the weekends, Doctor,' she replied, a statement that covered a multitude of half-truths, and an entirely acceptable one because the outdoors bug had bitten deep and the 'Bankies still had a reputation for going to the hills long after there was full employment. 'And when he can he takes an extra day or so. This is how he came back this time.'

'Has he a history of chest trouble? Does it run in the family?'

'Who knows, Doctor? We weren't the only people orphaned in 1941.'

'Oh, I'm sorry, I should've remembered.'

'Aye, chum,' she thought, 'ye should.'

'Well, he really is very ill, Mrs Ryan, I hope when he recovers you won't let him roam around too much in future.'

'Jimmy Ryan is his own man, Doctor, he answers to no one, and he wouldn't appreciate anyone, least of all me, telling him what to do.'

She was off work for a month with Jimmy with no money coming in, so Big Kenny's cash in the Post Office took a hammering during that time. His recovery took longer though, somehow he couldn't quite throw the illness off completely, and even when he was up and about he was still breathless. During the night she would be conscious of him easing himself into a sitting position in bed and trying to take deep breaths, and sometimes he would get up and sit in the darkened living room while the others slept. She would rise and ask if he wanted anything. 'Nothing,' he would reply. Did he perhaps want some company? A shake of the head. 'Nae use keepin' you awake as well,' he would say, and she would go back to bed. She didn't sleep, of course, and had they been truly man and wife he would have realised that. Instead she lay wide awake in the bed and stared into the darkness. There was something wrong, but she couldn't quite put her finger on it. It lay there like a heavy threat she couldn't see properly; she could feel it, though.

But Jimmy recovered slowly and by the spring she had almost forgotten her forebodings. 'A touch o' Granny Mirren's Celtic twilight there,' she thought wryly. He went back to work and soon they had returned to the familiar pattern of absences. While he had been ill she had tried to find out about his disappearing acts.

'Where dae ye go?' she had asked.

'Naewhere in particular,' he had replied.

'Dae ye see anybody, Jimmy, an auld pal mibbe?'

'No' really.'

She had the distinct impression that he wasn't deliberately hiding anything. In her mind she imagined him as he was at home, neither happy nor sad, but just existing, only somewhere else. She would listen to the wind and watch the rain running down the windows sometimes and hope someone was looking after him, hope he had found a dry bed somewhere, but she really couldn't see him leading a double life. Jimmy floated about the lives of the rest of the family and sometimes in and out of them, without having any impact; they had learned to live with the ghostly spectre that had once been Jimmy Ryan. He was a one-dimensional, lost soul that no one could reach and who felt no need to reach anyone else. Though she couldn't think what she had done wrong or what else she could have tried to get through to him, she still felt, and always would, that she had failed Jimmy.

'Now, look here, you old crone,' said Dr Drew Hall as he slid a needle into her arm to take another blood sample, 'I'm sending you for a spirograph in the morning, and I don't want you showing yourself up and eating it or anything. Right?'

Marion winced as he removed the needle. 'I thought you were kidding about that blunt needle yesterday.'

'Well, that will teach you not to be cheeky to your betters, won't it?'

'You bring a better to this bed and I'll be cheeky to him.'

Marion replied. 'Meantime I'll practise on you, Elbow Licker.'

'Right, that's it! I'll be bringing along a hammer to get tomorrow's needle in, you evil witch!'

'So tell me, what do you expect from this test then?'

'Ah, can't pronounce spirograph eh? Well, you blow into this tube thingie and it pushes a pen thingie across a graph, and we then have a reading.'

'I know what it is. It's just that you never answered properly

last time I asked. I want to know what you expect it to show in my case?'

'Are you accusing me of being deliberately evasive? It'll show your lung capacity. In language simple enough for you to understand, how well you can blow, an exercise at which I have no doubt you have had plenty of practise, madam.'

'If I had the slightest understanding of what that sad piece of innuendo meant I'd slap you across the kisser.'

'I doubt if you even have the slightest understanding of innuendo!'

'So what do you expect from this spider's graph then?'

'I expect to see your lung capacity slightly down, seeing as you are recovering from an attack of the Broon Kittens.'

'So what will that tell you then? You already know I had bronchitis.'

'The truth? Bugger all. In medical language, it will be viewed as only one in a series of associated tests that as a whole will lead us to guess at a diagnosis. Got that?'

'And when do I get the rest of the tests?'

'The main one is the bronchoscope –'

'I know about that too.'

'Kindly don't interrupt! Where is it written that you can interrupt a genius at work?' He was struggling with the syringe and several glass phials, and a pile of forms scattered out of his hands and fell on her bed.

'A genius! Can't hold a conversation and some bits of paper at the same time!'

'As I was saying,' he said with mock dignity, 'that's where we send a tube down into your lungs and have a butcher's at what's going on, and if we want we can take a tiny bit for analysis. I'm trying to arrange that at the moment, but the lads what do it are busy.'

'Unlike the patients, of course, who have all the time in the world!'

'Now that's sarcasm,' said Dr Hall, pointing a finger at her and narrowing his eyes. 'Ve vill not stand for ze 'Bankie sarcasm in our vards!'

206

And with that he clicked his heels and executed a very bad goosestep out of the ward, to the chuckles of his adoring female patients. Stooping into a deep bow at the door he acknowledged the laughter and blew kisses to his audience.

'I bet you sat in puddles for attention as a wee boy,' Marion called out.

'My dear old biddy, my arse is still wringing wet after wallowing in that big one in Castle Street this very afternoon! Good night, darlings!'

Marion settled back on her pillows. He was a good doctor, the boy Hall, he managed to seem light-hearted even when he was explaining to you that you might have cancer and were about to be told precisely how long you had. Service with a smile every time.

The Boyle family had moved into Langfaulds Crescent too, with Agnes's elderly mother, Sarah Sweeney. They now lived along the road from the Ryans and on the left, at 9F. Standing at her living room window Marion would often see Rab the Rhymer cycle off, his bike laden with camping equipment and fishing gear. It was one more thing that annoyed Pape, his son's defection to the countryside at every possible opportunity. Overtime was much prized in the yard and was granted along tribal lines – it depended on whether you had been part of the Boy Scouts or the Boy's Brigade, Catholic or Protestant. But Rab the Rhymer turned down overtime slips every time they were offered by a foreman, and while others were fighting for them. He didn't want overtime, he wanted to take off for the hills, and sometimes he didn't arrive back till Tuesday, missing an entire day's work. 'Ach,' he'd say, 'Ah was oan ma way back, an' it was a smashin' day, an' Ah thought tae masel', "Why ruin a good day?" So Ah just turned the bike roond an' headed ower the Switchback an' on to Loch Lomond.' He always gave his mother his dig money, but to Pape, who had had to fight for work all his life, his son's attitude was an insult.

Discovering a link with the life she had in Second Avenue

had been a bonus for Marion, and she was happy to be gradually sucked into the Boyle family. And the more she got to know them, the more her own family life seemed glaringly dull and abnormal. The fact was that the Boyles fought like pigs; their home resounded to arguments, raised voices and slamming doors, instead of the deathly quiet of 2E Langfaulds Crescent. Pape would usually start it by complaining about what he regarded as his son's Communist leanings, and his alleged support for the many trade unions in the yard, that Pape was convinced were bringing Brown's to its knees.

'Unions? Unions?' Robert would laugh at him. 'The Union men in Broon's are every bit as bad as the bastards at the top! Have ye no' noticed, Faither, that a' the union men are made foremen? Dae ye think it's because they're good at their jobs, like, are ye *that* daft?' He turned to Marion, 'When Ah was still an apprentice we went on strike −'

'Again!' Pape interrupted.

'Aye, *again*, Faither. We were standin' ootside the yard in the pourin' rain an' this big car draws up, an' a chancer wearin' the best suit Ah've ever seen or ever will, pops its napper oota the windae. This is oor Union man. "Ye're daein' fine, boys," he says. "Keep it up, we'll win yet!" "Wait a minute, Mac," Ah says, "whit's this 'we' crap? We're apprentices, we don't get any strike pay for this, but we've tae 'keep it up'?" "That's the rules," he says. "But we pay oor union dues tae," Ah says, "an' it seems tae me that a' we get oota it is some ponce in a big car tellin' us that 'we'll win'."' He turned to his father again, 'That's your Unions for ye, every wan on the take like a' the rest, an' daft auld buggers like you know it fine. Ye jist choose no' tae dae anythin' aboot it, jist as ye chose a' these years tae dae nothin' aboot the workin' conditions in the yard!' As he argued he walked from room to room getting ready to go out, and kept reappearing in various stages of the transformation between working clothes and civvies.

'The Unions have got us better wages!' Pape replied.

'For Chrissake make up your mind, man! Wan minute it's *ma* Union, full o' Reds, an' the next it's *your* Union full o' wage improvements! And as Ah keep sayin' tae ye, it's no' always aboot money. There are men killed and injured on every ship because safety is nonexistent, an' naebody does anythin'. Look at wee Harry Stewart the other week when he got hit wi' that spanner that fell aff the deck in West Yard. Whit did they dae? They brought in the insurers an' put pressure on daft wee Harry tae accept the first offer o' compensation. £20 they gave him! He coulda been killed!'

'Harry's no' right in the heid, ye know that!' shouted Pape, getting up from his chair and following Robert about.

'Aye, Faither,' Robert shouted back, '*Ah* know that. *You* know that. The whole bloody yard knows that, an' no' wanna ye raised your voice to help him, did ye?'

Pape's dark hair had more silver mixed in these days, making him look more like a badger, Marion thought, if a slightly older and at that moment an angrier one. He and his son stood nose to nose, shouting into each other's faces, staring into each other's eyes, but Robert's fingers still managed a perfect knot in his tie. 'Neither did you!'

'Ye're right, Faither, the electricians didnae jump up an' doon aboot it, an' we woulda had your support if we had, wouldn't we? Harry's wanna *your* lot, the big, strong, harumscarum black squad, an' whit was it noo that other big, brave riveter said? Oh aye, Ah remember noo, "He shoulda been merr careful!" Wee Harry has probably never seen £20 in his life before, but he was due a damned sight merr. If he wasnae right in the heid afore, he's a damn sight less noo wi' the imprint o' a spanner in his skull!'

'The black squad are hard men,' Pape shouted, his eyes bulging and spittle flecking the corners of his mouth, 'the black squad *made* Broon's!'

'Aye, Faither, hard frae ear tae ear every wan, an' ye're right, they made Broon's whit it is right enough. That's why *we're* in this position the day, because your lot did nothin' about Broon's in your day, when ye had the chance!' He threw his jacket on and made for the front door. 'See ye later, Ma,' he said to Agnes, who all this time had been clearing dishes from the table and taking them to the sink as though World War III wasn't happening around her. 'Ah'm goin' for a pint, Ah won't be late. Cheerio, Marion hen!' And with that he disappeared.

'Ye see?' shouted Pape at Agnes. 'Nae bloody sense, that boy o' yours!'

'Ach be fair tae yersel', Pape,' she replied calmly, 'Ah couldnae have done it withoot your help.'

'Naw, naw, that wan's no' mine, that wan's a' yours!'

'Well mibbe we should get a haud o' wee Father Sheridan at Our Holy Redeemer's in that case.' She changed her voice to that of a BBC announcer. 'Another Virgin Birth has taken place,' she announced in a mock upper-class accent, 'this time in Clydebank.' She threw the tablecloth over her head, 'Whit dae ye think, Marion? Would Ah make a passable Virgin Mary? Or would that be Virgin Agnes o' the Fifely?'

As the two women stood together laughing, Pape was still pacing back and forward, frustrated that the object of his wrath had walked out taking the last word by default. 'Disnae listen, he never bloody listens! Nae bloody sense, thinks he knows everythin'!'

'Ah hiv the feelin' ye're losin' the argument, Pape son,' Agnes said quietly. 'There's no much doubt where he got they character traits frae, is there?'

Pape lifted his newspaper and stormed out of the living room.

'Christ,' Agnes sighed, 'whit would ye dae wi' them, Marion? Clydebank's answer tae Laurel and Hardy!'

From the chair by the fireside came a voice. 'That the turn finished for the night, Agnes?' Mrs Sweeney asked. 'Can Ah turn the wireless oan noo? It's nearly time for "The McFlannels".'

210

'Aye, Mammy, that's them finished. Same time, same place the morra though. Put your programme oan, doll, ye'll get peace tae listen tae it noo that the floor show's over.'

'Is it always like this?' Marion asked.

'Naw, naw, hen,' Agnes said. She reached for the pack of Woodbines on the mantelpiece, took one out, put it to her mouth and lit it. 'Oor Robert's helluva bad at that,' she said absently, 'leavin' his fags lyin' aboot. Whit were we sayin'? Oh aye. Naw, it's no' always like this, Marion,' she said, like a comedian setting up a tag line, 'sometimes it gets *really* noisy in here! Fancy a wee cuppa tea an' a jammy dodger?'

It was early on a Monday evening, Jimmy was elsewhere and Davy was at the library. Davy was around the house less and less, either tied up in the library or, more likely, with the life of a student at Gilmorehill. She couldn't help smiling to herself when she looked at him these days, in his duffle coat and university scarf, and then there was the time he had tried a pipe: 'The Mad Professor!' she'd think affectionately. That Monday, as had become usual these days, it was just Marion and Colin at home when Robert Boyle arrived at the door of 2E, bearing in his hands four fresh brown trout. He followed Marion into the kitchen, with Colin in close attendance.

'Auld Aggie wondered if ye could use these fish,' he grinned, 'the whole family'll grow gills if they eat any merr. Ah had a good day at Loch Venachar yesterday, enough trout tae feed the multitude.' He laid the fish on the plate Marion handed him and put the plate on the table. 'Don't know whit attracted them, but then fish canny see the physog!'

Marion looked up at him sharply across the table. 'Robert, son, why dae ye always mention your scars?' she asked seriously.

He stared back. The silence stretched. 'Mibbe,' he said, 'mibbe because if Ah dae it won't be worth anybody else's bother tae mention them.'

'An' Ah mention them a' the time, dae Ah? That's why ye mention them tae me?'

'Naw, naw . . .'

'Son, they're only scars. They're no' as noticeable as ye think either, an' they'll quieten doon wi' time.'

They continued to look at each other.

'My Mammy's got lotsa scars, Robert,' said Colin brightly, breaking the spell. 'Look, Robert, look at this one!' He climbed onto a chair beside Marion and pulled her hair back to expose the big scar that ran round the back of her head. 'This is a horrible one!' he said with relish. 'It didnae heal right and it's a' bumpy!'

Marion was laughingly trying to resist her son, but glad he had been there, for no reason that she could understand. But Colin wasn't finished; he grabbed Robert's hand and pulled him over to where Marion stood like a prize exhibit. 'Feel it, Robert!' the boy urged. 'It's really *horrible!*'

She felt the rough fingers of his right hand moving across the impressive scar under her hair and his left hand resting lightly on her shoulder, and she shivered. She had no idea why, but his touch made her tingle, and she moved away sharply, her mind desperately trying to find an explanation for the sudden movement. Her eyes fell on the fish. 'Oh, great!' she laughed. 'Thanks a lot, Colin! Dae ye realise that his hands are a' fishy, an' noo he's made ma hair fishy tae?'

She heard Colin laugh with delight and Robert laughed too, but she couldn't bring herself to look at him.

'Listen,' she said brightly, 'aboot these fish. Ah've never gutted a fish in ma life.'

'Ye're jokin'!'

'Naw, honest. Ah'm a coward when it comes tae things like that, so Ah've aye bought them filleted.'

'Gies a sharp knife,' Robert said.

She handed him a knife, taking care that they didn't actually touch, and watched him slit the stomach of the first fish and start to remove the guts.

'Oh God!' she muttered, turning away.

'Well, make yersel' useful then,' he said. 'Don't jist staun' there makin' daft noises. Get oot the fryin' pan an' some butter!'

When she next looked the four trout had been expertly cleaned, but the heads were still attached.

'Well, take the heids off!' she demanded. 'Ah canny bear them lookin' at me like that!'

'Christ, but wimmen are peculiar!' he retorted, lifting the knife again.

'Leave the head on mine, Robert!' said Colin, who had been happily engrossed in the gory business from beginning to end.

'Right,' Marion grinned, 'so noo there's four big trout ready for the fryin' pan an' only Colin an' me in the hoose.'

'See whit Ah mean, Colin?' Robert said conspiratorially to the boy. 'No' only did Ah havtae catch them, but Ah hadtae deliver them an' gut them for her, an' noo Ah've got tae help her tae eat them as well!'

The boy shook his head like an old man, delighted to have been invited into a grown-up man's joke.

Sitting at the table the three of them presented the appearance of a happy family sharing a meal. For Marion everything seemed heightened, the sound of their voices, each look that passed between them, every movement, and she couldn't understand why. She looked at her son and saw how happy and relaxed he was, and it felt like a blow. This was the kind of scene he should be used to, the sort of domesticity he should take for granted, yet his eyes shone, his face was bright with the novelty of it and his voice was loud with enjoyment and excitement.

It was after ten o'clock when Robert left. He had undoubtedly been going out and had simply called in with the fish on the way, and the pubs would now be closed. She was glad that she'd allowed Colin to stay up till he went, because the protocol for bidding a neighbour goodnight didn't seem appropriate, and she didn't know what was. Colin chattered on, reluctant to let the only man he knew outside his family go, and he managed to extract a promise that Robert would take him fishing some weekend.

She stood at the window after he'd gone and watched him walking across the road towards 9F. He looked up at the window and waved. Marion caught her breath and had to stop herself from taking a step back; how did he know she would be watching? And come to that, why did she feel she shouldn't? Why the impulse to hide behind the curtains? She waved back, then she went into the kitchen to clear up before going to her bedroom. There she sat in front of the dressing-table mirror and, head down, out of curiosity she ran a finger across the big scar. There was no tingle, no shiver. Looking up she caught sight of her flushed cheeks and her shining eyes.

'Oh for God's sake, Marion, get a grip!' she chided herself. 'Anybody will tell ye that a red face doesnae suit folk wi' red hair!'

18

Auntie Maggie had moved out of Campbell Street into one of the new houses for single women. Now retired from Singer's she still did the odd bit of cleaning, and on Saturday mornings she worked in a baker's shop in Dumbarton Road. A day without earning something, no matter how little, was a day spent in agony for Maggie; every penny was a prisoner. Marion saw little of her these days, a situation that bothered neither of them unduly, but Colin visited Maggie every day after school. Whenever Marion and Maggie did meet there was a lively exchange of ideas, which Colin accepted as normal, perhaps because it never actually came to blows, but he still felt a little odd about his affection for both women.

'Ye don't *have* to go to Auntie Maggie's,' Marion said. 'Ye know that, don't ye?'

'I want to go,' he explained to his bemused mother, squirming a little. 'She's old, and sometimes she needs things done for her.'

'Like what?'

'Well, I get her bunches of sticks for her fire, an' her *Evening Times*, an' I make sure she's got enough milk.' He looked up at her sideways, his face colouring with embarrassment. 'That kinda thing. Y'know?'

Marion pulled him to her and held him, smoothing the stray lock of dark hair that always escaped. 'Ah'm no' sayin' ye shouldnae visit your Auntie Maggie, son,' she smiled, 'it's jist that Ah only went tae see her when Ah was your age if your Grannie Jean tied a big rope aroond me and dragged me!'

'But I feel sorry for her, Mum,' Colin murmured, 'she's all on her own.'

'As long as she's got her duster an' money tae buy polish Maggie will never be alone!' Marion laughed. 'But Ah'm pleased that ye think o' her, son, your Granny Jean would be that proud o' ye. Jist don't let her make ye feel ye *have* to go. She's aye been good at that!'

'Mum,' he asked quietly, 'can I take Uncle Iain's book to show her?'

Marion had to think fast. Iain's drawings had become precious to her and she didn't want them to leave the house except in complete safety, yet she could hardly tell her ten-year-old son that she didn't trust him to look after the book. In truth she wouldn't trust anyone on the planet, but Colin would feel hurt and insulted however carefully she phrased a refusal.

'Tell ye what,' she said, 'we'll go down together tomorrow night an' take the book. Ah haven't seen Auntie Maggie for a while, an' you're right, Colin, she's family, we should look after her.' Looking at his beaming face she felt ashamed of herself for being so underhand, but she consoled herself with the certain knowledge that an hour spent with Maggie would be sufficient punishment.

The house was smaller, so Maggie had sold a lot of her odds and ends. She had held onto the old Gingerbread clock that struck every half-hour though; all her life Marion had itched to put a hammer through that clock. And even with fewer bits and pieces around you would have sworn you were in Campbell Street, or in Jellicoe Street; no matter where she was, Maggie somehow contrived to make each home she took over the same as the one she had left behind. She sat in the same chair, on the same side of the fireplace, and – she swore to God this was true – wearing that same pinny. 'Pickled in vinegar,' Marion thought bitterly, 'wi' a nature tae match.' The old woman didn't see her at first, expecting only Colin to appear as usual. 'There he is!' Marion heard her say. 'Ma ain laddie!' and there was a real, honest-to-goodness smile across those thin lips. She looked up in surprise as Marion followed him in, and composed her features into their normal blank look. 'Oh, you're here tae,' she said, without any great approval. 'Ye must be wantin' somethin'!'

'Tae get oot fast!' Marion said to herself. 'Jist tae see your smilin' face, Auntie Maggie,' she said brightly, thinking, 'Beat that you auld bitch!'

Colin took Marion's bag, put it on the table and drew from it the book of drawings. 'This is it, Auntie Maggie!' he almost whispered. When he had that look of excitement in his eyes Marion would have sworn she was looking at his Uncle Colin at the same age. 'Now are your hands clean?'

Marion closed her eyes, expecting her son to be smashed to a pulp by one of Maggie's malevolent looks, but instead she heard an entirely unfamiliar voice say, 'Of course they are, son, Ah washed them specially, jist as ye said yesterday.'

He laid the book on her lap and knelt by her chair watching with barely concealed delight as she opened the cover.

'That's my Granda Tommy!' he said. 'You liked my Granda Tommy, didn't you, Auntie Maggie?'

Auld Maggie's eyes settled on the unsuspecting object of her devotion. 'Aye, son,' she said quietly, 'he was a fine man.'

In whatever grave her Da reposed, Marion thought, he would be rotating at a furious speed. Colin was anxious that every drawing should be looked at immediately. 'Let Auntie Maggie take her time,' she chided him gently.

'Leave the boy alane!' Maggie said, shooting her a cold, sharp glare. 'He's daein' nae harm!'

The venom was still intact; they were in the same universe after all, then. Maggie stared at the drawings in silence, until she came to one of Tommy and Jean together and, reaching into her pinny pocket, she pulled out a hankie and proceeded to dab at her eyes. Marion stared at her in shock. Maggie never cried. Maggie couldn't cry. If this woman was crying then she couldn't be Maggie.

'Would you like a cuppa tea, Auntie Maggie?' Colin asked kindly, his small arm more than reaching across the thin, bony shoulders.

'Aye, son,' she said, blowing her nose, 'that wid be jist the thing. You're a good laddie.'

Marion waited in total silence till Colin came back with the tea, unable to think of a word to say to Maggie as the old woman tried to compose herself.

'Here he is!' she said brightly, pushing the hankie back into her pinny pocket. 'An' ye found the gypsy creams tae! Clever lad!' The ceremony of the tea-taking and biscuit-eating took place with the customary avoidance of dropping a single crumb, then Maggie looked again at the book.

'An' ye say Iain did these?' she asked, looking up at Marion.

'So Ah'm tellt,' she replied, 'an' who else would draw oor family?'

'Aye, well,' Maggie said firmly, 'of course he woulda got it frae oor side o' the family.'

'Aye, sure, Auntie Maggie!' Marion replied, feeling for the first time that she was on safer, known soil. 'He couldnae get it frae the MacLeods could he? Or the MacDonalds, or Granny Kate's side, it would havtae be your side!'

'Ah'm tellin' ye! Ma faither, your grandfaither, was a fine drawer an' painter.'

'Aye, they tell me Hitler was a dab hand at the distemperin' tae.'

'Ye've always had a nasty tongue in your heid, Marion MacLeod!' Maggie spat at her.

'Well, thank God for that!' Marion replied. 'For a minute Ah thought Ah was in the wrang hoose, but it's you, Maggie, it's definitely you efter a'!'

There was a silence. 'You didnae know ma faither,' Maggie said. 'Oor Jean didnae know him either; a pity. He wis a fine wee man. Quiet an' a bit o' an artist. Came frae good folk. No' like ma mother, she wis a bad lot, wi' her drinkin' an a' that!'

'Aw for God's sake, Maggie!' Marion sighed. 'Your mother was a poor soul frae whit Ah know. She didnae have her troubles tae seek, did she? So she drank; she paid dearly for it, didn't she?'

'She had nae right behavin' like that wi' two bairns tae look efter!' Maggie said bitterly. 'She didnae bother aboot us!'

'Gie it a rest,' Marion said. 'It's 1958, the poor wumman has been gone for over forty years noo, gie her a wee bit o' compassion if ye have any. Ye survived, didn't ye? A helluva lot o' people didnae!'

'She'll be gettin' the poison darts ready for when Ah turn ma back,' Marion thought, but barbed reply came there none.

There was another long silence. 'Have ye seen that pal o' yours recently?' Maggie asked out of the blue. 'That Sal Devlin?'

'Ah've passed her in the toon a coupla times,' Marion replied. 'Why dae ye ask?'

'Nae reason,' Maggie replied. 'Jist that Ah heard that nae good man o' hers got the sack frae Singer's. The drink, of coorse.' Then with a dismissive sniff she remarked, 'It's nae merr than she deserves, right enough.'

'Noo whit the hell does *that* mean?' Marion demanded.

'She was a loose wumman a' through the War!' Maggie said, raising her voice. 'Ah remember, even if others choose tae forget!'

'Christ, aye, you would! Well, you balanced her oot, Auntie Maggie, ye've been stitched up that tight a' your life that you're waterproof!'

'Nae need tae be offensive! Ah was aye a clean-livin' wumman, ye can be sure aboot that!'

'Aye, but it would've been interestin' to find oot if ye would've stayed like that if ye'd had any offers, wouldn't it?' She prepared herself for an onslaught, but it didn't come.

'This must be a new game,' she thought grimly. 'She'll be lurin' me wi' a false sense o' security, then she'll plunge the knife in!'

When they got up to go Marion lifted Iain's book of drawings and put it safely in her bag.

'Can Ah ask ye a favour?' Maggie asked, Maggie who wouldn't have asked for air if she was drowning.

Marion stared at her. 'Here it comes!' she thought.

'The drawin' o' Jean an' your Da. Could Ah have it?'

Marion was aghast. 'Auntie Maggie, Ah don't want tae lose any o' them,' she pleaded, 'they're a' Ah've got o' ma family.'

'Ma family tae,' Maggie said quietly. 'Look, Ah'll put it in a nice frame, an' when Ah'm gone it'll come back tae ye.'

Marion didn't know what to do. It was such a little request, but at the same time it was such a big one. She didn't want to let the drawing go, but Colin was imploring her with his eyes and Maggie was dabbing with her hankie again.

'Aye, OK, Auntie Maggie,' she sighed, 'but you listen tae me. If this hoose ever goes on fire, Ah'll save this before Ah'll save you, an' Ah expect you tae dae the same. Understood?'

Maggie nodded and reached again for her hankie. 'Aw stop that!' Marion said. 'Ye've got what ye wanted noo, haven't ye? Ah'll get it framed for ye an' bring it doon.'

Sal kept popping into her mind over the next few days. She should have kept in touch, she knew Sal was in trouble, after all. So when the drawing of Jean and Tommy was ready she took it to Maggie and resolved to call at North Elgin Street on the way back.

It was a Sunday night and Davy was at home, so she asked him to keep an eye on Colin. As she passed the bedroom on her way out she heard Jimmy coughing and looked in. 'Ye a' right, Jimmy?'

'Aye, fine, Marion,' he said pleasantly, 'jist clearin' ma throat.'

'Wid ye like a wee cuppa tea?'

'Aye, that would be nice.'

She went back into the kitchen, made the tea and took it in to him. He was propped up in the bed, a copy of the *Sunday Post* in his hands, opened at The Broons.

'Thanks, lass,' he said.

As she walked to the bus stop she wondered if that cough was worse than usual, and decided that she would mention it to him later.

Auld Maggie took the framed drawing and placed it on a table by the window. 'Ah'm glad ye didnae bring oor Colin wi' ye, Ah've somethin' tae talk tae ye aboot,' she said.

'*Oor Colin?*' Marion wondered. 'Since when?'

'An'm needin' tae go intae hospital soon. It's ma heart. Ah'm told Ah must've had rheumatic fever when Ah was young, an' there's somethin' the matter wi' two heart valves. Had it for years.'

'Ye never said.'

'An' ye woulda cared a damn?' She raised a hand to cut off Marion's reply. 'Ah've been oan tablets for years noo,' she continued, 'but Ah might need a different kind. So Ah'm goin' in for tests. Ah'll be away aboot a week, so keep an eye oan the hoose for me, an' be careful how ye explain it tae oor Colin. Ah don't want him upset.'

'Is that it?' Marion asked, smarting inside that Maggie was concerned for *her* son.

Maggie shook her head. 'Jist like your father,' she said, 'ye're that smart your mouth's aye three steps ahead o' your brain. If anythin' goes wrang, there's a will made. *You* get *nothin'*. Everythin' goes tae the boy, whit's in the hoose, ma savings, the lot. A' for oor Colin.'

'Ma boy disnae need it!' Marion countered.

'Ah didnae say he needed it, Ah said he was tae get it! An' ye neednae worry, Ah'm expectin' nothin' o' you, Marion MacLeod! There's room in ma mother's plot in Dalnottar Cemetery, no' that Ah want tae lie next tae her, but there's nae sense wastin' money when Ah won't know any different anyway.'

'Look,' Marion said, 'Ah don't know what this perform- ance is in aid o'. Are ye tryin' tae make me feel bad because Ah've no' visited ye merr often?'

'Ye've visited *me* merr than Ah ever visited *you*! Cuts baith ways, an' ye've nae need tae look so surprised either!'

'If Ah'm lookin' surprised it's because you've actually got a heart, Auntie Maggie!' Marion replied. 'Ah'd have put money oan a lump o' stane, but Ah suppose these medical people must know whit they're talkin' aboot.'

'Which is merr than you dae!'

'Look, why don't we call this a draw, Auntie Maggie? Ah havnae got time tae stand here lobbin' ba's so you can lob them back.'

'Suits me. Good night tae ye. An' thanks for the picture.'

It was a queer world right enough, she mused on the tram to North Elgin Street. There you were getting on with life, doing your best, and something like that comes at you. She hadn't suspected that Maggie was on tablets for anything, never thought she was human enough to be ill, come to that. What did she do now? Was she supposed to turn up at the hospital every visiting hour with a bunch of flowers and a bottle of Irn Bru, and sit there making small talk? Did she go to the doctors and ask for a report on her dear old aunt, and if she didn't, would they think she was strange?

She got off the tram and made her way past the Co-op biscuit factory – how had she never noticed how sickly sweet the smell was? – over the bridge and into North Elgin Street. She looked at Number 10 and felt absolutely nothing. Her first home after she was married; she should surely have felt something? There was a light on in Sal's living room, but the garden and the outside looked shabbier than she remembered, unless her memory was playing tricks. She knocked on the door and it was opened by a girl of about fifteen.

'Is your Ma in, hen?'

'Is that you, Mrs Ryan? Come away in! Ma!' she shouted into the house. 'It's Mrs Ryan!'

She walked into the living room. Her memory hadn't been playing tricks. Sal's house had always been full of desperate little feminine touches, her antimacassars, her crystal decanter filled with coloured water, thanks to the brightest, if not the best, of English literature. It had all gone. Big Tony Gallagher was lying fast asleep on the couch. He was wearing a grubby vest and trousers and no socks or shoes. She noticed that his face was blotchy and swollen and he was snoring so loudly that she could've sworn the house vibrated each time.

'Marion, in here!' Sal's voice whispered. 'Don't wake the big bastard for Chrissake!'

Marion passed the couch on the way to the kitchen, and the alcohol fumes almost made her wince. There were four of her six children in the kitchen with Sal, all of them huddled around the cooker for warmth; it was like a scene from the workhouse. She had been about to ask, 'How are ye, Sal?' but decided in the circumstances that she didn't need to. Sal saved her the bother of thinking up another opening line.

'How've ye been, Marion hen?'

'Fine, fine, Sal,' she said brightly. 'Workin' hard, ye know. Ah was doon seein' Auld Maggie an' thought I'd jist drop in.'

'Whit age is yer Auntie Maggie noo, then?' Sal asked, her voice still in the whisper zone.

'Jist sixty past, Sal, but Ah know whit ye mean, she's been aboot as long as Methuselah.'

Sal laughed quietly. 'Ye'll have a cuppa, Marion?'

'Och, Sal, would ye mind if Ah didnae this time? Ah've still got Colin's school stuff tae iron an' Jimmy's workin' gear for the mornin' tae sort oot, and then there's oor Davy's troosers tae press,' she sighed. 'Ye know how it is?'

'Tell me aboot it!' Sal said a little too quickly, and immediately Marion knew that had she accepted she would have been depriving the family. Things must be bad. 'Look, Sal, ye know where Ah stay. That's really why Ah stopped by, tae ask ye if ye'd like tae come up for a bit o' a natter. Then tomorrow night mibbe? How would that suit ye?'

'Aye, Marion, that would be great! We havnae had a good gossip for ages.' She made no attempt to stop Marion from leaving, in fact there was a note of relief in her voice as she grasped the invitation and let Marion out of the back door instead of the front. 'It's better no' tae risk wakenin' him,' she said with a weak smile. As she pulled her cardigan sleeves down the movement caught Marion's eye. Sal's forearms were covered in yellowish purple bruises. She looked at the buttons running up to Sal's neck, Sal who believed in flaunting the gifts the good Lord had given her in plenty; the bruises must be all over.

Walking back down the road Marion felt despair and guilt at having deserted Sal. Then her eyes fell on Our Holy Redeemer's. Changing direction she strode up to the chapel house door and rapped it loudly. Father Sheridan opened the door.

'Good heavens!' he said jovially. 'It's the best cleaning woman outside the faith! Come in, Mrs Ryan!'

He led her to a seat by the fire, but she refused to sit down.

'Ah only want tae tell ye somethin',' she said firmly, 'then Ah've got tae get back tae the Fifely.'

'Now, you're not going to say you want to convert after all, are you?' he laughed.

'Naw. Father –'

'Or that you want your old job back?'

'Naw. Look, Father Sheridan, jist shut up an' listen!'

'Father Sheridan, eh? Must be *very* serious!'

She stared at him. 'That's it, then? Wisecracks ower?'

He nodded, the smile dying on his lips at the furious expression on her face.

'Jist alang the road there, in North Elgin Street, there's a pile o' your mob. The Gallaghers. Well, Sal isnae your mob, but she's supplied a bloody great army o' bairns, enough tae keep your chapel filled for generations.'

He sat on the edge of an armchair, his arms folded, listening.

'Dae you lot see it as your pastoral duty tae look efter the flock?'

Gerry Sheridan nodded.

'Well get your arse in gear an' hightail it alang tae Tony Gallagher's an' have a look at how his family are livin', then!' she shouted, pointing outside and leaning forward so that he couldn't help hearing each word. 'He's a drunk, he's been batterin' his wife for years, an' noo he's lost his job because o' the booze!'

'What can I do about it, Marion?' he asked.

'He's wanna your lot!' Marion shouted, 'Dae SOME-THIN'! Ah'll tell ye this, ma Da wis a good wee atheist aboot a quarter the size o' Big Tony, but if he was alive the day he'd go alang that road an' sort the big bastard oot wi' his two bare hands!'

'Marion, people don't always welcome interference, and the Church is reluctant to involve itself in private family matters.'

'Och, your arse!' Marion replied angrily. 'If Sal took wanna her bairns awa frae the Catholic school ye would be alang there like greased lightning. Ye'd a' be there, you an' a' your high-heid statue nodders in frocks, "involvin' yersels in private family matters", wouldn't ye?'

Father Sheridan nodded and shrugged. 'OK, Marion, as it's for you I'll look in tomorrow and see what I can do.'

'Holy Jesus Mother o' Christ!' she shouted, grabbing her head with angry, frustrated fingers. 'No' for *me*! Go alang there an' dae somethin' for Sal an' her bairns, her *Catholic* bairns, an' while ye're there, have a look at Sal's arms. It might gie ye an idea how bad things are! Ah don't care whit ye dae wi' Big Tony, as long as ye don't make a mess on the carpet. Right?'

With that she stormed out of the chapel house and leapt onto the platform of a passing No. 9 tram in Dumbarton Road. Tomorrow she'd go to the Post Office, take out some of Big Kenny's money and force Sal to take it, a present, a loan, anything as long as she spent it on her children. But first she'd make her promise that that big bastard wouldn't get a penny to spend on more drink!

It was later than she expected when she turned into Langfaulds Crescent, and in the dark a bike whizzed perilously close to her. She was still worked up about Sal, 'in fightin' trim' as her Da used to describe Granny Kate. 'You stupid sod!' she shouted out. 'Ye shouldnae be let oot on feet never mind oan wheels!'

The bike squealed to a halt.

'That you, Marion?'

'Aye. That you, Robert?'

'Whit ye doin' oot at this time?'

'Whit are *you* doin' oot at this time?'

'Ah'm jist back frae the weekend, spent three days fightin' the midges in Arrochar.' He had jumped off the bike and wheeled it back to meet her. 'Right, that's ma excuse, whit's yours?'

As he got closer he saw her face. 'Christ, whit's happened? Are ye a' right?' He held the bike with one hand and put an arm around her shoulder. His sympathetic tone achieved what sympathetic tones always did. She burst into tears of rage and he dropped his bike on the road to put both arms around her. It had all the elements of a good farce, and in the midst of her tears she started to laugh. Robert reacted with a mixture of confusion and embarrassment.

'Ah'll never understand youse wimmen!' he said, trying to make it sound as if he was joining in with some joke that no one had told him about. 'Wan minute you're greetin', the next you're laughin' – an' look at ma poor bloody bike!'

'Ah'm sorry,' she said, still unsure whether to laugh or cry. 'Ah've been tae see this pal o' mine. Mibbe ye remember her, Sal Devlin frae Second Avenue?'

'Big Sal!' he laughed. 'Her that ran a one-woman United Nations Social Club?'

'That's right,' she said archly. 'She made the best currant bun in Scotland, so ma Da used tae say!'

'Whit aboot her?'

So she told him how Sal had helped her when she went into labour waiting in the 'divi' queue in Alexander Street, about the day long ago when she discovered that Big Tony hit Sal and how she had done her shopping so that the neighbours wouldn't see the bruises. And tearfully again she told him how she had abandoned Sal when she left North Elgin Street, and how she *knew* she was abandoning her, but she still did it. Then she brought him up to date with the current situation, and how she had marched into the chapel house and shouted at Father Sheridan. To her amazement and rage Robert started to laugh.

'Ye jist ordered wee Sheridan tae get his arse in gear?' he chuckled. 'Ah mean, ye actually *said* that tae him?'

'Have you listened tae a word Ah've said? You're standin' there laughin' like an idiot, an' Ah've jist been tellin' ye aboot the state o' Sal an' her bairns! Ah sometimes think a' men have a screw loose, there's no' wan o' ye ever grows up!' She made to stomp off towards 2E, but he caught her arm.

'Ah'm sorry, Marion, but ye havtae see it frae ma point o' view. Ah mean, there's ma Faither trottin' alang there an' barin' his soul tae the wee man through the curtain every week. Confesses whit a big, bad bastard he's been an' how he's faithered the Devil himself, an' the wee man gives him a coupla Hail Marys and sends him oan his way clean as a whistle every time. Big Pape sees wee Sheridan as his ain personal link tae God, the man that'll stand beside him oan Judgement Day an' persuade the Big Yin tae gie him a paira wings an' let him intae heaven. An' Marion MacLeod jist marches intae his hoose an' tells him tae get his arse in gear!'

She stared at him, trying to keep her face taut with outrage.

'Noo, ye canny say it doesnae have its funny side, can ye?' She gave in and laughed. 'Aye, well, mibbe . . .'

'Listen, Marion,' he said gently, 'ye did whit ye could, ye did merr than most folk would dae for Sal. But ye canny take oan a' the cares o' the world. Ye canny look oot for everybody, ye know!'

His arm was round her again, and he pulled her close so that her head rested against his shoulder. She felt his lips touch the side of her forehead and suddenly realising what was happening she raised her head intending to pull back. But she didn't. She would go over that split second for the rest of her life, reliving what had happened and her feelings at that moment. She had made the decision not to pull back.

One gentle kiss on the lips, that's all it was, but it was the first she had ever had, and though later she consoled herself that it was late on a Sunday night when the neighbours would be asleep, deep down she knew that didn't matter. If it had happened in Hampden Park in the middle of the day with hundreds of thousands watching intently she still wouldn't have stopped him, and that was the truth. As Jean MacLeod had been fond of remarking, Granny Mirren and Granda Archie had a lot to answer for where Marion was concerned.

19

A kind of madness took over after that, she was sure that she became slightly insane. The kiss went no further and neither of them mentioned it, but she needed to be near him, to see him, to hear him talk. It was like a hunger that was never satisfied. Without discussing it they had taken a decision not to be alone with each other, but they took every opportunity that presented itself to be in the same company. And even when other people were around it seemed that they were alone within the company, communicating by looks that held a little too long, voices that were a little too gentle.

Looking back, all the signs were there, but she hadn't seen them because it was the time of her madness, when her mind had been elsewhere. Somewhere in the back of her mind she had noted a change in Jimmy, but in the little time she gave to thinking about it, she could always find plausible reasons for it. He had another chest infection a year after the first, and though not as serious, he again took a long time to recover. But he didn't eat properly, his here today, gone tomorrow lifestyle didn't allow for a sensible, regular diet. And it had been a bad winter, everyone had come down with something, and Jimmy had done the same. The breathlessness seemed more apparent, but maybe it had always been there without her taking any particular notice, perhaps it only seemed more apparent simply because it had been brought to her notice. He still went to work when he wasn't off somewhere, and at home there would be that characteristic little cough. Was that worse too, or was she just noticing it more? He didn't seem to be going away as often, but once again did she think that because she wanted him to go away? And God forgive her, she *had* wanted him to go away. She wanted him out of the way because it gave her the freedom to see more of her adoptive family at 9F. No, be honest, Marion. To see Robert Boyle. Maybe that was her only reason for missing Jimmy's deteriorating state of health, she missed it because she was thinking of another man.

In the late fifties there was a growing unease in the yards along the Clyde. After the War foreign competitors in Korea and Germany had been built up, as their governments, unlike successive British governments, invested heavily in shipbuilding. And these new shipyards were built with the demands of modern shipping in mind, whereas the traditional yards on the Clyde had changed little. There were many more welders than riveters it was true, but the yards hadn't kept up in other ways. This meant that waiting lists for ships built on the Clyde were longer than in other countries, and delivery dates were further ahead. With cheaper air travel there was no longer a huge need for the liners, the *Queens* that had made Brown's name famous the world over. There was less demand for naval ships, and orders for holiday cruise liners tailed off. Because of the closure of the Suez Canal oil tankers had to take the long way round instead. The logical progression was that bigger and bigger tankers were wanted, and Brown's couldn't afford to reconstruct the yard to accommodate the bulk carriers the market demanded. Gradually throughout the fifties the Clyde's share of world business declined, and one by one famous shipbuilding names began to go out of business.

To the men in the yards the thought of no shipbuilding on the Clyde was impossible, a kind of innocence rather than arrogance. They built fine ships, they did good work and they were proud of their skills; the notion that a Clyde-built ship might not be sought after simply didn't make any sense. There were frequent strikes, it was the way of the industry.

Industrial relations were abysmal because there was no trust between the men and the management. The rift between the old guard who thought like Pape Boyle, and the new, who sided with Robert, grew ever wider. There was strong resistance to changing working practices, to requests from management to learn new skills, because whatever management had asked of them throughout the entire history of shipbuilding on the Clyde, always turned out badly for the workers. Until the late fifties men were still laid off and had to sign on the dole whenever a ship was completed. They had come a long way to achieve the status of permanent employees, and based on past experience management would use any underhand tactic, any argument, to cheat them. It was clear that they had to keep what they had, the difference of opinion was over how to do that, but it was a strong difference that sprang from their souls.

Likewise up Kilbowie Road things were not going well with Singer's. The company had been the world leader in sewing machine manufacture, but the rest of the world had quickly cottoned on, and there was a build-up of strong competition from within Europe. Somewhat ironically Japan entered the industry upon the direct order of US General Douglas McArthur. After the defeat of Japan in 1945, McArthur decided that instead of producing munitions Japan should manufacture sewing machines, and Singer's would henceforth be banned from exporting to Japan. To make sure the seal had really been set on Singer's, American investment in Japan was to include the company's plans and patents to build up the industry, so that by the late fifties 300 Japanese companies were making over 2 million machines. It was little wonder, given the effects of the emerging competitors and their nationalities, that an oft-heard quip in Clydebank was 'Jist who *did* win the War, then?' But even so there was a stubborn belief that things would improve. This was *Clydebank*, a town that had survived, a town that *would* survive, because the rest of the world knew they produced quality goods, and the rest of the world would stay loyal to them. It was only *right* after all.

Davy's final exams were on at the University. After Easter 1958 the undergraduates stopped learning and started revising for the big event in June. The finals ran over six working days with a weekend break, after which the cauldron had to be entered again. If Davy looked haggard he was at least doing better than some, because there were various ways of cracking under the pressure; taking to the booze, going missing or having nervous breakdowns were common reactions. Davy was doing a double honours degree in English and History, but Marion never doubted for a moment that he might not pass, though she didn't realise till later that her blind confidence could have put more pressure on the boy. And he *was* a boy, even if he was twenty-two years old and had recently grown a passable beard. Because of Marion's determination, Davy Ryan, unlike his former schoolmates, hadn't gone straight into the Clydeside industries, and nothing made a lad grow up faster than the hard life in the yards. A university degree didn't bring maturity, that would come later.

The results were posted on noticeboards within the university and were published in the *Glasgow Herald*, though Davy didn't tell her when. He advertised his double first by coming home as drunk as a lord, throwing up on the stairs and falling in the door when it was opened after he'd tried unsuccessfully to find the keyhole with his key. Once on his feet again he danced her round the lobby then collapsed into a deep sleep mid-foxtrot. Unable to move the snoring dead weight, Marion sent Colin over to 9F for Robert Boyle to help her carry Davy to bed, and it was then, with great glee, that Colin told her that there was a mess all the way up the stairs. Marion got out the mop and bucket and with a good splash of Co-op pine disinfectant set about the stairs. It wasn't her turn, but she could hardly leave that lot to her next-door neighbour. In the meantime Colin and Robert carted Davy off to bed, and the only sense they could get out of him was several renditions of 'Roll Me Over', each one more graphic than the one before.

'Noo, what we havtae decide is whether the daft big lump was drownin' his sorrows or celebratin',' Marion mused, and just at that he appeared once more in the living room, asking if someone could kindly find his duffle coat so that he could go home to the Fifely. Robert persuaded him back to bed, promising to call him as soon as the next Central SMT bus came with his duffle coat.

'Ah'll stay a wee while in case he gets up again,' Robert grinned. 'Will that be OK wi' Jimmy?'

'Jimmy's away,' Marion said quietly.

Robert made no comment, he never did. 'Ah'd like tae stay till mornin', in fact, jist tae see the hangover hit poor auld Davy!'

'Sadistic bugger!' Marion laughed.

'It was a good thing Colin came ower anyway,' he grinned. 'Big Pape an' I were aboot tae murder each other again. Ah don't know if Ah'll be allowed hame again!'

'Whit was it aboot this time, the usual?'

'Aye.'

'Why don't the two o' ye pack it in?' she asked. 'Neither wanno ye can win.'

'He gets oan ma wick, that's why. Tae hear him rattle oan ye'd think he did me a good turn gettin' me intae the yard. He actually thinks Ah should stay there for the rest o' ma life oota some kinda gratitude tae him! It's like he found the golden rivet an' gied it tae me the way he talks aboot gettin' me started as an electrician.'

'Ye've got tae see it frae his side, Robert,' Marion said, settling down in the armchair opposite him at the fire. 'In his day he had tae fight for work every day tae keep his family. Can ye imagine leavin' the hoose in the mornin' no' knowin' if ye'd be able to feed your bairns? That kinda life must mark people, Robert. Tae him gettin' you oota the black squad, an' seein' permanent work comin', must seem like a dream, an' noo that things are gettin' shaky again he must be feelin' angry an' scared.'

'So he takes it oot oan me?' he demanded. 'It's a' ma fault?'

'Naw, of course no'. But ye'd think listenin' tae *you* that the state o' the yards is a' *his* fault!'

'Aye, ye're right, Ah know that. But Christ, Marion, ye see the conditions in Broon's; a' the yards are the same, an' tae hear ma faither ye'd think a secure job was the only important thing in life. There's nae safety, men are injured an' killed a' the time. In Fairfields the other day there was a fireball accident, aboot twenty men burnt, an' the bosses said, "We told them not to smoke, but they will persist."'

'Whit happened?'

'They were workin' wi gas, an' some gases are heavy an' sink tae the floor. Somebody threw doon a Woodbine dout and a fireball ran alang the length o' the boat.'

'But they're *constantly* told no' tae smoke, Robert!'

'That's no' the point, Marion! Whit that means is that men are working in conditions an' wi' materials they know nothin' aboot! They arenae trained, they're jist tellt no' tae smoke! Christ, they're grown men bein' treated like bairns. You know whit the bosses are like, they'd tell us no' tae breathe if they thought it would happen, it's a constant battle in there.'

They sat in silence, staring into the fire.

'An' *we* don't know whit a' that stuff is doin' tae us. Look at that bloody foul asbestos dust. It's everywhere, it gets in your nose, in your mouth, in your hair. They say it's safe, but somethin' that hellish smellin' canny be exactly good for ye, can it?'

'Aye, Ah know, Robert, but your father isnae responsible for a' that, noo, is he?'

'Ah know wan thing though,' he said bitterly, 'he thinks

he did well by keepin' me oota the black squad, but he shoulda kept me oota the yards a' thegither. You kept Davy oota the yards, an' ye'll keep Colin here oot tae, nae matter whit. He coulda done the same for me!'

'But dae ye no' think that's a generation thing, Robert?' she asked gently. 'You and me are the same generation, *we* think like that, but Pape could only think as far as his ain experiences let him, couldn't he? We went tae school, we mibbe didnae get the best education, but it was better than he ever got, it let oor generation see a way oot. Ye're blamin' Pape for things that arenae his fault.'

He looked across at her and smiled. 'Noo you're takin' Pape's problems oan, Marion. If ye dae that ye're finished.' He sighed. 'Anyhow, Ah'm thinkin' seriously o' gettin' oot.'

'Oh?'

'Ah was thinkin'. Ah spend a' week in that place waitin' for the weekends tae get away tae the fresh air. Why dae Ah no' jist go tae the country an' work there? Other people manage it, why no' me?'

'An' be an electrician?'

'Christ, naw! That's the last thing Ah'd dae, Ah *hate* it! Nae matter whit ye dae it comes back tae a coupla wires. A' that work an' every time ye're left wi' a coupla wires! Naw, Ah wis thinkin' o' the Forestry Commission mibbe. Can ye imagine Big Pape's face? Giein' up a trade tae cut doon trees! We'd need tae get wee Sheridan up frae Our Holy Redeemer's tae gie him the Last Rites!' The three of them laughed. 'Ach,' he said, 'we'll see. It's only an idea.'

Colin sat listening intently throughout as the conversation ran back and forth. It emerged that all those years ago, as she waited for Tommy MacLeod at the junction of Kilbowie Road and Second Avenue every night, Robert waited for Pape further up the hill at Crown Avenue. There they were waiting a few hundred yards apart at the same time, and neither knowing about it. And as Marion had gone up the hill to and from Radnor Park School every day with the

Protestant children, Robert had passed going down to St Stephen's with the Catholic children. On the night of the Blitz he had been in the Bank Cinema near North Elgin Street watching a film called *Maryland*, while Marion was in the La Scala watching Shirley Temple singing 'On the Good Ship Lollipop'. They had likely passed each other on the hill on the way home to be bombed. Later she had spent many hours trapped under the rubble and so had he, but unlike Marion MacLeod, Robert Boyle had been unconscious throughout.

'It was like the light had gone oot an' when it came oan again Ah wis in hospital.'

'Ah was conscious a lot in the dark,' Marion said. 'It took them a long time tae find me.'

'That must have been hellish, hen.'

'Aye, but Ah had –' she had been about to say 'my mother tae talk tae', but instead she said 'folk tae talk tae an' that kept me goin'.' She had never doubted hearing Jean's voice coaxing and nagging her into staying alive, but she had never told anyone about it either.

'Ah think that's why Ah hate bein' caught in any way,' she smiled. 'Ah hate things that are too tight, places that are too wee.'

'Is that why ye always unpin your hair as soon as ye get oota the yard gates?'

She looked up quickly. 'Ye noticed that, did ye?' she asked.

'Aye, Ah watch ye dae it every time. Ye take the pins oot then ye shake it free an' run your fingers through it. An' ye look as if ye'd taken aff a pair o' tight shoes!'

Colin, sitting on the fireside rug at his mother's feet, was beginning to nod off, so she used that as a way of breaking the conversation.

'My God, look at the time! Eleven o'clock!'

Robert took the hint and made a tactful withdrawal. 'Ah think Davy's oot for the night,' he grinned. 'Ask him in the mornin' if he'd mind giein' me the words o' that song he was singin'. He had a few verses there Ah'd never heard afore!'

'Listen, Robert, Ah'm really grateful for your help. Ah've ruined your night tae.'

'Naw, Marion,' he said softly, 'ye've made it. And see that long hair o' yours? Don't ever cut it. It's really, really . . . *braw*!' he said eventually. As she closed the door she laughed quietly to herself. Why did Scotsmen have trouble with certain words, she wondered. 'Beautiful', was one, for instance, and 'Love' was another.

Seeing Davy's name in the *Glasgow Herald*, 'the posh people's paper', was one of the highlights of Marion's life. It had happened, it had really happened, and he brought home two tickets for the graduation ceremony in the university's Bute Hall. He nodded towards the bedroom, where Jimmy had once again taken up residence, and said he could probably get another ticket. He and Marion looked at each other. 'Better no', son,' she said, 'he might no' be here by the end o' June.'

On the day, Marion and Colin went along to Gilmorehill in their best clothes, thanks to the blessed divi once again. Davy was sitting with the other 300 or so graduates in the front rows, all of them wearing black gowns. The relatives sat behind, and as each name was called in alphabetical order by the Dean of Faculty, the graduate would get up and step onto the stage from the right. It was a blistering hot day and Ryan being far down they thought it would take a long time to get to him, but there weren't many double firsts, and he was among them. They heard his name called, watched him shake hands with the Vice Chancellor, Sir Hector Hetherington, take his cap and scroll and exit from the left. It seemed so simple, so easy! No trumpets sounded a fanfare, no fireworks exploded in the sky, yet here was Davy Ryan of the Fifely, via Second Avenue and North Elgin Street, an educated man, and not just educated, but extra educated!

After the ceremony of the caps and scrolls was over, Davy came to find them, holding by the hand a blonde girl with blue eyes and a friendly smile. She too wore a gown with the English faculty's purple hood, the same as Davy.

'Marion, Colin,' he said, blushing furiously, 'this is Eileen. Eileen Callaghan.'

'Ah, well,' Marion thought, 'Father Sheridan *will* be pleased!'

Eileen Callaghan shook hands with both of them.

'I'm so pleased to meet you at last,' she said, 'I've heard a lot about you from David.'

'Well, you've got us beaten,' Marion replied, staring meaningfully at Davy, 'we haven't heard a word about you!'

The girl laughed out loud. 'That's what I thought!' she said. 'Look, would you mind if I introduced you to my parents?'

'No, no, that would be nice,' Marion smiled.

Eileen ran off, leaving Davy even redder than before.

'You big swine, Davy Ryan, or should I say *David*?' Marion seethed at him. 'You never told us anythin' aboot this! So it wisnae always the library kept ye busy, then?'

He was saved by Eileen and her parents, Dr and Mrs Francis Callaghan from Bearsden; in other words, rich folk, and it showed. As discreetly as possible Marion took in the quietly expensive clothes, Mrs Callaghan's jewellery, and most of all, their impeccably friendly manner. The only rich people she had ever seen were the bosses of the shipyards, but it was immediately obvious that the Callaghans were a different breed; they seemed genuinely decent people.

'Mrs Ryan, I'm Frank, my wife is Veronica. We've been dying to meet you, mainly because this lad here couldn't find the words to describe you.'

'I could find the words to describe him easily enough!' Marion replied.

'Well, he said you were like his mother, and that's clearly not true because you *must* be younger than him! And he said you were his sister, *nearly*, so as you can imagine, we are dying to find out. Would you please join us for lunch?'

Marion and Colin were taken to the Grosvenor at Central Station. It was the first time they had ever been in any restaurant, let alone a high-class one, but no MacLeod had ever been knocked off his or her stride and Marion was determined that no Ryan would be either. And it wasn't too difficult; you just let the Callaghans pick up whichever piece of cutlery was the right one and then did the same. They treated her with great respect, telling her how much they admired what she had done for David, and though she was basking in their admiration, she wondered how long the secretive big swine had known these pleasant people without saying a word to her about them, about the lovely Eileen in particular. She knew why of course. Scratch a double first, she smiled, and you'll still find a Scotsman underneath just like all the rest.

Miss Cairns was more respectful these days. Well, when you had a double Honours graduate in the family you deserved some respect, especially as Miss Cairns couldn't be sure that one day she wouldn't have Davy Ryan, alias Roger the Lodger, as her headmaster.

'The reason I asked to see you, Mrs Ryan, is that Colin is coming up to his Qualifying Exam, and we wondered what you had in mind for him.'

Marion waited. She had no idea where this was leading. She had in mind that Colin would pass; what else?

'You see, he is a very bright boy.'

'It runs in the family.'

'Yes, well. What we thought was that if you think it's a good idea he could take a few of the entrance exams for the bigger schools, like Allan Glen's or Glasgow Academy.'

'You mean fee-paying schools, Miss Cairns?'

'Yes, Mrs Ryan, that's why I wanted to have this chat. You see, I'm sure he would do well and be offered a scholarship, but then there are other considerations. There would be some parental contribution, and the uniform, travelling expenses, that kind of thing.'

'Oh, I see! Miss Cairns, if you wanted to know if Mr Ryan and I could afford to send Colin to a fee-paying school, you only had to ask. My late father was a strong Socialist, Miss Cairns, so that's something we'd have to think about. But there would be no problem about the extras if Colin passed the scholarship exams.'

On the way home she went back over her performance. The strong Socialist in the family had been Granny Kate, but hopefully the old battler would've understood why Tommy MacLeod had been given the credit. No she wouldn't, but it was too late to go back and change it now. 'My father' would somehow have sounded more acceptable to a conventional creature like Miss Cairns than 'my Granny', though Kate would have had a few words to say about that too. 'We would be perfectly willing to pay,' she had said. Oh God! Always in with both feet! Jimmy wasn't in the best of health, and what work was still around for her was curtailed by spells of looking after him. Not that she grudged it, of course. Half of Big Kenny's money had gone but, looked at another way, half of it was still there. The question was, how long would it last, given Jimmy's increasingly frequent illnesses when she had to take time off work to nurse him, plus those 'extras' for Colin? She had made sure Davy had his education, and if she was any judge he and Eileen would be marrying soon, so there would be no income from there. But if she had supported Davy, she would sure as hell support her own son, she decided. Whatever it took, she would find. But when did it end, this constantly climbing one mountain only to find another, bigger one behind it?

Maggie was back in hospital. It was the second time in less than six months. If possible she looked thinner lying against the pillows, her cheeks shiny red.

'These sheets are spotless,' Marion commented wryly for something to say. 'Ye didnae get up an' wash them yersel', did ye, Maggie?'

'Oh haud your wheesht! Ye canny get rid o' it, can ye? That Tommy MacLeod smart patter.'

'Well, Ah canny let the wee man doon, Maggie, just because he's no' here disnae mean his point o' view should be overlooked!'

'How's the boy?'

'He's fine. He wants tae see ye.'

'Tell him naw.'

'Well it's up tae you, but Ah think ye're wrong. Whatever he sees canny be as bad as he's imaginin', an' though Ah have nae idea why, the wean is awfy fond o' ye.'

Auld Maggie made a 'harumph' sound. 'Is he daein' well at the school?'

'Aye, fine. Better than fine. They want him tae sit tests for Allan Glen's or Glasgow Academy, but Ah'm no' sure.'

'Ye sayin' oor Colin canny dae it?' Maggie demanded, outraged.

'Oh he can dae it a' right. Ah'm no sure, though. Ah don't believe in fee-payin' schools.'

'Away tae hell! Ah know where *that* comes frae, that's Kate MacLeod talkin'!'

'An' whit if it is?'

'Look, the boy won't get in because he's got money, he'll no buy his way in. He's a clever laddie, no' some daft toff wi' money. He's got brains. Of coorse ye'll let him go! You've got your Uncle Kenny's money, haven't ye?'

After visiting hour Marion was stopped and told that the doctor wanted a word. As Marion was her nearest and only relative apart from Colin, Maggie had given her as next of kin. The outlook wasn't good, the chap in the white coat had said, Maggie's heart rhythm had been irregular for some time now, a common occurrence in patients with rheumatic heart disease, and adjusting her digitalis to strengthen her heartbeat had only had a limited, short-term effect.

'Can't you operate?'

'No, we can't. Cardiac surgery is making headway, but your aunt's condition is very advanced. It would mean replacing both the mitral and aortic valves in the heart, and her heart is too badly damaged for that to produce any improvement. And besides, her general condition isn't good. She wouldn't survive surgery even if it were a possibility.'

'So are you saying she's . . . dying?'

'I'm afraid the prognosis isn't good. She could go at any time.'

Well now, there was a turn-up for the books. First you find out that Auld Maggie has a heart, and then you're told it's about to give out. She would need time to think about this one, not least about how she'd tell Colin. But she didn't get it. At 3 o'clock the next morning there was a knock at the door and a big policeman stood there with some sad news.

20

It rained heavily all day, but Auntie Maggie's funeral was a triumph of neatness and decorum, she had arranged it that way well in advance. The local minister had already been approached and the form of the service agreed; Maggie had left nothing to chance or to the whim of her niece. Sitting in the church listening to him eulogizing Maggie, Marion had to admit that the old woman had had the last laugh. She was, apparently, 'the beloved aunt of the family, who had kept them going after the terrible events of the War. It was typical of her that she had taken into her home and raised not only her orphaned niece, but David, an unrelated orphaned boy.' Marion smiled as she remembered telling Auld Maggie all those years ago that people would think her a saint for letting her and Davy live at Campbell Street when they came out of hospital. Well, she had her reward now all right. And there was nothing that could be said, either, that was the beauty of Maggie's victory; without standing up and asking if the minister was at the right funeral, and that did cross Marion's mind, it was game, set and match to Maggie. Apart from the minister, Marion, Colin and Davy, there was no one there who had actually known Maggie. Agnes and Pape Boyle had turned up with Robert for Marion and Colin's sake, as had Sal and Tony Gallagher – at least she had the satisfaction of 'that Sal Devlin' seeing Maggie off! Despite all her years at Singer's there was not one ex-workmate. 'Ye see?' Marion thought. 'If it wasnae for me, Maggie, there would be naebody here but the minister, an' by the way he's wafflin' oan, he didnae *know* ye!' The only genuine mourner, the only one who grieved, was Colin.

As Maggie was buried at Dalnottar, Marion's mind was on the nearby memoral marking the mass grave of unknown, unclaimed dead of the Blitz, and after the service she took Colin to place flowers there for their family. She had come here before on her own, but she couldn't really connect it with the MacLeods; to her, if they were anywhere, it was in the Holy City, or at least the Holy City that existed still in her mind, because little of it remained in reality. Maybe if there had been some identifiable piece of grass that she knew for sure they lay under she might have felt something. In the distance she saw the Boyles at the grave of their children and almost felt a pang of envy. Agnes and Pape came here often, she knew, tidying up the grave, placing fresh flowers, talking to the children they knew lay there, whereas she could be standing on top of, or behind, or in front of what had been her Ma, her Da, her grandparents, great-grandparents, her brothers and –. But there was no 'and', because she couldn't say 'her sister'; no one knew what had become of Frances or where she lay. It had been in the back of her mind all these years, wondering, hoping she might meet someone who could take Frances and Marek's movements that night a step further on. At one point she had thought of trying to contact Marek, but even if he had survived the War, Poland was sewn up as tightly as the other Iron Curtain countries and there was nothing she could do about that. 'Maybe wan day,' she thought. 'Christ, my life has been full o' maybe wan days!'

After leaving the cemetery they went to the Boulevard Hotel for the traditional steak pie and ham spread, courtesy of Maggie's insurance policies. There were two insurance policies, one with the Co-op, naturally, and the other with the City of Glasgow, and between them they covered the funeral expenses with a good bit to spare.

'She was a good wee wumman,' Sal said gravely.

Marion looked around to make sure Colin was out of

earshot. 'Away tae hell, Sal!' she said. 'She was a thrawn auld bugger a' her days!'

Sal covered her mouth with her hand and laughed. 'Aye, but ye've got tae say somethin', haven't ye?'

'Ah see ye've brought Big Tony. He's no' touched a drop, either. Whit's brought this oan, Sal?'

'Well, Marion, that's a story! Ye know that wee priest frae Our Holy Redeemer's, wee Sheridan?'

Marion nodded.

'Well, a while back he knocked at the door an' in he comes. Big Tony was lyin' oan the couch, spark oot as usual, an' the wee man, Sheridan Ah mean, he grabs him an' heaves him ontae the floor withoot a word. The big fella jist lay there, so the wee priest gives him such a kick up the arse it near lifted him back ontae the couch again! 'Coorse that puts Big Tony intae fightin' mood, but before he can dae merr than roar like a bull, wee Father Sheridan belts him wan oan the nose! The blood was everywhere, an' Father Sheridan says tae him, "Don't you dare make a mess of that carpet, Gallagher!" an' he frogmarches Tony tae the bathroom an' makes him wash an' shave, an' a' the time he's shouting at him, tellin' him whit a big toerag he is. Me an' the bairns were standin' aboot wi' oor mouths hangin' open like goldfish. If we as much as whispered Tony would gie us the back o' his hand, an' there's that wee man orderin' him aboot!'

'An' that's a' it took?' Marion asked doubtfully.

'Naw, naw. The wee man had him doon at the chapel every night an' sent him oan retreats every weekend, seems he spent a' his time oan his knees prayin', an' that, an' being chanted at. He's no' touched a drop since, terrified o' wee Sheridan, he is. Who'd have thought it? He's such a mild wee man, no' a bad looker for a priest, either, is he?'

'Noo, Sal, you wouldnae!'

Sal doubled over laughing. 'Och, naw! Ma tea an' currant bun days are well ower, but if Ah had known the wee man was like that a few years ago, who knows? It would've been somethin' different, wouldn't it? A priest, Ah mean. Ah wonder if Big Tony would've been as handy wi' the poker then? There's only wan thing,' she continued, nodding towards her sober spouse. 'Look at him.' Big Tony was sitting at a table by the window on his own, his lips moving.

'What's he sayin'?' Marion asked.

'The rosary,' Sal said. 'The big clown's got religion noo! It's God this an' God that! Prays for everythin', he's likely seen a fly crawlin' up the windae there, or a bus goin' doon the Boulevard. Sometimes Ah think the booze was better, Ah canny go a' this prayin'!'

That night, when they were alone in the house together, Marion talked to Colin, conscious that he was hurting. She couldn't understand his devotion to Maggie, but there it was. Somehow he had reached something in the old woman that no one else had ever reached – except his Granda Tommy, of course, and he had never known it. She told him that Maggie had left him all her money, although they still didn't know how much it would amount to. Colin shrugged; he had no interest in the money. She already knew that he had mixed feelings about taking the exams for 'the posh schools', so she told him that Maggie had spoken the night before she died of her confidence that he would pass, and that he should go – all of it heavily edited though, being accustomed to discussions between Marion and Maggie, the boy probably replaced the missing comments.

'What Ah was thinkin', Colin,' she said, 'was that ye could use Auntie Maggie's money for things ye'll need at the school. What d'ye think?'

Colin shrugged again. He was sitting on the floor at her feet, staring into the fire. 'Do you think I could be a doctor?' he asked.

'Ye can be anythin' ye want, Colin,' she said, sitting forward and running her hand through his hair.

'I was thinkin',' he said, 'that if I could be a doctor I could help people who had the same illness as Auntie Maggie.' He looked up at her, his eyes brimming with tears that he was determined not to shed. 'Then it would be like helpin' her, wouldn't it?'

Christ! Maggie inspiring anyone! 'Aye,' she replied softly, 'that would be a good idea. She'd have liked that, son.'

'Did you really no' like her, Mum?'

How to answer that one? 'Och, Colin, it was just oor way,' she replied diplomatically. 'Auntie Maggie an' me liked tae argue, but she was family, wasn't she?' A half lie, but it had made him smile anyway, and wherever Maggie was, Marion had no doubt it had made her smile too. 'I had ma fingers crossed behind ma back!' she said to herself, and to Maggie.

With Maggie's day as the centre of attention over, all that was left was to clear out her house. Marion didn't want Colin to be there, so Robert Boyle offered to take him away fishing for the weekend instead, while his mother and Agnes carried out the last task. Before they left she asked her son if there was anything from Auntie Maggie's house that he might like. He thought for a moment. 'The clock,' he replied.

'Ye mean the clock that strikes every half-hour, Colin? *That* clock?'

'Uhuh, the big one. I like the sound of it, it's kinda friendly, and it'll be like havin' a wee bit of Auntie Maggie with us, won't it?'

She had never cleared out a house before, but she had heard plenty of stories of how heartbreaking it could be. She had already decided that Maggie's clothes would go to the Red Cross. 'That shouldnae be hard,' she thought wryly, 'half a dozen pinnies, a' the same!' Agnes could have what she wanted of the lino and the carpets, and the rest would be sold on to the shop down the road that specialised in secondhand household goods. The only two things she wanted were Iain's framed portrait of Jean and Tommy, and, well *she* didn't want it, but Colin did, that clock!

247

'Look at it!' she said to Agnes. 'A' my life Ah've hated the damn thing, Ah've fantasized aboot puttin' a hammer through it. It's the same as the wan in *High Noon*, Ah hoped the baddies would leave Gary Cooper alane an' shoot it insteed, an' it's the wan thing Colin wants! Ah'm tellin' ye, the auld besom will be hingin' aboot listenin' tae this an' laughin' hersel' silly. Mind ye, it would be the first time for that, when ye think o' it.'

'Makes ye think though, Marion,' Agnes said. 'Here we are clearin' away a' the life she had. Sad, intit? Ah widnae like tae think o' anybody goin' through ma things like this, but it'll come wan day!'

'The thing that's sad is that she didnae have a life, Agnes. Whit Ah'd really like tae find is some kinda scandal. Y'know, passionate love letters frae the minister, some bright red underwear ye could blow through. Somethin' that'd prove the auld misery was human efter a'!'

They finished the task and struggled homewards carrying the Gingerbread clock, and Marion invited Agnes in for a cup of tea. 'Marion, there's somethin' Ah've been meanin' tae say tae ye,' Agnes said uneasily, staring at the spoon as she stirred her tea. 'Ye can tell me tae mind ma ain business if ye like, but Ah hope ye won't be too offended.'

Marion had no idea what was coming. Had she inadvertently called Mr Boyle 'Pape' perhaps?

'It's aboot you an' oor Robert, hen. Ah know the two o' ye are auld enough tae know whit ye're daein', an' he's a' the man he'll ever be, but he's still ma son an' Ah don't like tae see him bein' hurt.'

'Agnes, Ah have nae idea whit the hell ye're oan aboot!' Marion protested. 'There's nae "you an' oor Robert", Ah'm a married wumman!'

'That's whit Ah mean, hen,' Agnes continued. 'We a' know ye have an awfy time wi' Jimmy, it canny be easy him leavin' ye a' the time for his fancy wumman, but –'

Marion drew herself up for battle. 'Noo, wait you a

248

minute!' she said firmly. 'Let me set ye straight aboot a few things here. Ma Jimmy has *nae* fancy wumman an' he disnae "leave me" as you put it! Ma Jimmy has an illness frae his days in the War, an' every noo an' then he has to go away because o' it.' She was making it up as she went along, but all the same she was quite pleased with the way it was turning out and she hoped her luck would hold. 'Jist because he gets oan wi things when he can an' disnae go aroond complainin' an' broadcastin' his business tae the world, he gets this kinda muck thrown at him!'

'Ah didnae –' Agnes protested, but Marion lifted her hand to silence her.

'An' as for your Robert, Ah can assure you that there's nothin' goin' oan. Any time he's been here it's been when Colin, Davy or Jimmy are here tae.' She swallowed hard. 'He's never wance said a word tae me, never laid a finger oan me, an' *you* should have merr respect no' only for me, but for your ain son!'

'Marion,' Agnes said kindly, 'Ah can see the way he looks at ye!'

'Well, mibbe ye should get yersel' a pair o' specs, Agnes, because ye're seein' things that arenae there! Noo Ah'm grateful for your help at Maggie's the night, but if ye don't mind, it's been a long day an' Ah'd like tae get tae ma bed.'

In the darkness of her bedroom she felt her face redden. She had acted in character, in the character she had perfected on the outside, at any rate. Suddenly thrust into the adult world after the Blitz, she had decided that attack was the best means of defence; her way of coping was to get the first blow in and hope that it would discourage the opposition. Everyone had their own way. Robert for instance joked and told stories to keep the world at bay, Marion attacked; even when she didn't really know what she would do next, it at least bought time to think. But she felt bad about attacking Agnes, and worse about lying to her. And she realised how stupid she had been. There *was* something between her and Robert. It hadn't gone beyond that single kiss, but it was there and they both knew it; she had stupidly gone along with it hoping that no one else noticed. And now she had no idea where she was or what to do about it, it must have been heading somewhere, no use kidding herself that it wasn't. There would be no point in pretending the conversation between herself and Agnes hadn't taken place, now she would have to keep up the pretence for ever.

And how was she to let the situation with Robert continue, or not continue, without telling him about his mother's remarks? Knowing him he would be furious and round on Agnes, and she didn't deserve that. She had only been looking out for her son, and however old he was he was still her son, just as Colin would always be Marion's. But the bubble had burst, she realised that; there would be no more secret shared glances, no more quiet, seemingly innocent words, because she would feel everyone's eyes watching, even if they weren't. The only thing that was of any value was spoiled and sordid.

At work the next day Agnes tried to make amends. 'Ah didnae know about Jimmy,' she said, and her sincere tone panicked Marion even more. Instead of welcoming the olive branch it made her feel worse about her deceptions and she reacted aggressively. 'Ah have nae intention o' discussin' ma business wi ye, if ye don't mind!' she retorted, and walked off in the opposite direction. Somewhere, if Gerry Sheridan and his lot were halfway right, there would be a big bloke with wings holding a book and a quill pen and keeping score. There was the poor minister who brought her and Davy the bad news about their families. He got screamed at and his Bible thrown against the wall. Now that *must* be a strike against her. And she had failed poor Jimmy. She had no idea how or what she *should've* done instead, but ignorance was no excuse; she had failed him. Another strike. There was that business with the Catholic hierarchy over Davy's problems with the Maths teacher, and Father Gerry Sheridan himself being told to 'get his arse in gear' over Sal and Big Tony. She wasn't sure about the fairness or otherwise of the last one in particular, but she suspected the bloke with the wings wouldn't give her extra points for either. And now poor Agnes Boyle, who had shown her nothing but kindness and concern, had been lied to and made to feel bad and then snubbed. All that had been accomplished since she was eleven years old, in seventeen years to be exact. When the trumpet finally sounded, she thought, she might as well trot on downwards instead of wasting her energy climbing the steps and knocking at the pearly gates on the off chance. But there were more immediate problems to be faced. Robert. How was she to deal with Robert?

21

But fate had its own schedule to keep, and it was to overtake the piffling little problems of a lovestruck housewife and mother in Clydebank. In Brown's the next day there was an accident that would change the lives of many people and end the lives of four. In the West Yard, where the berths were smaller than anywhere else, a ship was under construction. Because it was longer than the berth, the cranes wouldn't reach, so a temporary block and tackle had been cobbled together. It wasn't the first time such an arrangement had been made, and regardless of what was to happen that day, it wouldn't be the last. The makeshift crane was lifting a load from the dockside up and into the shell and something gave way. The arm broke free and swept across the side of the ship, where a team of painters was working from scaffolding. The scaffolding, caught by the swinging arm, was demolished like a matchstick construction. With a series of sickening crunches the scaffolding collapsed into the basin, together with the men who had been working on it. Four men died. The workers, as tradition dictated, knocked off for the day, but it rapidly became clear that the accident was a turning point for Robert Boyle in particular.

Going home on the bus that day the faces of the Brown's workers showed their shock, but none more so than Robert. Muted farewells were taken as the bus stopped and passengers got off, with the usual 'See ye the morra.' To everyone though, Rab the Rhymer replied tersely, 'No' me, ye'll no'.' A few hours later he arrived at Marion's door, the first time they had spoken to each other since the night he had brought Colin home.

'Can Ah ask a favour?' he said, his voice as agitated as his expression and the scars in his face bright red. 'Is it a' right if Ah stay here the night? Ah canny go hame,' he hurried on, 'Ah'm off the morra, Ah'm no' goin' back tae the yard, an' me an' that big bastard ower the road will kill each other if we're under the same roof!'

It seemed that Robert and Pape had argued as usual, only this time the events in the yard had added a new, deeper dimension; the deaths of the hapless painters had been the last straw.

Inside Marion's living room he paced back and forth. 'He disnae see it! D'ye believe that? He disnae see it! They men shouldnae have been workin' like that, it wasnae safe, anybody coulda seen it! An' still naebody will dae anythin' aboot it. They'll go back tae work in the mornin' an' argue ower a ha'penny here or there, but naebody will dae anythin' aboot the way they're treated. Ah said tae him that Ah wasnae goin' back, that Ah was finished, an' he said Ah was a coward! Gied me a' that crap aboot the yards bein' a man's work, an' Ah said it wasnae *this* man's work any merr. "Ye're no' a real man," he said, "an' ye're nae son o' mine." He says Ah should be grateful tae have a job, that he pulled a lotta strings tae get me intae the yard! Ah said tae him, "Nae doubt some clown thought they men should be grateful tae, but look at them, they're *deid* for Chrissake!"'

'An' ye're really no' goin' back, Robert?'

'Naw, Ah'm no', Marion,' he said wearily, sitting down and lighting a cigarette. 'Ah've been thinkin' o' gettin' oot for a while, an' this has decided me. The yards will be finished in ten years, daft auld buggers like ma faither won't believe that, but it's true. An' good bloody riddance tae, as far as Ah'm concerned!'

They sat in heavy silence for a few minutes. She tried to think of a way to lighten the atmosphere.

'Can Ah ask ye somethin', Robert?' she said. 'Since Ah was a wee lassie Ah've thought your Da shoulda been called Brock instead o' Pape.'

'Aye,' he chuckled. 'Pigswill! Right enough, suits the big bastard tae a T!'

'Naw! No' that! Because he looks like a badger!'

'You mean whit you mean, Marion,' he grinned wryly, 'an' Ah'll mean whit Ah mean!' He laughed for a moment and then was suddenly serious. 'Know whit he said tae me wance?' he said quietly. 'We were goin' at it hammer an' tongs as usual, an' he said, "Four bairns we had, an' *you* had tae be the wan that survived."'

'C'mon noo, Robert,' she said gently, 'ye were arguin'! The two o' ye say awfy things when ye get started, ye know that. Ah've heard some o' them, remember!'

'Aye, but he still said it,' Robert replied solemnly, then just as suddenly he recovered his sense of humour. 'Ah got ma ain back though,' he chuckled, blowing out a long, slow stream of tobacco smoke. 'Ah said, "Aye, but jist think, Da, the rest might a' have been like me, *worse* than me mibbe, then where would ye be?"'

Marion laughed with him, but she ached to put her arms around him. For all his bravado, for all the jokes and stories Rab the Rhymer told, she had always known that the front he presented to the world was a carefully crafted and very thin shell. Underneath it lay the real Robert, a quiet, sensitive man who could be easily hurt. Sensing that a dangerous intimacy was building up between them she changed the subject abruptly.

'Whit will ye dae noo then, Robert?' she asked almost brightly.

'Take aff, Ah suppose,' he replied. 'When auld Pigswill's away tae work in the mornin' Ah'll go ower an' get ma bike an' head aff somewhere. Ah'll get a job o' some sort. That's if it's a' right for me tae stay here, Marion? Jist say if it isnae.'

'Naw, son, don't worry,' she replied, 'ye're welcome tae

stay here. Davy's at his girlfriend's hoose, ye can have his bed.' An' damn the gossips! she decided.

That long night, as she lay in bed with Jimmy wheezing beside her, all she could think of was Robert only yards away. She felt ashamed of herself, but she couldn't help what she was feeling. In at least four households in the town families would be unable to sleep because of their grief and shock, yet all she could think of as she lay awake was that if Jimmy hadn't been there, Robert might not have lain alone.

Davy had been offered the chance to do postgraduate research at Oxford University. He had apparently dropped the idea of becoming a schoolteacher and wanted instead to be a university lecturer. 'Damn!' Marion said, teasing him. 'Ah really wanted ye tae be Miss Cairns' headmaster. Could ye no' dae that for a wee while, then move on tae Oxford?'

Davy tried to smile but he was finding it tough going. There was something else. He wanted to marry Eileen.

'An' that's it, is it?' Marion laughed. 'That's whit the long face is for? Well, whit's the problem, Davy, will her folks no' let ye?'

'I feel bad about it, Marion,' he replied, 'and you've every right to be annoyed. I've told Eileen we should put it off for a couple of years and pay you back.'

Marion was totally lost. 'Pay me back? For whit, Davy?'

'For everything you've done for me, of course!'

She stared at him, wondering when he'd start making sense. 'D'ye think ye could go ower that again, son? Ah don't have a clue whit ye're goin' oan aboot!'

'Without you I'd have gone into the yards like all the rest, Marion,' he began.

'Aye, so far Ah'm wi' ye. And?'

'Well, you made a lot of sacrifices, and here I am when I could be earning money to help out and pay you back, and I'm going off and getting married.'

All she felt was rage. 'Well, by Christ, Davy Ryan,' she

said savagely, 'Ah've brought ye up, but Ah've done a bad job o' it, haven't Ah? A' Ah did was gie ye what ye'd been cheated o', Davy, Ah gave ye the chance tae be educated. That was your *right*, it wasnae somethin' ye didnae deserve! Is that a' Ah managed tae get through tae ye, an' you a big clever laddie, that Ah had tae be paid back for giein' ye whit shoulda been yours tae start wi'?'

'But, Marion, you had the same right, yet you gave it up for me. That isn't fair!'

'Away tae hell, Davy Ryan! That's jist how things worked oot, you had nae merr control ower that than me. Ah had Jimmy, an' then Ah had Colin tae, Ah couldnae go tae school. Whit was Ah supposed tae dae? Stop you as well?'

'Don't be angry, Marion, please.'

'Aye, Ah bloody will be angry, Davy Ryan! Ye should never, *never*, be grateful for your rights, an' you should've known better than tae think Ah expected ye tae work for me. Ah mean, did ye have a figure in mind like, or a time? Did ye have it in mind tae work for say two years an' gie me every penny? Dae ye know whit they call that, Davy? They call it slavery! By Christ, ye might have your two degrees, son, but for a' your learnin' you're a daft big bugger!'

The wedding between Davy and Eileen took place in the summer of 1959, in a service that bore all the hallmarks of a favoured union of two Catholics. There was so much standing up, kneeling and sitting down to be repeated that Marion wondered if they were going for some record, and it seemed that little bits of business were being dreamed up as the service went on to make it go on longer. What was it with the Catholic Church? Did all this make them extra-married or something? And one priest wasn't enough; Father Sheridan, as Davy's parish priest, had been invited to join in with Eileen's parish priest. After what seemed like for ever the happy couple made their regal way down the aisle, with six wee girls in matching candy-floss dresses throwing rose petals before them. 'Some poor wee wumman will have tae sweep each an' every wan o' them up in the mornin'!' Marion mused.

Outside the church the various groups were being assembled for the photographer, and Marion found herself beside Father Sheridan.

'Well, ye made a meal oota that!' she said tartly.

'Yes, you got the full works to be sure,' he said, looking round to make sure no one could overhear. 'That was a full Nuptial Mass with Papal Blessing. Very impressive, but you couldn't do too many or you'd collapse with exhaustion, I'm telling you!'

'Was there nothin' else ye could think up? A quick tap dance doon the aisle scatterin' incense mibbe, or a coupla back flips?'

'Damn!' he said. 'I never thought of that! So we still don't have you converted, then, Marion?'

'Merr chance o' convertin' me tae gas!' she retorted.

He smiled at Colin who was standing at his mother's side. 'I haven't seen this young man in the congregation,' he said slyly.

'Naw, Ah had some control ower this wan,' Marion replied. 'He's jist aboot tae go tae Allan Glen's, we got the news yesterday.'

'Congratulations!' he said to Colin. 'But he could've gone to St Aloysius College you know,' he said, teasing her.

'Aye, only he got lucky!'

'Seen much of your friend Mrs Gallagher?'

'Noo, if you're expectin' some kinda thanks –'

'Heaven forefend, Mrs Ryan,' he said. 'The very idea! I just wondered how things were.'

'As far as Ah hear you'll know merr aboot that than me. Seems Big Tony's swapped wan obsession for another,' Marion grinned. 'Never oota the chapel these days.'

'Yes, very true. I have to be down there sharpish or he'd take over confessions for me. I have this recurring nightmare that I'll arrive to say mass one day and Father Gallagher will have it all in hand already!'

'Ach well, that's whit ye get for savin' souls, eh, Father Sheridan? Part o' the cross ye have tae bear as they say!'

'One day, Marion Ryan, you will go to the bad fire for remarks like that, you know that, don't you?'

'Aye, but it'll be the atheist hell, an' that's no' so bad. Noo ye'd better get your arse in gear, they want ye ower there in your nice wee frock for a photo with the happy couple!'

With Eileen being the only daughter of Frank and Veronica no expense was spared. The reception was held in the Callaghan home in Bearsden, a few miles down the road from the Fifely but, in terms of good living, a million years away. Marion had never seen a house like it, and neither had Colin. 'It's like a castle!' he whispered. They had managed to get Jimmy along to the wedding, the first time in living memory that they had been out as a family. It suddenly struck her that she was having to take his arm not as his wife so much as to steady him, as though he was an old man, when he was only in his mid thirties. When she looked at him the pallor of his face shocked her, and she noticed a slight blue tinge around his mouth. How had she missed that? She knew how, of course, because her mind had been elsewhere.

Robert had been gone for nearly a year. He was working with the Forestry Commission on Loch Lomondside, and not seeing him every day she began to understand why Agnes had noticed the connection between them. The enormous gap he had left in her life proved that once there must have been something there, and poor Agnes had seen it and been savaged for it. Davy had asked about inviting Agnes and Pape to the wedding, but Marion had stopped him. The truth was that she avoided them these days out of shame over how she had treated Robert's mother, though she knew that as far as Agnes was concerned, her coolness was the result of her comments, especially about Jimmy. Agnes had tried to make amends several times, but Marion had cut her dead. It was the only way she could remain in control, by keeping other people at arm's length. If she had let Agnes closer she would have been in a position to know where Robert was and what he was doing, and that was a bad idea, because she wanted to know so badly and had no confidence that she wouldn't do something stupid. Every now and again he would come back to Langfaulds Crescent to see his mother, and Marion would immediately leave her home and take a bus into town. Whether he came to her door or not while she was out she didn't know, and that was how it would have to stay. He sent postcards to Colin, and she read the few words on them over and over again, desperate for some contact at a controllable distance, so what might she do if he were to appear in front of her?

It was Frank Callaghan who noticed just how ill Jimmy was. The wedding reception was in full swing, with Davy's pals from the university making up for the lack of guests from his side. She sat with Jimmy, making as much conversation as she could and watching for signs that he had had enough, and all the time she kept thinking that he was too young to be looked after like this. Frank asked her to dance, and as they twirled around the floor, he broached the subject. Was Mr Ryan receiving any treatment? How long had he been ill? Marion's replies were vague, she had long regarded Jimmy as a sick man, but not in a medical way, and now here was this kindly doctor obviously thinking he was an invalid. She glanced across at him and realised that he was. It was like a confirmation of something that she had known somewhere in her mind, but it was still a shock. Years later she would think back to that moment and feel the shock all over again, and the question that shot into her mind – how could I have ignored this?

'Look here, Marion,' Frank Callaghan said, 'maybe I shouldn't interfere, but we're family now, after all, aren't we?'

Marion didn't reply, she was deep in her own thoughts.

'I don't know if Eileen or David would've told you, but I'm a consultant in respiratory diseases, and I think Mr Ryan might be having a few problems I can help with. Would it be all right with you if I arranged with his GP to see him at the Royal Infirmary?'

She nodded. How had she missed this? How?

The tests went on for months, and it seemed to Marion that they caused Jimmy more distress than they were worth at times. He breathed into things, he had stethoscopes and wires all over him, x-rays, blood samples, and then he'd have them all over again. She was glad that Frank Callaghan was dealing with it, because her instinct would have been to tell them to leave Jimmy alone, and she knew Frank wouldn't allow that. When he was finally satisfied he asked Marion and Davy along to the Bearsden castle where the wedding had been, and he told them that Jimmy was suffering from mesothelioma. They looked at each other; neither of them knew what it was. 'It's a form of cancer,' Frank said bluntly, 'and I'm afraid there's nothing we can do about it but make him comfortable.'

'Nothing?' Davy asked.

Frank shook his head. 'David, this is something that has to be dealt with, because he will steadily decline and need constant care. We will have to decide how that will be done and where. There is another factor. Jimmy will be expecting to be told the results of his tests. Do you want me to tell him?'

Neither Marion nor Davy could think coherently, never mind enter into discussions about the future. Marion felt sick and rushed out of the room to the bathroom, where she threw up all she could and then retched till her stomach muscles ached. This was no good though, she had to come up with some plan; there were things she had to think about and panicking wasn't helping. She had to get control of this; it was Jimmy she had to think of. And Colin. Dear God! The boy had lost most of his family before he was born, and he'd lost Maggie, now he would shortly lose his father. Even if Jimmy had never been a proper father, even if Colin didn't depend on him in any way, he was still his father.

It was decided that Frank Callaghan would visit Jimmy at Langfaulds Crescent with Davy and break the news to him. Marion sat by the bed and searched her mind desperately for something she could do to make it easier. Another wife might have held his hand, but she was Jimmy's wife; they had no normal kind of affection. Even so, he was a human being, a man who had done her no harm that he could've helped, he deserved some kind of comfort, if only she could think of some. His expression didn't change as he was told. He looked Frank Callaghan straight in the eye and took in every word, and there was no panic, no shock; it was as if he already knew.

'We have to decide how you're to be cared for,' Frank Callaghan said. 'There will be times when you will need nursing, Jimmy, and we can arrange hospital care very quickly.'

'Ah don't want tae go intae hospital,' was all Jimmy said, and he looked at Marion.

'He'll stay at home, Frank,' she said calmly. 'Ah'll look after Jimmy.'

'It could become difficult.'

'Ah'll look after Jimmy.'

After Frank had left, Davy tried to discuss the future with Marion. He and Eileen wouldn't be going to Oxford, he said, she would need their support. She stopped that dead in its tracks. She hadn't sent him to university to sit holding her hand; he and Eileen would get on with their lives as they had planned. Nothing had changed. She had always looked after Jimmy as best she could, the only difference now was that there was an end to that in sight. 'You're being stuck with the situation again,' Davy said miserably.

'The situation?' Marion rounded on him angrily. 'That's ma man you're talkin' aboot, Davy Ryan! If we want to be helpful, ye can talk tae Colin wi' me, because honest tae Christ, Ah don't know whit tae say tae him!'

They explained the situation to Colin as precisely as they could. His father was very ill and would get gradually worse till he died, they said, and he wanted to stay at home where Marion could nurse him. Colin nodded solemnly, his dark hair falling over his eyes. Davy and Eileen wondered if he'd like to stay with them in Oxford until . . . for a while. He shook his head firmly, shocked by the suggestion. He would stay at home where his mother needed him, and maybe he could help Jimmy too. As far as the outside world was concerned Jimmy had been ill for years off and on, and when he officially gave up work there would be little surprise. They decided that they didn't want anyone to know anything more than that, the burden was heavy enough without the sympathy of others to cope with.

Just as she was coming to terms with the situation she had a visit from Robert Boyle. He had come to tell her that he was emigrating to New Zealand, and he wanted her to go with him. She looked at him as though he were speaking a foreign language.

'Robert, Ah don't know if ye've heard, but Jimmy isnae well.'

'He's been no' well for years, Marion,' he replied. 'Everybody knows ye've had nae life wi' him.'

'He's ma man!' she said. 'Ah canny jist walk oot an' leave him! An' there's Colin tae consider.'

'Ah'm no suggestin' ye leave him behind! He'll come wi' us. Marion, ye know we should be thegither, ye *know* that as well as me!'

'Naw Ah don't,' she lied, 'Ah've nae idea where ye get these notions, Robert. We've aye been friends, good friends, but Ah'm a married wumman an' there's nothin' aboot that Ah'd change.'

The look in his eyes would haunt her for ever, the hurt, the pain, the betrayal, and many nights she would lie in her bed and relive that moment and sob into her pillow. He was the man she should have married, she had no doubt about that, in another life with no War they would have been together. Or if the bombardier on that fateful raid had let his bombs go half a mile away and missed the Holy City, in the normal course of events she would have met Robert Boyle, son of Pape, and married him. She would go over that other life in her mind's eye, her family still alive, Jimmy Ryan coming home and marrying Frances, the excitement of her Da that his Marion with the inquiring mind should be marrying his partner Pape's boy.

Fate was a weird thing. Sometimes she had imagined her mother as a teenager going out with Tommy MacLeod, being taken home to the Holy City to meet his parents and his grandparents. She saw Jean walking in and meeting the family she would end her days with, and she saw her walking into the house that had just become vacant, the house where she would have Colin, Iain, Frances and Marion, where she would play out those silly, happy scenes with Tommy and where she would die. It was as if some gods somewhere had planned the whole thing as a game, a diversion. 'We'll give them three children in three years,' they'd decided, 'and then they'll all be wiped out together.' But then one of them had said, 'Hang on, let's make it interesting. Let's give them another one, one that will survive, and we'll see what happens. We'll see what she makes of it.'

So in the revised plan her family had gone, but there was still scope to make something of it, only she'd messed that up too. She could've handed Davy on to his brother at the end of the War and still gone on to meet Robert, that's how the plan should've worked out. But she had fooled herself about Jimmy. She had tried to re-create her family with him, and so she had fooled herself that marrying him was really romantic, that it was what fate had intended. And Jimmy had married her because he was a lost soul like her, clutching at the familiar. She should have waited. Robert Boyle had been her fate, and now she had denied her feelings for him and turned him away, and in hurting him she had hurt herself even more. She had once vowed that she would marry the man who looked at her the way Jimmy Ryan had looked at Frances, and Robert had looked at her like that, even his mother had recognised it. And now she would never see him, never see that look again, and all she would have to remember was that other terrible look, when she cut him dead. If she could've traded places with Jimmy she would have.

She sank then to the lowest point of her life. It was worse than those hours spent under the rubble of Second Avenue, because then she had wanted to live; now she wanted to die. If there had been a way of simply going to sleep she would have taken it, and even the thought of Colin barely made her hold on. She had given up work to look after Jimmy, and now that Davy had moved out she slept in his old room to give Jimmy more space. It was the bed Robert had slept in, and like an animal she would sniff at the sheets in the vain hope of finding the slightest scent of him. In the mornings she would rise to put Colin out to school, then see to Jimmy and go back to bed; there was nothing else she wanted to do but sink deeper and deeper into the blackness until it smothered her.

And that's when Jean appeared again. She knew she must be in real trouble, because Jean MacLeod was talking to her again, telling her to get up, to raise her head, to take one breath at a time. But she didn't want to, she wanted to drift off, and still Jean pushed her and called her name. Her mother's voice talked to her in the dead of night, woke her in the mornings and refused to let her sink. When she protested that she wished she could turn the clock back and die in 1941, Jean sharply took her to task. 'Ye've got ma grandson

264

tae look efter!' she would say. 'Get up, Marion Katie MacLeod!'

But it seemed to Marion Katie MacLeod that she had spent her life surviving so that she could look after other people. No one ever looked after her or asked what *she* wanted, and she was tired of it. What she wanted was the life she should have had with Robert, the life she had a *right* to. Was that so much to ask?

22

It lasted a good six months. Some people would have called it depression, or a breakdown like the film stars had when they booked into expensive clinics in dark glasses, but working-class women in Clydebank didn't get such things. It seemed to Marion that she went into a kind of hibernation, she ticked over rather than lived, and then one day a letter arrived from New Zealand. Robert had written only a few lines. He was getting married to a girl called Susan. He hoped Marion, Jimmy and Colin were keeping well. There was no address. Instead of sending her down to deeper depths of despair it had a calming effect, but then maybe it was just coincidence, maybe the madness had run its course anyway.

Looking through rational eyes once again she saw that her son was lonely. Like her he handled things alone, but he was too young to handle what the Ryan family life had become, and instantly she felt guilty for retreating from him. Jean had been right, her grandson needed his mother. And Jimmy needed her strength too, he needed not only to be nursed and cared for, but to be cared about. At the time it didn't seem that the turning point had been so dramatic, but looking back at that dark time she knew she had only just survived it. She seemed from a distance to have been like a spoiled child in a sulk because she couldn't have what she wanted, who thought that by throwing a tantrum she could somehow get it. Well, that had gone. It should have been her, but Robert was getting married to Susan and there would be no turning back. Wherever he was, she hoped he would be happy, he deserved that. Now it was time to accept that this was the only life she had and get on with it.

As time went on Jimmy became breathless on less exertion and was almost entirely bedridden, an oxygen cylinder always by his bed. During those months she began to appreciate that he really was a brave man; he knew what the future held, knew there was no future, and he accepted it without crumbling. When he couldn't sleep she would sit by his bed in the night, reading to him or talking to him, something they had never done before, and if anything their relationship became real for the first time. She began to wonder if she had really tried to get to know him in the past, and if she had, what difference it might have made to them. They talked of their parallel experiences as children of the Holy City, and he would laugh gently as they discussed her brother Colin.

'He had nae fear, ye know,' he smiled. His voice was barely above a whisper.

'Tell me aboot it, Jimmy! The battles in oor hoose ower Colin! Ma mother seemed tae aye be greetin' ower somethin' he'd done.'

'Aye, an' she blamed *me*!' Jimmy laughed, the wheezing becoming louder. 'Ah began to think ma name was "Could ye no' have stopped him, Jimmy?" Ah mind the day we went oan the tram tae Glesca, an' when we got there nothin' would dae but we hadtae go on tae Airdrie. Airdrie! My God, it was the end o' the world! It was wan o' they trams wi' the wee closed bit at the end, whit was it they called them? Single ends, that was it. An mind the three o' us, Colin, Gino Rossi an' me, sittin' there as a' these strange places flashed past. Gino an' me wanted tae get off and turn back, but no' Colin. To Airdrie he was goin', come hell or high water. An' when we got there we found it was just like any other place! He was that disappointed, I think he thought the folk would be speakin' a foreign language, or they would be a different colour or somethin'.' He was quiet for a moment. 'Ah was glad ye called the boy Colin, Marion,' he said.

'He's called Colin Iain,' she said, and told him for the first time of her Da's opinion that if her brothers were split down the middle and put together they would make 'wan perfect laddie'. 'Ah threw in David tae, because Davy has been a good laddie a' his days tae. Well, nearly a' his days! Did ye know Ah wanted to throw him in the canal when he was five? Ma Da said it would dae him the world o' good, he wouldnae be a nuisance if he got a good droonin'.'

'My, but your Da was some man!' Jimmy said quietly. 'If Ah could've picked a man tae be ma faither, it would've been Tam MacLeod. Ah idolised your Da, did ye know that?'

'He wouldnae have been surprised,' Marion laughed, 'the wee bugger idolised hissel'!' She waited till the coughing fit set off by the gentlest of laughter had subsided, then went on.

'Ye idolised oor Frances tae, didn't ye, Jimmy?'

'Every fella in Clydebank idolised Frances,' he smiled. 'My but she was a beauty!'

'Ah've aye wondered,' she said, 'Ah've aye wondered, Jimmy, is that why ye married me? Because Frances was gone an' Ah was her sister?'

He looked at her sharply. 'Is that whit ye've been thinkin' a' these years? Marion hen, Frances was a stage we a' went through, it didnae last. Ah didnae go through the War thinkin' aboot comin' hame tae Frances or anythin' like that. A' that kept me goin' was the thought o' the Holy City, o' gettin' hame.'

'Then why, Jimmy, why me?'

'Well, lass, we've come through too much tae kid each other, haven't we? The truth is Ah don't really know. Is that too hard o' me?'

Marion shook her head.

'Ah shouldnae have married ye, Ah think Ah knew that

before we got married. It wasnae fair, ye were too young. Ah was selfish.'

'Naw, Jimmy . . .'

'Come oan noo, Marion hen, don't let us tell lies noo. Ye seemed so strong, ye had everythin' under control, an' Ah needed that because Ah felt Ah was goin' mad an' Ah didnae know whit tae dae aboot it. Ah thought you would help me, an' that was selfish. Efter a' ye'd been through ye deserved better.'

She put her head down and started to cry softly, and he put his hand out as if to touch her then pulled it back.

'Ye see? Ah canny even put ma arm roond ye. It's ma fault, Marion, no' yours, ye tried your best, but ye were jist too young. If ye'd been aulder ye widnae have married me, Ah cheated ye o' a better life.'

Somehow knowing that he'd been so aware all these years made it worse, the thought that he'd been torturing himself without her realising it made her feel even more of a failure. There they'd been, both of them knowing they had made a huge mistake, each of them blaming themselves, and neither able to even talk about it.

He stopped to catch his breath. 'It was the War did it,' he said. 'Ah canny explain it right, Marion, but the things Ah did in the War, somethin' happened tae me.'

'Were ye wounded, Jimmy?'

'Naw, no' a scratch. But it was like before being a Commando there was wan Jimmy Ryan, an' efter there was this other wan. Ah did a' the things Ah was tellt, followed a' the orders, but somehow it wasnae me. We had tae kill people, an' Ah was good at it; we had these daggers wi' thin, sharp blades, an' they taught ye tae kill a man withoot makin' a noise.'

Marion flinched, but she didn't stop him; he had never talked of his wartime experiences before.

'An' each time Ah did it, it was like this other Jimmy Ryan daein' it. Does that sound daft?'

269

'Naw, Jimmy,' she said, though she didn't truly understand.

'They would send us intae places behind enemy lines, special operations. We never knew why we were doin' it, we jist did as we were tellt. But Ah mind the first German prisoner we took alive, an' Ah suddenly realised he was jist like me. He wisnae Hitler or Himmler, he was jist a man daein' whit he was tellt tae, an' hopin' tae Christ he would survive an' get back hame at the end. An' Ah began tae wonder efter that. Ah never knew there were German Catholics, seems daft noo, but Ah didnae. Ah saw this poor bastard Ah'd killed, the dagger had caught oan somethin' glintin' roond his neck. It was a rosary, jist like the wan roond ma neck. It came as a helluva shock. Mibbe his mother had gied it tae him tae protect him durin' the War, jist like ma mother gave me the wan Ah'd been wearin' a' that time. An' Ah thought tae masel' aboot the priests an' ministers who said prayers ower oor men before they went intae battle. So the next German Ah saw Ah asked him, an' he tellt me they had the same thing. Ah couldnae believe it! Ah dumped the rosary efter that, an' Ah've hated priests an' ministers ever since. Whenever Ah see them Ah can almost feel the Commando dagger in ma hand!'

She thought back to when she had threatened to send Davy to the Protestant school, and the Catholic hierarchy had come to persuade her otherwise. They had asked to see Jimmy, and she had warned them that he might get violent if he saw them in his house. She had thought it was a white lie, but she had been speaking the truth after all.

'Is that why ye didnae mention gettin' married in a Catholic church, Jimmy?' Marion asked in surprise. 'A' these years Ah thought it was because o' me no' bein' Catholic!'

'Naw, it wasnae tae dae wi' you, Marion, it was tae dae wi' me no' wantin' any o' them near me. Ye were taught tae kill as a reaction, if anybody touched ye. There's a' sorts o' ways tae kill, an' it hadtae be done, Ah didnae doubt that. In the brigade naebody made any bones aboot whit we did, we knew we were daein' somethin' we hadtae dae. But the priests didnae know that, they didnae understand like we did, yet they mumbled their words ower a' they men oan baith sides an' sent them intae battle. Every time Ah saw wan o' the sanctimonious bastards in the street since Ah've hadtae stop masel'.'

That night in North Elgin Street when Davy had thrown a punch at him and Jimmy had nearly choked him, she'd tried to prise his fingers off the boy's throat one by one and didn't manage it. Jimmy had only just stopped in time. 'Ye touched me, son!' he'd almost cried. 'Ah canny help it, ye shouldnae have touched me.' Taught to kill by reaction, if anybody touched him. The thoughts whirled in her mind for days, of men like Jimmy turned loose after years of highly trained killing, killing silently and efficiently because they were required to. Turned loose onto the ordinary streets as though none of it had happened, and expected to be the ordinary men they were before the War. How many more were there out there? How many more who had become two people because it was the only way they could cope with what the War had obliged them to do. Jimmy was a Commando, his part in the War was more specialised, more concentrated, but what about men like big Tony Gallagher, for instance? Was that why he had become a drunk and a wife-beater? He was an ordinary soldier, but he had lived a brutal existence for six years, then they sent him home to his wife and the life he used to have, and expected him to fit in again. How could they? She remembered all the times she had heard women say of their men, 'He was OK till he went away tae the War . . . he was different when he came back.' How could they, any of them, be other than different? And their womenfolk never knew why, because men never talked about the War. Oh, they talked about the funny things that happened and the friendships, but she had never heard of any man talking about the terror they *must* have felt, the horror, the killing and the times they never thought they would see their families again. The War was over, but in many ways it would never be over, it would go on marking families for generations.

And one thought led to another. Before the Blitz she had been a happy child of eleven, one with an inquiring mind to be sure, but passive by nature, dependent on her family, who would always be there for her, to sort out her problems and help her over the hard times. But her experiences had changed her too. She had grown up too quickly and put on this aura of being responsible and able, but that was all it was, an aura. Inside she was still that child; she hadn't grown up, she was just pretending. It was all an act, and she knew only too well how often the act had nearly come undone. How many children were there out there like Colin, with a father marked inwardly by his experiences and a mother who was really an immature child herself? Until now.

Once Jimmy started talking it was as if he couldn't stop; the thought of imminent death seemed to have focused his mind and unlocked his tongue. Maybe all the men who had fought in the War would have done the same given the chance, but most went quickly, whereas Jimmy had time to think, reflect and voice his thoughts. Marion listened through many nights to things she would rather not have heard, but Jimmy needed to tell someone, and she was there. The names of foreign countries and places tripped off his tongue, places that you would've expected to hear mentioned as part of Big Kenny's exploits, but these tales were harder to tell and to hear.

'We were at Dieppe in 1942, that clown Mountbatten was tae blame for that. He's a hero tae some, but he was tae blame for a' they men bein' killed, an' there was nae need for it nae matter whit he says. There were aboot twenty o' us; only six survived. They said we'd get a medal. Comin' back ower the Chanel some officer frae another mob grabbed wan o' oor lot an' tried tae put him oan a charge for bein' "improperly dressed". We'd been workin' behind the German lines for weeks; we werenae in uniform, at least no' in any wan uniform. Oor fella had had enough, he gubbed the officer, felled him where he stood. Know whit they did? Took oor medal aff us! We hadnae even got it, an' they took it aff us!'

He told her of the Commandos being sent into the invasion of Italy in July 1943, when they had taken Sicily and prevented a vital bridge near Lentina being destroyed so that the following Allied armies could complete the invasion. 'Montgomery called the bridge efter us!' he said with a smile. Then there was Salerno a couple of months later, where the casualties were heavy, then the Anzio landing in January 1944 where they had expected to meet stiff opposition, but didn't. A few days later though, at Monte Ornito, they did, losing eleven officers and one hundred and seventy-two men. In April 1944 they had to take a piece of land between Lake Comacchio and the sea, but it had rained after weeks of drought and they had to drag their assault craft through thick mud that sucked men off their feet. Casualties were high and he had watched many die, friends who had been with him all the way through, killed because they couldn't move quickly enough through the mud. They had won through, of course, and one lad, a corporal, had won the Victoria Cross.

Being part of a special force he moved from one place to another, wherever the expertise of the Commandos was needed. He had spent a lot of his time back and forth with the men of the Eighth Army and he remembered Lady Astor, then an MP, accusing the Eighth Army of living it up in Rome instead of being back home preparing for D-Day. He never forgot the men of the Eighth Army and the long, hard campaign they'd fought across Africa and Italy. 'We were trained specially,' he said, 'but they were jist men ye'd meet every day, puttin' up wi' hell, no' able tae dae anythin' tae get oot o' the trouble they were in.' And he shared the righteous wrath they felt at Lady Astor's insult. 'There's a song aboot that,' he whispered, ' "The D-Day Dodgers", it's called.' He tried to sing it but had to stop, because of emotion she suspected as much as lack of breath.

While he had been doing all that she had been fighting to recover from the Blitz and then to stop Davy being sent to a children's home without her. She took on Auntie Maggie, went to work in Singer's, and all the time she wrote to Jimmy and he replied. His replies had been short and disappointing at the time, but now she imagined him taking time to write those letters and felt sad and angry at not knowing what he was going through.

Sometimes the horror of it got too much and she would stop him temporarily by talking about other things that she suspected might be related.

'Dae ye remember when Colin was born, Jimmy?'

He nodded.

'Why did ye run oot o' the hospital like that?'

'Because Ah'd hurt ye.'

'Ah'd had a wean, Jimmy, ye didnae hurt me!'

'But Ah did! The doctor tellt me ye could die. He thought by the name we were Catholic an' he said Ah should get a priest jist in case. Ye can imagine whit Ah thought aboot that! It jist seemed tae me that everythin' Ah touched Ah hurt. The War was ower an' Ah was still hurtin' people, even them Ah didnae mean tae hurt. Ah had thought the Jimmy Ryan Ah used tae be before the War would come back when it was finished, but Ah was still hurtin' people. If you'd have died Ah'd have killed ye, an' as it was Ah'd near killed ye. That's how Ah couldnae, y'know, touch ye efter that. It wasnae you, Marion, it was me. We were never really man an' wife, because Ah knew Ah'd only hurt ye, mibbe kill ye wan day.'

'Jimmy, Ah couldnae have any merr bairns efter Colin, Ah shoulda told ye that.'

'That has nothin' tae dae wi' it, lass. It was me, Ah *couldnae* touch ye efter that. There was somethin' wrang wi' me.'

'But where did ye go? A' they times ye went away an'
we didnae know if ye were alive or deid.'

'Ah couldnae help it, Marion. Ah'm sorry, lass.' His eyes
were glistening with tears.

'Jimmy, don't, please. Ah'm no' gettin' at ye, Ah'd jist
like tae know, dae ye understand?'

'Aye,' he sighed, 'Ah understand. Ah went tae the places
where Ah trained as a Commando, tae Achnacarry, Spean
Bridge, the Great Glen. Ye see that was the last time Ah'd
seen the first Jimmy Ryan, it was like that was the last place
Ah'd been him. This sounds crazy, Marion, doesn't it?'

'Go on, Jimmy, please.'

'It was like when Ah went back there, tae the days when
it was a' an adventure, before Ah'd actually killed anybody,
it was like Ah could be masel' again. So when somethin'
made me think o' the War again, somethin' would explode
inside ma heid, an' Ah'd go back up there, an' live ootside
like they taught us, an' climb and walk. An' it was quiet, an'
Ah'd feel like Ah was me again.'

'That was a' ye did?'

'Aye.'

'Dae you know, Jimmy Ryan,' she smiled, 'there are folk
in Clydebank think ye kept leavin' me tae go aff wi' a fancy
wumman?'

'Away!'

'Ah'm tellin' ye, whit a bloody reputation ye got yersel'!'

As he slept she thought about how disappointed her
brother Colin had been at not getting into the War. He was
the adventurous one, as Jimmy said, he had no fear, and he
had been so envious of Jimmy becoming a Commando. But
Jimmy hadn't been able to cope with it without thinking
about what he was doing, he was too human to be untouched
by the sights he'd seen and the experiences he'd had. It
occurred to her that the wrong man had been accepted when
they had gone to volunteer together, that Colin would have
been able to cope without a second thought. Colin had, as

everyone who knew him observed, including his mother, 'something missing'. What was missing was an insight into the consequences his actions had for others; Colin would have made a perfect Commando. He would have been able to come back after the War and never give a thought to the suffering he had seen and inflicted, whereas Jimmy hadn't questioned that awful things had to be done, and still didn't, but good man that he was, the horror of it preyed on his mind. And there it was again, that paradox she had noticed before, of this disciplined, efficient soldier, a member of an elite group, and yet there was about him a terrible, touching innocence. He was like a man looking through a child's eyes at awful adult things beyond his comprehension. Surely that made him a braver man than the fearless Colin? A truly brave man knows what he's doing, feels fear, feels revulsion and regret, but still does what has to be done, whereas those with 'something missing' don't have that insight, that level of feelings. Jimmy still had so much admiration for Colin, but he didn't see, never would see, that he was the worthier man.

23

Inevitably the word spread that Jimmy Ryan was ill; no one could miss the number of visits the doctor and the nurses were paying. The first to knock on her door was Agnes Boyle, desperate to patch things up between them and to help in any way she could. Marion invited her in and they sat together in the kitchen.

'Marion, aboot oor Robert –'

'Noo look, Agnes,' Marion said kindly, 'if we're gonny be pals again ye havetae understand that Ah don't have time for what was said before. It's a' forgotten. My only concern is whit's happenin' inside this hoose.'

'But, Marion, there's somethin' –'

'Agnes, stop! Ah don't want tae talk aboot your Robert.'

And so the subject remained closed between them, and as Jimmy slept for an hour here or there, Agnes would sit talking with Marion, or she'd do her shopping for her. Sal arrived too, which was more of a blessing, because Sal couldn't keep a mournful demeanour no matter how much she intended to. The problems of Big Tony's devotion to the Church were thrashed out regularly and helped to release Marion's mind from the long, slow process she was engaged in with Jimmy.

'Ah'm tellin' ye, Marion,' said Sal, 'Ah widnae be surprised if he put oan wanna they long black dresses an' the wee funny hat. He got his job back at Singer's, though things is bad there, but he prays there tae!'

Marion laughed.

'Ah'm tellin' ye! He goes intae the canteen an' before he

eats his dinner he kneels doon an' prays! Puts everybody right aff. Complains if anybody swears. Ah'm no' even allowed a "bloody" or "damn" anymerr withoot him drappin' tae his knees for an hour! An' as for the other, Christ, there isnae any. Ah was thinkin' the other night in bed – by masel' – while he was reading his prayer book. Know whit Ah think happened? Ye mind ma currant bun days? Well, Ah think a' that was some kinda premonition o' this. Ah was gettin' as much as Ah could because somethin' had tellt me that wan day it would a' dry up. Christ, dry up? Merr like *heal* up!'

'So ye'd rather have him drinkin' an' beltin' ye aboot, Sal? Is that whit ye're sayin?'

'Tell the truth, Marion, Ah'm no' sure aboot that, that's how bad it's gettin'. Know whit the bairns call him? Used tae be "that big nutter", or oan a good day, "Da". Noo they a' snigger an' call him "Father", an' the big eejit's that far away he disnae realise they're knockin' a rise oota him. Ah feel like abandonin' him on the steps o' Our Holy Redeemer's, only Ah think that nice wee man Sheridan is as sick o' him as Ah am. Poor wee bugger runs every time he sees Big Tony bearin' doon oan him. Bet he's cursin' the day he saved him! But nae worries, if he does, Big Tony will pray for him!'

And there was Colin to deal with. The boy was nearly fifteen years old and coping with the daily journey to Allan Glen's, deep in the alien territory of Glasgow. They had decided on the school partly at least because they had the 'Bankies' irrational and traditional prejudice against Glasgow, the city that begat Clydebank. Allan Glen's was still a Glasgow school, but it didn't actually have the city in its name, and that made them feel better about it somehow. In a way his longer day was a blessing, she felt, because it kept Colin out of the house more and gave him a life outside what was happening at 2E Langfaulds Crescent.

It was clear to her that the boy was caught between pity

for Jimmy and the feeling that there should be more than that. He had grown up barely knowing his father, unable to relate to him in a normal way because Jimmy couldn't relate to his son, or anyone else. And there was a sense of guilt about that, she knew, though it wasn't the boy's fault, wasn't anyone's fault. At first he seemed to cope with the process of Jimmy dying by keeping at a distance from the events in the bedroom that ruled the household, though she tried to encourage him to visit his father, because she knew he would look back on this time one day and regret it if he hadn't spent time with him. Slowly he began to copy what she did, sitting by the bed, telling his father about the events of his day and reading to him. It didn't matter what he read, he was making some sort of contact that would enable him to say a proper goodbye when the time came, and no one knew better than Marion how precious that could be in the years to come.

And Jimmy tried too; she would hear the low whisper of his voice as she worked about the kitchen, telling Colin stories of the Holy City, of the MacLeod brothers he was named after, and of his Granda Tommy, and she would hear them laughing together. Colin took Iain's cherished drawings of the family into the bedroom for Jimmy to see and he would listen intently as Jimmy told him a tale of each subject. He told him of Granny Mirren and Granda Archie's fights in the Gaelic, and how they didn't realise that the family understood the insults; he even had a passable knowledge of them himself. So, as Jimmy was dying, he brought to life for his son those he too had loved who had died before him.

Another visitor was Father Sheridan, alerted no doubt by Father Tony Gallagher. He stood on her doorstep looking uncomfortable. 'Can I come in? Would that be all right?'

'Well that depends oan whether ye're here as Gerry Sheridan or Father Sheridan,' she replied.

279

'Whichever you prefer,' he smiled, 'it's your house, after all.'

She served him with tea and biscuits and they discussed the exploits of his latest recruit from North Elgin Street, then he got down to the real business of his visit, as she knew he would. Would Jimmy like to see him?

'No.'

'Marion, I'm asking because there are Catholics who reject their faith all their lives, then turn to it on their deathbed. It might give him comfort.'

'Whit the hell is it wi' you?' she demanded. 'Are ye oan piece rates or somethin'? Look, if you went intae that room he might well use a' the strength he has left tae throttle ye – an' believe me, he could dae it, Ah've seen him nearly dae it wance an' that was enough.'

'Could we ask him?'

'Listen, Gerry, Ah know ye mean well, but ye've lost this wan; accept that. Ye don't know Jimmy, dae ye? Ye've never even met him, an' here ye are, tryin' tae claim for your ain somebody that would fell ye if he knew ye were even in his hoose. In fact Ah'd knock ye unconscious, never mind Jimmy, if ye tried tae get intae that room. He's no' a weak man. He's dyin', but he's wanna the strongest characters Ah've ever met. If he wanted anythin' tae dae wi' your church and your religion, Jimmy would say so. He's said the opposite, an' he's explained why. It convinced me, but it's nane o' your business, so Ah'll no pass it oan. If you an' me are tae stay friends ye'll take ma word for it an' accept that Ah'm doin' what Jimmy wants an' drop the subject. NOW. OK?'

'OK, but will you let me know when . . .'

'Noo that depends tae, oan whether ye intend makin' a mug o' yersel' an' mutterin' an' lightin' candles, or whether –'

'As a friend, Marion. I don't know Jimmy, as you say, but I know you. I'd like to be there, as *your* friend.'

'OK, Ah can live wi' that, Gerry, but Ah'm warnin' ye, nae funny business! Wan glimpse o' a rosary an' ye're history. Understand?'

The end came quietly and quickly. Jimmy had had a restless night, his breathing was laboured and he kept clutching, almost plucking at, his chest. She had spent much of the small hours sitting by the bed talking to him, then about 4 o'clock she had gone out of the bedroom into the kitchen to look for a newspaper to read to him. When she came back he was dead. She sat in the chair beside him, looking at him for what seemed ages before leaning forward and closing his eyes. It had seemed so insignificant; one moment he was alive, the next he was dead, and yet nothing else in the universe had been disturbed or had even noticed. The doctor was calling at 6 o'clock as usual, and there was no phone in the house. If she slipped out to a call box there was always the possibility that she might waken Colin and he could wander into the bedroom. She decided to wait. It was over; what was there for the doctor to do anyway? She removed the oxygen mask from his face, switched the cylinder off, then gently took the pillows from his back so that he could lie flat. Then she covered his face with the sheet, left the room and closed the door behind her. In the kitchen she made some tea, then sat down by the window sipping from her cup, to watch the dawn break over Clydebank. All she felt was relief. It was over for him. He didn't deserve such an end, fighting for every breath, didn't deserve to die at forty. But it was over.

24

When Davy arrived from Oxford he joined Marion and Colin in Langfaulds Crescent to plan Jimmy's funeral. Eileen hadn't made the long drive north because she was about to give birth to their first child. Davy a daddy, Marion could hardly believe it. Thanks once again to the Co-op Insurance Company there were no financial worries over the funeral costs. For as many years as she could remember the agent had arrived at every house she had lived in each Friday night, and after him came the Co-op milkman for payment, and then Byron the coalman, whose slogan, 'Fire on with Byron', stuck in the minds of every 'Bankie for their entire lifetime. The Friday night collections were a ritual in every household, and by Saturday morning most families had considerably less of their wages than they thought they had. At times like this it paid off though.

Now that the waiting was over Marion felt she had nothing to do; she hadn't realised how much her life had come to be occupied by Jimmy's dying, not that she grudged a moment of it. They had come close to knowing each other, as close as two basically unsuited people could come. Sitting at the kitchen table with his son and his brother she went over the conversations she had had with Jimmy in his final months. She told them of his torment about the War and his feeling that he was almost two people, one pre and one post War. Of how he had been unable to settle into normal life afterwards, and his agony that his experiences had left him so cut off that he couldn't relate to anyone, not even his family.

'You always said whatever was wrong with him was due to the War,' Davy said quietly.

'Och, don't make me oot tae be somethin' clever, Davy, it was jist a feelin'. Ah still couldnae dae anythin' aboot it, could Ah? Ah couldnae help the man.'

'But you tried, Marion, you made life as stress-free for him as you could, and you took care of him long after many women would have left or thrown him out.'

'Aye, well, we'll never know how much o' that was cowardice, will we? As Ah said, don't make me oot tae be anythin' special, Davy, Ah never knew masel' frae wan day tae the next whit Ah would dae.'

He reached across the table and covered her hand with his own.

'Right,' she said, 'we've a funeral tae organise, an' by Christ, it's gonny be wan that suits him. Nae flannel, nae priest, it'll be aboot Jimmy. Ah was thinkin', Davy, would you be uptae giein' a wee speech?'

'You mean a kind of eulogy?'

'Aye, that kinda thing. They usually have some craitur in a dog collar talkin' rubbish aboot somebody they didnae know. Ah'd like Jimmy tae have somethin' better.'

'Can I think about it?' he asked. 'He was my brother, but I didn't really know him, did I?'

'Well, that would be a good startin' point, no' think so? Ah want this to be honest, Ah want him tae be sent aff withoot lies.' She looked at Colin, anxious not to leave him out. It would be important to him in the future, when maturity had given him some understanding of his father, and therefore some pride in him, to have played his part in this. 'Is that OK, Colin?'

Colin nodded. 'Is he being buried, Mum,' he asked, 'or cremated?' Marion smiled; she had noticed that though she only spoke regular English when dealing with officialdom or foreigners, Colin, as Davy had before him, used it nearly all the time since he had moved into what she supposed were educated circles. It was natural, she imagined, that as they increasingly read and thought in what was regarded as proper English, they would speak it too. They had become truly bilingual.

'Whit dae you think, Colin?' she asked.

'Well, I've thought about it a lot,' he said. 'I hate the idea of the family all lying in the cemetery. I remember when Auntie Maggie died it was such a cold, wet day and when we lowered her into the ground we lowered her into a pool of water. I hated that. Then we covered her with cold earth and left her there.'

She bit her tongue; it seemed to Marion that Maggie had been delivered into the temperature she lived at. 'So are ye sayin' your Dad should be cremated, son?'

Colin nodded. 'And I've been thinking, Mum, about him being a Commando. Did you know that there's a Commando monument at Spean Bridge? I read about it a while ago. Do you think we could scatter his ashes there?'

The boy had given this a lot of thought, and she was proud of him.

'That sounds a good idea, Colin,' she smiled, and looking at Davy, she said, 'Maybe we could find oot aboot that. Whit d'ye think?'

'Colin and I will do that,' he replied gently. 'Any thoughts on music? I take it "Faith of our Fathers" is right out?'

Marion laughed. 'Aye, an' "God Bless the Pope" as well! Whit aboot that nice wan, whit's it called, "Morning has broken"? Ah keep thinkin' o' him oot there walkin' an' climbin' in the fresh air, mibbe he'd have liked that wan. If ye sing it quick ye can forget it's a hymn.' Then she thought again and remembered the time he'd tried to sing an Eighth Army song and couldn't. She told them about it. 'It was somethin' he understood, it meant somethin' tae him. I think it's called "D-Day Dodgers", dae ye think we could find that somewhere?'

'We'll find it. Look, Marion, there's something I need to

tell you, and I'm not sure this is the time to, but if I'm to give this eulogy I want it to be right, as you say, honest, so I want to mention this. About Jimmy's illness, did you ever wonder where it came from?'

Inquiring mind or not, she hadn't; people died from cancer every day, it was the great fear in everyone's heart because it was largely fatal. She shook her head.

'Well another name for it is asbestosis,' he said, looking at her. 'It's caused by exposure to asbestos dust.'

It hit her like a hammer and she tightened her grip on his hand and gasped. 'How do ye know?'

'It's a recognised cause. I found out that there have been government warnings to employers going back as far as 1930, there are people in America trying to have asbestos banned.'

'Are ye sayin' Jimmy knew that?'

'No, the workers were never told, they still aren't. But successive governments knew and didn't tell them, Turner and Newall knew and didn't tell them, and Brown's knew and didn't tell them either.'

'So Jimmy died because o' that bloody dust?'

'Yes.'

She slouched in her chair and sat wordless for what seemed a long time, then she straightened up. She wouldn't think about this now, if she did she'd go to pieces. She'd think about it later. 'Well, say that then, Davy son,' she said firmly. 'You say that.'

The funeral took place on a spring morning in 1963, with the sun just beginning to stir into warmth. She had no idea what Davy was going to say, he had simply told her that he had something prepared and had shown it to Colin already, and she was glad that he was giving the boy his place. There were people from Brown's there, people she had worked with and others who had worked with Jimmy, and Gino Rossi had turned up, the last of the three musketeers of the Holy City. And the old faithfuls arrived too, the Gallaghers, the Boyles, and sitting at the back, behaving himself as she had instructed him, sat Father Sheridan. When everyone had taken their places Davy got up to speak. 'I'm sure,' he told the mourners, 'that this will strike all of you as an unconventional service, but Jimmy Ryan's story isn't a conventional one, and the family decided that his funeral should be a tribute to *him*, rather than the usual kind of occasion. There will be no religious service, because my brother had a strong dislike of ministers, priests and religion. He had his reasons that he did not have to justify to anyone, and neither will I.

'I never knew my brother. When he went to war I was a wee boy. He was this hero, my brother the Commando, but when he came back, the truth is that I couldn't remember what he looked like. I daresay many men who went to war came home to find sons they didn't know and who didn't know them; well, I was a lot younger than Jimmy and that was the position we were in. What I had expected, what I wanted, was my hero brother, the Commando, with all his medals on his uniform, but what I got was a tired man who'd had enough. He had fought all over the world as part of a special band of men who did daring things in dangerous situations, who went into those situations knowing there was a very good chance they wouldn't come out again. But he wouldn't tell me about his experiences, or how many Germans he had killed; I was very disappointed in him I have to say. It was only recently that I discovered how deeply Jimmy had been affected by the things he had seen and done. He discovered that the average German soldier was just like himself. He wasn't fighting hand-to-hand with the German Reich, but with human beings like him, sent away from their families to fight. Jimmy still did what was asked of him, he never questioned that the War had to be won and that he had his part to play, but he never forgot either, because my brother was a very humane man.

'He was sent home to Clydebank at the end of the War and expected to live as though nothing had happened in those years of killing, as though by some magic he could unlearn all that training, and ignore all those honed instincts. They taught him to kill, but they didn't un-teach him. It happened to thousands of men, and they pretended all was well too, because to admit that it wasn't somehow questioned their manhood. It left Jimmy unable to get close to anyone, not to me, not to his wife Marion, and not to his son Colin. None of us could understand this sad, distant man, but Marion never gave up on him, Marion cared for him till the end, as she has cared for me and Colin all of our lives.

'And when Jimmy came home to a land fit for heroes, he was given a job in Brown's, the job that led to his death. He died of mesothelioma, a disease caused by exposure to asbestos, and as many of you here today will know, Jimmy was a "white mouse", a lagger; he spent his entire working life covered in asbestos dust. He breathed it, he swallowed it, it got into his ears, his eyes and eventually, his lungs. And though his employers had known for decades, no one ever told Jimmy that one day, one day soon, it would kill him. He was forty years old when he died the other day. That's the treatment a grateful nation gave to Jimmy Ryan, one of its true heroes.

'When the Commandos were disbanded in 1948, Winston Churchill said, "We may feel sure that nothing of which we have any knowledge or record has ever been done by mortal men which surpasses the splendour and daring of their feats of arms. Truly we may say of them, 'When shall their glory fade?'" Well, actions speak louder than words, except where politicians are concerned, and if I sound bitter, well that's because I am. The man in that coffin was my brother and I never knew him, and I am bitter about that. He *was* a hero, but he certainly didn't get his just deserts, and I'm bitter about that too. Marion, Colin and I were deprived of him, and he was just as deprived of us.

'But I'm also proud of him, because he never forgot the men he fought alongside, and all these years later he still felt outraged at that fine woman, Lady Astor, who had insulted

287

the Eighth Army. She said they were having a good time in Italy, instead of preparing to fight on D-Day. Jimmy knew better, and even on his deathbed he tried to sing the song you're about to hear, the anthem of the men who fought in Africa and Italy.'

In the chill atmosphere the strains of 'Lilli Marlene' rang out, with the words of 'The D-Day Dodgers' addressed to Lady Nancy Astor and sung by its composer, Scottish poet Hamish Henderson, himself one of the 'dodgers'.

> We're the D-Day dodgers, out in Italy,
> Always on the vino, always on the spree,
> Eighth Army scroungers and their tanks,
> We live in Rome, among the Yanks,
> We are your D-Day dodgers who live in Italy.

> We landed at Palermo, a holiday with pay,
> The Gerries brought the band out to meet us on the
>   way,
> They showed us the sights and gave us tea,
> We all sang songs and the beer was free,
> We are your D-Day dodgers, in sunny Italy.

> Naples and Cassino were taken in our stride,
> We didn't come to fight there, we just came for the
>   ride,
> Anzio and Sangro were just names,
> We only came to look for dames,
> Randy D-Day dodgers, in sunny Italy.

> On the march to Florence we had a lovely time,
> We took a bus to Rimini right through the Gothic
>   lines,
> Soon to Bologna we will go,
> And after that we'll cross the Po,
> We'll still be D-Day dodging, in sunny Italy.

Once we heard a rumour, we were going home,
Back to dear old blighty and never more to roam,
Then someone said, 'In France you'll fight!'
We said, 'No thanks, we'll just sit tight!'
Windy D-Day dodgers, in sunny Italy.

Look around the mountains in the mud and rain,
See the scattered crosses, some that have no name,
Heartache and sorrow are all gone,
The boys beneath them slumber on,
They are the D-Day dodgers who'll stay in Italy

Dear Lady Astor, you think you know a lot,
Standing on your platform and talking tommy rot,
You, England's sweetheart and her pride,
We think your mouth's too bloody wide,
That's from your D-Day dodgers 'way out in Italy.

At the end, before the button was pushed taking Jimmy's coffin for cremation, Colin held up his hand to Davy and then whispered to his mother, 'Can I keep his green beret?'

Marion looked at the beret lying on top of the coffin. Why hadn't she thought of that? 'Aye, of course ye can, son.'

Colin walked forward, lifted the beret, stood for a moment, bowed his head, then returned to Marion's side, the beret clasped to his chest. From behind them came the sound of Sal Gallagher sobbing. 'Good old Sal,' Marion thought, whose heart was so soft that she had served currant bun and tea to many foreign servicemen away from home in the War. Marion swallowed hard; this had to be done properly, she had to remain dignified and in control. Later there would be time for rage and tears.

As the coffin slowly descended, Marion, Colin and Davy led the mourners out to the strains of 'Morning has broken'. Outside, they shook hands with everyone who had attended and invited them to the usual reception. Father Sheridan was the last. 'Well,' he grinned, 'that was certainly an unusual service, but then you're an unusual woman, Marion.'

'Honest, Gerry, that's the word ye're lookin' for. Ye should try it sometime, but then again, if ye did, the faithful might twig that ye've been connin' them a' this time!'

Two days later the remaining Ryans drove to Spean Bridge in Davy's car, the first time in Marion's life she had ever been in a private car. The monument was unmissable, standing just off the road to Inverness, in the Great Glen. It stood 17' high, with the three 9' 4" Commando figures standing together gazing at the hills. It brought an instant lump to Marion's throat.

'Who made this?' she asked.

'Scott Sutherland of Dundee,' Davy replied.

'He must've met some Commandos,' she said. 'He must've.'

'Why?'

'Look at them!'

She didn't know how anyone could miss it. The figures were impressive to be sure, but there was something else, they looked innocent too. Cast into the features of their bronze faces was that expression of terrible, heartbreaking innocence that she saw on Jimmy's face, even when he was describing to her cutting the throats of men he knew were just like himself. They didn't look like Hollywood heroes, like something far removed from other men, other soldiers, they looked like men who got on with what they did because they could, and because they knew it had to be done. The three figures had a feeling of calm, quiet strength, but they looked like human beings, not killing machines, and whoever this Scott Sutherland was, she wished she could tell him how right he had got it. The Commandos *were* heroes, but they were men too, ordinary men who were called on to do those extraordinary deeds.

Then they took the urn to the Garden of Remembrance and between them they scattered Jimmy Ryan's ashes. When Davy had phoned the district council for details he had been told that the usual arrangement was that a minister scattered the ashes of dead Commandos on Remembrance Sunday. That was enough to decide the matter; no minister was laying hands on Jimmy, his family would perform this last rite for him. They stood together afterwards, silent in the quiet that Jimmy spent so much time returning to.

'This is where he belongs, isn't it, Mum?' Colin asked.

She reached out and pulled her son to her, 'Aye, son, it is. Ye did well tae think o' it.'

'I think we were expected to ask for official permission,' said Davy, with little if any conviction in his voice.

'Like hell!' Marion retorted. 'Efter whit he did, whit he went through, we're no' askin' permission o' some wee council upstart. We'll tell them we've done it. Whit are they gonny dae? Vacuum him back up?'

As they left she turned back briefly towards the garden. 'On ye go, Jimmy son,' she whispered softly. 'Away an' find him. Find Jimmy Ryan o' the Holy City again.'

25

Afterwards there had been periods of tears and rage, but then Marion had come to a decision. She removed her wedding ring and reverted to her maiden name. Marion MacLeod was who she was, she explained to Colin and Davy, she had never felt like Mrs Ryan, perhaps because she had never been Mrs Ryan. Whatever else she had been, she hadn't been a real wife to Jimmy, and it didn't matter whose fault that was, or wasn't; it was simply the truth. For the first time since she was eleven years old she felt that she had control over her life, she *was* Marion Katie MacLeod. If she had expected opposition or disapproval from Colin or Davy it didn't come, they both seemed to understand what she meant. But even if they hadn't, she had made her decision; it was a new era and she intended to make a fresh start.

Most of her time and emotion would be taken up for the foreseeable future in trying to provide for herself and her son. Big Kenny's money had seen them through Jimmy's illness and death, but she was left a widow at the age of 33, which meant she didn't qualify for a widow's pension, and she had a son to get through school and university and a roof to keep over their heads. At the same time the shipbuilding industry was in its dying throes, as was Singer's. In an attempt to turn the fortunes of Singer's the American HQ sent over its own kind into the top positions that local people had worked their way up to in the factory. Which was probably why in 1961 it was decided to demolish the Singer's clock. The local people were appalled. It had stood all those years, it had survived the Blitz and so it was to them a symbol of their survival against the odds, something that they could look at and identify with Clydebank. But it had been decided to build a new, smaller, more modern factory on the site, and in 1963 horrified 'Bankies watched their clock disappear in front of them. The final insult was that the hands of the clock were made into ashtrays, a sacrilege the 'Bankies would never forgive or forget. To the local people it was a precious link with the past, but to the Americans it was just a clock in the way of their new building, and they turned a deaf ear to the pleas of the townspeople. There was investment to try to rescue the factory, but not enough, and not in the right areas. Without investment there would be no improvement, and without improvement there would be no investment. The workforce demonstrated their growing feelings of insecurity, predictably, by an increase in industrial action; in the first six months of 1965 there were seventy-five separate work stoppages.

In the shipyards there was a similar story. Orders from central government for individual ships weren't what was needed, but it was what they got. The yards were outdated and the cost of updating them was too high, and all problems flowed from that, because it left them unable to compete with modern foreign shipbuilders. The feeling in the town was one of tension, of hanging on by the skin of their teeth and surviving day-to-day with no confidence about tomorrow. Marion got some work in Brown's, but it got less and less with the downturn in orders, so she did what everyone else did, she took any and everything she could find. She placed a postcard in the local shops advertising her services as a French polisher, but in a depressed area there were few in a position to think of such things, and looking back there couldn't have been many shops in the town she hadn't worked in. Finally she took a job as a nursing auxiliary at the Western Infirmary; looking after people was what she knew most about, but she had no qualifications and so she

293

became a skivvy. There was considerably less nursing than clearing up and cleaning, but it was steady work not too far from home and there was always the chance to take on extra shifts and earn more money. It crossed her mind that she could try to train as a nurse, but with Colin starting university in 1966, she couldn't afford to go to college to get the necessary bits of paper. Colin's desire to be a doctor had never waned, and he was given a place at Glasgow University Medical School, where he would remain for six years. Despite all her worries about the quality of family life he'd had in his childhood, Colin was OK, he seemed to have come out of it better than she'd feared.

Often when she was reviewing her life from the comfort of the new Holy City flat, she would look back over those days and years as the hardest, most tiring of her life. But she also knew that she wasn't alone; everyone in Clydebank was struggling. In 1968 the remaining yards came together as Upper Clyde Shipbuilders, and at Brown's the latest *Queen* was under construction, though no one had confidence that this meant things were any easier. There were problems with the new ship and Cunard had refused to accept delivery then refused to hand over the final £1.5 million payment.

The ship had been named the *Queen Elizabeth 2*, which had caused some comment in a nation sensitive to any suggestion that ERII of England was ERII of Scotland. At the time of the first Elizabethan age, Scotland had her own Mary Queen of Scots, who had been executed on the order of her cousin, Elizabeth I, and though there was no evidence that the Scots had benefited greatly from the reign of one royal lady rather than another, it was a matter of national pride. After ERII of England, ERI of Scotland, launched the QE2, assurances were hastily given that the '2' referred to the second ship of that name, not the second Queen Elizabeth. The explanation did not, however, convince everyone, and the suspicion that Scottish history had been slighted rankled on.

Across the road from 2E Langfaulds Crescent at 9F, Pape Boyle, who had retired without ever finding the golden rivet, watched the happenings in Brown's and declared that he had been right all along, the militants were killing the industry. Marion couldn't see why he should feel such fierce loyalty, especially as the asbestos situation was openly acknowledged and the number of men dying young from asbestosis was climbing. The workers in the yard, like those in Singer's desperately worried about their jobs, staged one dispute after another, until rumours gathered pace in 1971 that the yard was about to close. Then came the day at the end of July when Pape's 'militants', the yard shop stewards, took over Brown's. They would accept no redundancies and they would not have a sit-in, but, they told the media, they would have a work-in. Pape was apoplectic, but suddenly the entire world wanted to be part of what was happening in Brown's. The town became alive again, with politicians and all manner of personalities flocking to Clydebank to give their support to men who simply wanted the right to work. During the eighteen month work-in the town was suffused again with the kind of spirit that had characterised it in its earliest days, and Clydebank was rarely off the front pages of the newspapers and TV screens. It seemed that almost every day there were marches in support of the workers, and a public appeal brought in £485,000 to fund the campaign; the heart of Red Clydeside was still beating.

In truth, there was little work done, but that wasn't the important point of the work-in. The campaign captured the hearts of the country and a popular movement was born that forced the government into reversing plans for closure. Instead £40 million was invested to keep Upper Clyde Shipbuilders going – but not for long. The work-in may have reached that sentimental core of the Scottish psyche that its people prefer to deny, and it gave a new dimension to disputes in other industries thereafter, but in December 1972 Marathon Manufacturing took over Brown's yard to make oil platforms. John Brown's disappeared for ever from Clyde-bank. Robert Boyle had been only a few years out with his prediction; the shipbuilding era had come to an end in Clydebank.

And after similar agonies had been gone through in Kil-bowie Road, with the workforce being slashed regularly, Singer's would finally close in 1980. The twin landmarks of Clydebank, the massive ships under construction that towered above every street, and the clock that told you that you were in Clydebank, had been removed, leaving only memories of better days.

The Ryans, though, survived. In 1972 Marion was once again back at Glasgow University, to see her son being given his cap and scroll. Colin now had MB, ChB after his name, and after six months as surgical houseman and six as a medical houseman, he would be free to practise medicine anywhere he liked. Davy and Eileen came up for the ceremony with their three children, James MacLeod, Michael Francis, and Veronica Marion Ryan. They had remained in Oxford, where Davy was a bona fide, pipe-smoking English don. He had decided that instead of teaching children he would instead teach the teachers. He had found his own niche and he was happy with it, even if Marion secretly thought that his life lacked adventure. If Davy hadn't been family she might have thought his niche among the spires a trifle boring, but he *was* family, so wild horses wouldn't have dragged such an opinion out of her.

Colin did his housemanships at the Royal Infirmary, and being a clever chap he did them where the cream always did, in the Professorial Units. Not that this meant he worked any less or that he had an easier time; on the contrary, he worked longer and harder. It was a fact, he reported, that Professorial Units saw themselves as having a certain status, so any and every test going would be ordered, regardless of whether it was appropriate or not. This meant that their housemen were swamped by even more paperwork than other housemen, and they were expected to give a good account of themselves, because they had been admitted to the presence of the cream. Most of the time he was tired and irritable, but he found time to think of the future, and he decided to stick with his original ambition of becoming a heart surgeon. America was where it was all happening as far as heart surgery was concerned, so within a few years to America he went. With his mother's full support he went off to learn everything there was to learn about cardiac surgery, and all because his Auntie Maggie's life couldn't be saved all those years ago. But Marion couldn't help noticing that when he departed for the US, Colin left Maggie's 'friendly' old Gingerbread clock behind with his mother in Clydebank; an oversight she was *sure*. And the damn thing was still keeping perfect time, still striking every half hour.

His move made perfect career sense of course, but Marion reckoned that Big Kenny's influence was at work there too; all those postcards and stories throughout his childhood had made Colin aware that the horizon didn't necessarily end where Clydebank reluctantly joined Glasgow. The cards still arrived from Big Kenny, in fact he had written that he was thinking of paying a visit home, but he had said that before and it hadn't happened, so Marion wasn't surprised when he didn't arrive. He said the same thing in 1983, when he would, by Marion's calculations, be aged somewhere around 80 years old. He wanted to talk to her, he said, and just like before he didn't arrive. In 1985 she received a letter from a solicitor in St Lawrence, Canada. Big Kenny, he said, had died, aged 83, and he would be in touch about Mr MacLeod's estate at a later date. It wasn't possible of course. Everyone knew that Big Kenny was immortal, and even if some thought he was a myth, myths didn't die either. Big Kenny was, she decided, still alive and globetrotting until he himself told her otherwise. Big Kenny was a state of mind.

Just after that Pape and Agnes Boyle died within a year of

each other. She didn't go to their funerals, she took herself off instead to spend some time with Davy, Eileen and the children in Oxford; she knew the Boyles wouldn't mind. Not that she still carried a torch for Robert Boyle, of course, she was far too old for that kind of nonsense, she told herself. Then she told herself *that* was nonsense; romance was still alive and well, even if it had missed her. She didn't know if Robert would be coming home for Pape and Agnes's funerals, but if he did and he brought his family, it might be, well, uncomfortable, that was all. She supposed it was a time in life, when people started dying around you, then she laughed to herself. She still hadn't managed to grow up; natural deaths always took her unawares. After 1941 she had expected that no one would ever die again, because in her mind people only died in wartime. It always came as a shock when someone took the more conventional way out. And that was doubly stupid; look what had happened to Jimmy, and to all the other asbestos-stricken victims. You could hardly put that down to natural causes.

'You see, the thing is,' said Dr Drew Hall, 'the x-rays and the spirograph are OK. We would probably let you go with a telling off and a slapped wrist if it wasn't for your husband's cause of death.'

She knew this, of course. Clydebank by the 1990s had been awarded the dubious title of the asbestos capital of the world. Not only had the white mice and other ex-shipyard and ex-Turner and Newall workers been dying of asbestosis, but non-workers had too. Many of them had other causes on their death certificates. 'Lung Cancer' was a common one, and 'Heart Failure', that wonderful catch-all and cop-out; every human being eventually dies of a failed heart. What these 'causes' disguised, as they were intended to, was the quiet collusion of the local doctors in hiding the true story from the families of the dead. Doctors who came mainly from the middle or upper classes did not always regard their working-class patients as thinking human beings with feelings and rights like themselves.

Kate MacLeod's conviction that it was 'us against them' could be held just as strongly on the other side, and because of their class and their status, the doctors had considerably more in common with 'them' than with the patients who provided them with their living.

But gradually it had become clear over the years that the problem could not be buried with those who had worked with asbestos, and the cover-up began to fall apart. A woman who as a child had helped take her daddy's dust-encrusted boots off at night had contracted the disease. Bus and tram conductresses who had leaned across their passengers to collect fares on those 'yard specials' had also inhaled the dust from their overalls and were now suffering from asbestosis. And so it went on. Turner and Newall, the factory that had manufactured the asbestos used in the now defunct industries of the Clyde, had closed for good in the 1960s, though they kept other factories open. They had simply closed the gates of their Clydebank factory and walked away, leaving the area heavily contaminated. Later a private hospital had been built on the site, and as it was regularly used to treat NHS patients, the irony was that it could be dealing with sufferers of the pollution it was sitting on.

In the years after Turner and Newall left their contaminated material behind, not only were former workers becoming ill and dying, but so were those who had lived around Agamemnon Street, both during the working life of the factory and afterwards. The number of terminally ill people continued to rise, so that Clydebank had an instance of 1 in 2,000 affected, when the UK rate was 1 in 1 million. And included in those faceless figures were many of the women who had scrubbed the dust-impregnated overalls of their menfolk every weekend . . .

Marion understood that this was what was on the mind of Dr Drew Hall.

'OK, so you want to cut a lump out of me, but when?'

'Tomorrow morning. Didn't expect that, did you? You were dying to protest about the time it was taking, weren't you?'

'Not very clever phraseology in the circumstances, Dr Hall,' Marion remarked.

'Anyone ever tell you that you have a very sick sense of humour?'

But when tomorrow came there was another delay.

'What is it this time? Someone's Merc broken down and the Rolls is being cleaned?'

'I won't have this sarcasm!' Drew Hall retorted.

She looked at him; a nice lad, a nice-looking lad, and he was too tired to be having this conversation. The dark circles under his eyes made him look ill himself. She remembered Colin looking the same, and wondering if he'd get through his housemanship.

'You should be in bed,' she said.

'If that's an offer,' he sneered theatrically, 'I've had better!'

'That I doubt! Look, I need to know what the hold-up is.'

'What it always is,' he replied, suddenly serious. 'Too few staff to cope with demand. The bloke running this place used to sell Clark's shoes, he still thinks in terms of how much profit he can force out of the punters. I don't honestly know when we can get this thing of yours set up again. I'd be lying if I said I did.'

'Dear God, a conscience now!'

He smiled again, but weariness stopped it reaching his eyes.

'Well, Dr Hall, that's me out of here!' she announced.

'That wouldn't be wise.'

'Oh shut up, you old woman!'

'Marion, you really should have this test done.'

'The man I'm hoping to meet will be in Clydebank tomorrow, March 13th, if he's still alive, that is. The deal was that I'd be out by then.'

Drew Hall opened his mouth to protest.

'It's not your fault, son, I'll sign anything you want, but today I'm getting out of this bloody bed and heading home.'

'I'll get hell,' he said, looking pathetic. 'Does that mean nothing to you?'

'Do you,' she asked slowly, 'remember a Dr Frank Callaghan?'

'St Francis of the Royal? Christ, yes, we all know about the great legend. Are you going to tell me now that he once took a thorn out of your foot?'

'No. He told me my husband was dying. He was also my young brother's father-in-law.'

'Shit!'

'And have you have heard of Professor Colin Ryan?'

'As in "other famous son of the Royal now working with the even more famous cardiac surgeon Denton Cooley in Houston, Texas"?'

'You missed a bit out; he's married to Denton Cooley's niece,' Marion said sweetly. 'He's my son.'

'Your name's MacLeod.'

'Stranger things have happened.'

'You nasty, sneaky old bint!' Drew Hall gasped. 'If nature hadn't made me kind and courteous I could have insulted you without realising who I was dealing with!' He stared at her. 'Oh my God! When the Chief hears this he will have my balls! If he'd known he'd have given you the deference and respect due to your position, instead of treating you like any ordinary piece of dross!'

'Well, bugger all that, young Dr Hall, the reason I told you was to convince you that there's no way I can possibly walk out today and not come back to have that bit cut out of me. Now, lackey, tell someone to get my clothes.'

The second letter from the Canadian solicitor had knocked her off her feet. Big Kenny had owned a small but successful freighter business, and as he had never married and had named her sole beneficiary, she would get the lot. He couldn't say at the moment just how much that would be until the entire matter had been resolved, though it would certainly be a six-figure sum. She thought of all the desperate scrimping and struggling throughout the 1960s and the '70s, times when she often wondered if there would be enough to pay the rent *and* the electricity, and now here she was in her fifties, with real money and no responsibilities. And no idea what she wanted to do with the money. Davy and Eileen were fine, so was Colin. Who, what else was there to spend it on?

Then she remembered reading that new houses were being built on the site of the Holy City. That's what she would do; she would go back to where she belonged. Then what? She would get an education at last. For weeks she argued with herself about it. What did she need an education for? Why would someone of her age *want* to sit her Highers? Because, she answered, that's why. There had to be a better reason for taking herself off to Clydebank Technical College among all those young people; it wasn't as though she would need to get qualifications to find work, thanks to Big Kenny she was a lady of leisure. She thought about it a bit more; why was she thinking of doing this? To prove to herself that she could, she decided, to prove that she wasn't stupid, that was why.

26

She had been in hospital for a week, so there was a week's supply of newspapers behind the door including two editions of the *Clydebank Post*, the local paper. She flicked the pages of the first one eagerly for the latest news of the *Piorun* ceremony. The survivors from the OPR *Piorun* were coming back for the unveiling of a plaque at Rothesay Dock to mark their bravery on the night of the Blitz. Someone had mentioned the story to someone else, and gradually a head of steam had built up, and if Marek Nowak was still alive, perhaps he might be there. Marek was the key to her sister Frances's fate on that night. If she could find out for sure what had happened to Frances, where she had died, she'd give every penny she had. She didn't know why, but the need to know had grown over the years. Once it had just been there, in the back of her mind, a curiosity that she'd like to satisfy, but now it was eating away at her. Maybe she just had too much time on her hands and too little else to think about. There was nothing in last week's *Post*, so she picked up the latest edition and began looking through it. On the front page was a group photo of the returning Polish seamen down by the Dock. She scanned the faces eagerly; she didn't recognize any of them, but then why would she? She had known only Marek, and that was a long time ago. He lived on in her dreams though, standing in front of her, crying, and she couldn't hear what he was saying or answer back. She decided to call the *Clydebank Post* and ask if they had any names; was there a Marek Nowak among them?

'No,' said the voice on the other end of the phone, 'no Marek Nowak.'

Her heart sank. If he was dead, or if he was alive but not there, she would never find out. 'Thanks,' she said, 'it was just a thought.'

'There is a *Novak*, if that's any good,' said the voice, 'a Mike Novak.'

'No, it was definitely Marek Nowak. Thanks anyway.'

'Wait a minute. Let me phone the place where this bloke's staying, you never know. What's your number?'

She didn't think it would come to anything, a nice girl being kind to an old woman. She probably thought she was reuniting two wartime sweethearts after all these years, a nice little human interest story for the next edition of the paper. Then the phone rang.

'Is that Marion MacLeod?' a man's voice asked. He sounded American, but she detected something else in there too.

'Yes.'

'Really? Marion MacLeod, the little redheaded kid from Second Avenue?'

'Well, that was a long time ago, but I was once that little redheaded kid from Second Avenue! Who is this?'

'Well, my name's Mike Novak of Maine, but you might remember me better as Marek Nowak of Gdansk.'

It was true; at moments of high excitement you really could feel your heart jumping out of your chest. He would be at her door in less than an hour. What if there was some sort of mistake, what if it wasn't him? No, be reasonable, he knew who he was, it really was him. What if he didn't know? She would have to take that like an adult, that was all. But still, it would be a blow . . .

She opened the door as he knocked. Her memory of Marek had dimmed over the years, had gone hazy around the edges.

She scanned his face for a clue, for something familiar to latch on to. No, she didn't recognise him; she could have passed him on the street without a second glance.

'You've still got the red hair!' he said.

'You must have trouble with your eyesight!' she smiled. Inside she was screaming 'TELL ME!', but they had to go through the small talk. They sat facing each other across the fire.

'Last time I saw you was when you were in hospital,' he said. 'I don't expect you remember that. You were in a pretty bad way. In fact when I left I was told you wouldn't make it. I felt bad leaving you there like that, I can tell you, but there was nothing I could do.'

'I do remember that!' she said. 'I thought I had dreamt it! You were really there?'

He nodded.

'You were crying,' she said, 'I couldn't make out what you were saying, but you were crying.'

'Yeah, well, I was in a pretty bad way too, I guess.'

'Look Marek – Mike, I know I should offer you coffee and do all the polite things, but the fact is that I can't, not yet. There's something I need to know, something I've needed to know ever since the Blitz. They never found Frances. She's dead, I know that, I'm not harbouring any mad ideas that I might find her, but I need to know. Do you understand?'

'Of course I understand! I thought you knew, I thought someone would have told you.'

'There *was* no one. You were the last person to see her. I met someone once who saw you leaving the Masonic Hall after the bombing started. After that it's a blank.'

He looked upset. 'Marion, I'm sorry about this, if I'd thought for a minute that all these years you'd been wondering . . . I could have got in touch years ago, I feel such an idiot!'

'Marek, please, tell me NOW!'

'Yeah, sure, OK. Well, as soon as the incendiaries started

falling and we realised it was for real, Frances wanted to get home. We set off from the hall like you said, but by then the bombs were falling, and nothing would do but for Frances to get home to her family. We zig-zagged all over the place, trying to avoid the next bomb, but then it got real scary and I knew we had to stop and find a shelter. She was mad as hell! We argued about it, all these bombs falling around us, and I lost my temper with her. I just grabbed her, ran her through into a back court and into the first shelter I could find. She was still spitting mad I can tell you, yelling that she'd tell her father and her brothers and they'd kick the hell out of me. I had to get back to the dock to find out what was happening to my boat, so I just ran. I got halfway down the street again and I heard two huge explosions behind me. When I looked back half of the building had gone, but she was in the shelter, I reckoned she'd be OK. Only she wasn't.'

'Where was the shelter, Marek, can you remember?'

'Pattison Street,' he said. 'I put her in the shelter behind 5 Pattison Street. It's haunted me all my days. Why didn't I listen to her? If Frances had to die she should at least have died with her family in the Holy City.'

So that was it. Pattison Street. Everybody knew about Pattison Street. A huge bomb had hit Number 12 that night, killing 15 people. Some of those who had survived got out of the rubble, ran through Number 11 and dived into the safety of the shelter behind Number 5. As soon as they got inside it took a direct hit. Almost everyone inside had been killed. It was part of the folklore of Clydebank. She had never thought for even an instant that Frances could have been there too. So that was what Marek had been trying to tell her as he stood by her hospital bed, and in all the dreams she'd had since she had tried to make out what he had said. That was why he had been crying too, because he had forced her into the shelter and she'd been killed. So all these years that Frances had officially been one of the 'disappeared', what was left of her had been in the mass grave with the other unclaimed, unidentifiable bodies at Dalnottar. She was with the other MacLeods after all. Well, at least she knew now.

'Are you OK?'

'Fine, really. You've no idea what it means to me to know. Thanks.'

He put his hand into his pocket. 'I have something for you,' he said gently, 'I've carried it about with me all these years and I was hoping real hard that you'd pulled through so that I could give it to you.'

He pulled out a gold chain, and on it was Granny Mirren's gold cross from Uist. 'The old lady was so determined Frances should wear it for some reason.'

'The green dress,' Marion said, 'Granny Mirren thought wearing green was unlucky.'

'Yeah, well, it was getting caught in Frances's hair that night, so as soon as we were out of sight of the Holy City she took it off and asked me to keep it for her. I forgot all about it afterwards. It lay in my tunic pocket for about six months, and we were back at sea by then.'

Marion held out her hand and he placed it in her upturned palm. 'Granny Mirren believed the crucifix brought good luck,' she said, trying to control the tears running down her cheeks. 'She thought whoever had it would be safe.'

'Well, in a way she was right, wasn't she?' he smiled, but his own eyes were wet. 'I had it that night, and right through the War afterwards, and I was safe. How I wish Frances had kept it on that night.'

Next day, wearing Granny Mirren's crucifix, she went to the ceremony to unveil the plaque. The chain caught on her long hair too, but nothing would ever make her take it off. Father Sheridan was there in his official capacity, complete with full regalia and pious expression. He had aged well, the grey hair made him more handsome than ever; as Sal Gallagher always sighed, 'Whit a wee stoatir, whit a waste!' He saw Marion and nodded.

'No show without Punch, eh?' she whispered as he passed.

An almost imperceptible smile crossed his lips, then he saw the gold cross. 'That's a crucifix,' he whispered back.

'An' you withoot your specs oan tae!' Marion retorted.

'Does this mean I should get the Holy Water ready at last?'

'It means you never know when tae gie up!' she said. 'It belonged tae ma Catholic great-granny, the wan that married the Proddie frae Uist.'

'Oh,' he replied, 'so that's where the rot set in!'

'That's right, Gerry, an' noo you'd better put your po-face back oan an' join your mates before Father Gallagher there steps in!'

There was a good turnout, and the men of the ORP *Piorun* stood in a group, bashfully taking the applause of the 'Bankies. Sal and Father Tony were there too. Sal sidled up to Marion.

'See that big fella at the end there?' she whispered. 'Does he no' look helluva like the fella Big Tony donated the poker tae? Did ye no' notice he walks a bit funny?' She started to laugh, holding onto Marion's arm to support herself. 'Listen, there's somebody here ye might remember, turned up at ma door last night looking for ye. Said he remembered we were pals.'

As Marion started to turn round a voice said, 'You Marion MacLeod?' There was less hair, but the eyes were still the same, a vivid blue with that same gentle, mocking expression. She'd been right about those scars; they had calmed down. You wouldn't notice them if you hadn't carried a mental chart of his face in your head. 'Ah see ye kept your hair long,' he grinned.

'Aye Robert,' she said, 'somebody wance told me that it looked braw! I think he meant beautiful, but he was too Scottish to say it.'

He laughed. 'Whoever he was, he was right. Musta been a smart bloke.'

'What are you doin' here?'

308

'Ah get the local paper sent ower tae New Zealand. Been thinkin' aboot a visit for a while. Gettin' auld an' sentimental, been thinkin' o' comin' hame for good. Whit's that daft Yankee sayin'? "Bloom where you're planted", that's it. Ah've no' been back since ma Ma an' auld Pigswill died.'

'Robert Boyle!' she chided him, and heard that familiar chuckle.

'The same auld Marion then, still lookin' oot for other people,' he said, laughing gently. 'Ah knocked at your door when Ah was back, but ye were away,' he said quietly.

'Aye, Ah was doon in Oxford at oor Davy's place.' She looked around. 'Your family here, Robert?'

'Family? Whit family?'

'Well, Susan, is that her name?'

He laughed. 'Ah never went through wi' that, Marion,' he said. 'Did ma Ma no' tell ye?'

'Naw,' she said, and thinking back to when Jimmy was ill she said, 'Mibbe she tried tae, Ah'm no' sure. Whit happened?'

'Ah decided that the lassie deserved tae be somebody's first choice, no' ma second choice.' He was looking straight at her. It was there, she could swear to it, that look in his eyes, and she tried to will away the blush creeping across her cheeks. Blushing at her age, dear God whatever next? Young – no – *Old* Lochinvar on a white charger?

'She was a nice lassie, it wasnae fair.' He shrugged his shoulders. 'Ah was sorry tae hear aboot Jimmy, ma Ma wrote tae me aboot it. Ah thought aboot gettin' in touch then, but efter whit ye said the last time I saw ye, Ah thought it wouldnae be a good idea.'

That was a memory she didn't want to dwell on. 'Ah live in the Holy City noo,' she said brightly. 'Got a wee flat tae masel'. Would ye like tae come up, Robert?'

'Aye, Ah would.' They started to walk away. He held out his arm so that she could slip hers through. 'Ah hear ye've been ill?'

'Nothin' tae worry aboot,' she said, fingering Granny Mirren's gold cross. 'Ma mother always tells me when things are really bad, an' she's no' said a word.'

'Your mother? Christ, would that no' be a bit difficult, considerin'?'

'It's a long story,' she said. 'Ah'll tell ye if ye've got the time.'

'Ye realise,' he said, 'that if Ah go hame wi' ye it'll ruin your reputation for ever?'

'Holy Jesus, Mother of God, would ye listen tae the man! Even at this age he still thinks he's Rudolph Valentino!' Marion said, '*Amadain an diabhoil*!'

'Aye,' he smiled unsuspectingly, 'that Ah am!'

And arm-in-arm Tam the Teuchtar's daughter and Danny the Pape's son headed home to the Holy City.